In a fragile alliance, the natives are stirring uneasily under their foreign rulers. Rebellion is brewing, and at the heart of the conflict lies the bloody and powerful cult of the god Aoun, whose followers will stop at nothing to rid their land of alien domination. So civil servant Renille vo Chaumelle, scion of a proud, conquering line mingled with native blood, is conscripted as a spy and ordered to penetrate the fortress-temple known as the Fastness of the Gods. There he is to discover the secrets of the priests of Aoun and—if the chance presents itself—assassinate the head priest, named in legend as the god's own son.

But in the holiest depths of the temple, Renille finds there is more to the cult than his superiors suspect—far more than they will ever believe. What he learns leads him to the beautiful princess Jathondi, daughter of the native ruler, who is fated to be the crux of a violent confrontation between the fanatic followers of a flesh-hungry god and their arrogant overlords. Together, Jathondi and Renille must brave a whirlwind of revolution and apocalyptic magic that could shatter a nation, and open the long-sealed portal between heaven and earth.

"No one can create a fantasy world like Paula Volsky. She just _____ _____ _____ _____ better."—_A. C. Cr_

OTHER BOOKS BY
PAULA VOLSKY

Illusion
The Wolf of Winter

The Gates of Twilight

Paula Volsky

Bantam Books

New York Toronto
London Sydney Auckland

THE GATES OF TWILIGHT

A Bantam Spectra Book
PUBLISHING HISTORY
Bantam trade paperback edition / March 1996
Bantam mass market edition / February 1997

SPECTRA and the portrayal of a boxed "s" are
trademarks of Bantam Books, a division of
Bantam Doubleday Dell Publishing Group, Inc.

ISBN 0-553-57269-5

Published simultaneously in the United States and
Canada

Bantam Books are published by Bantam Books, a
division of Bantam Doubleday Dell Publishing
Group, Inc. Its trademark, consisting of the words
"Bantam Books" and the portrayal of a rooster, is
Registered in U.S. Patent and Trademark Office
and in other countries. Marca Registrada. Bantam
Books, 1540 Broadway, New York, New York
10036.

PRINTED IN THE UNITED STATES OF AMERICA

OPM   10 9 8 7 6 5 4 3 2 1

The Gates of Twilight

Prologue

It is held in the common memory of the Aware that doorways into that nether plane of existence inhabited by creatures calling themselves men sometimes open. Such events are unpredictable and largely inexplicable. The Aware, for all their superiority, do not rule the interdimensional portals. The atmosphere of the Radiant Level, whole and perfect unto itself, does not support the gross disruptions required to blast open the way into Netherness. The flawed air of the inferior plane, however—turbulent by its very nature, and therefore manipulable—invites experimentation.

One such experiment, performed in the second revolution of the Muted Epoch, bore significant consequences. A member of the human breed, toiling in Nether shadow, succeeded in breaking the barrier between dimensions. It was by no means the first of such successes. The fleeting manifestation of minute rips and tears in the substance of Radiance had been commonplace throughout the Muted Epoch. But this time, as never before, the opening was large; even sufficient to accommodate passage of an Awareness. And this time, as never before, the portal remained open.

An alien voice called faintly from the other side. The Aware listened, and pondered.

A shower of small alien artifacts rained through the gap. Some, instantly vanquished by the Radiant atmosphere, flashed and vanished. Others charred and blackened slowly. A few remained intact. These the Aware inspected, finding them crude and lightless.

A selection of small living things—some furred, some winged, some scaled—propelled by unknown means, came sailing through from Netherness. These immediately ignited, and wriggled, and stank, and died. Their remains the Aware fastidiously pitched back through the gap.

A pole, bearing a hoop attached to a fine net, poked through into Radiance, groped briefly, and descended upon a vagrant aetheric conflation. Pole, hoop, and net withdrew, bearing the conflation with them. There was silence for the term of a glowing span.

The plaintive, inviting voice on the other side resumed. Stronger and clearer, now.

The Aware considered the invitation. Few among them cared to squander their light upon the dim substance of the lower dimension. Communally conscious of their own perfection, they were largely free of curiosity's itchy taint. But not altogether free. Some among them, a few of the Anomalies, impelled by their own abnormalities, yearned for inexplicable things. Among these Anomalies, the greatest lucency belonged to the Presence Aoun.

Aoun, incomparably brilliant, might have brightened all the Level. Eschewing commonality, however, he asserted individuality—thus infecting himself with curiosity and ambition. Driven by these Anomalous passions, he dared the breach, passing from Radiance into the Netherplane of men. With him traveled a small band of his misguided admirers.

They squeezed through into the lower land known to its inhabitants as Aveshq, and what they found there exceeded all expectation. The subdimension was murky, slow, and foreign, as they had surmised. Beyond that, however, it was malleable, stupendously susceptible to Radiant influence. A thought, an intention, a casual desire—

any of these things, fueled by the force of the higher dimension, served to shape the coarse clay of Netherness.

The Presence Aoun, together with his followers, found themselves empowered beyond imagining. In Netherness, they ruled all force and substance. There, they were gods.

Initially, Aoun took leisure to learn the nature of his new domain, and to discover the limits, if any, of his new power. The first subject upon which he focused his attention was the being whose efforts had opened the doorway between dimensions. The creature was easily identifiable as female, for in Netherness, raw gender is for the most part apparent. She called herself human: her species. She called herself Bhudiprayd: her name. She called herself sorceress: her talent and her fantasy. She yearned for knowledge and dominance to feed internal hunger, and to this end she had studied for decades, sharpening brain and body to a lethal edge.

The Presence Aoun could recognize such hunger. Had she possessed Awareness, he might have honored her energy and accomplishment. As things were, however, she was fuel. She dreamed of ruling the entities she had summoned from beyond or, at least, of allying herself with them. Such dreams were foolish, for there could be no real alliance between pure Radiance and Netherly mud. There were reasons, however, to postpone her disillusionment.

Aoun, always inquisitive, communed with the human sorceress. There was much she could tell him of Netherness, its nature and inhabitants. He gleaned ample information. And when he had fully sampled the contents of her mind, there remained her body to experiment upon. The most ambitious of his projects involved an implantation of Radiant supradimensional essence within the woman's organs of increase. Following several unsuccessful attempts, implantation was effected, and conception occurred. The sorceress Bhudiprayd, anticipating eventual delivery of a hybrid superbeing destined to rule the world, settled herself to wait. Aoun likewise waited; an exercise in patience quite foreign to his nature.

He did not wait in idleness, however. Throughout the slow term of the woman's swelling, there was a new dimension to explore—a well of infinite potential, with a population of agreeable pliability.

The population, or humans, as they called themselves. Corporeal dross, their existence justified only by their capacity for adoration. But such capacity! Had Aoun never manifested himself, surely they would have invented him. As it was, they flocked to his worship, naming him Aoun-Father, Source and Finality.

Human adulation and fear were sweet to savor. The Presence Aoun found that divinity suited him. His Radiant companions, worshiped as lesser gods, seemed lamentably unappreciative of apotheosis, but they were limited in vision, and weak.

When the time finally came that the infant contained within Bhudiprayd's womb might fairly survive in the outer world, Aoun judged his period of waiting ended. The female body was as yet unready to deliver itself of its burden, but the disposable vessel had served its purpose. The God Aoun exerted his will. Nether-tissue parted, a fissure gaped, blood gushed, and the infant crawled forth from the maternal corpse.

It was a male, approximately human in appearance, yet displaying some evidence of its exalted ancestry, particularly in the other-dimensional radiance of its eyes. Before the sun of Netherness had set a dozen times, the boy could walk and run unaided. Another dozen sunsets, and he could speak to make his wishes known. He was born with a full set of luminous teeth, and from the very beginning manifested a marked preference for bloody meat, perhaps in recollection of his incarnadine emergence. Aoun-Father christened his firstborn KhriNayd, and tended the infant with care.

KhriNayd thrived and grew with a rapidity far exceeding the capacities of ordinary Nether-flesh. His intellect similarly flourished, and, at the close of four spans that humans call years, he was fit to take his place as First Priest, hybrid human/divine master of Aoun-Father's spreading cult. The triumph would have been complete, had Aoun's Radiant compatriots but demonstrated an appropriate enthusiasm. It was clear, however, that the lesser gods regarded KhriNayd-Son as something of an abomination. Within shared consciousness, they termed him "Beyond-Anomaly."

But they were small and narrow of mind. Aoun held their judgment of little account.

The years passed. The cult, rooted in fertile soil, expanded luxuriantly, overspreading the land of Aveshq. The bond between god/father and priest/son continued firm. Aoun was content as never before, His satisfaction marred only by the peevish insistence of the lesser gods, who now desired collective return to the Radiant Level. Should their leader refuse to go, they were prepared to abandon Him.

The threatened desertion suggested unspoken reproach. Piqued, Aoun made haste to shut the portal opened years earlier by the sorceress Bhudiprayd. The plaints of the thwarted lesser gods subsided to a sullen telepathic hum, easily ignored.

Serenity restored, Aoun-Father resumed His customary diversions, which at that time centered upon the construction of a vast stone temple, consecrated to His worship. The temple, product of ten thousand devoted human hands, was massive and impregnable as any fortress. It rose in the city of ZuLaysa, and its name was JiPhaindru, Fastness of the Gods.

Aoun looked upon His temple, and was as happy as His nature allowed. So He might have remained indefinitely, had not the passing years begun subtly to erode His power. The losses were scarcely perceptible, in the beginning; only such small failures as the imperfections of the Nether atmosphere might have accounted for. Gradually, however, they increased in magnitude and significance, until the creeping enfeeblement could no longer be denied. It seemed that supradimensional essence slowly but inexorably dissipated itself upon the dull air of the inferior plane. A brief return to the Radiant Level would surely have renewed Him. And now at last Aoun-Father regretted His haste in closing the portal, for He knew not how to reopen it.

Aoun reflected, and it came to Him that the Radiant essence, the very distillation of power, was capable at once of propagating and feeding upon itself. This truth recognized, the means of His renewal stood revealed, and He issued the appropriate commands.

KhriNayd-Son was swift to obey. To JiPhaindru came a score of human females—purchased, rented, stolen, or otherwise acquired. Each of these was Radiantly impregnated, after the manner of Bhudiprayd. Each accordingly expanded. When the moment was ripe, all twenty vessels were simultaneously emptied of contents.

The flame-eyed infants that crawled from the fleshly wreckage were visibly imbued with supradimensional virtue. Two of these Aoun-Father consumed, and the Radiant essence within them refreshed Him. Two more, and He was renewed, His divine powers wholly restored. The remaining hybrids were set aside for future use. A few of the females were preserved for eventual impregnation. The others served to fulfill their Father's needs, throughout the ensuing spans.

When supplies began to dwindle, KhriNayd-Son replenished his Father's larder. And now there were acolytes to assist him, for the worship of Aoun reigned supreme in Aveshq, and the faithful flocked to JiPhaindru. The priests required incessant replacement, for their human term of life was brief. But KhriNayd-Son, possessing supradimensional vitality, lived on to serve his Father.

The God Aoun, desiring witnesses to His triumph, now summoned the lesser gods to His presence. They did not come, and therefore He went forth to seek them.

They withdrew at His approach. They turned away from Him. And when He probed their shared consciousness, He then discovered their horror.

It was an infernal afternoon at the start of the swelter season, but the crowd racketing in the street outside the Vonahrish Residency in ZuLaysa appeared immune to heat. Of course, the crowd was Aveshquian, its members born to the climate. The steambath atmosphere so ennervating to foreign administrators dampened neither native vitality nor native hostility. Whizzing rocks pelted the outer wall of the Residency compound, and the air sizzled with howling abuse. Some of the insults were wonderfully inventive, but their beauty was lost upon the Vonahrish recipients immured within, who comprehended little of the local dialect. The accusations were likewise unintelligible, but their menace required no translation and, behind the wall, the Residency windows were shuttered tightly.

Similarly shuttered and barred were buildings all throughout this section of ZuLaysa known as Little Sherreen, in honor of the distant Vonahrish capital. The houses, shops, and offices—all neoclassically symmetrical in design, all constructed of imported cherry-colored brick, all seemingly lifted straight off the tree-lined boulevards of Sherreen—today appeared almost absurdly out of place under the glaring eastern skies. The streets ordinarily filled

with pallid expatriates today belonged to golden Aveshquians alone. The natives—for the most part a docile lot, as
their creed dictated—now displayed uncharacteristic fury,
and a westerner afoot in their midst might justly have
feared for his fair skin. Fellow countrymen went un-
molested for the nonce, even those clothed in the livery of
the Vonahrish overlords, but that could change in an instant.

The Aveshquian guards stationed before the Residency's big front gates were cognizant of peril. The uniformed figures stood motionless and upright, while the
faces beneath the stiffened visors of flat-topped dhurlies were professionally blank. But the dark eyes in the
bronzed visages shifted uneasily, and many a hand gripped
many a carbine with unnecessary force. Still, for all the
flying rocks and dung, the only missiles hitherto aimed
directly at the guards had been verbal, and even these consisted less of taunts than of pleas for racial solidarity.

A seething upheaval marked a point of fresh disturbance. Someone was pushing his way through the crowd.
For a few moments, loud commotion marked the newcomer's progress, and then a lone figure stepped forth to
confront the guards.

He was tall, by Aveshquian standards; lean, and
graced with the fluid eastern ease of motion so foreign to
the straight-spined, stiff-jointed Vonahrish. His voluminous tunic and baggy breeches of weightless, sand-colored
qunne might have belonged to anyone. Equally anonymous was the pendant bronze ushtra, ubiquitous triskelion
symbol of Triumphant Submission. But the embroidered
insignia decorating the polychrome zhupur wound and intricately knotted about his waist identified him as a member of the moderately prestigious Order of Divergence. A
wide-brimmed hat of woven waterfiber shaded his face,
but couldn't disguise the glitter of keen eyes, their apparent blackness belied by green highlights. The black-green
eyes, together with prominent facial bones and a long,
thin, arrogantly aquiline nose, marked the newcomer as a
northerner, possibly one of the mountain tribesmen. The
lines etching the eyes suggested an age near thirty. But the
mouth, chin, and jaw, which might have revealed so much,

were shrouded in gauze dust-wards depending from the hat.

He made straight for the gates, and the exhortations arising in his wake failed to slow his progress. Pleas and reproaches soon gave way to vituperation. "Traitor" was the commonest term of derogation, followed by "lickspittle," "yahdeen-vomit," and others of far more exotic description. The northerner appeared deaf, but not blind. When a beetle-browed graybeard sporting the gold-starred insignia of the professional Birthwitness attempted to trip him with an outstretched parasol, he effortlessly sidestepped the obstacle.

"Worm-prick!"

"Servant of chaos!"

"Nameless, prinked-up Nameless!"

The furious voices beat at his back, but the northerner ignored them. When the guards halted him, he drew some sort of paper from one of the folds of his zhupur. They scanned it briefly, and let him go in.

The wooden gates groaned shut behind him and the clamor subsided, but the shouting remained quite audible. Before him rose the Residency, irreproachably elegant, restrained in design, alien to this place. The grounds were manicured but uniformly ochre in hue, for the sprinkler system, powered by native muscle, and required to maintain a Vonahrish-style green lawn, had recently failed. The ornamental shrubberies, clipped into ruthlessly regular form, were as yellow-brown as the grass.

The native guards patrolling the parched courtyard paid no heed to the newcomer; save for legitimate credentials, he would never have won his way past the gate. Thus he proceeded without incident to the front door, where his pass was reexamined. Again he was admitted, and now found himself in the formal foyer incongruously echoing the pretentious proportions of the Palace of Justice, in Sherreen.

The place was unusually empty. The petitioners, malcontents, and entrepreneurs of all varieties wont to haunt the premises were not in evidence today. He made his way unchallenged across the foyer. Nobody troubled him as he mounted the broad central staircase. He was halfway to the second story before the inevitable hand descended upon his shoulder, and the inevitable angry voice demanded, "Here—where d'you think you're going?"

The intruder turned innocent green-black eyes upon his interlocutor—a hefty Vonahrish corporal of the Second Kahnderulese Regiment of Foot, clad in the authentic Vonahrish buff and gray, none of your native hirelings—a real Esteemed. He gaped.

"You drunk? You stupid?" the corporal inquired. "None of your kind beyond the foyer. Go back. Understand? Forbidden." There was no response, and he spoke louder. "FORBIDDEN! You hear?"

Hearing was one thing, comprehension another. The native shrugged and waggled ingratiatingly, a course guaranteed to stoke the other's rage.

"Get out! You'll be whipped! You'll be written up in the book! You'll be locked up and notated! You'll take a number!"

"Number? Esteemed?" the intruder breathed.

"Number, Pissie!"

This last unflattering epithet referred to the subtle golden tone of the Aveshquian complexion, but the newcomer's ignorance deflected insult. Flexing another winsome shrug, he resumed progress up the stairs, and the corporal waxed wroth.

"HALT!" The bellowed command produced no result. The corporal roared upon a different note, and uniformed figures converged upon the intruder.

"Throw that thing out," the corporal directed.

"Esteemed—most Esteemed—" A fervent flapping of wrists conveyed Aveshquian distress. "This one seeks the ear of the august Protector—"

"What's that?"

"The most tremendous Protector vo Trouniere. If I might be admitted to his presence—"

"Damned brass!"

"Forgive your servant, Esteemed. This worthless one implores a moment—but a single, fleeting, insignificant moment—with Protector vo Trouniere."

"Listen, Pissie," the corporal suggested. "The Protector's time is valuable. Too valuable to waste on pig-shit like you. Now you just haul your sorry yellow ass out of here while you can still walk."

"But I beg you, Esteemed—upon my very knees, if you desire it—for I bear a message of grave import—"

"Grave's the word—yours, if you're lying. What message? Who from? Let's see it."

"But it is meant for the tremendous one alone."

"You just give it here to me. If it's worth reading, I'll see it delivered."

"No, no, Esteemed, I am most strictly charged—"

"Search him," the corporal ordered, and a couple of his men stepped forward to lay hands upon the intruder.

"Ah, spare your servant this shame! I am of Divergence, do not defile my Order!" Piteous, singsong-accented pleas rang through the foyer. An interested group of guards gathered at the foot of the stairs.

"Check that rag around his middle," the corporal directed. "That's where they hide things."

"Gentlemen—Esteemed—you wrong me—" The captive wriggled violently.

"Sir, he's slippery as an oozie," one of the soldiers complained. "Permission to bash 'im a good one?"

"Not worth bruising your knuckles on. Just strip it raw and throw it out. Teach it some decent respect. Then you can search through the clothes."

"Yes, sir."

"No! Pity, gentlemen, pity!" The wriggling grew frantic. "By every god there is, by the Source and Finality Himself, I swear to you—"

But the nature of the oath was lost, for a sharply authoritative new voice now cut in to demand, "What is this, a carnival? Corporal, explain yourself."

Soldiers and captive looked up. Several steps above them stood a burly, barrel-bodied figure attired in civilian garb of dandified perfection: lightweight linen frock coat of elegant Vonahrish cut, checked strap trousers over polished boots, fashionable fawn moiré waistcoat, ivory silk cravat, gold-headed walking stick clasped in one coarsely formed, beautifully manicured hand. His starched shirt tabs, sharp and pointed as lethal weapons, stood mercilessly erect. The face above them was broad and wide-

mouthed, its peasant bluntness of feature mitigated by exquisitely groomed reddish moustache, imperial, and side
whiskers. Hair and garments exuded a powerful waft of
expensive imported perfume.

"Assistant Secretary Shivaux. Sir." The corporal
snapped a salute conveying all the respect due from a
lowly noncom of the Kahnderulese Second to an official of
the governing Aveshquian Civil Service, and one of the
Protector's right-hand men, to boot.

"Well?"

"Intruder, sir. This here Pissie—beg pardon, sir, this
yellow-fellow, that is, this *native*, he just came barging up
the stairs, cool as sherbet, demanding to see the Protector."

"And?"

"Claimed to be carrying a message. Wouldn't show it
to anyone—"

"Save the tremendous one," the culprit interjected.
Both Vonahrishmen ignored him.

"And so," the corporal concluded, "we were searching him, naturally."

"Naturally. And then?"

"Then?" The corporal appeared mystified. "Throw
'im out, of course."

"I see." Assistant Secretary Shivaux reflected a moment or two before inquiring mildly, "Without interroga-
tion?"

The corporal, sensing quicksand, said nothing.

"Those savages out there in the street are ready and
eager to drink blood," Shivaux continued in the same pen-
sive tone. "They are vicious and treacherous at the best of
times, and doubly so now. Has it never occurred to you,
Corporal, that this native's intrusion, at such a juncture, is
scarcely coincidental?"

"Spy, sir?" the corporal inquired.

"Drawing the attention of the entire Residency upon
himself? Hardly. Diversion, perhaps."

"Whose, sir? Assassin?"

"Quite possible. If so, we shall want the names of his
confederates."

"Being as there are any, sir."

"Oh, be certain there are. Have you not wondered, Corporal, how this yellow-fellow gained entry today?"

"Bamboozled the guards at the gate. They're fools, sir. I'll twist their tripes."

"They are quite probably blameless," Shivaux opined. "The yellow-fellow presented them with false documentation of some sort. You will discover it when you search him."

"Depend on it, sir."

"And where should such a thing as this acquire counterfeit credentials, without assistance?"

"You make it sound like plots, sir."

"Perhaps."

"Pissies don't hatch plots. They haven't the brains for it," the corporal declared.

"There you are quite mistaken. These Àveshquians are barbarous and morally inferior, but never devoid of cunning. Many, in fact, possess a kind of convoluted subtlety beyond comprehension of the rational western intellect. It is in their blood, no doubt. Never underestimate the native powers of duplicity, Corporal."

"No, sir."

"As for this fine fellow here"—Shivaux descended to prod the captive's shoulder playfully with the head of his stick—"I don't doubt he'll prove communicative."

"He will by the time we're done with him, sir," the corporal promised.

"Your assistance will not be required. Watch. I shall demonstrate. Now then, boy—" Shivaux addressed the captive directly. "You have recognized the error of your ways?"

"I am dust, Esteemed." The culprit bowed his head.

"Precisely. You wish to cleanse your spirit?"

"Ah, most truly!"

"There's a good boy. You will redeem your name and Order, and possibly save your own filthy little life into the bargain, should you succeed in satisfying me now. You will do so by answering all questions put to you, completely and without reservation. You will begin by telling me your name, your intention, and the names of your accomplices."

"Accomplices? Esteemed? This word?"

"Do not pretend ignorance. It is a crooked course, and dishonorable to your Order. Why are you here?"

"Esteemed, I bear a message consecrated to the Protector's vision. I carry no poison in my heart, for I am loyal to the glorious Republic of Vonahr, and—"

"Who dispatched you?"

"I am sworn to secrecy."

"May I not persuade you to reconsider?"

"Esteemed, I am sworn—"

"So am I, and I will cleave to my oath. Look at this." Shivaux raised his gold-headed cane. "What do you see?"

"A stick, handsome and costly, as is all that belongs to the Esteemed, even unto the heavenly fragrance, gorgeous and potent as the breath of ten thousand gardens, gracing the Esteemed one's person and garments—"

"Enough of that. Atop the stick?"

"The golden head of a Vonahrish falcon. Very beautiful, very finely wrought—"

"Just so, boy, but you miss an essential point. The falcon is a bird of prey. Note the raptor's killing beak, the wicked point, the cutting edge, all sculpted and honed to perfection. Beneath the gilded covering lies tempered steel, strong as any blade. Can you imagine the result, should such a golden beak impinge upon a human eyeball?"

"Esteemed, I—"

"Don't speak. Only consider, briefly. Use your imagination. I will not disturb your cogitations."

"Esteemed, you confuse me—"

"Then I will state the matter very simply. Answer my questions, or I will thrash you with my stick. In the heat and confusion of the moment, an accident may possibly occur, involving the falcon's beak and one or both of your eyes. Are you still confused?"

"Alas, I am lost! Aoun-Father, guide me! Am I mad, or are there not international treaties, charters, contracts, and other such awesome inky magics prohibiting the mutilation of my countrymen?"

"Difficult to say, boy." Shivaux shook his curled head. "Alas, I am no lawyer. You yourself are free to investigate the matter, upon your departure. I am told that the public Hall of Records in the city of Lanthi Ume, some three months' journey by land and sea to the west, contains facilities for the use of the blind. Perhaps you will find them useful."

"Oh, Esteemed, I—"

"You will state your name. Your name, boy!" The gilded falcon hovered.

"Softly, Shivaux—you already know it." The alteration in the captive's voice commanded attention. The singsong native rhythm vanished and he was speaking perfect Vonahrish, his intonation that of the old aristocratic class once known as Exalted, in the time before the great popular revolution of the last century had obliterated all titles of hereditary privilege. Shivaux, whose own accent was quite dissimilar, stiffened at the sound of it.

"Release me," the prisoner requested quietly, and such was the respect yet accorded an Exalted voice and manner, even in the days of the Vonahrish Republic, that the startled soldiers automatically obeyed. They loosed their hold without demur, and Assistant Secretary Shivaux's face purpled. The newcomer let fall his gauze dust-wards, thus exposing the lower portion of an angular, clean-shaven countenance. When he doffed his wide hat, it could be seen that the bronze-gold tone of his complexion terminated abruptly, and that the narrow band of skin skirting his hairline was of a western fairness. The hair itself was thick, innocent of pomade, and a sun-streaked brown in color, lighter than any Aveshquian's.

There wasn't a one of them that could fail to recognize him now.

"Chaumelle." The soldiers uttered the name with a mixture of amusement and chagrin. "Chaumelle's pulled another one." The corporal's face was red with embarrassment, but he couldn't repress a guffaw, for there was no resisting the outrageousness of Deputy Assistant Secretary Renille vo Chaumelle's notorious eccentricities. An icy glance from Assistant Secretary Shivaux quelled all mirth.

"Perhaps you would be so good as to explain your little charade, Deputy?" Shivaux's voice was under tolerable control, but his face remained revealingly flushed. "Do you seek to offend, or are we to assume that you attempt humor?"

"I should not so presume, Assistant Secretary," Renille murmured, with the Exalted nonchalance that his immediate superior in the Aveshquian Civil Service found so unspeakably galling.

"Enlighten us, if you will."

"I trust it has not escaped your notice that the street before the Residency is crammed with enraged citizens. In order to win past them safely, I resorted to Aveshquian costume."

"Ah, very resourceful. I congratulate you. It is a role you assume to such perfection, it can hardly be called a disguise. In time of trouble, the natural instincts come to the fore, do they not?" Assistant Secretary Shivaux curled a smile.

If the shot hit home, no sign of it appeared upon Renille vo Chaumelle's artificially darkened face. But he had had a lifetime in which to steel himself against such taunts. His family was of the oldest aristocracy. The official abolition of Exalted rank and title in Vonahr had scarcely diminished the vo Chaumelle prestige. Even the great scandal of wild Sisquine vo Chaumelle's mad decision, some ninety years earlier, to wed a northern Aveshquian princess, had proved socially survivable. And indeed, the subsequent fanatical adherence to perfect Vonahrish form and convention upon the part of Sisquine's descendants had all but erased the stain of that mésalliance. She had been a princess, after all, and many of the northern Aveshquians were actually as fair-skinned as Vonahrishmen. It might have been possible to forget Sisquine's indiscretion altogether, had not the matter self-advertised from time to time upon the faces of family members. There were those black-green Aveshquian eyes; the thin, aquiline Aveshquian nose. Renille vo Chaumelle had inherited both. His compatriots ordinarily pretended not to notice, a courtesy of which the beneficiary appeared unappreciative.

"There are few among us Vonahrish," Shivaux continued cordially, "to whom such a ploy would have occurred. The western imagination does not ordinarily travel such twisting paths. There are fewer yet who could have carried it off so well, but then, you've many an innate advantage. To be sure, the narrow-minded might deem recourse to falsehood unworthy of a gentleman, but such caviling detracts nothing from the luster of your accomplishment."

"Falsehood, Shivaux?" Renille appeared uncomprehending.

"Those allusions to the message that you carry—the oaths of secrecy—in short, those barefaced lies, so typical of the native—"

"Assistant Secretary, rest assured that I have spoken truly, even truly as you spoke just now in promising to put out both my eyes, an atrocity in violation of all existing written treaties. How, I wonder, should you have explained such a breach of international contract to the Protector? Was he likely to condone it? Or shall I conclude that news of the incident should never have reached vo Trouniere's ears?"

"Come, this is childish." Assistant Secretary Shivaux's assurance did not waver. "I spoke to discipline a recalcitrant yellow-fellow, as I thought. You do not imagine I intended to carry through on the threat?"

"Certainly. Otherwise, you are guilty of falsehood unbefitting a gentleman. What am I to think, Assistant Secretary?"

"More of duty. Less of amateur theatrics and formerly-Exalted attitudinizing." Shivaux, visibly striving to suppress all outward signs of rage, manufactured a tolerant smile. "The masquerade is amusing, but so much wasted effort, I fear. You might as well have continued your holiday in pursuit of ZuLaysan temple dirges, or some other project of similar import. The Protector is unlikely to find time for you today."

"I'm here at his request." From his zhupur, Renille drew forth a document, the same he had displayed to the guards at the outer gate. The summons bore the signature and seal of Breuve vo Trouniere, Resident Vonahrish Protector of the native state of Kahnderule.

Shivaux barely glanced at it. "Follow me," he snapped. Salvaging his authority as best he could, he turned and hurried up the stairs without a backward glance. Renille followed at a leisurely pace. Behind them both, the soldiers were snickering audibly.

Up the stairs they went, and along the dim, suffocating corridor to the Protector's antechamber, where the clerk examined the summons, vanished briefly into the office beyond, then reappeared to usher the two of them in. As he stepped over the threshold, Renille resumed the upright, comparatively rigid carriage of a Vonahrishman. Baiting Assistant Secretary Shivaux was good sport, but the Protector was another matter altogether.

Vo Trouniere's sanctum was dim and marginally bearable of atmosphere, its deeply recessed windows masked with screens of woven rushes, dampened to cool the air; its lofty ceiling hung with immense wicker fans, swinging upon cords manipulated by a quiet native niibhoy squatting in the corner. Otherwise, the furnishings were entirely western in style. Protector vo Trouniere himself sat behind the immense desk—a grizzled, rawboned, middle-aged man, deeply tanned by the Aveshquian sun; grim-lipped, long-jawed, and prematurely wrinkled of face, his high forehead grooved with choleric lines. He looked up, and his brows rose at sight of his Deputy Assistant Secretary's native garb, but he registered no displeasure; rather the contrary, in fact.

"Ingenious, Chaumelle," vo Trouniere observed, almost affably.

"Expedient, sir." Renille concealed his surprise. Ordinarily, the Protector was less than tolerant of colorful unorthodoxy.

"Got through the streets without trouble?"

"Yes, and brought a letter for you." Renille handed the other a sealed missive.

"From—?"

"My uncle, sir, at Beviairette."

"I see." Vo Trouniere dropped the letter into his in-basket. "No problem with the rabble at our gate?"

"They took me for one of themselves, sir."

Shivaux's lip curled.

"Good. Very good." The Protector's approbation astonished both listeners. "And would they have done so, had you spoken aloud?"

"Sir?"

"Their lingo, the native jabber—you speak it, don't you?"

"There are some twoscore separate and distinct dialects spoken throughout Aveshq, Protector. No one, to my knowledge, has mastered them all." Noting his superior's impatience, he concluded, "I'm familiar with half a dozen, fluent in three."

"Including the local chatter?"

"Kahnderulese. The Queen Tongue. I grew up with it."

"Excellent."

Another unexpected response. Usually, the Deputy Assistant Secretary's interest in native language, history, and culture was regarded as an amusing, if inappropriate, oddity. Not today, however. Renille inclined his head in wary silence.

"Take a chair, and I'll tell you why you're here. You, too, Shivaux," the Protector commanded. "I want you to hear this."

They obeyed and, in that wordless moment, the angry shouting in the street outside rose clearly to their ears.

"They've been bleating and blocking traffic out there since early this morning," vo Trouniere remarked. "Does either of you know why?"

Shivaux shrugged.

"The murdered astromages," Renille replied at once. "The ZuLaysans think it our doing."

"Can it truly be claimed that the ZuLaysans think at all?" Shivaux inquired.

"So deliberate a suppression of the Script itself attacks the very integrity of Order," Renille observed. "Or so the more zealous of citizens believe. They are correspondingly aggrieved."

A newcomer to Aveshq—or any number of profoundly insular Vonahrish residents, for that matter—would not have understood him. His two listeners, professionally obliged to deal with the natives, experienced no such difficulty. Aveshquian astromages—uniquely empowered to interpret divine intention as set forth in the configuration of stars existing at the precise moment of an individual's birth—performed the crucial assignment to Order that determined social status, thus setting the limits of opportunity, and fixing an infant's place in the world for all time to come. To westerners, the arbitrary inflexibility of it reeked of barbarism. In Aveshquian eyes, however, the symmetry and regularity of Order, beautiful as geometry, excluded the deadly influences of chaos. An absolute submission to the will of the gods, expressed in the design of the social hierarchy, represented personal spiritual triumph. The astromages, literate in the Script of the Gods, served as indispensable interpreters and guides. Thus, last night's fatal assault upon three of ZuLaysa's most prominent star-seers signaled an attack upon the fabric of human civilization, upon the very essence of human identity.

"And who fitter to launch such an attack than soulless Vonahrish invaders?" Renille continued. "They believe we would corrupt their spiritual wholeness, demoralize and ultimately destroy them as a people. Sometimes I suspect they are right about that."

"Here it comes, we're in for it now. You, boy"—Shivaux addressed the silent niibhoy—"fetch us a soap-box."

Renille ignored him. "Their fears are such that—"

"The worst of them are devilish," vo Trouniere interrupted. "The best—those educated in Vonahr—are inflated with goodness, and far more dangerous than the worst. And the majority are sheep, willing to be herded by best or worst."

"In short—indistinguishable from ourselves," Renille murmured.

"From some of us," Shivaux amended, amused.

"But who's herding them now?" the Protector inquired. "Who's goading them to the point of stampede?"

"Those damned witch doctors of theirs," Shivaux replied. "Those butchering bastards they call priests. Those murderous, yellow-faced—"

"VaiPradh," Renille concluded dryly. The Aveshquian term he employed translated quite directly into Vonahrish as "the Filial." It was the title chosen for themselves by the acolytes of the hungry native god known as "Aoun-Father," whose more gruesomely exotic rites of worship had, only within the past twenty years, been outlawed by the revolted Vonahrish authorities.

"Correct," vo Trouniere concurred. "VaiPradh. Busy, of late. Out there, stirring the pot night and day. Making progress, too. The mutiny in the Ulurri Light Horse was led by Aoun-worshipers. The riot in Xansu Gardens—VaiPradh's ushtra emblems were found chalked up all over the walls, afterward. The attack on Nesse v'Igne's household, in Vale Poorule—the slaughter of the family—same story. The uprising at Flower-of-Light Plantation—not three days' travel from your uncle's Beviairette, Chaumelle—that was VaiPradh again."

"Perhaps the murder of the astromages as well," Renille suggested.

"To lay at our door." Shivaux nodded. "There is the characteristic native deceit."

"Possible, but unproved," vo Trouniere returned. "In any event, the violent episodes increase in frequency, trouble's flaring all over Kahnderule, but nowhere more so than right here in ZuLaysa."

"Inevitable." Renille shrugged. "We stand in the shadow of the Fastness."

The vast temple known as JiPhaindru, the Fastness of the Gods, befitted its title, for it rose gaunt and impregnable as any fortress at the hot heart of ZuLaysa. Ancient beyond reckoning, origins clouded in legend and myth, JiPhaindru remained as yet inviolate to western eyes. Originally—or so popular wisdom had it—the holy fires of numerous deities had burned beneath the temple roof. Over the course of the ages, however, the lesser gods and goddesses had dwindled. Hrushiiki and Nuumahni had departed, together with ineffable Ahrattah, clockwork-minded Ubhyadesh, and the others, until at last remained only Aoun-Father, Source and Finality, the One Truth. JiPhaindru belonged now to Aoun-Father alone.

"The present KhriNayd's the worst within memory," vo Trouniere observed.

It was impossible to know where one KhriNayd left off, and the next began. The name itself, denoting intimate ties to the Aoun-Father, stretched back forever, its true nature lost in the mists of antiquity. Supposedly, the First

Priest␣KhriNayd was literal and actual son to Aoun-Father—representative of the Father's power upon the physical plane, leader of VaiPradh, absolute master of the faithful. In theory, there existed but the one, original KhriNayd-Son, a being of remarkable longevity. In fact, it might be safely inferred that the title passed unobtrusively from one native zealot to the next. The mechanics and frequency of transference were deliberately obscure, but the reality was obvious: "KhriNayd," supposedly an individual's name, was in fact an office whose requirements dictated resistance to foreign rule.

"Insofar as it's possible to judge, the successive KhriNayds are virtually indistinguishable—their similarities no doubt designed to foster the myth of an immortal leader," Renille told them. "The present First Priest merely upholds the policies of his predecessors. The abrupt increase in anti-Vonahrish activity coincides, of course, with our ban upon their rites. It would seem that VaiPradh takes unkindly to foreign interference."

"Think we should have kept out of it, do you?" Shivaux inquired. "Live and let live—eh, Chaumelle?"

"I think we might, with a little care, have avoided the dangerously disadvantageous position in which we now find ourselves."

"Dangerously disadvantageous." Shivaux barked a laugh. "You've made your affinity for these savages clear enough, but I never before knew that you're afraid of them. This is rich."

"A native population outnumbering the foreign occupying force by hundreds of thousands to one is hardly to be sneezed at, even by so redoubtable a soul as the Assistant Secretary," Renille suggested.

"A formless mass of yellow-fellows armed with knives and spears."

"The native contingents of the Kahnderulese regiments are rather better disciplined and equipped than that."

"True, and reliably loyal to Vonahr."

"Loyal as the Ulurri Light Horse?"

"The exception that proves the rule. Bah"—Shivaux affected to share a private joke with the Protector—"this

native costume he wears has inspired Chaumelle to new
heights of timidity."

"Chaumelle is quite right," vo Trouniere informed his
disappointed subordinate. "We are vastly outnumbered.
VaiPradh's opposition is damnably effective, and the loyalty of the native troops is compromised. The present
KhriNayd-Son has succeeded in rousing the populace to
such fury that we Vonahrish stand in danger of expulsion
from Kahnderule, if not outright annihilation."

"The solution is clear enough," Shivaux returned
without hesitation. "These yellows want firm rule. A touch
of the whip is indicated. The VaiPradh witch doctors have
flourished upon our sufferance long enough. I say, loose
the Second Kahnderulese upon JiPhaindru. Raze the place,
chase the priests from their rats' nest, and hang this
KhriNayd animal above the ruins of his own temple. That
is language they will understand. Proscribe the entire cult,
and there's an end."

"An end indeed," Renille approved. "I congratulate
the Assistant Secretary. He's sought the one surest means
of uniting Aveshquians against us, and he's hit it upon his
first attempt. Formidable. Defile and destroy their oldest,
holiest temple. Murder their priests. Suppress their reli-
gion. And they'll rise against us, never resting until they've
driven the last Vonahrishman from their land. This is
surely diplomacy at its finest."

"Diplomacy is for equals. We deal with a subject race,
suited by nature and by inclination to servitude." Shivaux
assumed an air of forbearance. "What is their own beloved
creed, but 'Triumph in Submission'?"

"That is the Vonahrish translation," Renille told him.
"But the Aveshquian truth of it may work for or against
us."

"It's worked for us well enough throughout the past
two centuries and more. There's no reason it shouldn't
continue to do so, provided we stand firm. Bad time to be
losing your nerve, Chaumelle."

"Bad time for spectacular blundering, Assistant Secretary."

"Bah, you're weak-livered, that's all. It's in the blood,
I suppose."

"Is cowardice hereditary, Assistant Secretary? For that matter, is stupidity?"

"Enough." The Protector's upraised hand forestalled Shivaux's response. "The two of you bicker like market women. Chaumelle is correct, as it happens. An attack upon JiPhaindru is likely to touch off a full-scale rebellion. Moreover, the benefits are questionable. Leveling the building gains us nothing, should this KhriNayd elude us. We aren't even certain that he's in there at all. Legend has it that he crouches at the center of that temple like some sort of antique monster at the heart of a maze, but it's never been confirmed. Perhaps the outlawed rites continue behind those walls, justifying armed intervention. Maybe there's an arsenal there, or some sort of training academy for native incendiaries. The fact is, we don't know, and we can no longer afford ignorance. Which brings me to the object of this afternoon's meeting—"

"If I'm not mistaken," Renille suggested, "you want me to play the spy for you."

"Ugly term, but accurate. We need information. You're the man to get it. You see, I deal plainly with you."

"Your unwonted approval of my native costume is now explained. You hope to send me into JiPhaindru, disguised as an Aveshquian."

"I wouldn't trust a native for the job, they haven't the fiber. And you're the only one among us Vonahrish capable of pulling it off. The right sort of face, knowledge of yellow customs and habits—language—you have them all. Those odd scholarly enthusiasms of yours will serve a useful function at last. It's all remarkably fortunate."

"Remarkably. I'll let you know when I've decided."

"Decided what?"

"Whether I choose to accept the assignment."

"It isn't a request." Vo Trouniere's affability evaporated.

"The obligations of a civil servant don't include violation of Aveshquian holy places, sir—you might consult the third article of the Treaty of Mandijhuur, should you require confirmation. I can scarcely be compelled to it."

"Don't be certain of that."

"Oh, bear with him, Protector." Assistant Secretary

Shivaux permitted himself an undisguised sneer. "His reluctance is only natural. It's a risky undertaking, after all."

"He's Vonahrish." The Protector sat inflexibly upright. "He'll do his duty."

"Duty. One of those sanctified but essentially nebulous concepts, like honor, or justice," Renille observed. "Interpreted according to custom, caprice, or convenience."

"Don't waste your facile freethinking on me, Chaumelle—I haven't the patience." The Protector's natural choler was rising. "Anyone with an ounce of decency knows his duty on instinct. If that doesn't include you, then I'll explain. It's your duty to protect Vonahrish interests in Aveshq, whatever the personal cost. Does that clarify matters?"

"Not entirely. It's not clear, for example, that Vonahrish interests in Aveshq actually merit protection."

"There, his true colors." Shivaux didn't trouble to conceal his satisfaction.

Vo Trouniere, apparently stunned by the sacrilege, said nothing.

"We westerners have established our trading ventures here," Renille continued, "practiced commercial exploitation upon a grand scale, divested the natives of property and enfranchisement—"

"Most of them had none to begin with." The Protector had found his voice.

"Deliberately suppressed their culture—"

"What culture? Temples, taboos, talismans, twaddle—"

"Taken all, and given—"

"Civilization," vo Trouniere snapped. "That's what we've given. We've taken these unwashed savages in hand—educated and guided them, ministered to their needs, remedied their moral defects as best we may, corrected their worst faults, lifted them from barbarism— given far more than we've ever received in return. If you can't see that, then what are you doing in the civil service?"

"Oh—" Renille shrugged. "I was unsuited to the military or the clergy."

"That does it." The Protector's overtaxed patience broke. His face suffused, and the gray brows bristled. "Are you a fool, a coward, or both? I've ignored most of what's said about you. I've been fair, given you the benefit of the doubt, but now I must wonder. You have the vo Chaumelle name, but what sort of stuff are you really made of? Is it sound, or rotten at core? Are you one of us at all?"

Renille habitually deflected such queries. "You spoke just now of plain-dealing," he observed, "and yet, when you described this proposed excursion, you omitted a fairly obvious point."

The Protector's silence was revealing.

"Slip quietly into the temple, sniff around, listen and observe," Renille mused. "Locate First Priest KhriNayd, the mysterious KhriNayd-Son, archenemy of Vonahr, author of our current woes. Find him if he is there, and then—slip quietly out again, to carry the news back to the Residency? I think not."

"Are you one of us at all?" the Protector repeated.

"You expect me to eliminate KhriNayd."

"That is premature. His whereabouts are presently unknown."

"I'm no assassin."

"This murder-cultist's death would preserve Vonahrish lives and property."

"Then arrest him. Give him a trial. Execute him as an enemy of the state."

"Drop the false naïveté, we've no time for it. I expect you to consider your obligations to your country and your compatriots."

"These are not the sole considerations."

"They are the ones that must always come first. Any gentleman, any man of honor, would know as much. Any Vonahrish schoolboy would know, provided he *was* truly Vonahrish." The vein in vo Trouniere's forehead bulged. "But what are you? Are you anything at all? Well?"

Renille's face was expressionless beneath its mask of artificial color.

"Useless, as I would have expected," Shivaux opined.

"You may as well recruit a full-blooded yellow, Protector. Better than nothing."

Vo Trouniere's reply died unspoken. A commotion of some sort had arisen in the antechamber, and such was the temper of the times that the hand of the Protector flew to the desk drawer, wherein reposed a loaded pistol. The office door banged open, and two women strode in, trailed by the frantically remonstrating clerk. Both intruders were clad in Aveshquian fashion, with floating translucent draperies, fringed zhupurs intricately wound and knotted, wide-brimmed gauzy hats, and parasols. The garments were of silk, richly embroidered, but unmistakably aged, rubbed almost threadbare in spots. The bhibhiri, or decorative finial topping each parasol, bore the golden wreath emblematic of Effulgence, the Order of priests and royalty. But the fabric covering the collapsible frames, though clean, was worn to the point of shabbiness.

One of the women was tall and gaunt, regal of carriage, with deep-socketed fanatic eyes blazing in a narrow, fierce countenance. The gray streaks plentifully marbling her black hair, and the bitter lines marking her face, conveyed an immediate impression of senescence, but closer inspection disclosed an almost undiminished vigor. She was, in fact, not more than forty-eight years of age. Her companion was some twenty-five years younger, and half a head shorter; small, slight, and seemingly fragile, light and graceful in all her movements. The girl had the great, blue-highlighted black eyes and hair characteristic of many patrician Kahnderulese. Her complexion, ivory faintly warmed with gold, suggested northern blood, and the clear, fine cut of her features was likewise northern.

The clerk was babbling. "*Protector, I tried to explain*—"

"Understood. Leave us," vo Trouniere commanded, and the clerk withdrew. The Protector rose to his feet, and bowed slightly. Renille and Shivaux did the same—an almost unheard-of display of Vonahrish deference to a pair of native women. As for the niibhoy in the corner, he had obeised himself and now crouched, nose pressed devoutly to the floor. For none present failed to recognize the hereditary ruler of the state of Kahnderule. Foreigners had dominated Aveshq for the past hundred years or more, and yet, through courtesy or expedience, many of the ancient royal houses had been permitted to retain their gorgeous, empty titles. The Ghochalla Xundunisse possessed no particle of real power, but technically qualified as a monarch; while her young daughter, the Ghochanna Jathondi, possessed princessly status.

"Madame. We are honored," the Protector remarked with patent untruth. "Will you be seated?"

"Such ceremony. Such gallantry." Like most educated natives, the Ghochalla Xundunisse spoke fluent, slightly singsong Vonahrish, her voice a rasping contralto. She curved a razor smile. "I will stand, but I thank the good Vonahrish Protector vo Trouniere for his courtesy. The warmth of this reception reassures me. As my three written requests for a meeting have gone unanswered, almost I had begun to doubt my welcome in this place. Now I perceive my fears to be groundless."

"An unfortunate oversight, Madame." Diplomacy was hardly vo Trouniere's forte. Embarrassment and impatience warred visibly upon his face. "A regrettable administrative error."

"An error. To be sure."

"The parties at fault shall be severely reprimanded—"

"I tremble for them."

"—and you may be certain such negligence will not repeat itself."

"The Protector is most reassuring."

"And now, Madame, how may I serve you?"

"Easily enough, if you will. You may commence by accepting a small gift."

"Impossible, Madame. Vonahrish law prohibits me from doing so."

"There is true rectitude. Be at ease, Protector," the Ghochalla Xundunisse advised. "I bring but a token, of no value other than sentimental. Here, take it." Into his reluctant hand she pressed her offering.

Vo Trouniere looked down. Upon his palm lay a couple of discolored marble chips, a lacquered splinter of wood, and a plaster fragment. Frowning, he demanded, "What's this?"

"OodPray, Protector," the Ghochalla replied. "I bring you the crumbling scraps of OodPray Palace. Do not hesitate to accept them—the supply is plentiful, for each passing day witnesses new deterioration, and the broken relics lie everywhere. When disintegration is at last complete, and nothing but foundation stones remain to mark the site of Aveshq's most glorious palace, then perhaps these mementos will assume the significance of historical curiosities, and they will be sought after. For the present, however, there is no shortage."

"Very pretty. Madame, you've made your point." Vo Trouniere tossed the fragments down on his desk. "I am sensible of your difficulties and, as always, I offer my sincerest sympathies."

"Your sympathies, sincere or otherwise, are useless to me. I require your practical assistance." She spoke as a queen to a subject.

"We've discussed this matter in the past, more than once, Madame. I trust I've made the Vonahrish position clear."

"The Vonahrish position must change."

"Impossible."

"It *shall* change!" Passion blazed, and she paused a moment to compose herself. "I shall explain, and then you will understand why this must be."

"Madame, it's quite useless—"

"Silence. You will hear me, and this time you will comprehend." The Ghochalla drew a deep breath, and spoke with rigorous self-restraint. "Try to envision, if you can, the misery of the conditions we endure at OodPray. The great palace of my ancestors—ancient beyond knowledge, magnificent beyond description, one of the marvels of the world—is falling to ruin, utter ruin. The roof leaks and threatens collapse. The walls crumble. The rains enter, and the dampness is perpetual. Mildew and rot corrode the hangings, the statues and holy images. Worms assail the furnishings, beetles gnaw the carven screens, and bats nest in the corridors. The treasures of the ages perish, and all gives way to filth, decay, and a squalor indescribable. It is a shameful fate to befall OodPray. It is shameful to all the state of Kahnderule, that her Ghochalla and Gho-

channa should live in wretchedness. And this shame must
be laid to the charge of Vonahr alone. It is Vonahr that has
deprived us of our revenues, Vonahr that has unlawfully
withheld the tribute promised our family, Vonahr that has
broken all promises, reducing a royal Effulgent House to
direst poverty. In all justice, it is now Vonahr's obligation
to make amends. You will tender us such sums as required
to restore and maintain the palace of OodPray, in fitting
state. This small reparation scarcely begins to address your
debt, but I am tired, and willing to content myself with
little. Now, I have spoken very calmly, very clearly, and
you must surely see at last where your responsibility lies."

"Ghochalla." Vo Trouniere breathed a sigh. "It is not
the first time that you have, as you put it, spoken clearly.
There are certain realities, however, that you refuse to acknowledge. I have tried to clarify matters, and Assistant
Secretary Shivaux here has likewise tried—"

Xundunisse shot Shivaux a glare of loathing. "He is a
viper disguised as a pig. I will have no dealings with that
one."

"Nevertheless, it is to the Assistant Secretary that such
petitions as yours are customarily addressed—"

"Petitions! Am I a humble suppliant, entreating your
notice, that you speak of petitions? Or am I Ghochalla of
Kahnderule, demanding what is owed me?"

"Mother," warned the young Ghochanna Jathondi,
very quietly.

"Nothing is owed you, Madame." Assistant Secretary
Shivaux entered the debate. "Not so much as a single
zinnu. What does it take to get that through your head?
But listen carefully, and I'll state the facts for you one
more time. There is not, and never has been any 'tribute'
promised your family by the Republic of Vonahr. There
was a pension, and a generous one at that, granted to your
uncle, the Ghochallon Ruzhir, and his direct descendants.
Ruzhir, a notable bon vivant, exhausted your family fortunes at the gaming tables. When he died without issue,
passing the title to his younger brother—your father, Madame—the coffers were empty. At that time, of course, the
condition of direct descent being voided, the pension
ceased. From start to finish, Vonahr honored the terms of

the agreement, and there is no legitimate complaint to bring against us. Now, then, Ghochalla—did you manage to grasp it that time?"

"What is this foolish monkey-chatter from this perfumed viper-pig?" Xundunisse inquired. "I do not hear him." She addressed herself to vo Trouniere alone. "There were sums promised my kinsman the Ghochallon Ruzhir. We are of one House, one blood, one flesh, Ruzhir and I. Had he left debts, I must have paid them. Conversely, what was owed to him is inherited by me. Who of sound mind can dispute so simple and obvious a fact?"

"There's no point in trying to talk to this woman." Shivaux shook his head in disgust.

"Our laws and customs differ greatly, Madame." Vo Trouniere's face was tight with impatience, yet he strove still to maintain a semblance of courtesy. "Perhaps it seems unjust to you, but you must accept the fact that, by our own lights, we have honorably discharged our obligations. However, if you're truly in want, there are agencies to which I would encourage you to apply for assistance—"

"Agencies! Assistance!" The Ghochalla's self-command slipped, and her voice rose like heat from a fire. "Here is insolence beyond endurance! You would offer charity—to me! To me!"

"Mother, please," Jathondi appealed softly. "Your promise, remember your promise."

"I promised forbearance, Ghochanna—I did not promise martyrdom. I did not promise to suffer the vilest insult!"

"Mother, believe me, this uncontrolled anger will only make you look—"

"How? How will it make me look? It would seem that I already look like a beggar!"

"By no means, Madame," vo Trouniere attempted. "Quite the contrary. The treasures of OodPray are renowned throughout Aveshq, and beyond. It occurs to me that you might consider liquidating certain assets—"

"Liquidating? What is this? What does he say?" Xundunisse demanded.

"He means, we might sell the furniture and artwork,"

Jathondi explained. She spoke flawless Vonahrish, without the slightest trace of a native accent.

"This is madness. Or else it is a dream. The treasures of our ancestors, the inheritance of our descendants, the personal belongings of our House—he is saying we shall sell them for money? That the royalty of Kahnderule shall barter and haggle, soiling ourselves with commerce? Is it possible?"

"Your knickknacks are falling to wrack and ruin. You just said so. Best unload them now, while you can still turn a profit," Shivaux suggested brutally.

"Better to burn them than profane them thus! Better to blast them in the furnace that is Irriule, Land of the Gods! Rather than stoop so far, I would starve!"

"Then turn your hand to some employment. Take in needlework. Take in boarders. Paint china. Teach classes in dancing, or flower arrangement, or something. In any case, support yourself. Cease burdening others."

"Really, Shivaux, your bluntness—" vo Trouniere complained.

"I say it's best to face facts squarely, sir," Shivaux returned. "In our own country, we've done away with royalty, nobility, hereditary privilege, all such trash, and we're the better for it. There's no place left for blue-blooded parasites. The day of kings and queens is over, and this woman should understand that the world doesn't owe her a living."

"Oh, you Vonahrish, with your arrogance, your blindness, your contempt for our ways—you are the wolves of the world." The Ghochalla's voice was infinitely bitter. "Despoilers of all nations, tyrants and destroyers, you are the bane of humanity. You come from across the sea, with your ships that are fortresses, your weapons that none may withstand, your demons' devices. You overrun our lands, devour our wealth, deceive and make puppets of our kings. You defile our temples, scorn our laws and learning, despise our traditions and our magic. Barren of intellect, you pretend to take us for savages, when you yourselves are the godless barbarians. You take away everything that we are, everything, leaving us naught but shame, and servitude, and despair."

"Mother—" the Ghochanna Jathondi appealed.

"You degrade us as a people, you exploit and humiliate us. You think us finished, beaten, your servants there for the whipping. But I say this to you, and to all your paste-faced kind—I say, do not be too sure. Do not exult in your triumph, it is early yet."

"Mother, remember the Balm of the Spirit—!"

"You and your fellows of the pack, beware." The Ghochalla was flame-eyed and steel-faced. "It will not always be thus, in Aveshq. Remember, there is magic to aid us—and there are the gods! Someday the wheel will turn, you will be flung down, and the ones you have trodden underfoot will rise to throw off your foreign yoke. They will cast you forth, and you, deprived of our life-substance that sustains you, will sink in obscurity, ever lower, until at last your dire name has fled the world's memory."

"This yellow belongs in a madhouse," opined Shivaux.

"I only hope I may live to see the day—ah, how deeply I long for it! To see my country cleansed of alien taint, purified and free, the old ways restored—there is the true desire of my heart! I would give my life to hasten that day by a single hour! Do you hear me, Vonahrish wolves?"

"Mother, stop this!" The Ghochanna Jathondi now spoke in Kahnderulese, believing the language incomprehensible to the foreigners in the room. "Stop it this instant!"

"Are you one of them, then?" Likewise switching to the native tongue, Xundunisse rounded on her daughter. "Are you their dupe, their slave, their thing? Has your schooling in that cursed land of theirs shriveled the Aveshquian heart within your bosom? Traitor, I see that it has!"

"That is false, as you well know! And lower your voice, Mother—these men take you for a madwoman."

"I care nothing for them! I care only for OodPray—our home, our treasure—decaying before our eyes, because these Vonahrish cheat and rob us! Of all their crimes, this is the blackest!"

"The louder your voice, the less they will hear. Please, listen to me, Mother!"

"Listen to what? You say nothing! You comprehend

nothing! You care nothing for OodPray, you are like these westerners here. You do not recognize the majesty—the ancient glory—the meaning. OodPray." Xundunisse's harsh voice cracked. The tears rose to her eyes. "Ood-Pray . . ."

"Royal Ghochalla, I will help you save the palace if I can." For the first time since the wretched interview began, Renille spoke up, in Kahnderulese. "I cannot promise success, but I take my oath, I will try."

Startled, Xundunisse turned to regard the still, hitherto silent figure in native garb, finally noting the incongruity of Aveshquian features and light, sun-streaked hair. Eyes narrowing, she demanded, "You are—?"

"Renille vo Chaumelle, Deputy Assistant Secretary to the Resident Protector."

"That is a Vonahrish name, yet you speak with an Aveshquian tongue. You are not quite one of them, I think. Nor are you one of us. Explain yourself."

"Royal Ghochalla, I am a Vonahrish civil servant. I have not the authority to personally resolve your difficulties. Such influence as I possess, however, is at your service."

"That is courteously said," Xundunisse conceded grudgingly. "I had not believed the Vonahrish capable of grace or courtesy. But you are not truly of their breed, and perhaps that accounts for it."

"Perhaps. I share your concern for the great palace—"

"Do you so? You have seen it, then?"

"From the outside, several times. Once, by moonlight."

"Yes, yes, that is the way it is meant to be viewed! The illuminated fountains—the Violet Dome—the Crystal Archways of Shirardhir the Superb—"

"Rare and beautiful beyond compare. They must be preserved. I'll do all in my power to see that they are."

"Yes. Yes. Do so. That is satisfactory. I shall expect your best efforts. You will abandon all other concerns and distractions until such time as this matter is resolved. You will keep me apprised of your progress." Rage seemed to bleed from the Ghochalla Xundunisse, leaving her tired and drained, though indomitably erect as ever. She turned to her daughter. "My will is made known. We are done with this abominable place."

"Then let us go home, Mother."

"Protector vo Trouniere, I take my leave now," Xundunisse announced in Vonahrish.

"As you wish, Madame." Unable to follow a word of the Kahnderulese exchange, vo Trouniere was taken aback, but rallied quickly. "I'll provide you an escort from the compound. I shouldn't advise you to confront the crowd at the gate without protection."

"I do not require protection. They are my people. Master vo Chaumelle, I bid you good afternoon."

"Ghochalla." Renille bowed.

"Come, Ghochanna." Without another word, Xundunisse turned and swept from the office.

The Ghochanna Jathondi dutifully followed. An instant before she exited, her great blue-black eyes met Renille's, and she silently mouthed, *Thank you.*

The door closed behind her, and only then did Renille realize that he wasn't sure which language she had used.

There was silence for a few moments, and then vo Trouniere demanded, "All right, Chaumelle, what was that all about? You certainly smoothed her feathers in a hurry. What did you say?"

"I told her I'd assist her if I could. I made it clear I'm not in a position to guarantee results."

"Soothing but noncommittal. Excellent. Actually, if you could find some loose change to squeeze out of the budget, I wouldn't mind granting the Ghochalla an allowance. I feel rather sorry for the old girl," vo Trouniere confessed.

"I doubt that she'd welcome your pity, sir."

"No, but she'd welcome our subsidy soon enough," Shivaux remarked. "Crazed old harpy belongs in a public hospital, but isn't so far gone that she can't manage to keep her palm outstretched. These natives, they're all of them natural-born beggars. Can't deny that some of their women have fine faces, though. That young one. Did you notice the mouth, the skin? Too bad those damned draperies hide so much."

Deputy Assistant Secretary vo Chaumelle and Resident Protector vo Trouniere exchanged discreetly disgusted glances.

"Check the accounts," vo Trouniere commanded. "See what you can do for the Ghochalla. She is confoundedly down and out."

"Down, but not quite out." Renille stepped to the window. "Look here. Watch."

The other two joined him. Seconds later, they saw the Ghochalla Xundunisse and her daughter emerge from the Residency to make their quick way across the courtyard. There was a brief parley with the guards at the gate, and then the great wooden doors swung wide to reveal the riotous crowd. Those watching from the Protector's office could only view Xundunisse from the rear. They neither saw her face, nor heard her voice. But they saw her lift one old-ivory hand, and they saw the mob restrain itself. They waited for a couple of minutes, and they saw the crowd grow calm under the influence of her inaudible words. A few moments more, and the great human clot began to dissolve. Presently, a path opened through the thinning protoplasmic mass, and there at the end of the way awaited an ancient but still splendid gilded fhozhee, three-wheeled, drawn by a single huge and dusky human hurrier clad in the purple, black, and gold of Kahnderule. Xundunisse and her daughter entered the fhozhee, which sped off in a cloud of dust. The crowd quietly dispersed.

"You see that? There is a moral authority with her, even yet," Renille observed. "Real power, albeit intangible. Don't discount it."

"You're quite right. It never does to underestimate the resources of the enemy." The Protector smiled grimly. "Which brings us back to our original topic of conversation, Chaumelle—your descent upon JiPhaindru. You remarked, I believe, that you could not be compelled to it. Think again. Perhaps it's slipped your mind that members of the Aveshquian Civil Service adjudged guilty of heinous insubordination in time of civic peril are subject to imprisonment for a term not exceeding two years. This is demonstrably a time of civil peril. Have you stopped to consider the effect of your conviction upon your family? The vo Chaumelle line is ancient, proud, and celebrated in

Vonahrish history. How shall these formerly-Exalteds endure the public degradation of one of their own?"

Renille was silent.

"Console yourself. No one constrains you to murder, or at least, no such commands will be committed to writing. When you meet the present KhriNayd, don't suppose yourself obliged to kill him." Vo Trouniere produced another wintry smile. "Only remember your duty—but by all means, let your conscience be your guide."

2

He could pass himself off as a native, but that wasn't enough. The role he undertook demanded preparation of an unusual nature, and the tutoring he required was not to be found in ZuLaysa.

Upon exiting the Vonahrish Residency, Renille vo Chaumelle made his way through comparatively quiet streets to his own lodgings at the foot of Havillac Boulevard, where the Gates of Twilight marked the limit of the enclave known as Little Sherreen. Beyond the great silvery portals ZuLaysa continued, wholeheartedly Aveshquian, with only the street and shop signs in Vonahrish, and the presence of buff-and-gray-clad soldiers, to reveal the dominance of foreigners. Here at the boundary, Vonahrish and Aveshquian voices mingled, and the guards at the gate were ever-vigilant to repel the incursion of native beggars, mhuteezi, street-gamers, snake-shimmies, jukkha vendors, and other such undesirables.

Not today, however. The morning's howling invasion had driven the guards from their posts, and now the wretched plaintive Nameless, the blossom-girls, and musicians were plying their respective trades within the normally sacrosanct precincts. Presently the guards would return to eject them all, but for now, business was good.

Renille walked into his own lodging house, a tall and narrow structure indistinguishable from hundreds lining the streets of any substantial Vonahrish city. The concierge at the desk glanced up from his ledger, momentarily startled; then, recognizing his eccentric tenant beneath the native disguise, subsided without a murmur. Renille ascended two flights of stairs to his own rooms, a modest three chambers occupying the southeast corner of the third story, overlooking the Gates of Twilight. His promotion to Deputy Assistant Secretary, and the accompanying salary increase, might easily have permitted a transfer to grander quarters, and many of his compatriots urged the move upon him. He had not, however, as yet brought himself to relinquish his present view out over the Gates, to the purely Aveshquian realms beyond.

He walked into the sitting room, where western armchairs, fat sofa, and brocade curtains warred with eastern carpets, wicker ceiling fans, ivory curios, wave-bladed weapons upon the walls, and a corpulent, appalling sandstone image of the Goddess Hrushiiki. His sole servant (too few for dignity—his position demanded no less than four domestics) dozed in an overstuffed chair. The factotum—a wizened and gnomelike Nameless, theoretically unemployable—woke and leapt to his feet. The master issued orders, and the servant swiftly packed a valise. While the packing progressed, Renille stood staring out the window at the natives promenading the street below. They were comfortable, as comfortable as the climate allowed, in their light, voluminous tunics and trousers, their wide, gauze-shrouded hats, and airy sandals. Whereas he, now obliged to don Vonahrish attire—

He considered the western uniform, with its mercilessly starched sharp collar tabs, its choking cravat. Perhaps, if he'd never known anything different, such garments wouldn't have seemed so galling, but as it was—? Unendurable. He would retain his Aveshquian garb so long as practicality allowed and, perhaps, a little beyond.

The packing done, Renille issued a few final instructions, and then he was out the door, valise in hand, down the stairs, past the incurious concierge, and back on the street again. Through the Gates of Twilight he passed, effortlessly blending with the Aveshquian crowd, and through the teeming streets he made his way to Central Station, another western oasis in the middle of ZuLaysa. There he purchased a second-class ticket to AfaHaal, at a price less than half of what might have ordinarily been charged to an Esteemed, in the unlikely event that a Vonahrishman of any degree should opt for second class.

Second class aboard the brand-new Aveshquian railroad might have been deemed nightmarish by western standards, for the carriages were solidly packed with perspiring, garlic-breathed native travelers; women generously draped, men conspicuously armed, infants not infrequently unclothed. There were elbows aggressively or defensively jabbing, tongues shrilly wagging, belongings bulwarked—and such belongings: suitcases, carpetbags, bulging knapsacks and bundles; wicker hampers of food, water bottles, vacuum flasks, jugs of wine and fermented milk; tin boxes, oilcloth garment bags, leather-covered trunks, and shoe cages. And then, there was the livestock—the avians, reptiles, insects, cats, baby ruminants, and others permitted to travel in a second-class compartment. Adult sheep, cows, goats, Whooping-dogs, and apes were consigned to the baggage cars, but that left plenty for the beast-loving among the passengers to commune with.

Renille vo Chaumelle didn't mind any of it. There was something curiously liberating in the crush and stir, the noise and the smell. Ordinarily, he relished neither dirt nor squalor. But here, every twitch and yelp and pungent vapor seemed a release from Vonahrish constraint; and here, he was thoroughly at ease.

They never realized that he wasn't one of them. As ZuLaysa receded and the train chugged west across the dusty plains, under skies that seemed to reflect the yellow tint of the parched grasses below, he added his own voice to the raucous babble, joined in the exchanges of jokes, opinions, fairy tales, and biographies, telling many a monstrous lie in his perfect Kahnderulese, and never was his nationality remotely imagined. Despite the killing heat in the compartment, he never once removed his hat; a peculiarity that drew some jocular attention, but nobody guessed the reason—nobody ever suspected the revealing light color of the hair beneath.

The harsh yellowish skies dimmed and dulled. Night drew on, the lamps were lit, and the train whistled on along its new tracks, through all but unrelieved darkness; for the lights in the occasional tiny village or isolated hut died early, and nary a star glittered down through the dusty haze overhead. At this time, the native stewards servicing the first-class passengers came in to turn down the spotless coverlets in the sleeping cars, to lower the mosquito netting, to distribute the iced drinks. But the passengers in second class slept sitting upright amongst their bundles upon the unpadded wooden seats—those that could sleep at all. Despite all his habituation to Aveshquian ways, Renille vo Chaumelle could scarcely shut his eyes in such surroundings. But he didn't regret his own insomnia, for two seats back traveled a mhuteez, or mendicant-magician, more than willing to entertain his wakeful fellow passengers.

The ragged, hollow-cheeked fellow wasn't much of a magician, of course. Had he possessed greater talent, he wouldn't have needed to beg. But, like most of his kind, he possessed an artifact—a talisman, charm, or gewgaw of some sort, supposedly imbued with marvelous power. In this case, the revered item was an unprepossessing lump of dingy brownish matter, shot through with veins of a smooth, glassy substance. Unremarkable though this artifact appeared, the owner proudly proclaimed it "a part and substance of Irriule, the Beyond-Country, Land of the Gods, drawn by secret occult means through the Portal Between Worlds, a holy relic ablaze with ineffable potency!"

They always made such claims, it was part of the ordinary mhuteez patter. There was considerable variety in the type and magnitude of miracles coaxed from the divine relics, but usually they didn't amount to much—and this specimen was no exception. In the wake of the mhuteez's prolonged mumbling and abandoned grimacing, the glassy veins threading the holy lump began to glow—quite faintly, yet in the dim, thick atmosphere of the second-class compartment at midnight, the light was quite perceptible. Brighter waxed the glow, and its colors changed, veining the lump with luminous violet, then red, orange, yellow, green, blue, and back to violet again, whereupon the light faded and the artifact resumed its original appearance.

A minor show, nothing astonishing, yet Renille rewarded the mhuteez with two zinnus; as large a gift as he could bestow without focusing attention upon an improbably flush second-class traveler. Such performances, despite their frequent crudity, never failed to intrigue him. Humbug and cheap trickery, his Vonahrish compatriots opined, and he was reluctantly inclined to agree, but skepticism hardly lessened the fascination. For these petty native magicians, with their extravagant claims and their absurd posturing, performed feats that apparently defied explanation. Of course, a skilled western sleight-of-hand artist might do the same, yet somehow, here in Aveshq, amidst the temples and the images of the gods, the magic was not so easily dismissed.

West through the dark, with periodic stops to disgorge sleepy passengers into what seemed a black, humid void.

Around noon of the next day, the train pulled into the smart new station at AfaHaal, upon the banks of the great Gold Mandijhuur River, and there it halted with a certain finality, for AfaHaal was the end of the line. The railroad, incomplete as yet, penetrated no further westward into Aveshq and, thereafter, the journey would continue by river barge.

Valise in hand, Renille hurried to the waterfront, where the vessels-for-hire abounded; everything from tiny rowboats, to sailed rafts, to downstream gliders. But his destination lay a distance upriver, and the conveyance best suited to his purpose in terms of comfort and dependability was the yahdeen-drawn barge, of which there was no shortage.

"River-runners! Water-whackers! Fat, fine, fast, furious, ferocious!"

The cries of the yahdeeneers arose on all sides. Renille lost no time in booking passage—once again, at a price a fraction of what might ordinarily have been charged a Vonahrish Esteemed—upon a barge designed for comfort, despite its small size, with a clean cabin and painted canvas awnings.

Up the Gold Mandijhuur, and the yahdeeni lived up to their owner's promises in all respects, for they were indeed great, fat, strong aquatic beasts, able to brave the current without rest for hours at a time, courageous and untiring. That they were also belligerent, treacherous, and frequently intractable could only be regarded as the inevitable counterbalance to their virtues. Too often to note, the journey was interrupted by the abrupt dive of one or the other of the yahdeeni pair. A deep, grumbling moan—the pettish shake of a massive, broad-snouted head—and then, without further warning, a vast wrinkled posterior, colored golden brown as the surrounding water, presented briefly to the sky and, an instant later, a vigorous descent followed by shuddering shock throughout the boat.

Then all progress would cease, while the fulminating yahdeeneer violently plied his poles, his reins and spiked goaders; while the river roiled, the barge rocked, and water drenched the deck. The delay might vary in duration, but eventually the ministrations of the yahdeeneer, reinforced by the buoyancy of the many inflated floaters attached to traces and harness, would force the errant creature back to the surface. Even then, the contest of wills was not necessarily concluded, for a thwarted yahdeen was capable of deep malice. There always existed the possibility of a swift, sudden turn within the harness; a huge gape of enormous, yellow-toothed jaws; dank blast of foul breath; and then, the powerful projection of a vomitous stream—a loathsome mess of partially digested fish and vegetation—spewing forth to coat yahdeeneer, decks, and any passengers in the vicinity with reeking slime. Vengeance accomplished, the beast would subside amidst hoarse wheezes of triumph.

But the journey wasn't always fraught with conflict. Sometimes, for as long as an hour or two at a stretch, the barge glided upstream without hindrance. And then it was quiet, so quiet that the lapping of the water against the hull, the creak of timber or harness, the snuffling complaints of the yahdeeni, seemed to fill all the world.

AfaHaal was well behind them now, and the terrain about them was changing as they proceeded northwest. Gone were the yellow-brown dusty expanses, the yellowish dusty skies. The flood plain of the Gold Mandijhuur comprised the richest soil in all Aveshq, most of it now possessed by wealthy Vonahrish planters. The land along the river was irrigated and highly cultivated, its fields a distinctive shade of blue—for here the crop of choice was tavril, source of the azure spice prized for its color and pungent flavor throughout the world. The scent of the famous bilobed leaves sharpened the air for miles about. The sap that stained the fingers of the pickers likewise saturated the dark soil, and the heavy runoff from the fields along this stretch of the Gold Mandijhuur dyed the yellowish water a spectacular, if faintly alarming, shade of green. The air, while damp and suffocating, was comparatively free of dust. Blue sky and blue fields merged indistinguishably in the distance.

The blue world deepened to purple. The sun went down in an exuberant splash of rose and gold and violet. Color faded from the atmosphere, darkness soothed the overtaxed human eye. The barge dropped anchor for the night. The yahdeeni fished, grumbled, ate, and rested, while the yahdeeneer slept. Renille sat on deck, a river-chilled flask of orange-clove tea in one hand. Upon his wrists and the back of his neck lay coolers, sluglike creatures scooped from the river, and commonly regarded by Vonahrishmen with a disgust verging on horror. But he discovered no such antipathy within himself, and even the most squeamish of westerners could hardly deny the coolers' astonishing ability to drain heat from human flesh. He used them native-fashion now, and felt the better for it. Above him, searing white against illimitable blackness, blazed the Basilisk and Nuumahni Heaven-Dancer, constellations never glimpsed in Vonahr from one end of the year to the other. Before him, tiny points of white light, reflecting the stars overhead, hovered low above the fields. Very pretty, very beguiling, if only one did not know them for what they were—firestingers, named for their light and also for the lingering acid heat of their voracious bites. Fortunately for the field workers, firestingers were nocturnal. Fortunately for *him*, they rarely if ever ventured beyond the bank.

Renille expelled his breath, wishing to prolong the moment. He had rarely known such peace. It was all quite perfect—or would have been, but for pesky thoughts of the journey's end, the inevitable confrontations, the unavoidable return to ZuLaysa, and the unenviable if not uninteresting task that awaited him there. Then there were the peripheral distractions, the faces circling through his mind; condemnatory vo Trouniere, contemptuous and contemptible Shivaux, bitterly passionate Ghochalla Xundunisse, to whom he had made a promise, beautiful Ghochanna—what was her name? Jalousie? Jealousy? Jasmine-y? Jathondi. That was it. Jathondi. Beautiful? A matter of taste. Intelligent, educated, and self-possessed, beyond question. Apparent strength, despite apparent fragility. Beautiful? What difference did it make? He was thinking like Shivaux.

Thank you, she had said, in silence. Her walk, the poise of her head.

Beautiful.

Likely to end as fourth wife to some aged princeling, who'd give her the pox on their wedding night.

Renille drained the last of his tea, set the empty flask aside, and rose abruptly. Stripping the coolers from his neck and wrists, he tossed the creatures back into the water and withdrew into the cabin for the night.

He emerged in the morning, transformed. Gone was the Aveshquian of the Divergent Order. In that native's place stood a fair-skinned, light-haired Vonahrish Esteemed, clad in shirt and trousers of khaki-colored cotton, a pith helmet upon his head. The yahdeeneer regarded the river, the sky, the universe.

It wasn't possible to suppress all last traces of schoolboy amusement. Renille tried, and failed.

In the mid-afternoon, they reached Beviairette Plantation. Renille tipped the yahdeeneer, disembarked, and made his swift way along the narrow path snaking up the rise from the landing to the house. A group of naked bronzed toddlers played in the blue dust of the path and, young though they were, they were swift to crawl off, making way for the Esteemed. Their guardian—a dusky, dumpy young woman, brass insignia of the laborsome Order of Flow dangling from her zhupur—bowed deeply as he approached, freezing into the requisite bunch-backed crouch of submission. He had glimpsed her face briefly, and it was familiar—she'd certainly been working about the place upon the occasion of his last visit, some year earlier—but he did not recall her name. Her behavior, of course, was perfectly apt and appropriate, but something in the exaggerated humility of her attitude galled him.

Stop groveling. Stand up straight. Look me in the eye.

He bit the words back. They were useless, worse than useless, as he knew from past experience. Twenty-one years earlier, as a boy of ten freshly arrived at Beviairette and freshly fired with liberal notions gleaned from studies of the last century's great Vonahrish Revolution, he had indeed dispensed such advice to house servants, native playmates, and field workers alike. At least one of his listeners, a nine-year-old niibhoy, had taken the young master's instruction to heart, stoutly refusing to bow in the presence of the Most High Esteemed Nienne vo Chaumelle, master of Beviairette. In consequence, the niibhoy had been whipped bloody, to the great improvement of his character.

"You see the consequences, Nephew." Uncle Nienne's righteous words still rang in Renille's mind, over two decades later. *"This is all your doing, the result of your folly. It is time you learned that we have standards to maintain, traditions to uphold. We are Vonahrish, and of Exalted blood, at that."*

"Exalted titles are gone, now. I think they should be, too." His own youthful response. *"And we may be almost all Vonahrish, but remember we've got—"*

"Hereditary titles have been abolished, for the benighted present, but that loss cannot undermine the inherent superiority of a natural ruling class, nor does it alter the code of our kind. We treat our inferiors kindly, provided they prove tractable, but without excessive indulgence. That is best for all."

"But Uncle, what's inferior about them? And how can we say they're inferior, when we ourselves have got—"

"We maintain at all times an appropriate distance between master and servants."

"But why should they be anyone's servants, when it's
their country? And why should we vo Chaumelles pretend
to be so much better, when we've got—"

"One of the oldest, highest, most glorious of
Vonahrish names—"

"—when we've got—"

"—A proud Vonahrish heritage—"

"—Aveshquian blood in our own veins?"

Horrid silence, dreadful look upon Uncle Nienne's
face, and he knew in that instant that he'd spoken the
unspeakable, uttered the unutterable, and that his uncle,
who hadn't much cared for him to begin with, would now
dislike or perhaps hate him forever. Too late to take the
words back, the damage was done, and he hadn't really
wanted to take them back anyway.

"If you are so misguided as to cite the incident of
Sisquine vo Chaumelle's regrettable aberration, be advised
here and now that this is a matter never alluded to."

What language. What ridiculous, inflated, stilted idi-
ocy. He could laugh at it now, but twenty years earlier
there'd been nothing remotely amusing about it.

"We are Exalted Vonahrish, Nephew, and we maintain Vonahrish standards in all things. Here at Beviairette,
we neither flag nor deviate. If you wish to become a part
of our household—if you wish to remain at all—you will
accept and abide by our standards. You, with your unfortunate face, must exert an extra effort to overcome the
disadvantages of Nature. Are you willing to do so? If not,
are you prepared to make your own way in the world?"

Of course, it had been an empty threat. The old
Vonahrish codes by which Nienne vo Chaumelle set such
store absolutely obliged the uncle to undertake full pater-
nal responsibility for his orphaned nephew—to shelter,
feed, clothe, and educate the boy as his own son. At age
ten, however, Renille had known nothing of this, and the
prospect of homelessness, beggary, and starvation in the
dusty streets had quite simply terrified him.

"I'll try, Uncle." Even now, the remembered words
seemed to stick in his throat.

"Very well. You are permitted to remain upon a trial basis. At the conclusion of a three-month period, we shall review your record."

Insufferable ass. But the menace had seemed very real back then, and for a considerable span, he had dutifully striven to overcome the deficiencies of his unfortunate face. He had really tried, too—conscientiously aiming for perfect Vonahrish style and confidence, perfect Vonahrish form—but a troublesome fondness for his Aveshquian playmates and servants, who favored him for his unfortunate face, had impeded him at every turn. He had never managed to satisfy his uncle, and when the widower Nienne took unto himself a second wife, the sweet-smiling Tifftif v'Eriste, bad went to worse, for sweet-smiling Tifftif was, if anything, narrower than her new husband. And the presence of a half-grown nephew-by-marriage, blighted with Aveshquian features, strong will, and alien tastes, was almost more than she could bear.

She had never hesitated to make her displeasure known—or felt. With a sweet smile. There had been the slaps, the public reprimands, the suspension of privileges—for his own good. The verbal cataloguing of his many faults—in order to improve his character. The starvation, isolation, dehydration—to make a better boy of him. Uncle Nienne had always supported her decisions.

It would have been a fairly unendurable time, but for the kindness of the house servants, several of whom had befriended him. Chiefest by far among these had been Sohbi—back then, a widow, over thirty years old and therefore ancient, despite her smooth golden skin, straight spine, and black hair. She'd smelled of tavril, soap, and luruleanni flowers. She'd had a big nose, crooked teeth, blue-stained fingers, and she was magnificent. She'd been the housekeeper, and it was she who had taught him to speak Kahnderulese like a native; how to walk, sit, stand, and gesture, Aveshquian-style; how to eat with a jishtra, the native scooped knife; how to read the flight of fire-stingers; how to wrap and knot a zhupur two dozen different ways; how to recognize the various insignia of Order; how to be, for hours at a time, something other than the burdensome unwelcome interloper he knew himself to be.

He'd been about twelve when Sohbi remarried. Within the year she'd died in childbirth, and he might have sickened with grief, but for the last and perhaps the greatest of her favors—an introduction to her graying kinsman, the umuri Ziloor. An umuri—or Aveshquian savant-guide—conducted youthful scholars through the allegorical Palace of Light, whose imaginary but precisely mapped chambers, galleries, and secret passageways represented the huge diversity of human knowledge both worldly and spiritual. An umuri knew the myriad divisions and their connections, the separation and interdependence of the various levels, the rich content of the chambers. No mortal mind encompassed the whole of the vast edifice, but Ziloor probably came closer than most. Having amassed such knowledge, the sage desired nothing more than to share it with the world, and the young Renille had proved eager to learn. Ziloor had already guided him all the way through the First Antechamber at the time of Sohbi's death, and the great treasure of the First Antechamber was, as any educated Aveshquian would know, the Balm of the Spirit . . .

Ziloor had helped him then. Ziloor might help him now. Before seeking the sage, however, there were certain unavoidable preliminaries to endure.

At the crest of the rise before him loomed Beviairette, an expensive architectural monstrosity. Named in honor of the Beviaire in Sherreen, former dwelling of Vonahrish kings, Nienne vo Chaumelle's plantation house aspired to the splendor of its famous model. But the great stone columns, baroque ornamentation, and heavy magnificence of the original, so impressive in a parklike Sherreenian setting, were absurd reproduced in wooden miniature upon a sunbaked Aveshquian hilltop. Even as a boy, Renille had disliked the house; it wasn't until he'd visited Sherreen, however, that he'd understood why.

Up the hill, and now the path was flagged with imported stone, bordered with imported shrubs that never throve. He came to the front door, and knocked. One of the houseboys admitted him, took his bag, then ushered him with many a deep bow into the drawing room, where the Esteemeds were variously deployed upon the gilt-and-brocade Vonahrish fauteuils and settees. A decorous group clustered about the sideboard, whereon stood the silver ice buckets housing slim bottles of white wine, urns of iced coffee, cordials and tisanes, bowls of Vonahrish fruits, plates of walnut sugar-biscuits, glacéed chestnuts, pastel petit fours—all such postluncheon refreshments as might have appeared upon a Sherreenian table.

Evidently, a house party was in progress. Renille recognized the faces of visitors from the neighboring plantations, those that lay within a day's journey of Beviairette. Affluent Vonahrish planters all; the men garbed in linen suits, the women laced into tiny-waisted, voluminously skirted western gowns mercilessly ill-suited to the Aveshquian climate. Faintness, indigestion, heat stroke, and palpitations were common complaints among the distaff Esteemeds. Little wonder.

Why, Renille wondered for the thousandth time, do they try so hard to pretend they've never left Vonahr?

Nienne vo Chaumelle stood in the center of the room, his wife at his side. Both of them spied Renille, and identical expressions of startled displeasure briefly froze each face. Tifftif recovered first, swiftly bending her lips into the habitual smile. Teeth and eyes aglint, two plump hands outstretched, she rushed forward. Flinging both arms about her husband's nephew, she planted a patch of quick little kisses upon each of his cheeks.

He managed to keep himself from recoiling. There was no call for discourtesy, after all. Her breath was bad, he noted dispassionately. The peppermint pastilles she'd chewed in the recent past failed to disguise the effects of chronic dyspepsia. At first glance, across the room, she'd appeared youthful, almost unchanged over the course of two decades, save for a moderate increase in girth. But she was forty-eight years old—*About the same age as the Ghochalla Xundunisse,* his mind registered, *but how different!*—and it showed in the sag of the flesh beneath her chin, the darkness pouching under her eyes, the grooves bracketing her lips. She was short, barely reaching his shoulder, and unhealthily pallid under her rouge. Hard to believe she had once seemed so intimidating.

"Renille! ReNILLE!" Tifftif's voice soared an ecstatic octave. "You wicked scoundrel! How could you? You never let us know when you are coming! You astonish us, you overwhelm us! But never mind, I forgive you anything, as you know I always must! It is so wonderful to see you again!"

More kisses rouging his cheeks, and this time he couldn't perfectly conceal his repugnance. She felt his muscles stiffen beneath her hands, and her eyes took on a sugar-crystal glitter. As always, he wondered why she bothered with the pretense. Presumably, she thought it obligatory.

"Tifftif." He inclined his head. Throughout his life, he had never addressed her as "Aunt," except by way of deliberate provocation.

"I declare, dearest boy, you are handsomer than ever! How you must break poor feminine hearts, in the city!"

Commonplace social protocol demanded a compliment in return. He looked down into her fleshy, powdered little face, and couldn't think of one. His mind went blank, while the smile hardened upon her lips.

Fortunately, Uncle Nienne arrived. A pudgy, pompous little man, precise in manner and attire, with, fortunately for his peace of mind, no trace of Aveshquian heritage revealing itself upon his face.

"Nephew," Nienne intoned with careful civility. "I bid you welcome, as always."

Exactly as always.

"Uncle," Renille returned ceremoniously. "I thank you for your hospitality. As always. I don't intend to impose upon your generosity for long, however."

"Never say *impose*, Renille—" Tifftif admonished, wide-eyed. "This is your *home*."

She'd sung a different tune, twenty years ago. *"One more impudent word out of your mouth, you Pissie-nosed little mongrel, and I'll see to it that your uncle turns you out. I can do it, too. He'll do anything I ask."* His cheek still remembered the not infrequent, stinging impact of her palm. And then, in front of guests, *"Darling boy, you have brought youth and joy to our home!"* Nauseating.

"The years cannot change you, Tifftif." Renille smiled sourly.

"La, Cavalier Gallantry!" She dropped a gay curtsy, affecting to take the remark for praise.

"I apologize for this unannounced arrival," Renille continued, "but circumstances pressed. I've come upon two errands. One is to report the delivery of your letter, Uncle, to the Resident Protector."

"Bah—" Nienne scowled. "I've thought it over. I should never have let you talk me into that. Beg asylum in the Residency? Undignified and unnecessary."

"It may well prove entirely necessary," Renille countered. "In the event of attack, you'd be vulnerable, here at Beviairette. You couldn't defend the house for a single night."

"There will be no such attack, Nephew. It is folly to imagine otherwise. Perhaps a few among the pickers are fractious, of late, but I think it unwise to exaggerate the significance of such trifles."

"No doubt vo Cheresse, over at Flower-of-Light, thought the same. Unfortunately, he's unavailable for comment. His family members are similarly silent."

"Vo Cheresse was—unlucky." Nienne stirred uncomfortably. "There was treachery among his house servants, as I heard it."

"And you imagine it impossible that yours are anything other than loyal?"

"Certainly it's impossible," Tifftif declared. "We are always good to our yellows, they are members of the *family*. They would die for us!"

And would you return the favor, I wonder? Aloud, Renille merely observed, "These are difficult times, and you'd do well to heed the signs. Your servants, devoted in the past, may not be so any longer. Oh, many of them are, no doubt, but there are always exceptions to be found and the Filial are skilled at such detection. VaiPradh is at work throughout Kahnderule—"

"Those cannibals aren't permitted upon my land." Nienne folded his arms. "I won't have it. Any of that sort shows his face here, and he'll be whipped off my property."

"Provided that you spot him, but do you suppose they wear labels? And do you think you can keep your servants and pickers from listening? No, Uncle. You cannot silence VaiPradh, any more than you can expect to defend Beviairette. That's no reflection upon you personally—every Vonahrish planter along the river is equally disadvantaged. And I say to them all exactly what I say to you. Be wise. Prepare to withdraw upon a moment's notice. A return to Vonahr wouldn't be a bad choice—"

"That is utterly absurd. Out of the question."

"As I expected. Very well, then I repeat my original advice. Be ready to run for ZuLaysa and the Residency there. The compound, at least, is capable of withstanding an assault."

"You exaggerate. You are too much the alarmist." Nienne vo Chaumelle spoke without conviction. He and his wife exchanged uneasy glances.

"I only wish I were, Uncle."

"Well, then—to humor you, I followed your advice, and dispatched that fool letter to vo Trouniere, didn't I?"

"You won't regret it, I think."

There was a moment's comfortless silence, a condition unendurable to Tifftif vo Chaumelle. "We have listened to the prophecies of doom. Now let us speak of something more *agreeable*," she suggested.

"Another time, perhaps," Renille told her. "I've still my second errand to perform. I need to consult Ziloor."

"Ziloor? That ghastly old crackpate? Oh, but ReNILLE—I'm sorry, but—"

"He's down in his old spot, beside the well?"

"You won't be finding him there, anymore," Nienne said.

"No? Why not?" Dread twinged across Renille's mind. Ziloor—dead? He was an old man, and frail. If the umuri had died any time within the past several months, Nienne would probably have deemed the matter unworthy of mention in his infrequent letters. Tifftif, far more perceptive, would have saved the revelation for the moment of maximum devastation. Just like them both, predictable, and yet he found himself unprepared.

"The old boy packed up and cleared off weeks ago. Didn't even ask my leave to go. Extraordinary behavior." Nienne shook his head.

Not dead. Mortality thwarted, for now. The rush of relief was almost painful. He let no emotion touch his face.

"Why would he clear off?" Renille appeared casually inquisitive.

"Oh, wounded pride, I suppose. A fit of the sulks. He's quite the little yellow prima donna."

"And what wounded his pride, Uncle?"

"County Board held its semiannual a couple of months ago, and we ruled a ban on the teaching of that Palace of Light claptrap."

"A ban. I see. May one venture to ask why?"

"It is my firm conviction that such mumbo-jumbo mysticism exerts a harmful effect upon young native minds. It retards their development, fosters superstition, builds resistance to change, to progress, to all beneficial influence—"

"Such as ours, no doubt. Perhaps you might recall that the Palace of Light is part of an Aveshquian tradition dating back at least two thousand years that we know of, and—"

"That is just what's wrong with it. Filled with anti-quated foolery. Did you know, they actually claim that Palace has a room containing a silver waterfall five hundred feet high, ten thousand golden stars, a herd of gazelles, and a diamond fish that swims through the air? In one room. Now, that is ludicrous."

"It isn't meant to be taken literally, Uncle. It symbolizes—well, never mind. Possibly you overestimate the potential harm."

"I do not think so." Nienne vo Chaumelle drew himself up stiffly. "It was my moral duty, as I saw it, to make my opinion known to my fellow Board members and, happily, I discovered a number among them to be of like mind—enough to carry the vote. So the Palace of Light is now officially condemned in our county, as in so many others. When old Ziloor was informed of the decision, he packed up and cleared off."

"Without so much as a by-your-leave," Renille murmured. "Well, Uncle, no doubt you're well rid of such an ingrate, but the fact is, I need to consult him. To do so, I must track him down, and so, if you'll excuse me—"

"Oh, but you can't be leaving us so soon!" Tifftif seized Renille's arm. "We shall all be quite desolated! Everyone's dying to hear the latest from ZuLaysa. My niece Cisette will be inconsolable if you do not speak to her!"

Renille smiled down into her knowing, sugar-crystal eyes. The alternating coquetry and coldness of pretty Cisette v'Eriste had galled him persistently for the past two years and more, as his uncle's wife had long since divined, but he wasn't about to let her know she'd struck a nerve.

"*Do* promise to stay at least an hour!" Her smile remained fixed in place. Her fingers dug into his arm.

"How can I refuse?" he inquired, to make her let go.

"Dear Renille! You have restored the sunshine!" She let go. "Now, you must go pay your respects to Cisette. Otherwise, she will be wretched, and who could blame her? See, there she is, over there"—Tifftif pointed—"with her new baby."

Her baby?

Renille's eyes followed the pointing finger to the girlish figure standing at the far end of the room. At a distance, she looked slender and small-waisted, shapely and graceful as ever, but the brown-gold head was bent lovingly over a cloth-wrapped bundle.

Cisette—the laughing, teasing, frivolous young Cisette—married and a mother? Since his last visit? Married to whom?

Renille turned and started toward her, ignoring his uncle's wife's candy smirk. Straight across the long drawing room and, as he drew near, he saw that the baby in her arms was remarkably ugly, puckered and brown, with broad nostrils, and a wide lipless mouth. It flashed across his mind that she must have taken a native husband, else the infant could never have been so swarthy, but that was impossible, it could never happen—

Cisette v'Eriste lifted eyes that were still the bluest in the world; smiled to reveal dimples that remained the most enchanting he had ever seen.

"Renille!" she exclaimed, her voice high and flutelike as ever. "Come here and meet my beautiful little bonbon!"

Her beautiful little bonbon's jaws gaped. A purplish tongue some fourteen inches in length shot forth to snare a passing housefly. Tongue and fly withdrew, bonbon mouth snapped shut.

A Forest Baby, one of those jungle amphibians named for their disturbing resemblance to human infants; shunned as ill-omened by Aveshquians, but often kept as pets by Vonahrish women and children. It wasn't the first Renille had ever encountered, but this time he'd been taken unawares, and thoroughly deceived. A curious disgust filled him.

"His name is Momu the Magnificent. He loves flies and flattery, for he is dreadfully vain. I absolutely dote on him, I am his slave and, of course, he knows it. He takes shameless advantage, but what can I do?" She shrugged helplessly. "I'm in love."

"Lucky Momu. I wonder if he appreciates his good fortune."

"Oh, no." She pouted. "He's a brute, in every sense. He treats me quite abominably."

"Perhaps that's the secret of his success. Yet you seem to thrive on ill-usage. Maternity suits you."

"Does it? Really? Oh, but that makes me sound so *old,* so staid, so dull! Quite ancient!"

"What are you, all of twenty-two?"

"Beast, I am only twenty-one! Do I really look older than that?"

"You look entirely delightful, as always."

"There, that is better, you have redeemed yourself. As a reward, I'll let you hold Momu."

He hadn't the smallest desire to hold Momu. "Oh, he looks quite comfortable there in your arms, as any intelligent creature would. Let us not disturb him."

"I think, perhaps, he *should* be disturbed." An adorable frown creased Cisette's smooth brow. "He is far too comfortable; it has made him too sure of his power over me. I shall teach him a lesson, for his own good. I shall make him jealous." Shifting the Forest Baby's weight to one arm, she stepped forward a couple of paces, placed her free hand on Renille's shoulder, rose on tiptoes to approach his lips with her own, then veered at the last moment to barely graze his mouth before landing a soft kiss upon his cheek. For a moment she lingered, allowing him to breathe her flowery scent, then stepped back, apparently abashed by her own boldness, eyes downcast to display a double fringe of luxuriant lashes. "There now, Master Momu—that will show you!" she fluted sternly.

Vintage Cisette v'Eriste. Transparent, but effective nevertheless. A wholly artificial naïveté scarcely diminished the allure of perfect white skin and strawberry lips, about which there was nothing artificial whatsoever. A year earlier, the teasing kiss would have had him pestering her for a private meeting in the conservatory. This afternoon, he was curiously indifferent. Not that her skin had lost anything of its bloom, yet he found himself thinking of another, very different face—fine-boned, ivory faintly touched with gold, framed in blue-black hair—a face that somehow seemed more real and immediate than the one actually before him.

"Am I too hard on my poor Momu, Renille?" Cisette lifted concerned blue eyes. "Am I cruel and wicked?"

"Moderately naughty, at worst." He smiled, to conceal his growing impatience. Odd. Cisette's affectations had often frustrated or even infuriated him, but never before this afternoon had he found himself bored. He needed to be out tracking down Ziloor. He had promised Tifftif an hour, however.

Cisette blinked. Sharp behind her infantine mask, she had not missed his unwonted indifference, and now she set out to recover lost ground, plying him with smiles and wide-eyed admiration.

Typical again. Had he requested an assignation, she'd have feigned coldness, made him beg for a while before granting her consent, and then, in all likelihood, she'd have skipped the appointment, leaving him to wait until hope and patience finally failed. Any sign that he was drifting away, however, and the itch to reassert power waxed urgent.

Today she was quite resistible, and he found himself observing her performance with detached amusement, even while admiring her prettiness. He traded inanities with her for another few minutes before disengaging himself to circulate about the room, thereafter acquiring certain information. From Quisse v'Ieque, dapper master of

JewelLeaf Plantation, he learned that fully a third of the local planters, alarmed by recent happenings, had dispatched their younger children to relatives back in Vonahr. Laillie Bozire, white-haired matriarch of Azurenne, described the recent rash of desertions among her pickers. And one of the Beviairette houseboys informed him that the umuri Ziloor had repaired to an abandoned riverside hut standing at the northern extremity of the vo Chaumelle property.

The hour ended, and Renille made good his escape.

Outdoors again. Well into the afternoon now, and the shadows were starting to stretch, and the heat was merciless. The Vonahrish pith helmet was fairly effective in keeping the sun off, but a broad Aveshquian hat of woven waterfiber would have been better. The cotton shirt was reasonably comfortable, but a loose Aveshquian tunic of qunne would have permitted freer air circulation . . .

Back down the hill to the landing, then a brisk stroll north along the Gold Mandijhuur. Twenty minutes later, he reached Ziloor's hut, a tiny affair of baked mud brick, with a thatch of river grasses. The door was open. A child's piping voice issued forth:

"The Balm of the Spirit rests in the First Antechamber, its vessel standing in plain sight, yet hidden. For the Antechamber is designed to foil the vision of Man, and it is not by means of the physical senses that its contents are perceived . . ."

Familiar words. Ziloor was teaching.

Renille drew near and looked in. The umuri sat crosslegged upon a mat of woven reeds. Facing him sat a black-haired little urchin sporting the Order of Flow insignia upon his sleeve. Just one student. In the past, Ziloor had instructed as many as ten or twelve at a time. The effect of the County Board's ban was only too evident.

His shadow fell athwart the mat. The young student turned to discover a lean Esteemed framed in the doorway. Instantly the lad prostrated himself, nose to the clay floor.

"Ah, see how well he has learned." Ziloor's black eyes gleamed. "How admirable a state of humility has the child achieved!"

Renille was mute.

"Go, child," the umuri advised. "Return tomorrow."

Renille stepped aside. The student was on his feet and out of the hut in a flash.

"Come—enter," Ziloor invited. "Master vo Chaumelle honors me."

Renille entered, and sat. The interior of the hut was even smaller and plainer than his former teacher's previous lodgings alongside the stables had been. Woven mats, water jug, cup and bowl, nothing more. "Why are you speaking Vonahrish?" was all he could think of to say.

"Why, in what other tongue shall I address so eminent an Esteemed? Deputy Assistant Secretary to the Resident Protector vo Trouniere, is it not?" Ziloor inquired. "A most impressive title. A most successful career. I must congratulate the fortunate Master vo Chaumelle."

"How long will you stay angry, Umuri?"

"I do not know, Ren. How long will you suffer your people to outrage us, without lifting a hand?"

"My uncle told me of the ban upon Palace of Light. I'm sorry."

"You are sorry. That is good of you."

"What do you expect me to do?"

"What you can."

He hadn't changed. He was emaciated, gray, shriveled, shabby, snake-eyed, and unyielding as ever. No compromising with Ziloor.

"I can direct the matter to the Protector's attention, by way of my immediate supervisor, but I can't guarantee a prompt response."

"He is such a very busy fellow."

"Yes."

"But you will undertake this tremendous exertion. You will address the appropriate authorities, when you get around to it. As befits your position, you will go through the proper channels. That is the correct expression, is it not? Proper channels?"

"Yes."

"And an excellent expression it is. I would congratulate the Deputy Assistant Secretary upon his perfect propriety, were I not prey to a certain misgiving. The Esteemed vo Chaumelle has caught me wandering the forbidden precincts of the Palace. Does his perfect propriety now compel the Esteemed to address the appropriate authorities—to go through proper channels—in short, to turn me in?"

"I'll overlook that insult."

"Rather should this humble one cut out his tongue, than offer an offense to the Esteemed."

Goaded, Renille demanded, "What do you want of me, Umuri?"

"Only that you be what you once were—open of heart, flexible of mind, hopeful of spirit, hungry for knowledge. You were once the most promising of my scholars. A pity you'd not ventured beyond the Rainfall Gallery before quitting the Palace of Light."

"Yours is not the only palace, Umuri."

"Indeed not. You have learned much in your Vonahrish schools. You have learned how to be a true Esteemed. You have forgotten all else."

"My fellow Vonahrish would scarcely agree. I am no more a true Esteemed than I am a true Aveshquian, or a true scholar."

"That is by your own choice, or lack thereof."

"Perhaps. I hope you'll approve my present choice, however."

"Which is—?"

"To learn all I can from you of VaiPradh. That is why I've come to Beviairette."

"Ah? A questing soul, so rare among the Vonahrish." Ziloor appeared innocently gratified. "You contemplate religious conversion?"

"I contemplate fraud. I mean to enter JiPhaindru, in the guise of an AounSon upon pilgrimage."

"To spy?"

"That's what it amounts to."

"Such daring in the service of Vonahr. Such dedication. No doubt your compatriots are properly appreciative."

"No doubt. Umuri, I seek your knowledge."

"You dispensed with it years ago."

"I need your help."

"Why should I give it?"

"Because, quite simply, VaiPradh is far worse than Vonahr. You resent the Vonahrish ban upon your teachings, and rightly so. But that's a local prohibition, and in all probability, short-lived. Should Aoun-Father's faithful win the ascendency they aim for, what will be their policy, I wonder, toward those seeking knowledge in the Palace of Light? Toward those whose minds or hearts cannot embrace the perfect submissiveness embodied in the symbol of the ushtra?"

"The Filial are blood-drinking barbarians, beyond doubt. The Vonahrish are likewise barbarians, but of a different stripe."

"A very different stripe. Umuri, a state dominated by such murderous fanatics as VaiPradh fosters, shames itself in the eyes of the world."

"So much you managed to discover in the Second Antechamber, before you abandoned the Palace for good."

"Ziloor, you must help me. Your convictions obligate you."

"Do not depend on it. So, then. What, specifically, do you ask?"

"Teach me all you know of VaiPradh—enough that I may pass myself off as one of them."

"That cannot be accomplished in an hour."

"How long?"

"Days, at least."

"Time well spent."

"Very well. Let us see if anything of your old quickness remains. Or has an excess of Vonahrish air and conversation stiffened your mind, along with your tongue and your backbone?" Ziloor switched then to the Kahnderulese language. "We shall commence with the Great Invocation, known to all of Aoun-Father's faithful. No, do not seat yourself there. Outdoors, in the sun. Remove the hat."

"Good thought. My skin—"

"Wants color, Esteemed. We cannot have you approach JiPhaindru looking like a cup of skim milk."

* * *

He spent the next four days with Ziloor, returning to his uncle's house only once, to collect his bag and a quantity of lampblack. During that time, he learned much of VaiPradh ways and beliefs, some of them so fantastic as to border on the farcical. Perhaps more important, he renewed his feel—once so perfect—for Aveshquian subtleties of language and attitude. Certainly Ziloor's taunt of "stiffened" tongue and backbone was a gross exaggeration, and yet it was true that he had lost something almost indefinable in recent years. Now, he regained it. He was as finely attuned to Aveshquian rhythms as he had ever been in his life, and his thoughts came in Kahnderulese.

For four days, he sat hatless in the sun, and his tan deepened until his color nearly matched that of his teacher, who took, sardonically, to calling him "son." He used the lampblack to manufacture a passable dye for hair and eyebrows, and when he surveyed the results in his shaving mirror he was genuinely startled, for the face looking back at him from the glass was altogether northern Aveshquian.

Dawn of the fifth day, and time to take his leave, for he had assimilated all that his teacher knew of VaiPradh. Cool gray light of morning, and Renille vo Chaumelle—brown-faced, black-haired, clad in loose garments of qunne—stood facing his host before the door of the riverside hut. It did not occur to him to shake hands. He bowed, Aveshquian style.

"Umuri. I thank you."

"Scholar. I am pleased to note that the Ren I once knew is not entirely lost. For that one, there is a gift." Ziloor drew a small drawstring bag from some inner recess of his tattered robe.

Surprised, Renille took the bag, opened it, and shook forth the contents into one hand. He held an airy, globular network of countless interwoven filaments—each thread hair-fine, yet rigid, inflexible, and remarkably strong. He pressed lightly, and felt not the slightest yielding beneath his fingers.

"Squeeze with all your power, Scholar," Ziloor advised.

"Umuri, I will break it."

"Not in this universe."

Renille obeyed. The seemingly delicate filaments resisted. He increased the pressure. No results. "What is it?" he asked.

"It is a true artifact of Irriule, Land of the Gods. So swore upon his future grave the magician from whom I acquired it, forty years ago. Crystalline aetheric conflation, he named it—fashioned by the huge mind of Ubhyadesh."

"He would part with such a thing?"

"At a trifling price, and for one reason only. Bafflement. He was, it seemed, incapable of coaxing forth the smallest hint of a miracle. Consistent failure bruised his spirit, until at last he wished only to rid himself of a constant shame. For forty years and more, the divine relic has lain dormant. No one has solved its mystery, and yet I am assured the artifact is genuine. Now, it passes to you."

"Umuri, I am baffled in my turn."

"No matter. Keep it. Display it often. Spin tales about it. Mere possession of Irriulen substance will greatly enhance your credit among the Filial. Assuming they do not kill you out of hand, they will regard you as blessed."

"May I prove worthy of the gift. Ziloor, most generous of the wise, farewell." Once more, Renille bowed deeply, then turned to make his way along the riverbank to the Beviairette landing and the boat that would carry him downstream along the Gold Mandijhuur, back toward ZuLaysa and JiPhaindru, Fastness of the Gods.

3

 It was hotter and dustier than ever, the day he got back to ZuLaysa. The sun blazed down through a dirty yellow haze, and the air was thick with clinging grit. Exiting the train at Central Station, Renille promptly lowered his gauze dustwards. Within seconds, every exposed inch of skin was coated with grime and his eyes were smarting. No matter. He was accustomed to it, and the accretion enhanced his disguise.

Two days earlier, he had disposed of his valise and his Vonahrish gear in AfaHaal, vending the western articles at a good price. Now, he carried his few remaining possessions in a big square of oiled cloth slung native-style across his back. In one hand, he grasped a staff of redtooth wood, incised with the ushtra, and marked with the ovoid symbol of the holy pilgrim. His bearing was virtuously humble, his eyes aglow with spiritual exaltation. Thus transformed in character, he passed from the station, out into the streets.

Colorful. Cacophonous. Stinking. Exhilarating. The familiar Aveshquian stew of stimuli, simmering in the heat of late afternoon. Renille made his way through tortuous, narrow streets, clogged with wagons and fhozhees. The shops and booths were reopening now, at the end of the long midday break, and they would remain open well into the night. The beggars, napping in the shade these past three hours, were once again awake and vociferous, while the children—weasel-faced, light-fingered little creatures who seemed never to sleep at all—were darting everywhere, whining for alms or employment. This last hope was farfetched on the part of the many Nameless ragamuffins, with whom no Aveshquian of Order would ever have deigned engage in commerce. Not all of them were Nameless, however. Here and there flashed the Order of Flow insignia, whose possessors Renille eyed with interest. Not impossible to hire one of them to carry a message to the Residency, informing vo Trouniere of his return—

No. A pilgrim, new to ZuLaysa, would send no such message. Most certainly not by way of some sharp urchin capable of noting and recalling the incident. Vo Trouniere would have to wait for news.

On through the streets he advanced, his gait the plod of a footsore traveler, his wide eyes apparently devouring marvels. From time to time he slowed his step to gaze about in slack-jawed countrified wonder. Twice he stopped to ask unnecessary directions, and once he paused to indulge a curiosity that was perfectly genuine. The open space surrounding the Nabarqui Obelisk contained a throng of shouting citizens, clustered about a makeshift funeral pyre. A burning was in progress, despite the recent Vonahrish ban upon open-air cremations within the city limits. Intrigued, Renille drew near. His interest deepened as he noted the artificiality of the corpse. A crudely carved wooden figure lay amidst the flames. The dummy was clad in the gray and buff of a Vonahrish officer of the Second Kahnderulese. Its stick wrists were lashed together with rope. Blotches of red paint bloodstained the uniform.

Fabric blazed, wooden limbs ignited, and a chorus of exultant howls arose. Renille turned to his nearest neighbor, a substantial laborer of Flow.

"Where are the parents of anger?" he asked, in pilgrim-persona.

"In Little Sherreen, among us." The Flowman's eyes never left the pyre. "These foreigners kill our astromages. Only last night, Kydhrishu-in-Wings perished in pain."

Kydhrishu-in-Wings was, by popular consensus, preeminent among the astromages of ZuLaysa. No one ever had or ever would exceed Kydhrishu's stellar fluency.

"A great loss, a tragedy. And yet, submission be victorious." Renille applied reverent lips to the ushtra carved into his staff.

"Submission be stomped, you holy hayseed. You think this murder the will of the gods? It is the will of Vonahr."

"Here are huge mysteries. What method of killing?"

"Poison."

"Delivered by what means?"

"Who knows the craft of the disOrdered? For it is their doing, beyond doubt."

"Aoun-Father guide me. How is this known?"

"Common knowledge. These Vonahrish oozies plot destruction of the spirit."

"Why should they do so, my brother?"

"The better to ruin and rule us. This is known. Listen, they go further. Behind closed doors, they teach the sons of the Nameless to solicit women of Order. Thus is the taint of Nameless chaos infused throughout Aveshq."

"This, too, is known?"

"Be certain of it. Be certain of this, as well. There is no triumph in submission to the enemies of the gods. There, the honor lies in resistance. Should we drive the foreigners from our land, or better, kill them to the last man, then shall we enjoy Aoun-Father's favor."

"Lightning speed His name." Another labial reverence of the ushtra. "It would seem that my brother heeds the teachings of the Filial."

"They have eyes," the other returned. "And they are our own."

"Divine wisdom illumine our thoughts. My brother honors the will of the Father?"

"Your brother is tired of meddlesome foreigners. We have our own ways, our own gods, and it is for us to follow our own path. There is the kernel of it."

"There indeed." Role and reality momentarily merged. "Although, it must be said, these Vonahrish offer certain worldly gifts—mechanical and medical marvels—of which even the gods might desire us to avail ourselves."

"Gifts? Bribes." The son of Flow grunted. "And I tell you—"

But his sentiments were lost, for a detachment of the Second Kahnderulese now arrived upon the scene to disperse the crowd. A few warning shots cracked the air, and ordinarily so much sufficed to break up a peevish gathering. Not today, however. The angry Aveshquian voices rose, the creative taunts took wing, and a shower of stones pelted the troop. Undeterred, the soldiers advanced in perfect order, carbines clubbing right and left to sunder passage through the human mass. They reached the pyre and paused there, thwarted, for the roaring flames were momentarily inextinguishable. The native audience, however, was not to enjoy the spectacle. The Vonahrish captain uttered a command, and his men turned to raise and level their guns.

"ZuLaysans, DISPERSE," the captain bellowed.

Motionless, indecisive pause; a few suspenseful seconds that seemed endless. Then collective nerve broke, and the muttering Aveshquians began to fade away by twos and threes. The reluctant retreat picked up speed, and presently the site was clear of civilians. The victorious soldiers of the Second Kahnderulese waited there until the funerary fires sank to manageable levels. Then they scattered the pyre, stamped out the remaining flames, and marched away.

Renille had been one of the first to leave. Long before the last of the unruly had departed the vicinity of Nabarqui Obelisk, he was already several streets away, pushing on toward the center of the old city. His progress was steady, but not too swift, for he was supposedly a stranger to ZuLaysa. One section of his mind almost automatically occupied itself with maintainance of the charade, but for the most part his conscious thoughts anchored on the scene he had just witnessed. Another unpleasant manifestation of increasing native hostility, but no real harm done. And yet there had been that moment, that protracted moment, during which the outcome had hung in the balance. No violence this time, but another day . . . ?

He walked on, and the buildings rising on either side were dingy and ramshackle, scarred by the tenancy of

anonymous multitudes. Another quarter mile or so
brought him to the remains of the wall, ancient beyond
knowledge, formerly enclosing all the city. ZuLaysa had
overgrown its wall centuries earlier, but sizable stretches
of masonry remained intact, and the original bas-relief serpents coiled yet across the great stone lintel once surmounting the long-vanished main gates.

Through the Python Gates and into the Old City, as
the section within the wall was known, and now the afternoon was dying, and the long shadows were pooling in the
breathless streets, building darkness from the ground up.
On along the crooked little alleyways until the constriction
vanished, and he was standing at the edge of a broad circular space, known as Jaya, "the Heart," at the very core of
old ZuLaysa. No tradesmen hawking their wares, here; no
peddlers, mhuteezi, musicians, or beggars; no taint of commerce polluting sacred ground. At Jaya's center rose
JiPhaindru, Fastness of the Gods—a stark, graceless construction of black basalt, massive and impregnable as any
fortress. A high wall of black granite, fit to withstand an
army, girdled the temple. The ironbound gates, however,
stood wide open, for the faithful were never turned from
JiPhaindru's courtyard. The wall above the gates bore the
great carven symbol of the ushtra.

Bowed head advertising a suitable humility, Renille
advanced to the gates, passing painlessly beneath the ushtra, where few if any westerners had preceded him. Nobody hindered him, accosted him, or, indeed, appeared to
take the slightest notice. He might have been invisible. In
which case, the prickling sensation at the back of his neck,
the queasy coldness assailing him the moment he set foot
on temple property, were inexplicable.

He glanced about him. Twilight now, and the old red
lanterns in the temple courtyard were already glowing.
Ruby light fell upon black stone flagging, sealed, waxed,
and rubbed to an improbable luster. Here and there about
the courtyard crouched the bunch-backed faithful, down
on their knees, rags in hand, devotedly polishing. Others
knelt within the prayer niches cut into the granite wall at
irregular intervals. From the niches issued an incessant
drone of chanting. But these minute human manifestations

were scarcely noticeable, their existence all but eclipsed by the spectacular monstrosity looming at the center of the courtyard.

There towered a gigantic figure of black marble, its smooth surface reflecting the lantern light in red gleams. The figure stood upright, appendages extended, but the exact number of members was impossible to judge, for all such details were lost beneath billowing folds of sculpted cloth. The unknown artist had been a master, somehow imbuing marble with the flexibility of black silk to create an illusion of fluid fabric draping an unimaginable form. The head surmounting the improbable body was swathed in a deep, sculpted hood. A great gilded mask hid the face. The mask seemed designed to express the concept of luminescence, for it was edged with wavy rays, like the representations of the sun in traditional Aveshquian art. The features were amorphous, all but undefined, save for elliptical black voids suggesting eyes and open mouth. Evidently these were windows to a hollow interior, from whence issued a greenish radiance, fitful and sickly, but startlingly visible in the deep twilight. Baskets of fruit and grain, loaves of flat bread, bowls of nuts, flasks of essence, vials of elixir—all the varied offerings of the pious—ringed the base of Aoun-Father's image.

For a moment or two, Renille stood staring. Then, recollecting Ziloor's instructions, he dropped to the ground, which he kissed three times in time-honored style, and crawled forward, pausing here and there along the way to bestow additional kisses upon the pavement. At the foot of the statue he halted, pressed his forehead to the flags, and there crouched motionless, arms outstretched, imploring palms presented to the god.

He could hear the drone of the faithful at their prayers, the slap of sandaled feet on stone, and the humming of insects, millions of insects. The minutes passed, and the humming intensified. Presently he felt the first sting on his bare wrist; then the next. He didn't so much as twitch, for immobility was one of the criteria by which his seriousness of intent would be gauged by his unseen observers—if such there were. Devout silence and stillness set him apart from the ordinary transient pious of the courtyard, advertising an uncommon grandeur of spiritual aspiration.

Time crawled. Renille appeared petrified. Already the obligatory quiescence was beginning to gall him, but the ordeal, as he well knew, had scarcely begun. It would take more than a moderate display of zeal to convince the Filial of his worthiness.

The bites were starting to itch. *No scratching.* The sweat at his temples was trickling down his face, and he wondered for the first time whether excessive moisture might not cause his black hair dye to run in revealing rivulets. For the moment, his wide hat would conceal such a mishap, but later . . . ? He would have to experiment with the dye formula, perhaps try increasing the wax content. A ridiculous concern, but it served to keep his mind off the bugs, the sweats and itches, the mingled boredom and apprehension, the pressure of unseen eyes.

Twilight sank into night. The red lamps burned on, the faithful at their prayers droned on. Quiet figures emerged from JiPhaindru to gather up the offerings deposited at the foot of Aoun-Father's statue, but Renille did not lift his eyes to inspect them, for such a lapse would have counted heavily against him. He was aching, now; muscles cramped, joints protesting. Damp patches prickled his skin, and the insects were swarming about him in clouds, but he never stirred. The mosquitoes feasted undisturbed and, for a time, he suffered intensely. Then his training came to the fore, and he diverted himself with a mental review of all that Ziloor had told him in recent days of the Filial and their ways. This led naturally to older recollections of earlier sessions with the umuri. Ziloor, seated cross-legged in the dusty blue shade beside the well at Beviairette, leading a young Vonahrish explorer through the Palace of Light. Ziloor, parsimonious of praise, yet visibly pleased with his student's quickness. Ziloor, guide and gadfly, throwing wide the door of Infinity's Closet, that tiny cubbyhole encompassing unlimited space, wherein the mind ranged immeasurable distances . . .

Now he opened the closet door again. His thoughts went flying far from JiPhaindru's courtyard, and the physical miseries retreated to the shadowy edge of awareness.

His mind returned, hours later. Dead of night, and the prayerful voices had ceased, but the red lanterns burned yet. Muscles, ferociously aching. Hands and wrists, ferociously itching. Atmosphere, ferociously hot. Hardly a sound to be heard in the universe. Even the mosquitoes had retired. Yet in the midst of that sultry stillness, he still felt the weight of invisible regard, perhaps from JiPhaindru's central dome. At that moment, the temptation to raise his head and seek the source was all but irresistible.

He didn't move. Presently returning to Infinity's Closet within the Palace of Light, he was once again outside of time.

The breaking of dawn recalled him to the world. The lamps had burned out, and gray morning light played somberly upon the black pavement. Now at last Renille rose stiffly to his feet and made his way to the western corner of the courtyard, and a convenience to which even the holiest of pilgrims was occasionally obliged to repair. Such interludes would not be held against him, provided they were infrequent and brief. He took the opportunity to gulp a little water—a very little—from his bottle, and to splash a few drops upon his face, taking care to avoid drenching the falsely darkened brows. No food, however, and now he was beginning to feel the lack.

Back to his crouching post at the foot of the statue, and soon the sun came up, and the light beat down upon the heat-absorbing black flagstones, and thirst began to trouble him in earnest. Recourse to the water bottle might not have disqualified him, but would surely have lengthened the term of his protracted obeisance. He abstained.

Once more, the tireless voices droned from the niches in the wall, sandaled feet slapped the courtyard, and the visitors deposited their gifts. By mid-morning, the extraordinary devoutness of the stranger-pilgrim had impressed itself upon all observers—many of whom, in token of approving encouragement, scattered flower petals upon the holy man's motionless form.

Renille barely noticed. Consciousness was far away, and sometimes lapsed altogether, but he could not have said how often or how long he slept. At dusk, when he rose to visit the western corner again, his legs were shaky, and the courtyard seemed to tilt. This time, he was comparatively liberal with the water, allowing himself enough to restore equilibrium, if not comfort. No point in killing himself to demonstrate his zeal, much as the Filial might appreciate the beauty of the gesture. No food, of course, but that denial scarcely seemed a hardship, for extreme thirst had driven the hunger clear out of his mind; had, in fact, driven nearly everything other than itself clear out of his mind.

Back to his place, now marked with growing drifts of withered petals, back to the detestable groveling posture, and now the lamps were burning again, and the air was still hot, but the furnace intensity of the daylight hours had waned. The insects were out in force, again. Time to flee to the Palace of Light—whose discipline, he suspected, was all that kept him from running mad—but not so easy to gain the threshold this time, for the distracting gnat-thoughts flitted uncontrollably about his brain. He had crouched in the courtyard for a miserable night and day. Now the second night was under way, and the Filial had not seen fit to recognize his existence. Perhaps they never would. His wordless suit, judged by unknown standards, had been wordlessly rejected, and nothing remained to the rejected petitioner beyond an uncomplaining submission to the decrees of fate, followed by a tastefully prompt withdrawal. And then? Ignominious return to the Residency, confession of failure, explanations that would sound like excuses?

Not yet.

Mental escape was increasingly difficult, but once again he managed it, dispatching consciousness to far realms wherein he wandered until a touch upon his shoulder brought him back. He opened his eyes and raised his head. Starless, moonless dark. The red lamps illumined a silent courtyard. Beside him stood a robed figure, motionless, face lost in the shadow of a deep hood.

"*You have been recognized.*" An electric whisper.

For a moment, taking the remark literally, Renille stiffened. Then, recollecting the ritual phrases taught him by Ziloor, he realized that the masters of the temple, whoever they might be, had chosen to acknowledge his pres-

ence. In ceremonious expression of his gratitude, he struck
his forehead hard upon the pavement.

"You are admitted."

Nicely timed. Dead of night, and no witnesses. When
the pious returned to their prayers in the morning, they
would find the steadfast pilgrim gone, his fate a mystery.
Received in honor, or mutely rejected? No one would
know.

"Rise and follow."

Easier said than done. The endless hours of immobility had taken their toll, and now his limbs had rusted.
Clumsily, he hauled himself to his feet. The robed herald
was already some yards distant, gliding soundlessly for
JiPhaindru's central portal, which for once stood ajar.
Renille hobbled after, through the door, which his guide
barred behind them, and now he stood within the temple
itself—in all likelihood, the first Vonahrishman ever to do
so. His sense of unseen observation intensified. Almost, he
might have imagined the building itself awake and aware.

It was a vast, cavernous, ill-lit stone pile, old as the
skeleton of the world. Dark basalt, granite, marble, everywhere. Sterile, stark, devoid of ornamentation. Tremendous vaulted ceiling, all but lost in the gloom overhead.
Atmosphere dank, comparatively cool, heavy with indefinably disquieting odors. But no time now to look, for his
guide was disappearing through a square-cut opening at
the far side of the vestibule, and there was nothing for it
but to follow.

Out of the vestibule, along an endless echoing corridor, hellishly lit with red lanterns, and it was easier now to
keep pace, for the excited surge of his blood was fast restoring life to deadened extremities. Another couple of
turns, another doorway, and he found himself standing at
the bottom of a room like a dry well.

The chamber—a black rotunda no doubt designed to
intimidate the impressionable—was far taller than it was
wide, with lofty curved walls supporting a steep coffered
dome. A pale of polished columns edged the circumfer-
ence. Midway between the floor and the base of the dome
ran a circular gallery, upon which stood a number of motionless figures. Renille counted quickly. Ten of them,

hooded and dark-robed like his guide. Faces lost in shadow. Palpable pressure of invisible eyes, gazing down from imperial heights. Here were the Filial, at last. Perhaps KhriNayd-Son himself was there among them.

Instantly, Renille prostrated himself. A thin stream of prayerful chanting dribbled from his lips. Speech was difficult, with mouth and throat so parched. Inwardly, he prayed for interruption.

It came at last:

"Humility gladdens the Father. Speak, and He will hear you."

No whispering, this time. The priestly voice rang through the rotunda, whose shape somehow lent superhuman resonance.

Renille rose to his knees. Respectfully, he doffed his wide hat, but the skullcap beneath remained in place, sparing observers the affront of an uncovered head.

"Sons of the Father." His voice emerged a hoarse, wretched croak. No advantageous acoustics down here at floor level. "This lowly one—a pilgrim aspiring to no name of his own beyond the most excellent title of Aoun-Son—has journeyed hither from northern HinBhoor, in hope of enlightenment. We faithful of HinBhoor, while zealous and strong in devotion, confess ourselves weak in knowledge. Remote and isolated in our mountain stronghold, we follow our own ways, and who is to judge how far, in the course of time, we have wandered from the true path? It is here in the city of ZuLaysa that the Source and Finality first manifested Himself. It is here in His own fortress of JiPhaindru, where His presence is immediate, that His worship continues in its purest form. It is therefore here that this pilgrim comes in search of instruction. Sons of the Father, I ask you to teach me the true ways, to show me the rites and ceremonies performed in accordance with His wishes. Guide me, shape my spirit, bend me to His will, that I may carry wisdom to my brethren in HinBhoor and the mountains beyond. Train me, that I may light the holy fires throughout Aveshq. Upon my knees, I beg this boon. Sons of the Father, favor me." He had to stop there. Voice and topic were exhausted. Bowing his head, he waited.

Long, nerve-racking silence. If they conferred in whispers up there on the gallery, he heard none of it.

"What proof of your devotion do you bring us?"

That one was easy, he was prepared. "I bring the collected offerings of HinBhoor's faithful. Three hundred zinnus, joyously rendered unto the keepers of the Father's fastness." He placed a purse, bulging with the profits of his recent AfaHaal transactions, upon the floor before him.

"You ask much. Where is proof of your worthiness?"

"The Father Himself has blessed the temple at HinBhoor. It has not been two months since a great light filled this humble one's dreams, and a voice of wonder spoke from the light, bidding me dig beneath the southern cornerstone of the temple. I obeyed, and thus discovered a divine relic. Behold—" Renille produced and displayed Ziloor's artifact. "A marvel. The very substance of Irriule, land of the gods. By this sign has the Father manifested His approval of an unworthy one's endeavor." A real pity the Father hadn't taught an unworthy one how to use the thing.

Renewed silence. Bad luck, should they decide to keep the purse but kick the donor out. Silence, lasting forever.

"Pilgrim, the Father smiles upon you. Tarry among us for a time, and learn the true ways."

Renille touched his forehead to the floor. When he looked up again, the gallery was empty. He rose, leaving the purse on the floor but returning the Irriulen relic to his zhupur, then turned to the doorway where his guide beckoned. The robed figure mutely withdrew and Renille followed, without question or comment. Among the Filial, he knew, a voiceless reverence customarily reigned. In any event, his thirst was reaching intolerable levels, and the last thing he wanted was conversation.

Gloomy corridors, and then a large chamber evidently serving the initiates of JiPhaindru as communal sleeping quarters. The three small night-lights glowing overhead shed their faint rays upon a polished stone floor, dotted with thin mats, upon which reclined an unconscious population of priests. Renille took a second look at the night-lights. They served, he noted, as the glowing eyes and mouth in a vast sculpted face. Aoun-Father's image—or rather, the image of the mask obscuring His visage—gazed down from the ceiling. His luminous regard, fixed upon the slumbering faithful, no doubt fostered the holiest of dreams.

Tearing his eyes from Aoun's, Renille looked about him. The guide had already vanished. The priests slept on. Best to join them, for he dared attempt no exploration of the temple tonight. Like any Aveshquian pilgrim, he carried a sleeping mat of his own, which he withdrew from his pack, unfolded, and spread out on the floor. Then, at last, he was free to gulp down the remaining contents of his water bottle. The killing thirst subsided and, for the first time in hours, he noticed his own fatigue. Lying down, he shut his eyes. Despite the pressure of the Father's scrutiny, he was asleep within seconds.

In the morning, he began to discover the dreariness of the neophyte AounSon's life.

A whispering roused him from slumber. Renille opened his eyes. Dawn, probably, but he wasn't sure, for the windowless chamber was artificially illuminated. Voices all about him; muted, jumbled, overlapping. He recognized the cadences of the Great Invocation, which Ziloor had succeeded in branding upon his mind. Good thing, too, for now it appeared that repetition of the long chant was the first matinal duty of the faithful. Hunching into a crouch, he bowed his head and commenced. His memory proved generally reliable. Only twice in the course of the Invocation did the precise wording elude him, and then his voice dropped to such a garbled mutter that the lapses went unnoticed. It took a good seven or eight minutes to get through all the verses, and when at last he concluded, and cast a covert glance about him, it was to discover his fellow Filial whispering indefatigably.

Three full repetitions required, most likely. One for the Gods, one for Man, one for the Beasts—the universal verities, finding symbolic representation in the three legs of the triskelion ushtra. He resumed chanting and it seemed endless, but at last collective vocalization subsided, the final voice faded, and the AounSons rose to file mutely from

the chamber. Through the gloomy corridors they trooped
in devout silence broken only by the rhythmic tap of fingernails upon the bronze ushtras dangling from their
zhupurs. *Clickclickclick,* pause, *clickclick,* pause, *clickclick.* The same swift sequence, repeated endlessly. Ziloor
had described this voiceless temple language, had even
taught him a few of the sequences. The one he now heard
was commonplace. Triple click aurally representing the
legs of the ushtra; two double clicks for *ahv,* twenty-
second letter of the Aveshquian alphabet, the first letter of
the Source and Finality's august name. Renille's fingers
started moving. *Clickclickclick.*

Presently they emerged into a small inner courtyard
where the faithful performed their austere ablutions. By
the dim light of early morning, Renille inspected his fellow
AounSons. Weedy and undernourished, most of them. Pallid as the natural Aveshquian complexion allowed, yellow
tint of skin unhealthily pronounced. Garbed in shabby
wrappers of qunne, with drab zhupurs and yellow-gray
skullcaps. Faces expressionless, dark eyes intent. Neophytes, he saw at a glance. Humblest of the Filial, lowly
temple drudges, with nothing of the authority owned by
last night's robed figures.

There was no conversation. Even the tapping of fingernails suspended itself for the moment. Minutes later,
the group repaired to the refectory for a meal of gruel and
flat, tough-textured bread, washed down with tepid water.
A good twenty minutes of fervent prayer preceded ingestion. The AounSons sat cross-legged upon the bare stone
floor, droning out the mind-numbing phrases of the First
Self-Renunciation:

". . . *Utter surrender to the will of Finality offers the
only true freedom.*"

"*Self bars the way to the Source.*"

"*Nonentity is Infinity, which is the mind of the Father.*"

Renille mumbled dutifully, allowing no disdain to
touch his face. Communal abasement concluding, he was
free to wolf his grayish breakfast. No talking during the
meal. A sparse clicking of fingernails on bronze, nothing
more.

Breakfast concluded, and now one of the authoritative, robed figures appeared at the doorway. A deep hood shadowed the face, obscuring personal identity, in accordance with the Father's desires. The neophytes bowed and straightened as one. The robed AounSon gestured, quick hands sketching silent commands. Renille watched intently. Ziloor hadn't prepared him for the hand signals, probably hadn't known of them. Unlucky, but a yokel-pilgrim from HinBhoor might be excused his ignorance. Perhaps.

The faithful exited in clumps of five and six. Presumably, the hand signals communicated assignment to various work details. Renille waited. An imperative priestly finger flicked. That gesture, at least, was intelligible. He joined the next departing group, and soon found himself scrubbing iron pots in a granite kitchen. Scrubbing, which continued uninterrupted for the next two hours, was followed by communal prayer, then by an interlude of meditation, and then by a stint of heedri feeding. Heedri, the giant insects whose bioluminescence powered countless night-lights and, more significantly, glowed from the facial cavities of Aoun-Father's many sculpted images scattered about JiPhaindru, required periodic tribute of live flies and masticated nough-cane. He chewed cane until his jaws ached, and then he spent an hour trapping flies.

Prayer. Lugging of water from well to kitchen. More prayer. Filling of scarlet lamps. Trimming of wicks. Polishing of holy images. Priestly gathering at sunset for the ritual of the Lesser Invocation. Meditation, again. Prayer and a niggardly dinner of flat bread and thin vegetable soup. Fingernails tapping bronze ushtras; no other conversation. At last, tired and mentally dulled, back to the sleeping quarters and the ceaseless pressure of Aoun's glowing stare.

A typical day in the life of the devout.

They were welcome to it. Idly, he wondered what fears or obscure ambitions held these men to such an existence. Voiceless and incomprehensible of impulse, they seemed to him more alien than the heedri.

Renille lay thwarted and wakeful upon his mat. About him slumbered the humbler of the Filial. Above him glared the Father's vigilant eyes, internally fired with *heedrishe*, the insect light. The hours had proved unrewarding. He had labored to the point of exhaustion, prayed and meditated to the verge of stupefaction, and learned nothing. Never alone, and never free of observation, he'd neither roamed the temple nor questioned the silent faithful. Even now, he dared attempt no exploration. Frustrating, but no great matter. Come morning, his luck was bound to change. Lulled by this thought, he slept.

But his second day duplicated the first. Work, prayer, ritual, meditation, execrable food. Grim corridors, grimmer inhabitants. No conversation, no investigation, no revelations. Early to sleep, beneath the eyes of greenish flame.

The third day, instead of filling lamps, he peeled vegetables in the kitchen.

The fourth morning, he learned the correct wording of the Abnegation, previously known to him in sadly truncated form. That afternoon, he added half a dozen new fingernail-tapping sequences to his repertoire. The Father, he reflected, would doubtless approve his progress; the Protector, on the other hand, would not. No chance to snoop, however. No privacy, no respite. No sight or word of KhriNayd, either, until the dawn of the fifth day, when the robed figure presenting itself at the doorway of the neophytes' dormitory actually spoke aloud, in tones clear and penetrating:

"Be it known to all that the First Priest KhriNayd-Son proclaims the imminence of Renewal."

Renille blinked. For days, he had listened to Filial voices uplifted in prayer and invocation. Now, unexpectedly—ordinary speech, and a reference to the invisible First Priest, who was, it might be inferred, lurking somewhere about the place. On the verge of revealing himself, perhaps. And what was this imminent "Renewal" all about? His quasi-brethren furnished no insight. They were mute as always, but their eyes gleamed with pleasurable excitement, and their enthusiasm found outlet in a hailstorm of clicking.

Renille's fingernails tapped bronze. Conscientiously, he practiced one of his newly acquired sequences. Collective emotion cooled by slow degrees, and assignment to daily toil began. The pilgrim from HinBhoor scrubbed floors, prayed, chewed nough-cane, masticated and meditated, scraped burgeoning vegetation from the ceilings, chanted, doused walls and ceiling with caustic solution to suppress the growth of mold, prayed, killed unwelcome snakes in the refectory, prayed, licked the Father's sculpted image clean in traditional style, prayed, kneaded dough in the kitchen . . . In short, a day like any other at JiPhaindru, until sunset, at which time a new door literally opened.

The kneading and shaping of dough was completed. The flat loaves were ready for the oven. A moment's pause to beg the Father's blessing and, in that instant, a hitherto-locked door in a shadowed alcove swung wide to reveal an inner chamber. A robed figure loomed on the threshold. A peremptory finger crooked.

Renille and his sole companion of the moment—a runtish, frizz-haired neophyte, much given to sotto voce chanting—obeyed the voiceless command at once. Following their summoner through the doorway, they found themselves in a small auxiliary kitchen, well ventilated and well equipped, wherein the doubtless superior meals of the privileged among Aoun's faithful were prepared. Upon a table sat a pair of silver trays, laden with bowls of worked silver and crystal, containing food fit for a ghochallon's table. The perfume of expensively rare spices wafted from the bowls. One of the dishes—the glazed sapphire-eel coiled upon a bed of blue tavril-hued rice—was customarily reserved for members of the Effulgent Order alone. More remarkable yet were the lush chains of luruleanni blossoms wreathing each tray. Such luxury and plenty were foreign to this place. Dinner for the invisible KhriNayd-Son?

Priestly hands danced in silence. The frizz-haired runt bowed low, and took up one of the trays. Renille did likewise. The runt departed, with an air of purpose. Renille followed.

Through the main kitchen they hurried, along the stone corridors, and up the stairs. The urge to question his companion was irresistible. Renille's fingernails tapped the bottom of the silver tray in a simple interrogative sequence, to which there was no reply.

Along a murky little passage, to a jarringly anomalous door—ornate, heavily carved in high relief, painted in bright colors, and securely barred. Balancing his tray on one hand, the runt drew the bar with the other, pushed the door open, and went through. Renille trailed his companion into a room tricked out like a seraglio in a madhouse. It was all he could do to keep his face a blank. Certainly, he couldn't stop his eyes from wandering. The chamber, like many within JiPhaindru, was windowless. The air was still, hot, and choked with floral perfume. Gauzy pink hangings softened the granite walls, colorful thick rugs covered the floor. The lamps were brass and colored glass, with dangling crystal lusters. The furniture was massively upholstered, stuffed with down and crusted with golden embroideries. There were bulbous hassocks, gilded tables inlaid with jasper, and a number of fringed divans, two of them occupied.

A couple of girls reclined on couches. They were young, not more than thirteen or fourteen years of age. Both were small, noticeably pale by Aveshquian standards, with round little faces, nondescript features, empty eyes. They wore expensive silks of screaming yellow and purple, with golden ushtras dangling from embroidered zhupurs. No symbols of Order in evidence, however. The voluminous draperies failed to disguise a pair of distended bellies. Both girls were hugely pregnant, no doubt due to deliver in a matter of days.

A small, private harem? The tenants were scarcely more than children. Singular appetites, these Filial had. And what would become of the new little AounSons, now so near emergence? Raised within JiPhaindru, to swell the ranks of the faithful? Not a bad source of future zealots. Trained and indoctrinated from infancy on, they'd surely mature to serve the Father well.

The two girls hardly glanced at the newcomers. Their eyes locked on the food. The runt deposited his tray on one of the low tables. Renille similarly disposed of his own. In a flash, the girls were off their couches, across the room, and down on their knees. Ignoring the scoop-bladed jishtras set out on the trays, each attacked her meal with bare hands. They ate avidly, but not desperately, not as if they'd been deprived. As they chewed, small birdlike cooings of pleasure escaped them.

These were young animals, devoid of human speech. Or so he imagined, until one of the gravid creatures lifted her head to observe:

"Good."

Her companion nodded. "Pretty. Good."

And both intoned as one, *"Praise unto the Source."*

Eating and cooing resumed.

The runt was bustling about, plumping cushions, smoothing fringes, flicking invisible dust from the lamps. These small domestic chores completed, he drew back to the doorway, halted, and bowed deeply to the two occupants, dipping low as if to an image of the Father Himself. Renille performed a similar obeisance.

The girls giggled. One of them poked the other's ribs, and the giggling expanded; an agreeable sound, but indefinably odd, as if, in the absence of example, the youngsters had devised their own particular version of human laughter.

The two men exited, and the runt barred the door. Renille stifled all impulse to communicate. No questions, no talk, no clicking—no point. Then it was down to the refectory for a dreary dinner, followed by a span of Ritual Stasis, followed by cleansing of privies in the inner courtyard, followed by—

Throughout the evening, he maintained the impassible demeanor that his role demanded. Behind the expressionless front, his mind spun. The two young girls, captive in the midst of gaudy luxury. Their adolescent giggles, characteristic neither of hapless prisoners, nor of Aoun-Father's grim priesthood. Their swelling bellies. KhriNayd's work? Others? Perhaps a number of the highest Filial enjoyed access? And finally, their voices. Light, high, juvenile voices. Inarticulate, yet surely capable of answering simple questions.

The likelihood of an interview, however, appeared remote.

That night, he lay upon his mat, with Aoun's gaze

burning down on him. There was no evading that regard, for the Father was all-seeing, all-knowing, His vast presence permeating the temple . . .

Renille shook his head, scattering superstitious fancies. Insects. Luminous insects inhabiting the cavity behind the sculpted mask lent spurious omniscience. That was all.

Annoyed with himself, he rose from his mat and made for the door, picking his way among neophytes seemingly dead to the world. Yet, as he walked from the room, the skin between his shoulder blades prickled, and he sensed more strongly than ever the pressure of invisible eyes. Imagination? He moved quietly but without furtiveness, heading for the inner courtyard and the privies there— surely the most unexceptionable of nocturnal excursions, but it required conscious effort to refrain from slinking and sneaking along the corridors.

It was the first time he'd ventured from the dormitory before dawn, and now he discovered JiPhaindru by night a place transformed. Gone were the drudging neophytes— the floor scrubbers, the wall scrapers, and idol lickers. In their place glided silent robed figures, of the sort he'd encountered upon his first arrival. They were not much in evidence by day. Perhaps they slept then. Now they were awake, intent upon their nameless errands, and their shadowy silence spoke of knowledge, potent yet dwarfed by the power of the huge unseen presence.

Those fancies, again.

He had never felt so conspicuous. Hooded heads turned to mark his progress. There would be no discreet probing of forbidden temple recesses tonight.

Then when?

The days were passing. He had learned nothing.

When?

Not tonight.

The inner courtyard was empty. Nuumahni Heaven-Dancer, blazing in the black sky overhead, was for once his sole companion. He took the opportunity to try several of the doors spaced about the courtyard perimeter. All locked.

Back to the sleeping quarters, the snores of the neophytes, the glare of the Father's eyes. Another profitless night. And sleepless. He was still wide awake at dawn, when the faithful rose from their mats, and the Great Invocation commenced. He droned out the verses without effort, for by now he knew each syllable by heart.

A cryptic announcement: *"Be it known to all that Renewal is nigh."* Happy response from the AounSons.

Renewal?

The usual early morning assignments, and now many of the hand gestures were easily intelligible. To the kitchen, this morning, and a purge of resident geckos. After that, a scouring of algae from the water jugs. Then the door to the inner chamber opened, and there were voiceless instructions, and two meals on a single tray for him to carry upstairs to the pregnant odalisques. This time, he was to go alone. Finally.

He went.

Today, the girls sported silks of crimson and bile green, freighted with gold. The childish little faces glistened with heavy cosmetic paint.

Two heads turned as Renille entered. Two pairs of kohl-rimmed eyes lighted with pleasure at sight of the food. He deposited the tray, and the girls hauled their swollen selves to the table at once. Amidst much cooing and squealing, they fell to. For a couple of minutes he busied himself with small tasks about the room, then stood watching them. When the tempo of their chewing slowed, he spoke.

"Honored ladies. All is to your liking?"

Both girls turned to goggle up at him. Their astonished mouths fell open. Cooing and squealing ceased. It was as if no one had ever addressed them directly before. Perhaps no one had. He repeated his query, speaking slowly and very distinctly. Their faces did not change, and he wondered if they understood his words. Another dialect required? But no, he'd heard them speaking in Kahnderulese hours earlier.

The two girls looked at one another, then back at him.

"Aeh?" one inquired.

"The food, honored ladies. It is satisfactory?"

"Food. Good," replied the girl in crimson.

"Pretty. Good," concurred the bile-clad girl.

"*Praise unto the Source,*" they intoned as one.

Progress. Encouraging.

"What are your names, Honored?" Renille essayed.

The question seemed to exceed their capabilities. Two puzzled young brows creased.

"How are you called?" he amended.

They mulled it over for a while.

"Chosen," the red one replied at last.

"Blessed Vessel." The green one pressed a hand to her belly.

He imagined he'd extracted their names, until the red girl likewise pressed her belly, and echoed, "Blessed Vessel."

One chosen, two blessed vessels. Unenlightening. "How long have you been here?" he asked.

They stared, apparently without comprehension.

"Here," red Chosen finally replied. "Good. Beloved of the Father."

"Chosen," proclaimed the green girl.

Two chosens.

"*Praise unto the Source.*"

Mentally impaired, both of them, he was beginning to suspect. Evidently not dissatisfied with their own captivity, however. Or perhaps simply unaware.

"Where do you come from?" he attempted.

"Down."

"Down?"

"Below. With Chosen."

"And where was that?"

Blank looks. Vacant eyes wandering. The novelty of attempted communication was fast diminishing, and their attention was starting to flag. But there was at least one topic certain to engage their interest.

"Babies," he suggested.

"Aeh?"

"Babies." He pantomimed cradling an infant, then pointed to one of the distended abdomens. "Soon."

"*Praise unto the Source.*"

The chorus commenced to wax tiresome.

"Praise." Suppressing all visible frustration, Renille

touched reverent lips to his ushtra. "And the most fortunate father—?"

"*Praise Him.*"

"The father is—?"

"*He is Source and Finality,*" both girls droned like
adolescent automata.

"And His son is the First Priest KhriNayd." Renille
radiated fervid piety.

"KhriNayd-Son."

"First Priest."

"—Visits you here, perhaps?" Renille inquired.

"Here," the red girl informed him. "Good."

"Chosen," proclaimed the green girl.

"*Praise unto the Source.*"

The conversation was neither informative nor safe. It
wasn't the place of a neophyte to question and, in any
case, the chosen heads were clearly empty. Departing with
a bow, he left them to finish their meal in peace.

The corridors were deserted. It was one of the many
hours given over to prayer, and the AounSons were now
assembled in the inner courtyard. His absence among so
many would go unnoticed. Probably.

Eyes scanning left and right, he advanced. Low,
arched ceiling, featureless walls, red lamps. Nothing much
to see, and in any case, what was he actually looking for?
Iron-strapped door to the left. He tried it. Locked. Straight
ahead, a T-shaped intersection, with a narrow stone stairway ascending to unknown regions. Deep recess beneath
the stairs, bizarre sculpted image of Aoun-Father occupying the recess. Image in need of a good cleaning, he noted,
mind working like a neophyte's. Voices and footsteps descending the stairs, and he couldn't afford to be caught
sightseeing.

Renille slid into the recess, hunkering down behind
the statue. The voices descended, receded, faded away. He
peered from his hiding place. The corridor was empty
again, but still he didn't chance emergence, for instinct was
tingling coldly along his spine. There was the familiar
sense of being watched, back again, and too strong to ignore. Delusion? The eyes of the Father?

The cavelike place in which he crouched was larger

than he had supposed. His outstretched arm failed to encounter the back wall. The inner reaches were lost in shadow, slimed with fungi, but otherwise empty; or so he imagined, until his groping hand closed on a human limb. It was small, warm, and alive. Its owner jerked back with a squeal. Renille controlled the impulse to do likewise. His heart jumped and his grip tightened. His invisible captive wriggled desperately. Sharp teeth gnawed at his arm, and he suppressed an unFilial curse. The struggle did not cease until he had secured two wrists, so thin he might grasp both in one hand. The unseen went limp.

He drew his prisoner forward into the light. The red glow from the corridor illumined a small, sharp-featured face; tangled, unwashed black hair; a slight, gawky form. It was a girl, Aveshquian, probably about twelve or thirteen years old. The body beneath the knee-length tunic of qunne was just beginning to mature. She was staring up at him with scared but curiously appraising black eyes.

"You tell, I tell," she announced, her voice a threatening child's, her accent slum-ZuLaysan.

"What do you tell?" Instinctively, he whispered.

"You and Blessed Vessels. I listen, outside door. You inside with them. Questions. Talk. Forbidden. You tell what you see, I tell what I hear. Believe it."

"What I see?"

"Me. Here. They catch me, they put me back."

"Back where?"

"Down. With Chosen. Below. *You* know."

"Below?"

"Below? Below? This AounSon a parrot bird?"

"Where the Blessed Vessels come from? What the two in there just spoke of?"

"*Them.*" The girl's nose wrinkled. "Stupid ones. Always here, whole lives, know nothing. Not like me. *I* remember."

"Remember what?"

"Out there. Streets. People. Fhozhees. Jukkha vendors. Before. I remember. Not like stupid cow-yahdeens in there. You let me go, now? Hurting me."

"Apologies, young one." He relaxed his hold on her wrists. "You will not run away?"

"I do not run. I am not fearing you. Hear this, you tell on me, I tell on you."

"I hear." He released her.

"Aaah. Better." She sat back, rubbing her wrists. "Maybe I lie a little. When you come in here, seize me in the dark, then I am very afraid. But not now. Now I am thinking, others afraid, maybe."

"Maybe. What is your name, child?"

"Chura, I am once called. Out there, before. They call me Chosen, here. But I remember. Chura."

"When was before? When were you out there, among the fhozhees and jukkha vendors?"

"Long time back."

"And how long since you were down below, with the Chosen?"

"Long time below, with know-nothing Chosen. *'Praise unto the Source.'* All they say. Then—out. Days and nights, I am out. No food. Scraps, two, maybe three times. You got food?"

"Not with me, but—"

"You bring food to lard-head Blessed Vessels. Maybe they leave some."

"The gods willing."

"You give me scraps?"

"If I can. Are you telling me that there are other girls—Chosen—kept somewhere in this building?"

"Sometimes many, sometimes few. Right now, many. Below. Underneath. *You* know."

"No. I am a stranger to this place."

"You know kitchen?"

"Yes."

"You go kitchen?"

"Sometimes."

"Get bread? Give me some?"

"Didn't they feed you—down there? Below?"

"Bread. Gruel. Other things. Two times each day."

"Then why do you not go back?"

"No." She shook her head, snarled locks whipping. "Never go back."

"The priests abuse you, no doubt. The condition of those two Blessed Vessels in there speaks for itself."

"What is 'abuse' meaning? When time is ripe, the Father Himself comes to the Chosen, she is Glorified, and then she is Blessed Vessel, carrying His child. Then—Renewal."

"The Father Himself? Renewal?"

"It is surely a parrot bird. What AounSon of JiPhaindru does not know all this?"

"A new one. Then you got out because you do not wish to carry the Father's child?"

"My time is near. I become a woman, and they all know. They whisper, and point, and say, 'Soon.' Dumb cow-yahdeens. But they are right. They think I am glad, but I am not like them. *I* remember from before. Jukkha vendors. And I do not want to be Glorified, or Blessed Vessel. So I am out."

"Why have you not fled JiPhaindru?"

"AounSons at every door. Day and night."

"If you got past them, where would you go? Have you family in ZuLaysa?"

"Three brothers, five sisters. Not enough food, so my mother sells me to the priests of the temple."

Sale of superfluous children. Repellent to Vonahrish sensibilities, but commonplace in Aveshq. And not the worst of possible fates, as far less appetizing alternatives existed. In the absence of a purchaser, unwanted girl babies were routinely drowned at birth. At least the "Chosen" of JiPhaindru were assured of shelter and food. Still, enforced concubinage—virtual slavery, in supposedly enlightened times—

"Are there other Chosen like you, who wish to leave?" Renille asked.

"Why does the parrot-bird squawk such lard-head questions? What does he seek of this one?"

"Knowledge."

"Then he must pray for it or pay for it. You pay."

"I've only a few small coins—"

"Aeh! What should I do with them here? Food. You bring me food. Here. Then I answer questions."

"This AounSon desires to feed the hungry one, yet the task is far more difficult than she supposes—"

"Do it, Parrot. You think of something." The black

eyes gleamed. "Else maybe I madden with hunger. Maybe I run to the priests, I beg their bread, I tell what I hear between new AounSon and Blessed Vessels. I tell the questions he asks. Better if this one not so hungry."

"Far better. Then wait for me here in the hour following sunset. I will try to find a way."

His observations of the past days suggested a method. In the late afternoon, when the sharp hand clap of a robed priest released the neophytes from their various attitudes of Ritual Stasis, Renille remained frozen in place. He was crouched before one of the Father's multifarious graven images, much as he had once groveled at the foot of the great statue in the outer courtyard. Now, as then, the sheer persistence of his petrifaction implied an ecstasy of self-abasement meriting the respect of the faithful. No one presumed to shake a commendably fervent AounSon from the throes of self-abnegation, and thus, when the neophytes withdrew to their drudgery, he stayed where he was, forehead pressed to the floor.

The hours passed. Paralyzed, suspended in time, he dreamed. Presently the approach of a small priestly parade, en route to the refectory, signaled the hour of sunset. An anonymous hand scattered approving rose petals over his still form in passing. The measured footsteps receded. He didn't stir. The distant chanting voices faded, and quiet descended upon JiPhaindru. The red lanterns burned on, and now at last he rose from his place to wander away, paroxysm of piety concluded.

He made his way through the building without incident. Perhaps unseen eyes marked his progress, but he never encountered a soul. Up the stairs to the second story he drifted as if in a dream, along the corridor to the recess wherein a ravenous runaway Chosen, who still remembered her own name, might or might not await him.

Chura, she had called herself.

She was there, just where he had left her. She'd probably been hiding there all day. As he squeezed in behind the statue guarding the entrance, he heard her quick, excited breathing and then her voice:

"Parrot? You bring food?"

"Bread. A few pijhallies. It is little, I know, but all I could safely carry away without—"

"Give me!"

"Where is your hand? This parrot has not the eyes of an owl."

"*Here.*" She approached on hands and knees, and a stray beam of light caught her face for an instant, reddening the avid eyes. "*Give me!*"

He extended the morsels in her general direction, and felt them snatched from his grasp. She fed ferociously, in urgent gulps interspersed with animal grunts. His eyes had adjusted to the dark, and he could see her now—open mouth crammed full of bread, jaws laboring. Poor little wretch.

He expected her to devour all that he'd brought, but she surprised him. When the gulping and grunting finally abated, a couple of pijhallies remained. She stowed them away in one of her pockets, then looked up to meet his questioning eyes.

"For later," Chura explained.

"Eat, child. I will find a way to bring you more."

"Maybe you do, maybe not. For now, I save them."

"For now. But what of tomorrow? And the day after? You cannot live in such fashion forever."

"Cannot live in any fashion forever. So it is all one."

"Not so. You might leave this place."

"So wise, this parrot. Maybe the gods themselves squawk through his beak. He tells me how I get out, past AounSons at door. For he is knowing all things."

"Perhaps I can help you."

"You bring more bread?"

"Better than that."

"There is no better."

"There is the city, beyond JiPhaindru's walls. There is freedom, and sunlight. There are the jukkha vendors."

"There is a parrot cheeping like songbird. So pretty."

"Daughter of Doubt."

"Son of Ignorance."

"Truly. This benighted one looks to Chura for enlightenment. She has eaten. Does she now consent to share her knowledge?"

"We make bargain. Ask."

"Good. Tell me, then—during the time that you have been out, have you explored much of this temple?"

"All."

"Where?"

"Top. Bottom. Middle. Everything." She flapped a careless hand. "The priests, they do not see me. I am like air. Like shadow. Go where I please."

Except to the kitchen, little girl? Aloud, he merely observed, "You might tell me what you have found here."

"Why is Parrot asking of me? Why not ask his brethren? What kind of AounSon, this?"

"Remember our agreement. This parrot asks questions. Chura answers."

"Truth. Listen, then. Top of JiPhaindru—for priests, *real* priests, that are knowing things. Not for statue-licking, slime-scrubbing, heedri-feeding low ones like Parrot. Up top, they are walking by night, and they are talking, not working."

"What do they speak of?"

"I am not hearing many words. They jabber of the Father's—ah"—she groped—"His—victory. Yes, this is it. Victory. I do not care. Up top, food good, but I am not getting any of it."

"What do they say about the Father's victory?"

"This and that." She shrugged. "Monkey-chatter. Most of them. But wivoori, they do not talk much."

Wivoori, Aoun's own devoted priest-assassins, were named for their traditional reliance upon the services of the lethal little reptiles called wivoors. Winged, elegantly sinuous, armed with the deadliest of venom, and reliably responsive to the commands of its master, the well-trained wivoor was regarded by many an Aveshquian connoisseur as the ultimate weapon. The rapport between night-stalking human wivoori and reptilian wivoor reputedly verged on the supernatural, but it was a relationship dismissed by Vonahrish authorities as largely mythical. The very existence of such priest-assassins was questioned by western skeptics.

Perhaps their disbelief would prove misguided.

"How many wivoori, up top?" asked Renille.

"Aeh—" Another shrug. "Ten, twelve, maybe. Who knows? They come, they go, they play kissy-face with flying lizards. They do not see me, for I am like ghost."

"Doubtless. What more has ghostly Chura witnessed?"

"Up top, not much. Then there is middle, with low, slave-faithful, like Parrot. Wash pots, pray, fill lamps, pray. This you know."

"And below?"

"Below is big. There are the Chosen, the Glorification, the Assembly, the Wisdom, and the Holiest. There are the passageways in rock, and then there are—"

"Slowly, child. Explain these mysteries."

"Chosen, you already know. Down below, they wait. When time comes, the Father comes to them, and there, in that place they meet, is Glorification, and then they are Blessed Vessels. Fat cow-yahdeens ready to calve. You know."

"And the others? The Assembly, the Wisdom, the Holiest?"

"The Assembly—great room where AounSons meet for Renewal. The Wisdom—magic place, old scrolls in boxes, ugly pictures on walls. And Holiest—far below, lowest place of all. I do not go in Holiest. Forbidden. Stay out. But sometimes, voices in there."

"Whose voices?"

An uneasy shrug.

"What do they say?"

"I do not want to hear."

"Why not?"

"Do not want." She was hugging her knees tightly. Her face was averted.

"I see." He suspected she'd bolt if he pressed her about the voices. "Have you ever beheld the First Priest, KhriNayd-Son?"

"No."

"Then he is not here in JiPhaindru. Perhaps there is no real KhriNayd." He would rather enjoy reporting such news to vo Trouniere.

"KhriNayd here. Real. I do not see him, but I hear him behind closed door, sometimes. I hear him order wivoori to house of astromage called—called—"

"Kydhrishu-in-Wings?"

"This is the name. And wivoori, they say, 'Your will, First Priest.' KhriNayd-Son real. Believe it."

"I believe." The first piece of useful information he'd yet acquired, but it was a good one, confirming Filial involvement in the recent, politically incendiary astromage murders. This in itself would justify Vonahrish intervention; a thorough search of JiPhaindru, arrest of certain priests, including the mysterious KhriNayd, and close observation of Filial activity.

She might tell him more, however.

"What is Renewal?" he asked.

"Renewal is ceremony of purest and highest worship, wherein Blessed Vessel offers greatest gift of all unto the Father, thereby elevating herself unto the state of radiant tranquility that is the ultimate oneness with Infinity. Source and Finality merge, and the circle is complete. Praise unto the Source," Chura declaimed mechanically.

"This is what they teach the Chosen, down below?"

"Every day."

"You recite your lesson well, child, but can you tell me what it actually means?"

"Why? You think I am stupid?"

"Never. I seek your wisdom. What is the 'greatest gift' that you speak of? What is the 'circle'? What takes place during this ceremony of Renewal, and does First Priest KhriNayd himself preside over it?"

"No AounSon asking such questions, ever. No AounSon needing to ask." Chura's unblinking eyes held his. "Here is no priest, no pilgrim. What is he, then? You tell me, Parrot. Now."

4

For a moment, his wits froze over. This scrawny little she-rat had seen straight through him, and denial would avail nothing. He'd have to throw himself on her mercy. He'd have to buy her silence with quantities of bread. He'd have to flee JiPhaindru at once. He'd have to—

His mind resumed functioning. The lunatic impulse to confess subsided. If his face had changed expression, the darkness probably concealed it. No need to let the child know that her chance shot had hit home.

"It is not for Chura to question Parrot." Renille's tone was suitably lofty. "She holds to her bargain. Else no more bread, no pijhallies. This is certain. Understood?"

"Aeh." Chura scowled.

"Chura is partial to boiled rice? Flavored with ground spikkij?"

The scowl vanished. She nodded.

"She shall have it. But first, she will tell this one where to find KhriNayd-Son."

"What does Parrot want with First Priest? Why does—" Catching his eye, she broke off. "Bargain. Understood. In daytime, First Priest never to be found. At night, he is down below. I hear him in Holiest, sometimes. Not alone."

"Who is with him?"

Silent shrug. Averted face.

"Have you been in Holiest?"

She shook her head.

"Do you know what is in there?"

Another shake. Prolonged silence.

Holiest wasn't one of her stronger topics. She was ignorant, or fearful, or both. Time to change direction.

"Tell me more of Renewal," Renille suggested.

"Renewal is ceremony of purest and highest worship, wherein Blessed Vessel offers greatest gift—"

"Yes, you have said so. What is the greatest gift?"

"Gift of Renewal."

"And what is that?"

"It is—is—" Her brow creased. "What it is. Not spoken of."

"You do not know?"

"I am not stupid!"

"Assuredly not. Yet some matters are veiled in mystery, hidden from even the wise."

"Hidden, yes. These questions you are asking have no answers."

"All questions have answers, somewhere."

"Not spoken."

"Written, perhaps?"

"You are saying?"

"Chura spoke just now of the Wisdom, down below, containing scrolls in boxes. Such scrolls often preserve knowledge."

She shrugged.

"I should like to see them," Renille continued. "But I fear the Wisdom is inaccessible."

"Is what?"

"This one cannot enter there. He does not know the way. No doubt the place is guarded."

"Sometimes, priests about. Sometimes not. *I* know when. *I* know where. *I* go where I please. Like shadow, like ghost."

"Can Chura show me the way?"

"I lead you straight to Wisdom. I bring you past priests, I laugh at them. But only if you give me more bread. Rice and spikkij. Yes?"

"Agreed."

"Then hear. When robed ones climb stairs above, that is time to go. This happens soon. For now, we wait."

Renille considered. Well into the evening now, and by this time, the neophytes would have repaired to their sleeping quarters. Were his own absence noted, it was probably assumed that he remained where he had last been seen, frozen in Ritual Stasis. Now was the time to explore JiPhaindru, a chance that might never repeat itself.

"We wait," he agreed.

They sat in silence for a time, for the faithful were passing to and fro in the corridor, and even a whisper would have drawn attention. Renille studied his companion. She had taken one of the pijhallies from her zhupur, and was now devouring the thing—skin, seeds, and all. She must have decided that he could be trusted to bring her more. Progress, of sorts.

The air was thick and stifling. The silence was profound. In the midst of that great stillness, the stone walls throbbed with the presence of alien life.

Alien life? Colorful. All those Great Invocations and Self-Renunciations were softening his brain.

The quiet minutes trudged. Then, the measured tread of footsteps, and a voiceless procession drew near. From his hiding place, Renille glimpsed the dark sweep of their ample robes as they passed; perhaps six or eight shrouded figures. Footsteps ascending the stone stairs, and then, renewed silence.

"Now." Chura's voice was barely audible. "Like shadow, like ghost."

"Which way?"

"You follow, *I* lead."

She slipped soundlessly around the statue and out into the corridor. Renille did likewise. She was already several feet ahead; a thin, elusive little figure, gliding wraithlike through the reddish murk. Along the passageway she led him, down a narrow, moisture-slicked stairway, where the fitful light of the heedri caged in perforated sconces played

upon pallid fungi studding dank stone walls. Down the
stairs to a low, dim gallery that he had never seen before,
and here she paused in the shadowy stairwell, flattened
herself against the wall, and motioned him to do the same.
Seconds later, a brace of hooded figures stepped forth from
a tributary passage, crossed the gallery, passed beneath a
lateral arch, and vanished.

Renille felt an elbow jab his ribs. He turned to look
down into Chura's triumphant eyes.

I know temple, she mouthed.

For the life of him, he couldn't repress a smile—yet
another compromise of his professed orthodoxy. Not that
it mattered much. She'd already recognized the fraud.

Evidently deeming the way clear, she darted from the
stairwell. He followed her down the gallery and around a
corner, into a short spur of corridor terminating in a vast,
sculpted likeness of Aoun-Father's mask. The stylized
stone face stretched from wall to wall. Its eyes were empty
black holes. Its mouth, large enough to afford human passage, was obviously a doorway. A long, protruding stone
tongue served as a ramp from floor to gaping mouth.

A singularly uninviting entrance. But Chura hurried
up the tongue without hesitation, and he would have to
trust her, or else turn back. Already she had vanished into
blackness, swallowed alive by the Father.

He went after her, up the stone grade of the tongue,
ducking his head a little at the entrance, then through, and
into the mouth of Aoun.

He half expected to hear the sound of a gulp.

No noise, however, beyond the tiniest of whispers:
"This way!"

Dim, but not pitch-dark within Aoun's maw. Sullen
heedrishe, pulsing. He stood upon a small landing.
Chura's skinny figure, visible in faint silhouette, stood
poised at the head of another staircase. When she saw he'd
spied her, she began her descent.

Down, deeper, where the subterranean air was pungent with fungi, and weighted with time.

No sound. No breath. Motionless dead air. Down
into the place that Chura called *below.*

They were far underground now, and the passages

they walked were hewn through living rock; by what agency, he couldn't begin to guess. The walls flowed by in polished waves, so convincingly liquescent that once, in passing, he actually touched the cool surface, assuring himself of its solidity. Here, it seemed that molten stone had once congealed in an instant, and almost he might have imagined the passageways some freak of natural formation, had not their unvarying level straightness proclaimed artificiality. But surely, such miracles of engineering exceeded the capabilities of ancient or even modern Aveshquian builders.

No reasonable explanation suggested itself.

The heedri light was faint and fitful. Chura's slight form slid through deepest shadow, sometimes disappearing altogether. Around a perfectly right-angled turn she led him, and then another, and there was a barred door to the left, at which she jerked a contemptuous thumb.

"Chosen," Chura announced.

He paused to listen, but caught no whisper of sound. Presumably, the blessed inmates slept.

"No time now for cow-yahdeens. *This way.*" She tugged his sleeve.

He let her drag him away. The liquid walls flowed. Another door, and Chura's concise explanation:

"Assembly."

Along the corridor, another perfect ninety-degree turn, another portal.

"Glorification."

Peculiar, that one. Irregular, wavering outline; undulant surface; faint suggestion of luminosity about the edges. Dizzying to look at. Slightly sickening.

"No time." Another tug at his sleeve. *"Come."*

Down more stairs, but only a few of them, this time. Dim, foul air. Feeble, flickering gleam of light. And there before him, sunk deep in polished stone, a low, heavy wooden door, ancient and worm-eaten.

"Wisdom," Chura said. "Writing. Pictures. No food."

She was positioned oddly. Not quite facing him squarely, she stood with her back presented to the shadows cloaking the far end of the short gallery. Her shoulders were rigid, her arms tightly crossed.

Behind her, all but lost in darkness, yawned an opening or entrance of some sort, visible only as a deeper concentration of blackness.

"What is that?" Renille pointed.

"Holiest." She did not turn around to look.

"What is the purpose of that place? What is inside?"

"No time for that. Forget Holiest." Her fingers were digging into her arms. "You want writing, you go Wisdom. Quick! You have maybe half a prayer-time, before priests come, put the Parrot in a cage."

Half a prayer-time. About forty minutes, or so. She was right, he'd better hurry. Expecting resistance, he tried the heavy door. It yielded to the lightest touch, swinging open with nary a creak. Beyond the threshold—faint light, steadier than *heedrishe*.

"I hit door, you come out fast," Chura commanded. "Hear? Fast."

He nodded once, and went into the Wisdom, shutting the silent portal behind him.

He tried to take it in at a glance. Small windowless chamber, somehow exuding antiquity. Smooth, level walls, crowded with images, brilliantly colored, almost glowing. Not paint, not mosaic, or glaze, or enamel. Not any medium that he recognized at all. The pictures *were* actually luminescent, he realized; their muted radiance the sole, uncanny source of illumination. Backlit stained glass? He looked closely. Not glass. Luminous color, the like of which he had never encountered. And the images themselves? Chura had called them ugly, but that was hardly a fair description, for they possessed beauty, of an intensely alien sort. The perceptions that had shaped them were unfathomable, and perhaps that accounted for the girl's revulsion. The pictures ran in broad bands about the four walls, where distorted but recognizably human figures mingled with lucent, equivocal forms. A narrative of some sort was certainly intended, but its language was unintelligible to him.

Frowning, Renille studied the walls. Some of the human figures were female, and spectacularly fecund, all bulging breasts and bellies. Pregnant fertility goddesses? One such goddess, or woman, sporting distinctive braided coils of hair, appeared again and again. Initially, she was a lithe if improbably voluptuous figure. Later, she was robed in yellow, bathed in otherworldly radiance. Then, she was serene, distended, unmistakably fruitful. At the last, she lay surrounded by attendants, huge belly gaping wide open, tiny figure visible within, rays of light either entering or emanating from her womb. Then, the mother was gone, and the offspring alone remained, lapped in flame. And finally, all form was lost in the great light. Beyond question, miraculous events were depicted here, but their true nature remained obscure.

Chura had been right. Weird beauty notwithstanding, there was something repulsive in these images.

He'd do better to concentrate on the writings. At the center of the room rose a great stone pillar, its vertical surface pocked with niches, its niches filled with scrolls— far too many to read in the brief time allowed him.

He chose one at random. Heavy, fibrous paper, crisp under his fingers; sharp, clear inkings. Whatever it was, it couldn't be very old. Spreading the scroll, he scanned the contents. Modern Kahnderulese script, clerkly and precise. Date in the upper right corner, harking back some three years. Short phrases, arranged in columns.

One measure millet seed. Brass bowl, he read. *Twenty-six soapfruit. Wooden tray. Three braided loaves, each containing a silver zinnu, rendered in faith unto the Father.*

Evidently, the Father's priestly minions maintained finicking records of every bowl of grain or nuts ever deposited at the foot of Aoun's statue in the outer courtyard. Uninteresting.

Restoring the scroll to its place, he eyed the column, noting the carven stone borders surrounding a few select niches. Contents of unusual value? Stooping to a shadowed aperture piercing the stone a few inches above the floor, he drew forth a deeply yellowed document, and cautiously unrolled it. Sepia ink, copious writing, unknown language. Similar to Kahnderulese, he saw at a glance, but incomprehensible. No good. He put it back and chose another.

The oldest yet, he suspected. Brown, tattered, and so

brittle with age that almost he feared to tamper with it. Very gingerly, he unrolled the scroll. Despite his care, time-toasted crumbs of paper rained plentifully. The document was crowded with crabbed scribbles, faded and ancient. The language, this time, was Old Churdishu, the antique prototongue from which Kahnderulese and several sister dialects originally derived. He could read Old Churdishu, after a fashion.

Account of Events following upon construction of · JiPhaindru, Fastness of the Gods, in the city of ZuLaysa. Penned in the Year of the Great Fire by the hand of Fahjeed, Son of the Father, Scribe of the Temple—

There followed a list of indecipherable titles or offices. Skipping a few lines, he read laboriously:

*The years that followed brought weariness unto the Father. His labors were taxing, the atmosphere of our most imperfect world insufficient to maintain His divine vigor, and thus at last hungered He for the—*essence? Distillation? Concentrated substance? The term was unclear—*of Irriule, Land of the Gods.*

*The doorway between the—*great spaces? Worlds? Universes? Realities?—*stood closed. The will of Aoun-Father might have opened that door, and yet He stayed His hand, in mercy. For how should He abandon His worshipers? Without His guidance, Mankind was surely lost, and this He knew, as He knows all things.*

*Then He pondered, at length resolving to—*cultivate? Propagate? Instigate? Generate?—*the substance of Irriule within the universe of Men, for such a feat lay not beyond His power.*

Summoning His firstborn KhriNayd-Son to His presence, Aoun-Father made known His will, and KhriNayd-Son ventured forth from JiPhaindru for the first time.

There followed a confusing and only partially comprehensible description of the semihuman young KhriNayd's doings in the world of Men, culminating in the First Priest's triumphal return to JiPhaindru, with a score of human females in tow.

These Chosen ones, favored above all women save Bhudipraydh-Mother alone—

Who?

. . . were first among their kind to know the splendor of divine regard. The Father revealed Himself unto them, and, in that moment of—glory? Rapture? Transcendence?—*kindled within them the spark of Irriulen fire. Thus blessed, the twenty vessels of divinity awaited*—

Here, a short gap in the text, where the ancient ink had faded out of existence. Several lines later, legibility resumed.

. . . delivered of their contents, rendering the greatest of gifts. The Father accepted, consumed, and was thereby renewed in power and—godly fire? Radiant force? Magical light?

Next paragraph incomprehensible, filled with unfamiliar archaisms. Many references to Irriule, land of the gods.

And then:

. . . witness the totality of His victory, He summoned to His side the lesser gods, His fellow Irriulens, His companions of the past.

These undutiful ones came not at His call, and therefore went He forth in anger to seek them. They fled in fear at His approach, and when He named them, one by one, they would not answer. Then, He despised them as weak and fearful, thereafter denying them the glory of His presence.

The banished lesser gods and goddesses—Hrushiiki, Nuumahni, Ahrattah, Ubhyadesh, and the others—withdrew to the hills beyond ZuLaysa's walls, where the human sorcerer/ruler known as Shirardhir the Superb oversaw construction of the palace called OodPray. It was said that Shirardhir had chosen this site by reason of its—

The passage that followed was well nigh indecipherable, smudged and filled with unfamiliar words. The general sense was something to the effect that the site of the palace had been chosen for the sake of its air, or aura, or force, or something along those lines—that was in some way peculiarly conducive to the practice of human sorcery. One phrase, however, was reasonably clear. *Here, in the midst of unseen*—turbulence? Disruption? Vortex?—*the barrier between realities was thin and easily penetrable.*

Next line illegible, and then:

. . . *finally locating the vital*—flaw? Mistake? Weakness?—*in the atmosphere, proceeded to enlarge upon it, eventually blasting open the path to Irriule. For this feat of magic, Shirardhir the Superb won the gratitude of the lesser gods, who pledged friendship to the human sorcerer and to his children. Hrushiiki and Nuumahni together completed the construction of OodPray, thereby creating the greatest palace that ever was or ever will be. Then the lesser gods returned to their own world, leaving Aoun-Father to His solitary glory, and the doorway closed behind them.*

It is said that the locked portal between the worlds stands waiting to this day, its location known to Shirardhir's descendants of the Effulgent Order, who yet retain the friendship of the gods. It is by reason of this friendship that the Effulgent Order breeds ever—true? Faithful? Pure?—*unto itself, its children requiring no confirmation of their state by Birthwitnesses or others. Privileged above all are the descendants of Shirardhir the Superb, who yet retain power to open the door and to call, once in a generation, upon the gods of Irriule.*

Mythology. Tales of fantasy. Legend, offering some insight into the nature of Aoun's cult, and therefore of a certain academic interest. But nothing substantive, nothing of practical use. Renille replaced the scroll in its niche. Before he could choose another, he heard a soft tap at the door. Chura's signal. Time to leave.

Fast, she had commanded, and he was.

She said nothing as he emerged, but merely turned and hurried away, soundless as fog. He followed, emulating her stealth, but presently the urgent pressure of her hand upon his arm halted him, drawing him back into the shadows, where the two of them stood listening to the slap of priestly footsteps passing almost within arm's length of their refuge. Then on through the passageways and up the stairs, up from *below,* through the mouth of Aoun's great stone mask from the wrong side, and down the long ramp of a tongue—two unsavory morsels regurgitated by the Father.

Thereafter, Chura's pace slackened, and her tension eased a little. When he turned his steps toward a familiar gallery, she pulled him back, and now dared audible, if whispering, speech:

"This way. Better."

Through JiPhaindru's red-lit maze she led, with never a moment's hesitation, until they came to the mouth of the corridor leading back to the neophytes' dormitory, and there she halted.

"Bargain finish." Chura turned to face him. "You go back alone. Then you bring me rice and spikkij. Payment, remember. You owe."

"Truly. But I cannot get away again to meet you upstairs, it would be noticed."

"You better pay, Parrot! You do not cheat me! You *owe*!"

"I would not cheat you. Listen. You know there is a loose stone at the base of the wall in the southeast corner of the inner courtyard?"

"I find it. You think I am stupid?"

"If I leave a package of food behind that stone, can you get at it?"

"Easy."

"Very well. I'll leave your rice there tomorrow morning."

"You better."

"No fear. But after you've eaten it, what will you do? How will you live?"

She shrugged. "Like before."

"I cannot allow that."

"Nothing to you."

"Untrue. After tomorrow, search often behind the loose stone. I will leave food there for you as often as I can."

"This I believe when I see."

"Agreed. Only look there." He was strongly tempted to offer the absurdly courageous little creature escape from JiPhaindru. He could promise to take her with him when he himself departed. But she would scarcely understand, she'd certainly disbelieve, and she might possibly betray him to the AounSons if she thought she stood to gain. He said nothing.

"Maybe. Farewell, Parrot." She smiled maliciously. "Most unFilial of birds."

Then she was gone, swallowed in shadow.

Renille, wafting beatitude, made his way back to the neophytes' communal quarters. Presumably, his protracted absence had been excused on the grounds of acute spiritual exigency, for no one questioned him. If his anomalous entrance drew covert attention—and surely, it could not have gone unnoticed—there was no obvious sign. The faithful, to a man, appeared to slumber, and the glowing gaze of Aoun-Father shone impartially down on all.

Renille slept. In the morning, temple life resumed its customary dismal rigor, its monotony broken only once, in the hour following the morning meal, by a brief withdrawal to the inner courtyard, and the furtive deposit of a moist parcel in the space behind the loose stone in the wall. He hoped Chura wouldn't delay in claiming her reward. It was still early, but the heat in the courtyard was already intense. The food, in its miniature stone oven, would shortly bake and harden like clay in a kiln.

When he returned to check the spot in the late afternoon, the parcel was gone.

Thereafter, at least once a day, he contrived to leave an offering; sometimes no more than a handful of rice, sometimes bread with pijhallies and raisins, but always something. He caught no glimpse of Chura, but the hole was invariably emptied of its contents within a matter of hours, and he could only assume that she was active and, if not satiated, at least not famished.

No further opportunity to explore the temple presented itself. He learned no more of KhriNayd-Son than the old myths preserved in the Wisdom revealed. He had hearsay evidence of the First Priest's presence, of wivoori existence, of Filial involvement in the death of the astromage—but Chura's tales remained unconfirmed. The profitless days marched, and presently he began to suspect that his time in this place was wasted. He'd accomplished next to nothing, and the situation wasn't likely to improve. Humiliating to contemplate confession of his failure to vo Trouniere, but there was little point in putting it off.

Time to depart JiPhaindru.

When next dispatched to gather up the gifts deposited at the foot of Aoun's statue in the outer courtyard, he would quietly exit.

But his plans altered on the day that a priest appeared upon the dormitory threshold at the break of dawn to announce the immediacy of Renewal.

The day, suffocating even by Aveshquian standards, passed uneventfully. Renille toiled, and prayed, and sweated, as always. His fellow drudges did likewise. Their faces were characteristically impassive, but profound elation communicated itself in fusillades of clicking. Scores of fingernails tapped bronze ushtras. The clicking intensified throughout the day, reaching frenetic levels around sunset.

The sun sank in gaudy, tasteless splendor. The color splashed across the sky paled to subtler tones, then faded away altogether. Ash deepened to charcoal, then to black, and the first stars sparked overhead. The Filial addressed their evening meal, and in that interval, a slim crescent moon took the sky. Communal ingestion concluded. Ordinarily, a final prayer session would have preceded repose. But not tonight.

Dark now, black velvet wrapping the world, blinding the city, smothering the temple.

Well into the evening, deep in darkness now, and the Filial of Aoun-Father made their way in single file through the infernally lit corridors of JiPhaindru. Renille, all but invisible, shuffled dutifully among his fellows. Along the passageways they led him, down the stairway he had trodden only once, lower and deeper, until they came to the great stone mask of Aoun-Father, stretching wall to wall.

Into the Father's gaping mouth filed the faithful. Down the stairs, into the region of seemingly fluid walls, their illusion of liquescence heightened by the flickering of *heedrishe*. Past the abode of the Chosen, and this time, a faint girlish twittering filtered through the barred door. On along the corridor to the next door, which Chura had identified as the Assembly. Through it, and into the meeting place of the Filial.

The chamber—rectangular, vault-ceilinged, barbarically torchlit—conveyed an impression of echoing immensity, but its true dimensions were impossible to judge. Three undulant stone walls, veiled in shadow, were dimly discernible, but the fourth was invisible. At the front of the room rose a massive half-circle of twisted columns, carved of black stone and polished to a muted luster. Beyond the columns, the darkness thickened impenetrably. Behind that sable curtain, the Assembly might have extended into infinity.

A low, semicircular dais occupied the curved space before the columns. Atop the dais stood an object resembling a cross between an altar and a bed; high and blocklike in shape, but thickly padded, cushioned, and swathed in somber fabrics.

The chamber, despite its great size, was tolerably filled. All the priesthood of Aoun-Father must have been assembled in that place. There were the neophytes in their shabby gear; the robed acolytes; and the legendary wivoori, night-mantled and hooded, but recognizable by the elegant little reptilian killers riding their shoulders. The verification of wivoori reality was at least one substantive piece of information to carry back to vo Trouniere. With any luck, the impending ceremony would furnish more.

He noticed then that a number of glowing braziers stood spaced at regular intervals along the walls, and briefly wondered at this. The light furnished by the small charcoal fires was negligible, and the heavy atmosphere was already too warm for comfort—stifling, actually. His forehead was dewed with sweat, which he blotted discreetly. The wax-fortified blacking applied to his eyebrows would resist moisture up to a point, but he wasn't eager to test its limits. Slow curls of scented smoke rose from the braziers. The perfume was too sweet, almost sickening. He inhaled unwillingly.

A final dark file of robed figures entered the Assembly, and the door clanged shut behind them. One of those anonymous acolytes may have gestured or signaled—if so, Renille didn't catch it—or perhaps the Filial knew the procedure by rote, and needed no instruction. In any event, the silent AounSons swiftly deployed themselves about the dais in a big horseshoe curve. Probably, some unspoken order of rank or precedence governed the arrangement, but Renille, ignorant of such niceties, simply drifted into position amidst the lowliest. For the first time, he glimpsed the great ushtra carved into the floor at the center of the room.

Now there was a clear signal—two hooded figures, placed at the opposing extremities of the horseshoe, simultaneously gestured. Synchronized as some sinister corps de ballet, the AounSons sank to their knees; touched foreheads to floor three times, in token of extreme submission; and then, in unison, proceeded to drone out the endless stanzas of the Great Invocation.

No problem there. He'd long since committed every word to memory, or so he'd thought. But somehow those words were escaping him now. A phrase, a line, an entire verse—inexplicably gone. His chanting voice dropped to a mumble. He was a little giddy, he realized. Bad time for it. He breathed deeply, but the hot, cloying air failed to clear his head.

Endless recitation; some familiar, some not. He kept pace as best he could, hoping that his lapses went unnoticed. And then there was a robed figure (and where had he come from?) with a wide, shallow bowl clasped in one hand, passing along the curved line of the faithful, pausing repeatedly to toss a pinch of the bowl's powdered contents into each upturned priestly visage.

Renille looked up. The acolyte stood before him. Flick of a wrist, and the dark powder floated. Spores? A powdered herb? He didn't dare turn his face away. Surreptitiously, he held his breath, but not before a sharp whiff of the stuff had tickled its way up his nose. Weightless grains settled about his lips, and he resisted the urge to wipe them off. The acolyte passed on. Renille quietly expelled his breath to the bottom of his lungs. His giddiness was worsening. He didn't want to know what it was he'd just inhaled. Chancing a quick glance left and right, he discovered his fellow faithful still on their knees and droning. No obvious unsteadiness among them. The priest with the bowl had worked his way to the end of the line. Another, similarly burdened, was gliding from brazier to brazier, dusting the coals with powder. The smoke rising from the fires thickened, the nauseous perfume weighting the atmosphere intensified, and his senses swam.

Fresh air. He wanted it badly. Be lucky ever to taste it again.

Filial voices, still chanting, and now they seemed distant. Another repetition of the Great Invocation? No, they were onto the Self-Renunciation, now. Well, he knew that one, more or less. He commenced a fervent muttering.

He couldn't have guessed how long it lasted. He'd knelt there on that stone floor, babbling amongst the brethren, since the dawn of time. There was neither beginning nor end to it. So he imagined, until the first thin moan of alien music rose to cut the pious outpourings short.

It came from underground—a faint shrilling of entombed locusts, growing louder, gathering strength—and then there were AounSons grouped about the altar/bed, and a pair of litters bearing a brace of perilously pregnant adolescents. Blessed Vessel and Chosen, the two less-than-eloquent odalisques.

Renille blinked. The dais, empty a moment earlier, had magically filled. They had come from—thin air? The nether regions? *Correct.* There had to be a trapdoor in the dais, concealed behind the altar/bed. Priests and odalisques had entered from below. The musicians remained hidden from view, their dissonant high notes screeching from unseen depths.

Capable hands transferred the girls from litters to altar, where the two of them reclined, glazedly tranquil. The childish little faces were creased in identically moronic smirks. The kohl-rimmed eyes were round and lizard-empty.

Drugged?

With Chosen and Blessed Vessel, it was difficult to say.

He squinted through wreaths of perfumed vapors at AounSons, writhing as they chanted, bodies twisting and snaking to the rhythm of the music. Puppets. Mindless marionettes. He noticed then, for the first time, that his own torso was swaying. He didn't know the words to the communal chant, but cadenced gibberish was pouring from his lips. His hands were jerking, and he could feel the uncontrollable flutter of small facial muscles whose existence he had never suspected.

His body seemed not his own. He was one with the puppets, and an unseen hand pulled the invisible strings. For the first time since he had come to JiPhaindru, he was thoroughly afraid.

Drugs. In the smoke, in the air. Temporary.

Certain of that?

Don't think of it now.

His blurred gaze returned to the dais, and his eyes widened. The priestly contingent surrounding the swollen nymphets had vanished, no telling when. Before the altar stood a lone, motionless figure.

Voluminous robes of black shrouded the newcomer. A great mask of beaten gold hid his face. The eye and mouth apertures were heavily outlined in black, and from them glared a greenish light. The resemblance to the many sculpted representations of the Father occupying JiPhaindru was unmistakable, and no doubt intentional. But the form beneath the dark draperies was recognizably human, with shoulders and chest decked in at least a dozen luminous Irriulen artifacts—aetheric conflations similar to Ziloor's gift, but glowing with power. No such ornaments graced Aoun's images.

A man, only an ordinary human, beneath the theatrical trappings.

The light behind the eyes and mouth?

A trick, designed to awe the simple and superstitious.

Among others.

A priest, merely.

No. The priest.

A curious sort of internal chill told him he looked at last upon KhriNayd-Son. The hairs prickled along his forearms, despite the warmth of the air.

Music and Filial chanting swelled to a crescendo, then ceased. The kneeling AounSons waited in rapt silence. The charged pause lengthened.

The First Priest spoke.

As the first syllables issued from behind the mask, Renille tensed in every muscle. Never in his life had he heard such a sound emerge from a human mouth.

Cracked, ancient, yet powerful, penetrating, impossibly resonant, KhriNayd's voice seemed to echo through transdimensional caverns, seemed to vanquish barriers of time and space.

Absurd. He was waxing suggestible as any real Aoun-Son. Deliberately, he unclenched his jaw. The charlatan up there on the dais doubtless employed some artificial means of vocal amplification and distortion—perhaps some sort of simple mechanical device built into his mask. Clever, but quite explicable.

Explain it, then. What "device"?

Not the time to think about it. What was the fellow saying? That peculiar reverberation obscured the actual words. He listened closely. No wonder he hadn't easily caught the message. KhriNayd-Son was speaking in Old Churdishu.

Concentrate.

Difficult to focus his attention, with his vision so clouded, his head so muzzy, his limbs so leaden. *That smoke.* Difficult, but not impossible. The thing up there on the dais, the whatever-it-was behind the mask, was intoning some sort of ritual catechism, to which his listeners chorused rote response. No sense to it. Blather. Only a word or phrase distinguishable, here and there.

"How shall Infinity endure?"

He had caught that, clearly enough. And the answer: *"Through Renewal."*

And:

"What is the nourishment of Forever?"

"Forever feeds upon Itself."

"Who is the Father of the Father?"

"He is Father unto Himself."

"In Renewal, Source and Finality merge, and the circle is complete."

And:

"How shall He renew Himself?"

"He takes where He has given. He gives where He will take."

"The balance is perfect, whole, and eternal."

"The balance is Infinity, which is the mind of the Father."

Mystical claptrap. There was more of it, spewing from the First Priest, answered or echoed by the dutiful, drugged faithful. Pointless to keep track of such stuff, and for a time, he let it go. His mind drifted, floating on perfumed clouds of smoke. He was elsewhere, and then he was back again, recalled to the present by a ripple in the surrounding atmosphere. Something—vibration or mild shock—tingling straight through him. Strangling, unbreathable air. Moaning outcry of the Filial, battering his brain. Renille knuckled his swimming eyes, drew a gasping breath of scented vapor.

Impossible, metallic tones still reverberating above the priestly clamor. His ears were playing him tricks—no human voice possessed such resonance. He lifted his gaze to the black-swathed figure, motionless upon the dais. The hooded head was thrown back, the arms uplifted. And was it his imagination, or were the clouds of smoke beginning to thicken about the First Priest, the altar, and the simpering girls?

Distempered imagination. His head was spinning. He couldn't breathe, he couldn't think. His eyes were certainly not to be trusted, for now they told him that the smoke swirling about the dais was glowing with a greenish light of its own.

Wake up. Watch.

Again he rubbed his eyes, and his hand came away marked with black. The false color applied to his brows was dissolving. Bad, but reparable. And the rubbing helped, his eyes were a little clearer, and now the smoke veiling the dais was—brighter than ever.

No mistake, no trick of vision. The dense tendrils of mist were distinctly luminescent. Through that radiant haze he could still discern the upright motionless form of KhriNayd-Son and, behind him, the two young girls recumbent upon the altar. Still vacuously content? He pushed with his eyes. No. The juvenile faces had changed. Imbecile simpers had given way to a kind of stunned doubt.

Hot in the Assembly, unbearably hot, sickening perfumed air, waves of discordant sound, confusing and confounding—

If only they'd shut up for a moment, he might be able to think. If only he could breathe a few lungfuls of clean air—

He was drenched in sweat, and the room was beginning to revolve.

Pay attention.

Up there on the dais, KhriNayd-Son had moved aside, and now the view of the altar was unobstructed. There were the two little pregnant, painted girls, draped in silk and gold, wrapped in smoke, no longer smiling—

The faces, dimly visible.

Concentrate.

He looked, looked hard, and saw two frightened children. The young girls, evidently emerging from their stupor, were gawking about in wide-eyed incomprehension. One of them—Blessed Vessel, it was—tried to sit up and collapsed, too weak or dizzy to lift herself from the cushions. Abandoning the effort, she lay where she had fallen, head turning slowly from side to side, mouth working. The other, Chosen, sprawled limp and slack-jawed, tears from her kohl-rimmed eyes tracing black rivulets down her cheeks.

The vapor was thickening, the light waxing. The priestly pandemonium swelled, the unmistakable tones of KhriNayd-Son rising over all, but the words were unintelligible, lost amidst the feverish heat, the poisoned smoke, the glare, and the mass delirium. The light much brighter now, painfully bright, pushing its way into the dark, lost space behind the row of twisted columns, to reveal something that waited there, hovering upon the verge of visibility—something vast, misshapen beneath its cloak of shadow, radiant behind its mask, ancient and overwhelming. Something inexpressibly alien, fearsome, and profoundly magnetic.

He would have given his life for a clearer view of it.

And now, a new sound swelling the racket—a high, knife-edged keening, from the dais. Dimly discernible through the luminous cloud surrounding the altar were two contorted girlish faces, shrieking mouths wide open, staring eyes fully aware.

Still the light strengthened, until it seemed that the

thick mists flamed. The voice of KhriNayd-Son poured from the cloud, and the words were incomprehensible, yet there passed some unmeasured span wherein nothing else in the world was audible, nothing else in the world existed.

The impossible voice ceased. For an instant, the world resumed—feminine screams underscoring ritual Filial frenzy—and then the mists wreathing the altar flared to such unbearable brilliance that every human observer present, advanced level of personal sanctity notwithstanding, was forced to look away. The shrilling soared to intolerable heights, and ceased.

Renille instinctively flung an arm across his face. For several moments, he knelt there motionless, sightless, more than half dazed. At last, some subtle quiescence of the nerves told him he might once more use his eyes. Slowly lowering his arm, he looked up.

The bright mists swirled yet about the dais, but the scene was quite visible. The two girls, what was left of them, sprawled dead upon the blood-drenched altar. Their young bodies, split wide open from breastbone to crotch, gaped redly. The means of destruction was not apparent. KhriNayd-Son, presumable author of the deed, stood motionless at the foot of the altar, gloved hands empty of weapons.

Not the time to contemplate the mechanics of the slaughter, not with those twin ruined bodies quivering before his eyes, not with his addled vision playing him false again, telling him that the swollen dead bellies were quaking, telling him that the ragged edges of torn flesh were trembling, telling him of ghastly impossibilities.

Drugged hallucinations, but for the moment, appallingly real.

His efforts to impose mental control failed. The corpses continued to shudder and twitch. The wounds yawned. Amidst a wet commotion of fleshly fragments, the dead wombs yielded up their contents. Two dripping infants crawled forth from the maternal wreckage.

Save for a few distinctive deformations of the skull, their general conformation was human. But when did human infants ever possess the power to crawl at birth? And where was the human infant ever born with fingers that were tentacles, dwindling from sinuous solidity to sub-stanceless shafts of luminosity? And where was the human infant ever born equipped with eyes of searing incandescence, and teeth—little, plentiful milk teeth—glowing with their own otherworldly light?

The babies commenced to squall, their small voices peculiarly resonant—reminiscent, in a tiny way, of KhriNayd-Son's metallic tones.

Perhaps the First Priest sensed a kinship, for his gloved hands were careful as he lifted one of the red-dripping little beings from its raw nest.

The enormity waiting in shadow behind the pillars stirred, its movement visible as a shifting of huge substance, a fleeting shaft of fugitive light. The radiance surrounding the dais intensified, as if in response, until once more the glare was painful to behold. His eyes stung and watered, but this time, Renille did not look away.

Brighter and brighter, almost blinding, now. The infant's personal luminosity drowned in that vast radiance. Its body, bombarded and shot through with light, seemed to assume an impossible translucency.

Moments passed, and the illusion maintained itself. The bones were visible beneath the flesh, together with the ghostly organs, the veins and arteries, the intricate miniature brain. Light glowed from the inside out, and the brilliance inhabiting that quick heart, that perfect brain, exceeded the surrounding light. The two organs shone bright as suns.

Brighter, unbearably bright, charged with devouring energy that mortal flesh could not endure—

And did not.

The double flare, emanating from heart and brain, ripped the infant's body apart in a burst of flying gobbets and spraying blood. The morsels shot in all directions, some of them spattering KhriNayd's golden mask. Before the airborne ruins hit the floor, the thing waiting behind the pillars bestirred itself, advancing to the limit of its shadowy refuge.

Energy irradiated the corporeal remnants, set them aglow, shivered them in midair, and annihilated them. Every trace of substance vanished in an instant. Only the torn maternal carcass upon the altar remained to confirm the past reality of infant existence.

Renille found that his breath was coming in gasps. He was cold with sweat, and his stomach churned. Bowing his head, he drew deep draughts of air. The giddiness receded, and he lifted his eyes in time to witness the flaring consumption of the second infant. Around him, the Filial voices rose in unbridled exultation, and the First Priest poised upon the dais spread his arms to gather in the sound, and the entity behind the columns rippled and seemed to drink the light.

Was it all his own drug-muddled fancy, or was that thing back there expanding, increasing in power?

Not clear. He couldn't think about it. The noise, the heat, the intense collective passion, overwhelmed him. Insanity ruled. For a time, he was submerged, and part of it.

The madness passed at last. Individuality reasserted itself, but confusion persisted.

Better that way. He wouldn't have to think about what he'd seen.

So easy to avoid thought. The Filial lunacy raging about him could easily fill every cranny of his mind with itself.

And if so, what then? Assimilation into—what?

Perfection.

He seemed to hear the otherworldly voice of KhriNayd-Son echoing through the darkest reaches of his mind.

Unity. Wholeness. Totality.

Garbage, Renille answered, with extraordinary effort, but without words.

Purpose. Belonging. Hope.

"Lies." He spoke aloud that time, in Vonahrish, an appalling blunder. But surely it went unnoticed, for his whisper lost itself in the priestly pandemonium.

Didn't it?

Palpable power charged the atmosphere, and he knew without question that it radiated from the thing in the shadows, the thing that terrified and attracted him. Energy hot in his brain and his nerves, shared energy, linking him to all the others; to the Source, to the Filial, to KhriNayd-Son—

And vice versa.

He knew in an instant that he was known, felt the invasive comprehension pressing upon his mind. He sensed himself bathed in invisible light, singled out, naked object of remorseless scrutiny.

Overexcited imagination. His disguise was perfect.

KhriNayd-Son stepped to the edge of the dais. The pulsing light of a dozen Irriulen adornments shot reflected daggers off the golden mask.

Radiant blades laying bare mind and heart.

Ridiculous fancy.

"There is a stranger here among us." KhriNayd's ineffable tones projected a certain terrible kindliness. "Let us welcome him."

Renille knelt motionless. He was, no doubt, invisible; perfectly camouflaged and lost in that priestly throng.

"Let us befriend him."

The holes in the golden mask aimed themselves straight at his face. He stared back, transfixed. The glare behind the mask illumined the recesses of his mind. He could feel the heat of it inside his skull.

Confusion stirred the ranks of the kneeling faithful. The stranger in question remained as yet unidentified. Renille scarcely noticed. He was alone with KhriNayd-Son, and the thing behind the columns, in an otherwise empty universe.

"Let him know the Source and Finality."

The words chilled him to the heart, but it took a moment for his conscious mind to register the fact that KhriNayd-Son had spoken in Vonahrish.

Madness. Delusions.

"Come. Approach. Experience oneness."

Words oddly stressed and accented, but Vonahrish speech, beyond question.

Disobedience unthinkable.

Unconscious of his own action, Renille rose to his feet. He took a step forward. Another, and the magnetic force drawing him waxed as he neared the dais. The sense of alien presence within his mind was overpowering, and the longing to merge, yielding every shred of individual identity, was all but irresistible.

Unity. Wholeness. Totality.

Words spoken aloud, or echoing inside his head?

"Reveal yourself. Speak your name."

Spoken aloud, by KhriNayd-Son, in Vonahrish.

Renille hesitated on the verge of reply. There was no point in holding back. Useless even to try, for the First Priest's comprehension was supernatural. Moreover, there was something beautiful in the prospect of surrender to a force too vast to withstand. The soothing loss of identity, of perpetually troublesome selfhood; the beauty of—what was that term they used? Self-renunciation. That was it.

"Speak your name."

Self-renunciation. No more wondering who or what he was. No more confusing internal duality, no more divided loyalties, no more sense of exclusion.

"Your name."

Purpose. Belonging. Certitude.

"Vo Chaumelle," he muttered, unaware that he had spoken aloud.

"There is the truth," KhriNayd said. "Thus we begin."

Words coming from the outside, or inside?

Self-renunciation. A highly desirable state, much prized by the Filial, who chanted on about it endlessly.

Like the mindless, primitive fanatics that they were.

What mental crevasse had that last thought sprung from? It set his memory afire.

He had once listened to their fervent, mindless droning, and found it repellent. It had taken an effort of will to feign convincing piety of his own. Strange that he'd forgotten that, for a moment. Strange that he had almost been willing to forget that he was Renille vo Chaumelle, a Vonahrishman, of sorts, former pupil of Ziloor the umuri. And Ziloor had taught him of the Palace of Light, wherein existed a closet containing all the universe. That closet was his mind, and its door could be closed at will, closed and locked against all intrusion, either violent or insidious . . .

But the hinges, it seemed, were rusted.

He shut his eyes and strained his will. There was great resistance. *Harder.* Much harder. A mental paroxysm forced shut the recalcitrant closet door.

"Oneness. There is the deepest hunger of your heart."

Words that struck chords. But coming from the outside, unmistakably.

Renille blinked. He found that he stood at the foot of the dais, all recollection of his approach lost. The altar's dreadful cargo stank of blood and raw offal. KhriNayd-Son stood above him, close enough to touch. The radiant Irriuliana still shot rays off the golden mask, crowning the First Priest with light. The closing of the closet door had blocked mental encroachment, yet something of the connection must have persisted, for Renille caught the fleeting echo of alien sensation. Behind the mask seethed ancient obsession—immeasurable ambition, a will vast and deep beyond knowledge—and something more, unlooked-for, and almost indefinable. Anger? Frustration? Thwarted desire? Something of that nature, some sort of eternal canker. Underlying all, the deep throb of primal power, emanating from the dark beyond the columns.

Gone. All psychic contact broken, and Renille was himself again, a little dazed but inwardly his own, alone in the midst of the Filial. The greenish fire that was KhriNayd's regard blazed down at him. Had the First Priest actually addressed him in Vonahrish? Moments earlier, he'd been sure of it, but now—?

"Accept the gift of the Father."

Kahnderulese. How had he thought otherwise? Unconsciously, he shook his head in rejection of the Father's offer.

"Take what you so greatly desire."

A new note in that extraordinary voice. Mockery?

And KhriNayd-Son added, very deliberately, "Vo Chaumelle."

The sound of his own name cut straight through the lingering mental mists. He recognized a death sentence when he heard one, and reacted instinctively. A strenuous spring carried him up onto the dais. Behind him rose cries of Filial outrage. He now stood on a level with KhriNayd-Son, who still towered above him, or at least appeared to, for the great golden mask disguised the wearer's true height. The glare behind the eye holes was insupportable. Renille turned away from it, glancing confusedly about in search of escape. Scores of AounSons stood between himself and the sole visible exit, but the darkness beyond the columns might conceal a second door. Circling the altar, he made for the shadows—and froze well short of their shelter, stopped in his tracks by an almost tangible wave of inhuman sentience, rushing from the darkness. His mind was damnably clouded. He must have stood there petrified for at least a couple of seconds, during which time, the equally motionless KhriNayd-Son waited, silent and disquietingly attentive.

The paralysis broke. Turning from that unapproachable blackness, he spied the trapdoor through which Chosen and Blessed Vessel had been introduced; a sizable square void, shielded from audience view by the bulk of the altar. A couple of long paces brought him to the edge. KhriNayd-Son made no move to hinder him. Curious buzzing in the air. Wrathful shouting of the faithful? Unclear. Before him, narrow stairs plunged into nothingness. Renille descended. As he went, he heard the voice of the First Priest pronounce a single word:

"*Wivoori.*"

The syllables were freighted with an incongruous amusement.

Instantly, a detachment of dark-mantled figures sprinted for the dais. The small reptilian wivoors, sensing the imminence of murder, took wing, swooping in tight, disciplined curves about their masters. Renille caught a single glimpse of running men, of soaring lizards, and then he was through the trapdoor and down the stairs, submerged in the *heedrishe*-flickering dimness beneath the Assembly.

Above him, the interrupted ceremony resumed.

He was hurrying along an unfamiliar passageway (so many unknown corridors, he was lost, perpetually lost), and his head was fogged, but not so muzzy that he couldn't hear the footfalls behind him. Never any voices, however, for the wivoori needed none. Through the hallways, branching in all directions, and he had no idea which path to follow. Stone maze, locked away from the air and light, no way out.

He glanced right and left. Granite, everywhere. Drumming of leathern wings, and here were the wivoors, driving straight at his throat. He struck one aside with his fist, and the reptile hissed and dropped to the floor, trailing a broken wing. Setting his heel upon the creature, he pressed.

Resistance for an instant, and then a crunch of bone giving way, a sound hideously satisfying. Blood and a smear of meat underfoot, and then there were others, wheeling about his face. He struck out, connected, struck again, and he was free of them, free and running.

Echo of swift footsteps behind him, and he fled blindly through the maze. Brain still fogged, but one fact clear; to get out, he needed to ascend.

Stairs? Ladder? Ramp?

Nothing but featureless, windowless tunnels. Door on the left. He opened it. Storage closet. Useless, and the delay had cost him, for now the pursuing footfalls were closer. On along the passageway, *Probably a dead end.* But no, for there before him at last, rose a steep spiral stairway.

Up, quickly. No light in the stairwell. Rough stone wall beneath his right hand, and he felt his way up in the dark. Then, through a doorway, and out into one of the numberless red-lit corridors. JiPhaindru was riddled with such, and he might have been anywhere.

Move.

Turning right, he broke into a run. Next turn, another right, but an instant too late, for the wivoori were near again, and they'd spotted him. He heard a low, sharp whistle, and the signal sent a couple of winged lizards hurtling down the corridor. No outrunning the creatures, they were too swift, they'd already reached him. One he struck aside in midair, smashing the light body hard against the granite wall. The second arrowed at his face, and he flung a protective arm across his eyes. He felt something sharp— claws or teeth—slice through the fabric of his sleeve, grazing the flesh beneath. Catching the serpentine neck, he twisted. Bone cracked, and the wivoor went limp in his hands. He dropped the carcass, turned, and ran.

Still lost in the labyrinth, no idea which way out, *all exits guarded,* and the fresh gash on his right arm was already aflame. Fire was eating its way along his veins, and his clouded brain was starting to heat about the edges.

Wivoor fangs, used as counters in the gambling games of Death's dungeon.

The old piece of Aveshquian lore floated to the surface of his mind.

On through JiPhaindru's bowels, and the heat licking about his thoughts was mounting to a blaze. Still no idea where he was, and the leaden weights were dragging his limbs—

Wivoor poison. You're done.

Left turn. Ascending ramp. Left turn. Still lost, and the gray fog in his head was taking on a tinge of red.

Which way?

What difference?

He pushed straight on. His eyes were blurred, but his ears must have been unimpaired, for he heard the reptilian hisses sizzling the air behind him. Hiding place?

None.

Exit?

Final.

He was going to die in this place, he realized; probably within seconds. Should have killed the First Priest when he'd had the chance, strangled that monstrous mountebank with his bare hands, in plain sight of the entire nightmare congregation, in view of the Father Himself. *He was there. Real. Impossible. Real.* Should have somehow found a way of sending word of what he'd witnessed back to vo Trouniere. *News, Protector. These Filial fellows have got themselves a prime specimen of a First Priest, partial to human sacrifice. Got themselves a pretty lively god, too, fond of ripping the live infants out of adolescent wombs. Thought you'd like to know.*

Too late now.

Murky red light played on featureless stone walls. He'd still no idea where he was, until he rounded another turn and came upon a familiar landmark; the sculpted image of Aoun-Father, occupying a deep niche underneath a flight of stairs. He'd got his bearings, finally. He was up on the second story, just down the corridor from the ugly bower of Blessed Vessel and Chosen. He had once found refuge within that niche. Maybe the place would serve him a second time.

Around the statue, and into the darkness beyond, where he crouched, lungs laboring, and right arm burning. Moments later, a voiceless dark band of wivoori glided by without pausing. He watched almost disbelievingly.

"You give them the slip," remarked a small voice, behind him. "But they come back soon."

"Chura," he said, then turned his head. She was just barely visible in the dim light filtering in from the corridor. Skinny as ever, long fringe of black hair all but obscuring the shrewd eyes.

"Hello, Parrot. You lizard bait, tonight?"

"Yes indeed."

"Why? They catch you talking to cow-yahdeen Chosen?"

"No. But they catch me."

"Because I am not telling them about it, you know."

"I never thought you did."

"Lizards get you?"

"Touched an arm."

"Tooth? Or claw?"

"Not sure."

"Hurting?"

"Enough."

"Aeh." She made a face. "Claw—maybe not so bad. Tooth—say good night."

"I know."

"Either way, you need a—ah—magical mud—" she groped.

"Poultice."

"This is the very thing."

"I won't find one here. Have to look elsewhere."

"You mean, outside?"

"This parrot means to fly the cage."

"Dead bird."

"Still squawking."

"Listen, you do not do this. No way out. Else I am going myself, long ago."

"You have waited long enough, then. Help me, and I will take you out of this place tonight."

"Help how?"

"You know your way around JiPhaindru better than I."

"Much better. Next to me, you are like baby, like blind baby."

"Then lead the blind, as you led once before. Guide me to some forgotten exit."

"Monkey chatter. No exit forgotten here. All locked, no keys. Or else, AounSons there to guard the way."

"Many AounSons?"

"Sometimes."

"But not tonight. Most of them have gathered in the Assembly."

"Maybe." An uncomfortable shrug.

"Then bring me to some humble door, lightly guarded, and I will deal with the priests."

"You will deal, lizard-bait? You, poultice-picker?"

"Believe me."

"No. I do not believe, and I do not guide. They catch you, they kill you, and then there is no one to give me rice and spikkij."

"There is no one to give you rice and spikkij if I die of wivoor venom, for want of a poultice. There is no one to give you rice and spikkij if I survive the poison but remain here trapped within JiPhaindru, for then I must hide, as you do. In short, the days of rice and spikkij are over. On the other hand, you might leave this place with me tonight, and then you will be free amongst the jukkha vendors. The choice is yours." He believed he'd managed to conceal all traces of desperation.

"Jukkha vendors?"

"Hundreds of them, out there." He hoped she wouldn't take too long thinking about it. His right arm ached viciously, and that wretched sense of dizzy weakness was worsening by the second. And how much time left before the wivoori returned? He studied her covertly. Her head was bowed, unkempt hair obscuring her face. If she didn't make up her mind quickly, he'd have to take his chances alone.

He was gathering his depleted energies, on the verge of rising, when she spoke:

"You sure you can deal with priests?"

"Entirely sure." *Liar.*

"Then I will lead you. And then you owe me again."

"Yes."

"You owe me *much.*"

"Truly."

"You pay once, you pay again."

"I will."

"You better. When we are out, you give me money. And things."

"Agreed. But get me out."

"Ah, such a sad bird-squawk. Where are you, without Chura? Follow, then." Without awaiting reply, she flipped the hair back from her face, rose to her feet, eyed the hallway, and swung herself around the Father's image.

He followed in silence. He could only hope she knew what she was doing.

And it seemed that she did. He couldn't begin to keep track of the complex route she plotted. The passageways were featureless and indistinguishable, the twists and turns innumerable. Within moments, he was lost. But Chura never faltered or hesitated. Either her knowledge of JiPhaindru was great as she claimed, or else she was extraordinarily lucky, for she managed to keep the two of them clear of the priests. Throughout the course of their meandering trek, they never encountered another living soul. No doubt the great majority of Filial remained in the Assembly to witness the conclusion of the Renewal.

And the wivoori? What of their vaunted skills? Had they been thrown off track so easily? No sign of them, however.

On through JiPhaindru's bowels, Chura's meager little figure gliding soundlessly before him, until she reached an intersection, where she paused, back pressed flat to the wall. Renille likewise halted, then leaned forward minimally to peer around the corner. A few feet from him, an AounSon sat cross-legged on the floor before a door. The door was small, the guard was not. A hulking human monolith, with a cudgel laid across his knees; impassible and unpassable.

Weapon. Renille scanned the immediate area in search of a stick—a loose stone—a heavy lantern—anything. Nothing in sight. Beside him, Chura stirred. He looked down to meet her insistent gaze.

DO *something*, demanding eyes signaled unmistakably.

The ocular prod drew results. An idea did occur to him then, and swiftly he unwound the zhupur from his waist, folding and refolding until he grasped a fabric band of convenient length, weighted at one end with the bronze ushtra. His right arm was all but useless. Transferring zhupur and ushtra to his left hand, he paused a moment to eye the makeshift weapon. Pathetic. Ridiculously inadequate against an armed and enormous AounSon. Wobbly and poisoned as he was, he'd probably be knocked flat before he managed to strike a single blow.

A sharp elbow dug his ribs. Chura, scowling, flapped an imperative hand. When he failed to respond, an audible grunt of impatience escaped her. The guard raised his head at the sound. Instantly she strode forward and rounded the corner, revealing herself to startled Filial eyes.

Renille watched, aghast, as she halted before the astonished priest to inquire clearly, "Aeh, AounSon, you let me out?" He didn't respond, and she elaborated, "Open door? And no one ever is knowing."

Still mute, the guard rose to his feet.

The young girl danced back a few paces. "I am *weary* of JiPhaindru," she explained. "Bad food. See, I am all skin and bones! Only look!" Turning from him, she lifted her tunic to expose her bare buttocks. "Skinny, just like I am saying!" She wiggled for emphasis.

He wheeled to goggle at her, and the broad back presented itself to Renille, as Chura doubtless intended.

Best chance he'd ever have. Advancing in silence upon his preoccupied target, Renille swung the zhupur with all the strength of his left arm. The flying ushtra struck the guard's temple, drawing blood. The injured man staggered, but stayed on his feet. His hand flew to his wounded head. The cudgel dropped from his grasp.

Discarding the zhupur, Renille scooped up the fallen club, raised the weapon, and tapped the other's skull. The guard went down, hit the floor hard, and lay unmoving.

"At last. So slow, this parrot," Chura complained. "AounSon finished?"

"No."

"You never get past him without Chura, you know."

"I know. Try the door, indispensable one. Arm's no good." He spoke a little breathlessly. Wivoor venom was starting to squeeze his lungs.

Chura complied.

"Locked," she reported.

Renille knelt to search his recumbent victim. Quickly he located and appropriated an iron key ring. The AounSon stirred and groaned.

"Hit him again?" Chura suggested helpfully.

"No. Here." He handed her the key ring. "Find the right key, open the door."

"Me?"

"I would be slow. Eyes not so good."

"*Mine* are sharp."

"Then hurry."

She fumbled at the lock, trying key after key. The AounSon opened uncomprehending eyes, and Renille lifted the cudgel. The yielding snap of the lock spared him the necessity of using it. Chura pulled the door open, and a puff of night air entered.

"Come! Quick!" she commanded, and a leathern flutter underscored her words.

Renille looked up. His vision swam in the red gloom, but he caught a dark flash of movement overhead. Quick, winged form swooping, diving. A thin shriek escaped Chura. A wivoor clung to her throat, venomed claws deep in her flesh. The miniature dragon head lanced back and forth, in two flicker-quick strikes. Then came the proverbial third, fangs buried to the jaw, poison glands draining. Too late, he was on his feet, club swinging to knock the reptile from its prey, a second blow to kill it in midair. Chura dropped to the floor, mouth wide open, gulping for air.

Hopeless. Even as he knelt beside her, he knew it.

Concentrated wivoor venom, maximum dose, straight into the neck. Fatal within seconds. There was nothing he could do for her, nothing anyone could do.

Sliding his left arm around her shoulders, he held her tight, and wondered if she could feel it. No question of lifting her. Not enough strength left in him to do it, and no place to carry her, no help to be had.

Her face was contorted, staring eyes aimed blindly over his shoulder—

Blindly? Almost without volition, he twisted to follow her gaze, and a second wivoor shot straight at his face. He swung the cudgel, and the lizard dropped. He killed it, then turned back to find Chura livid in the red light, stiff lips dripping bloody froth, outflung limbs still jerking. He gathered her up again, uselessly. She was already gone, slight body limp in his arms, and now the priest-assassins were in sight, flowing blackly along the corridor, steel in their hands and poison winging above their heads.

Renille dragged himself to his feet. A hand clutched at his ankle—the dazed guard's hand—and he kicked it aside. Head spinning, right arm burning, he staggered through the open door, out into the warm night air.

He recognized the place at once. He stood at the deserted southwest corner of the outer courtyard, where the nauseous stench of rotting refuse repelled even the holiest of the Filial. Before him rose JiPhaindru's unbreachable wall. No climbing it, but a short sprint would bring him to the main gate, which always stood open. He glanced back over his shoulder, to glimpse Chura's corpse sprawled on the floor, shaky guard struggling to rise, wivoori rushing past them both without a glance, wivoori gaining on him—

Renille made for the front courtyard at a pace approaching a canter, his best present speed. Around the angle of the building he hurried, past the Father's statue, past the prostrate faithful, straight on toward the open gate. The praying pilgrims raised their eyes to stare, but nobody lifted a hand. *Don't look behind.* Another few seconds, and he was through the gate, clear of the temple, out upon the open space known as Jaya, the Heart. At the far edge of that paved clearing rose the shops and tenements of the

Old City, and once he reached that shelter he'd be free, for the wivoori would never follow him there. In fact, they probably wouldn't pursue him beyond the boundaries of JiPhaindru's grounds.

Or so he attempted to convince himself.

He sped on, crossing the open space that seemed endless, then plunged at last into the mouth of an alleyway, where the hot shadows swallowed him alive.

He paused, panting. Safely cloaked in darkness, he turned to look back upon Jaya, the Heart. Across the moonlit expanse rushed four wivoori. Their pace was swift, and they were coming straight for him.

5

 For a moment or two he stood stupidly staring. It took forever to get his legs moving
again, and even then his pace was sluggish.
Faster. His body ignored the command.
His arm flamed, and he was curiously short
of breath. More than a little dizzy, too, but it didn't matter, they'd never be able to follow him through the alleyways. He was sure to lose them within seconds.

Sure to lose himself, as well. He didn't know his way
about this snarl of black little streets, shadowed by countless overhanging balconies. Then he emerged from the
darkness into the dusty, baked square surrounding a public well, and the moonlit scene swam before him. He
knuckled his eyes, to no avail.

There were idlers loitering about the well, enjoying
the comparative coolness of the night air, and they were
gawking at him—or at least he thought they were. Hard to
be certain, for the faces were a pallid blur, but one thing he
knew; *too exposed.* He wanted the shelter of the alleys.
The distance was inordinate, however, for he was running
across the open square, weaving and staggering like a
drunken clown, and the far side receded as he advanced.

One of the idlers called out something as he passed.
Query? Insult? Warning? The words were meaningless, but

he glanced behind to behold a patch of corporeal darkness flowing toward him. Four wivoori? Five? Unclear. There seemed no end to the Father's resources.

The Father.

Real.

And the Vonahrish didn't know.

Would never believe; would label him a liar or a lunatic, if he told.

The world was black around him again. He was weaving along another anonymous, fhozhee-width streetlet, with the wivoori somewhere close behind, and almost he wanted to stop there, just to end it.

The drumming of wings reached his ears, a sound that served as a spur. Straight on through a sultry void he lurched, until his outstretched arm encountered a barrier, along which he groped blindly. The way was fetid and sightless for a time, and then a flicker of *heedrishe* quickened the gloom. One of the lesser passageways, opening into the inner courtyard of the temple? No, he was free of JiPhaindru, and the light wasn't *heedrishe,* but only an ordinary candle, guttering behind a screen of perforated tin. The cheap lantern surmounted a splintery door set into a tall fence of unpainted boards. Below the lantern hung a metal disk, customarily a symbol of Order, but this one was quite featureless. The absence of self-identification proclaimed Nameless habitation. In short, the place was spiritually tainted.

He wasn't much concerned about the aura, tainted or otherwise. He pushed, and felt rather than saw the door yield. Unlocked, of course. The Nameless, like lepers, need hardly fear intrusion. He went through, heard the door swing shut behind him, and found himself in a forgotten lot, probably the former site of some long-gone tenement or warehouse, presently choked with weeds and dotted with makeshift shelters. Huts, constructed of packing crates. Lean-tos, built of sticks, garbage, oiled cloth. Cooking fires here and there. Smell of smoke, oil, onions, tavril, sewage. Dimly realized human forms. Clouds of smoke, swirling everywhere, or was it only his own failing vision?

He thought he heard a whistling, behind him. He tottered forward a few steps, and then he was prone, with the ground under his cheek. There was a vibration of footsteps, voices above, and then, nothing.

He had only a vague sense of time passing, of alternating dark and light. There was pain, a great deal of heat, weakness, and confusion. There were dreams, dreadful dreams that carried him back to JiPhaindru, where the Renewal was in progress, and the flame-eyed infants, crawling forth from the ruined bodies of their mothers, were caught in the light, blasted and consumed. And then the Thing waiting in darkness fixed Its gaze upon him and he was absorbed, lost in It, all selfhood gone, and the true horror lay in the pleasure of that loss. There were human forms bending over him, disappearing and reappearing at irregular intervals. There was water poured down his throat, over his face and body. There were unbearable ministrations to his arm, senseless babbling that must have been his own, and protracted sleep.

It was morning and the sun was still low in the east, when next he opened his eyes. He lay upon hard-packed dirt, with a bundle of rags beneath his head. A flimsy lean-to roof slanted overhead. An unpleasant odor filled his nostrils, an unpleasant buzzing filled his ears. Flies, big ones, were circling persistently about him. He looked down at himself and knew at once the source of the odor, and the object of insect interest. The carcass of a wivoor was bound securely to his right forearm, covering the wound. The reptile had been dead for hours, or possibly days. Intolerable. He pulled at the bindings, and found himself too weak to release them. For now, he and the deceased lizard were one.

"Leave it alone."

The voice was peremptory, the accent city-slum. Renille turned his head at the sound. A woman stood between himself and the daylight. His slow gaze traveled up a scrawny figure clad in rags, pausing briefly at the hands to register knuckles arthritically swollen, before ascending to the face, which was lost in shadow. Only a simple headdress of threadbare muslin shaded her against the Aveshquian sun. There was no symbol of Order to be seen. Nameless, without a doubt.

"Poison comes from wivoor, and wivoor draws it out again," the woman continued. "This is known. Do not pick at the lizard."

His zhupur, with its ushtra and its other symbols, was gone. His person was as devoid of Orderly identification as her own. Moreover, he had entered freely in upon this Nameless enclave, something that no Aveshquian of Order would have stooped to under any circumstances, for death was preferable to spiritual pollution. Good. Illness not-withstanding, his memory seemed to be functioning. When he spoke, in Kahnderulese, he matched his accent to hers. But his voice came out astonishingly faint, a mere whisper.

"I obey you in all things, my sister." By granting her that title, he implicitly acknowledged his own Nameless-ness.

"Ah. How I rise in this astonishing world. Now I am sister to nothing less than an Esteemed. Indeed, this lowly one deems herself unworthy."

So much for attempted camouflage. He found himself curiously devoid of alarm. Perhaps he simply hadn't the energy for it.

She advanced a couple of paces, and now he could see her better—remorseless raptor eyes, set in a face harshly lined, and aged. But the wisps of black hair escaping her headdress showed no trace of gray. She was probably younger than she looked, a common characteristic among Nameless females. Kneeling at his side, she checked the bindings on his arm, and adjusted one of them. He gasped.

"There is yet pain? Esteemed?"

"Some. Why does my sister call me by that title?"

"Your sister heard you chattering Vonahrish in the madness of your fever. The fine, pure Vonahrish of the high and the great."

"A trick of my tongue, to mimic the flour-faced fat fellows."

"Truly an agile tongue, a double tongue. It is also a trick, then, to falsely blacken your brows and your fair western hair? Esteemed?"

"Falsely?" *Parrot.* Chura's mocking voice echoed in his head.

"Falsely. Else why should your Esteemed sweat wash the color away? And why should I find little packets of black waxen stuff in your pocket?"

"You searched my pockets?"

"Assuredly. Have I not the right? Have I not tended your wound, saved your life, and does that not grant me possession of all that you have?"

"Where is that written?"

"In the sewers, but when does an Esteemed lower his eyes to read there? Believe. Your life is my gift to you, and your return gift must look to equality. You carried but a sorry few zinnus upon your person, and these I have taken, but they are trifling, they are nothing. Where shall you find the resources to match my gift?"

"In my heart, my sister."

"A generous heart, I trust."

"And what of—?"

What of the Irriulen artifact, he meant to ask. What of Ziloor's aetheric conflation? Had she appropriated that as well? If so, he'd have to persuade her to return it. But his tongue failed, the clouds gathered, and a sighing exhalation plunged him back into darkness.

When he emerged, the light had changed, and the shadows had shortened. It was probably near noon. A touch had awakened him. A furtive little hand was exploring his pocket. He made a grab, but he was slow. The intrusive hand's owner eluded him with insolent ease and then, to complete the insult, didn't trouble to run away.

Renille squinted. An emaciated boy of some ten or eleven years squatted a few feet distant. The child was barely clothed in rags, like any Nameless urchin, but a deeply sun-bronzed skin could not obscure an unusual refinement of facial features. His large eyes glowed with intelligence and fire. Almost, he might have belonged to the Order of Wings, or at the very least, Divergence.

"Useless. I have already been picked clean," Renille informed the delinquent.

"Not clean." The response was brazenly casual, the accent gutter.

Insult, or statement of fact? Pressing his good hand to his pocket, he felt the irregular contours of Ziloor's artifact. Still there. Evidently his rapacious benefactress had failed to recognize its worth.

"You are truly a stinking Esteemed," the boy observed, with amusement.

Another insulting accuracy. During the hours that he had slept, the dead wivoor bound to his arm had ripened, to the delectation of the flies, and now the stench was overpowering. He gagged on it.

"Get this thing off me," Renille suggested.

"Dead wivoor draws out wivoor poison. Very good for you," the boy returned piously.

"Dead wivoor draws flies, and that is all. Help me with it."

"Why should I do this thing? The Esteemed cannot pay. He has already been picked clean, or so he says."

"Consider it an act of charity."

"Ah, *charity*, lovely as roses in the sight of the gods. We in this place know much of *charity*. But, alas—this worthless one cannot oblige the Esteemed."

"Because—?"

"Because Knobs would toast my heart on a skewer." Without awaiting reply, the boy bounced to his feet, calling out at the top of his lungs, "Knobs! He is awake! She bade me let her know," he added parenthetically.

Knobs. Typical nomenclature of the outcast class. The Nameless, true to their title, identified themselves by means of description. In this particular case, most likely a reference to the swollen knuckles.

"Knobs—your mother?" Renille essayed.

"Mother? Pah!" The boy spat eloquently.

"Would Knobs toast your heart for giving me a cup of water?" His thirst raged.

"Ask her yourself!" The boy scowled, and then appeared to relent, for he added, with a touch of challenge, "There is no cup. If the Esteemed thirsts, then he must drink from the ladle, touched by many Nameless lips."

Renille nodded, and the boy's large eyes widened. After a moment, he dipped a ladleful of water from a clay jug in the corner, returned, hesitated, and inquired, "You will truly do this thing?"

Again Renille inclined his head, and managed, with vast effort, to raise himself on one elbow. The boy knelt at his side, applied the ladle to his lips, and watched in clear amazement as he gulped every drop of the contents.

Indescribable relief to his parched mouth and throat. Allowing himself to fall back, he shut his eyes. When he opened them again, the woman identified as Knobs stood before him. About her clustered some half-dozen starveling children, of varying ages. Correction. Five of them rickety and ragged. The sixth, a boy of seven or so, was plump and moistly pallid, tolerably well clothed, in garments devoid of holes. This one clung tightly to the woman's skirts. None of the others touched her.

"So. He grows stronger," Knobs observed.

"He has drunk our water. Out of the ladle that we ourselves have used," the would-be thief announced with an air of wonder.

"And where is the miracle in that? He is Esteemed, and these westerners, being soulless, fear not spiritual pollution," Knobs returned, as if stating the obvious. "Greenface, you are stupid as you are worthless."

"And you are like a dried-out rat-turd propped up on two crooked sticks," Greenface returned promptly.

"Little crab-louse, you wait—" Freeing her skirts, she jumped for him, fist upraised, and he danced nimbly away. "Out of my sight!"

"Out of your reach is good enough," he taunted.

Stooping swiftly, Knobs snatched up a rock, straightened, and threw. Greenface dodged, and the missile whizzed past his ear to strike the slanting roof with a solid thunk. The boy wiggled his tongue at her in a gesture of obscene insult.

"You go hungry tonight!" Knobs informed him. "No gruel!"

"Little to lose, tastes like slops."

"And tomorrow!"

"Better yet. More left for your flab-cheeked darling." Greenface cast a contemptuous glance upon the plump lad lately clinging to the woman's skirts.

"Do not speak of my Oozie thus, he is worth ten of you, and someday he will have a name! You have earned yourself a whipping."

"When you catch me, old fart."

"Vermin, you will never eat again!"

"Words, words. Starve me, and when I am dead, where then are your profits?"

"Ah, but he is so very wise, this young one, he knows all things. Only tell me, clever Greenface, when you are dead, *who in all the world is to notice the loss?* Who is to speak of it, who is to spread the tremendous news? Aeh?" She paused, awaiting reply, of which there was none. Her gimlet gaze shifted to the children clustered before the lean-to, piercing each in turn. "Who is to know or care if any of you nits live or die?"

Several of the smaller children began to cry. Even the well-nourished Oozie appeared moderately perturbed.

The lachrymose lull offered opportunity to make himself heard. "Goodwoman Knobs, I ask your assistance." Renille no longer attempted to maintain the Nameless fiction, and his speech altered accordingly. "In mercy's name, relieve me of this carrion."

"There is gratitude for you!" She rounded on him. "Has the Esteemed forgotten that this carrion, as he calls it, has drawn the poison from his body?"

"But surely, even if that is true, the task is now complete, and—"

"He is a physician, this one? He is far too high, too learned, and too modern to believe in these quaint Pissie remedies? They are such children, these yellow-fellows, after all. Then let him believe in this. Had my husband not killed this same wivoor with a stick, the Esteemed himself would now be cold and dead. For the priests that hunted never dreamt that their quarry should seek refuge in such a Nameless haven as this. But the wivoor, wiser than its masters, flew over the wall in hot pursuit, and should have finished its prey, but for us."

"I am most grateful—"

"How then will you demonstrate your gratitude?"

"Alas, I find cogitation difficult, with such a stench

assailing my nostrils, and so many flies circling about
me—"

"Is there no end to your complaining? Very well, you
shall have your will. On your head be it." Knobs knelt at
his side and loosed the bandages.

The reptilian remains slid to the ground, taking the
flies with them. The flesh thus revealed was coated with a
poultice of clay, moistened with aromatic infusions; ingre-
dients far more instrumental in his recovery than putre-
fying wivoor flesh, in Renille's unspoken opinion.

"There." Knobs sat back on her haunches. "Are you
now content?"

"Comparatively."

"Then it is time to speak of repayment. Much time
and many precious medicines have been expended upon
the Esteem's behalf, and surely it is only just—"

"I have a thought, Knobs," interrupted the boy
Greenface, who hovered at the edge of the shelter, just
barely out of reach of his guardian's fists. "A most excellent thought. Perhaps this reptile-ridden Esteemed has
family outside, kinsmen willing to pay for his gruel. Perhaps they will send you two zinnus a month, or even more,
to keep him alive, and to keep him out of their sight. Perhaps you might add him to your zoo. There is a chance of
profit, here."

"Out," Knobs commanded.

"Hear me," Greenface persisted, wide-eyed. "You
have already stolen his coin, and it was not enough, so
what remains? Ransom, perhaps? But no, for none here
has learning enough to pen the note. Alas."

"Another word, and I turn you out, to fend for yourself in the streets." There was no reply, and Knobs added,
"And the rest of you whelps, as well!"

Muted sobs from the threatened children.

The scene was not without interest, but Renille
couldn't focus on it. His head swam, and his lead-weighted
eyelids drooped uncontrollably. He let them fall, and was
instantly dead to the world.

Gray twilight when he next awakened, alone this
time. He was parched again, ravenous, but somehow feeling healthier. Still indecently weak, however, as he discov-

ered when he tried to reach the water jug. Impossible to stand, or even to sit upright. It was all he could do to drag himself on hands and knees across the few feet of packed dirt separating him from the clay vessel. Reaching his goal at last, he paused to rest, before dipping the ladle and drinking deeply.

Much better. Mind clearer, raw sensation in the throat diminished, but hunger keener than ever. He drank again, then lay flat on the ground beside the jug, and worked his brain to divert his attention from the sharpening ache in his belly.

Questions. The wivoori—gone for good? Evidently it hadn't occurred to them that even the most desperate of quarry might seek refuge among the Nameless. They had passed this spiritually soiled site without pausing, and that had been—how long ago? Hours? Days? He had no clear idea. In any case, how long before they thought to retrace their steps? Not that they would deign set priestly foot upon polluted soil—he was probably safe as long as he remained here—but, having divined his presence, might they not set watch upon the place? More likely that they'd simply launch their willing wivoors over the fence, for the little reptiles had proved themselves admirably free of class prejudice.

He'd do well to leave, as quickly as possible. Return to the Residency, inform vo Trouniere of his discoveries. Probably be dismissed as a liar or a lunatic, but at least he'd have done what he set out to do. Sound plan, with one drawback—he wasn't going anywhere, not yet. He was too weak to stand, much less walk, without so much as a single zinnu to hire the sorriest fhozhee.

Send word, then. Write a message. *With what? On what?* No paper or ink among the illiterate Nameless. Diluted dye compound, if Knobs hadn't stolen it, on scraps of qunne torn from his tunic? Not impossible. But then, how to post it? No money to hire a messenger, and probably no one willing to accept a guarantee of payment upon delivery. Perhaps, however, the offer of an unusually substantial reward might tempt some Nameless to chance it—?

A small motion caught his attention, and he turned his

head to discover the child Oozie standing at the edge of the shelter, a bowl of gruel clutched in one grimy hand.

"For wethtern dithOrdered," lisped Oozie. Sticking a couple of pudgy fingers into the bowl, he withdrew a gob of damp substance, conveyed it to his mouth, and swallowed. The child, unconscious of impropriety as any savage, performed this operation with an air of habit, before setting the vessel down on the ground beside the invalid.

"Thank you." Raising himself on one elbow, Renille regarded the offering. A small portion of thick, grayish gruel, retaining the imprint of Oozie's fingers. Ugly, but downright appetizing, such was his hunger. There was no spoon. He'd have to follow the child's example. Dipping his own fingers, he ate, and the internal ache gradually subsided.

Oozie watched in openmouthed interest. Finally, he pointed and spoke. "You give me thome of that."

"Too late, child. I have eaten it all."

"You give me!"

"None left. See?" Renille displayed the empty bowl.

"Not fair! I tell Mama! Then you are thorry!"

"But—"

"Thnake-thtomach, you jutht wait and thee!" Oozie dashed from the lean-to, yelling for his mother.

For a few seconds, Renille listened to the receding juvenile howls, then applied himself to the task of licking the bowl clean. By the time he had finished, Oozie was back, along with his mother. Beside Knobs stood a man, middle-aged, grizzled, and droopy, with a sheep's mild face, and a mournful air of resignation.

"He eats," Knobs observed. "What little we have, he takes. Such are the Esteemed."

"He eatth *all,*" Oozie complained.

"Aveshquian children go hungry—"

"Not that one," Renille muttered.

"—but the westerner takes, with never a thought of our need," Knobs concluded.

"Goodwoman, you are well aware that I am presently penniless. However, should you or one of yours consent to carry a message to the Vonahrish Residency, I think it more than likely that—"

"And yet the gods have inspired me," Knobs resumed. "They have shown me the way. There is a means of restoring fair balance, within the reach of all, provided the Esteemed proves just, and wise."

"Wise?" *Parrot.*

"The Esteemed knows how to read?"

Odd question. Did she mean read Kahnderulese, or Vonahrish? Didn't matter, he had both. He nodded.

"This is as the gods bade me expect. Itch—" Turning to the sheep-visaged man beside her, she clapped her hands smartly. "Show him."

Itch at once obliged. Dipping into his pocket, he produced a handful of tattered documents.

"*Show him!*" Knobs commanded. "My husband," she explained to Renille, "whose valor, and skill with a stick saved you from certain death, possesses the innocent heart of a child. Without guidance, he is lost." She turned back to her consort. "*Show him!*"

Itch let fall the papers. Renille looked. Some in Kahnderulese, some in Vonahrish. The light was dim beneath the lean-to roof, but he was able to make out the words.

"What are they?" Knobs demanded.

"This one—bill from a rug merchant in Bishnalli Street, dated last month. Ten thousand zinnus. Must be quite a rug," Renille told her. "This one—tailor's bill, summer dress grays for a major of the Second Kahnderulese Regiment of Foot. Threatening legal action. Two months old. How did these come into your hands?"

"Do not think of it," Knobs advised. "The others?"

"Personal letter from Miss v'Isseroi at New Fabeque Plantation on the Gold Mandijhuur, to her sister, Madame vo Doliet, in Little Sherreen. Six weeks old. Why did Madame never receive it?"

"No concern of the Esteemed's. What more?"

"Letter of condolence to Vif Pinille, in Havillac Boulevard, upon the death of his Forest Baby, Chocolate Miracle. And this one—addressed to Under Secretary vo Crev, penned by the hand of one Rashtizia Flame-Blossom, at the House of Delight, in Snake Alley, demanding immediate remittance of eight hundred zinnus, in exchange for her cooperation in the affair of—" He looked up. "This was never meant for strangers' eyes. Where did you get it?"

"No matter. Read. Read," Knobs urged.

"I think not."

"You refuse me this small favor? I save your life, feed you and tend you, and this is how you repay me?"

"I'll gladly repay you, and generously, if you will only carry a message to the Residency—"

"Do not add falsehood to base ingratitude. Both are hateful in the eyes of the gods. And if you will not do this thing, then I say unto you—"

"Not important." Itch spoke up for the first time, his voice a mournful bleat.

Knobs turned a glittering eye upon her spouse.

"Not important," Itch repeated. He sighed. "He has read enough of it. Under Secretary vo Crev. That is all we need."

"It is *not* all. We need—"

"Nothing more, for now. Reflect."

She did so, briefly. "Well. Perhaps. The Under Secretary vo Crev will doubtless reward the bearer of his Rashtizia Flame-Blossom's message. Or, if he fails in generosity, Madame his wife may prove the more appreciative."

Itch breathed an affirmative sigh.

"We will send to the Under Secretary in the morning," Knobs decreed. "In the meantime, there are other writings?"

Itch considered.

"*Well?*"

"Soon," Itch decided at last. "Dust begs, and cuts purses, at the Gates of Twilight, tomorrow morning. Tonight, Shadow cleans privies and pockets at Central Station. Should they prosper, there are sure to be new writings."

"Praise the gods. The documents will come to us, and the Esteemed will read them aloud."

"The Esteemed will not," Renille informed her.

"Surely hardship and privation have clouded my senses. My ears deceive me. I did not hear the Esteemed."

"You heard me. No reading of purloined letters."

"The Esteemed is still delirious. He knows not what he says."

"No extortion, no blackmail. At least, not with my assistance."

"Ah, he is so clean, so virtuous, so pure of heart, this one! He is so perfect, too noble for this dirty world! From what heights he looks down upon the rest of us poor mortals crawling in the muck! What does he know, this spotless spirit, of want, or misery, or the struggle to own a Name? He is so far above all that!"

"Struggle to own a—what?"

"He is above reproach—above gratitude, too," Knobs continued, with gusto. "He is above paying his debts, this one!"

"What sum do you name?"

"What sum is the Esteemed's life worth? But no, he will not settle upon a figure, for he is above sordid commerce. Only let him know this. Until he consents to read the writings aloud—until he performs this one small favor that we ask of him—until that time, he may consider himself above sharing our poor bread!"

"Or gruel?" Oozie inquired.

"Or gruel, my own."

"More for me! You promith?"

"With all my heart."

"Thee? I told you!" Oozie bent a triumphant smirk upon the invalid.

Renille looked to Itch, who answered the glance with a tiny, melancholy shrug. No help there. "There is surely another medium of exchange," he suggested.

"Good! You think about it, then! When you see the way, you let us know! Until then, you do not eat! Ingrate!" Whirling, Knobs stormed from the lean-to, dragging her son by the hand. Itch followed.

Renille lay watching them go. The light was fading. He soon lost track of his hosts. They were gone, but hunger remained. The bowl of gruel had helped, but not enough. He needed to change Knobs's mind, or else to depart; one or the other. But he wasn't strong enough to stand, much less walk, and wouldn't be for hours or days to come.

He meant to ponder the problem, but his thoughts drifted. He closed his eyes, and promptly fell asleep.

He woke in the morning, hungrier than ever. He lay on the ground, beside the water jug. A detestable stink fouled the sultry air. He turned his head. A few feet away, the flies thronged about the rotting wivoor carcass, which no one had troubled to remove.

Time to end this nonsense. Time to get up and walk straight out of this place.

Wivoori waiting outside?

Probably not.

Best if one of the Nameless were to check the street for him, before he ventured forth. Best, and about as likely as snowfall.

Get up.

Drink, first. He turned to the water jug. The level of its contents was rapidly sinking. Not much left. And when it was empty—?

He sucked up a ladleful of thick water, rested a little, and then attempted to rise.

No good. Jelly muscles. Cannonball head. Mouse lungs. Rest a while, and try again.

He was on his fourth try, when someone spoke:

"Not yet."

The boy Greenface stood grinning down at him.

"Not yet strong," Greenface elaborated.

"And not likely to become so, without food," Renille returned.

"Alas, there is hunger?"

"Ask your guardian."

"She-wolf! I ask her nothing!"

"Well, Knobs has decreed that I shall have nothing more to eat—"

"This she often does to me, also."

"—until I reveal the contents of certain personal letters that her husband or his associates have stolen."

"So. You must do it, then."

"No."

"Why?"

"You might say I have moral objections. You might also say I don't like having my arm twisted. It fails to engage my cooperative spirit."

"This is foolishness. You will not eat."

"You're a fine one to talk. Just yesterday, Knobs ordered you from her presence. You disobeyed, and called her names, thereby forfeiting your dinner and your breakfast. Why did you do it?"

"Because I love to plague her." Greenface thought a moment. "And because she cannot make me do what she wants."

"There you are."

"Perhaps this is empty talk. Perhaps the Esteemed does not read because he cannot."

"Will not, rather."

"You truly possess the art?"

"Of reading? Learned when I was child, a few years younger than you."

"Me, I am no child. I have *never* been a child."

"Perhaps you will come to it, later in life."

"Aeh." Approaching, Greenface squatted. "*I* should like to learn reading."

"Not a bad ambition. Certainly not unattainable."

"I cannot pay a teacher."

"Not all teachers demand payment." Ziloor's face was there in his mind for a moment, and gone again.

"There is no teacher would suffer a Nameless shadow to touch so much as the tip of his shoe."

"I know at least one who would. In any event, that is an Aveshquian attitude. Among the Vonahrish, no such prejudice exists."

"Truly said, for the Vonahrish despise us all, equally."

"Some Vonahrish are free of bigotry."

"Let the Esteemed prove it," Greenface challenged.

"How shall I do so?"

"You teach me to read."

"I?" Renille was nonplussed. Weakness and hunger must have dulled his wits, for he hadn't seen it coming.

"If all that you have said is true, then you will do this thing. This very day. This very hour."

"It is not quite as easy as that—"

"Aeh! Now the truth comes!"

"Listen to me, Greenface. You cannot learn to read in a single day. It's a task requiring weeks of study, and I'll not be here that long. In fact, I'll be leaving as soon as I'm strong enough to walk. Or even sooner than that, if anyone here can be persuaded to carry my request for assistance to the Vonahrish Residency—"

"Then you teach me what you can, while you are here."

"I—"

"Teach me, and I will bring you bread, when nobody watches. Believe, I can do this. See?" Greenface fished in his pocket to bring forth a desiccated crust. "And I can get more. Truth."

"Where did you—" Breaking off, Renille gestured, and Greenface instantly stuffed the bread back into his pocket. A moment later, Knobs and her dejected consort stood before them.

"So—what new mischief is this?" Her expression was unwontedly affable.

"Mischief?" Greenface echoed, sweet-faced.

"Get out of here, Worthless," Knobs advised, without rancor. "The Esteemed and I have business to conduct, and you are in the way."

"What business?"

"No concern of yours."

"The Esteemed is like my brother. He does not mind if I stay."

"Out!"

She took a step toward him, and Greenface prudently retreated a few yards, then paused to loiter within earshot.

Knobs paid the boy no further attention. Turning to her husband, she commanded, "Show him."

Itch obeyed without demur, producing a trio of sealed envelopes.

"New writings," Knobs explained unnecessarily. "They come to us just now. The Esteemed will read them aloud."

"I thought we had settled that question last night," Renille said.

"Ah, but that was *last night*." Her apparent good humor did not falter. "Doubtless, the Esteemed has pondered greatly, since then. Doubtless he has reconsidered. His heart has softened."

"Hard as ever," Renille assured her equably.

"So much for his heart. But what of his stomach? A little empty, by now?"

Renille was silent.

"Nor is the passage of time likely to mend matters. In fact, I fear the very opposite." Knobs shook her head in regret. "But no, I am wrong, for here is food aplenty. Should the Esteemed whose ungrateful life I have saved hunger, here is wivoor meat to satisfy his appetite." Her gesture encompassed the maggot-riddled lump of reptilian putrefaction.

Renille kept his face a blank.

"Perhaps you go too far—" Itch attempted.

"*Stay out of it!*" Knobs cut him off, without turning her head, and her spouse subsided at once.

"Be wise," Renille advised. "Carry a message of mine to my countrymen—"

"Pah, do you think the guards of the Second Kahnderulese would let one of us Nameless through the gate? And for what, indeed? A zinnu or two in grudging reward? That does not begin to address your debt!"

"I can promise you—"

"Promise nothing. Spare your throat, else you will dry it out." A thought struck her. She peered down into the water jug, and scowled. "Aeh, but this water here is thick with scum. It is not fit to drink." Upending the vessel, she discarded the contents. "There." Knobs smiled. "When the Esteemed is ready to read, he shall have good, clear water to refresh him."

"Truly, you have forgotten prudence," Itch remonstrated.

"Enough!" Her voice lashed, and her husband winced. "I have forgotten nothing! It is you who forgets his own son! Oozie must have a name!"

"But—"

"Oozie *shall* have a name! No matter what it costs! We will give him this! Hear me, Husband, I will not be opposed. And we will do what we must do." Her raptor eyes returned to Renille. "And you, ingrate—you will help us, or you will never more taste water. Think upon it." Turning, she stalked away, without a backward glance.

Gusting a martyred sigh, Itch trailed in her wake.

Now what?

"She has got you, you know. Well and truly snared." Greenface was back again, and evidently expecting no reply, for he continued without pause, "The proud Esteemed would rather perish of thirst, than sacrifice his honor."

"Not really."

"But he need neither thirst nor yield, for *I* shall secretly bring him bread, *I* shall fetch him water. Provided, of course—" Greenface did not need to reiterate his terms.

Renille eyed the triumphant urchin. "Do you know the alphabet?" he asked.

Teaching Greenface proved unexpectedly easy, even pleasurable, for the boy was uncommonly quick. They began with the alphabet—the western alphabet, for Greenface, like most urban Aveshquians, spoke fluent Vonahrish and, even in childhood, realized that his best chance of future advancement lay within the social structure of the resident foreigners.

"I shall learn to read and write Vonahrish, and then, when I am grown, I am clerk in the counting house, in Little Sherreen," Greenface declared. "I wear white jacket, bring home salary twice a month, live in furnished room in nice boarding house, maybe Luruleanni Street, eat meat stew three times a week."

"Good thought. Write me out the first ten letters, both capital and small, in order. Pay particular attention to your downstrokes, they are sloppy."

"Sloppy! You are blind!" Greenface wiggled his tongue rudely.

"Yes, sloppy. You want to be clerk in counting house, you learn to do it right."

"Yahdeen-crap!"

"First ten letters. Now."

"Lizard-bait!" Greenface's complaints were largely pro forma. Taking up the sharp-pointed stick that was his writing implement, he began to trace the letters in the dirt. For a time, he applied himself to this task, but it was too easy, and presently, his mind began to wander.

"When I am clerk in counting house," Greenface resumed, "I walk into the Nirienne Gardens, in Little Sherreen, and nobody draws his hem aside, to dodge my shadow, because they do not know. They do not guess that I am Nameless, I fool them all. I am good as anybody, going where I please, and doing what I want."

"And what do you want?"

"I come back here, to this place. I walk up to Knobs. She sees my white jacket, she knows I am salary-man, she asks for money. She begs, she talks so nice, she fawns like a hungry dog. I listen, I nod. When she is finished, I spit right in her face. Then I laugh. Then I walk away, and never come back."

"Now, there's a worthy goal for you. Yes, that is certainly something to strive for."

"You make fun of me?" Greenface frowned.

"Well, I cannot blame you for disliking her. She's a distinctly unpleasant creature."

"She is rotten meat!"

"But at least, for an orphan such as yourself, she's better than nothing. She feeds you, at any rate."

"Who says I am orphan?" Greenface demanded.

"I assumed—"

"Wrong. I am no orphan. My parents, they are here in ZuLaysa. So, too, are my brothers, my sisters. They live in big house, nice neighborhood. JaiPheel Street. Sometimes, I go watch house, watch them coming in and out."

"I see."

"You do not believe me!"

"I have not said so."

"I see it in your face—you think, 'Poor beggar brat, he dreams, he makes up tales.'"

"You put words in my mouth, Greenface. Let's return to your lesson. I asked you to write out the first ten letters."

"Piss on the letters! You think I am liar. You think you know everything, when you know nothing. I tell you, my father is big man, rich man, Order of Wings. He has big house, with ushtra carved above the door. Ushtra—meaning, you know, 'Triumph in submission.' Submission to the will of the gods." Greenface grimaced. "My father, he is pious, so pious. When I am born, the moon is dark, the stars are in flux, and I cannot be assigned to Order. Most families, they would bribe Birthwitness to swear falsely— this is often done. But my father bows his head, humbly submitting to the will of the gods, and so I am Nameless, forever. I cannot stay, to pollute house with disOrder, and so I am given to Knobs, who is paid every month to feed me moldy gruel, and to beat me when she can catch me."

"How do you know all this? Knobs has told you?"

"Yes, but I do not believe, until I follow her to house in JaiPheel Street, where she is paid. They toss coins to her from window, so they do not have to touch her shadow or breathe her air."

"And you think this family your own?"

"I do not think. I know. The others—the brothers, the sisters—they look like me."

"Have you ever spoken to them?"

"Spoken to them—ha! They would turn away, if I came near. They would not look upon me, they would not hear my voice."

Renille had no answer.

"But that is nothing to me, I do not care about it." Greenface shrugged. "They are welcome to their cleanliness, and their Order. I would not dirty their perfect house. Triumph in submission—much joy may it bring them! Let them crawl to the gods! *I* shall be a clerk at the counting house, a salary-man with a white jacket, and I will crawl to no one. But first, I learn to read. You teach me. Not much time. Go on, teach!"

"Very well. I'm happy to do it while I can. You are a clever scholar." Renille raised himself to a sitting posture.

"I am?" Greenface looked at him. "Truly?"

"Truly. Now. You've learned your letters well, and you are pretty good at writing them, even if your downstrokes are somewhat—"

"My downstrokes are most excellent, they are—"

"Sloppy. No matter. You can work on that at your leisure. Now is the time for you to learn that each letter of the western alphabet represents a certain sound. Write out all the letters in the dirt, and I will show you—" Renille broke off, suddenly giddy.

"Ah, wivoor venom still with you. Here, you drink this." Greenface proffered water in a glass bottle scrounged from some garbage heap.

Renille splashed a little on his face, then gulped the rest of it down.

"Now, you lie down. There, that is right, you lie there. You are hungry? Here—" Greenface offered a crust of bread. "You eat, grow stronger. Go on. Eat."

"No, thanks. Better eat it yourself, else put it away. You don't want Knobs to see."

"She will not."

The boy's optimism was probably well-founded. Throughout the past thirty-six hours, Knobs had suspected nothing. Periodically, she had come to demand the prisoner-invalid's assistance with the purloined letters, only to suffer repeated defeat. She'd displayed frustration, and some puzzlement, but no awareness of deliberate subversion.

"You'll land yourself in trouble," Renille warned. "If Knobs should catch you—"

"What can she do? She beats me, but she does not kill me. She talks with a big mouth, but truly, she would not lose her monthly coin."

"The other children—are they like you? Nameless, but with Ordered families paying for their care?"

"All but that lump, Oozie. He belongs to Knobs, she dotes on him. She skimps on food, shaving every quarter-zinnu, until she saves enough to buy her son a name."

"What do you mean, buy him a name?"

"One day, she bribes Birthwitness, she bribes astromage, she buys all the documents, seals, tokens needed to assign Order. This is often done, but it is expensive, very expensive. Takes many years to save that much money."

"Think she'll do it?"

"Someday. Nothing she would not do for her own darling boy. And then, what happens?" Greenface laughed unkindly. "When Oozie gets his name, he no longer knows her, she does not exist. He walks away, he forgets her. How I shall mock her, then!"

"Will you?"

"There is that look, upon the Esteemed's face again."

"What look?"

"As if he is watching a worm. From high above."

"Not true. I believe I understand. When I was your age, I lived under the guardianship of my uncle, who was married to a woman not unlike Knobs, in some respects." *Wonder how Tifftif would enjoy that comparison?* "I hated her with all my heart," Renille continued, "and often I dreamed of avenging myself upon her."

"Ah—I know how this is!" Greenface's eyes lighted with interest. "Did she beat you—this woman?"

"Slapped me, often enough."

"Slapped—pah, that is nothing!"

"Locked me in the closet, from time to time."

"Closet? This is never happening to me."

"Wasn't my favorite way of spending the day."

"And did you at last avenge yourself?"

"No. I at last grew up. Then I looked at my uncle's wife, and saw that she was small and unimportant. Someday you, too, will grow up."

"And I will know how to read—"

"But only if we return to your lessons. Let us try again." Very carefully, Renille sat up. The giddiness had passed. For the moment, he was all right. "Write out the letters. We must go fast. I will only stay until I'm able to walk, and I don't think it will be long, now."

Far underground, at the deepest level beneath the temple of JiPhaindru, the chamber known as Holiest was utterly dark. This was a matter of no concern to the two occupants, neither of whom required illumination. Their conversation would have confounded a human eavesdropper, for much of it was voiceless. The telepathic capacity of the younger, however, could not equal the abilities of a true Presence, native to the Radiant Level. Therefore, part of the dialogue was spoken, after the fashion of Netherness, in the tongue known among men as Old Churdishu.

Stripped of its incomprehensibilities, and rendered in purely human terms, the exchange would have run more or less as follows:

"Father. Enormity." It was the junior—indescribably ancient, by human standards, and yet, by far the younger of the pair—entreating the other's attention, which was not forthcoming. After a moment, he called, with increased emphasis, *"Aoun-Father."*

Several repetitions were required to elicit response, which came in the form of an emotional wave.

Gigantic petulance. Some confusion. Impatient inquisitiveness.

"You know me. You have not forgotten."

Increasing impatience.

"I am KhriNayd." These words, spoken aloud in tones barely qualifying as human, produced the desired result.

Firstborn.

"Yes." Recognition, at last. Something resembling a sigh lost itself in the darkness. "I come unto Your presence in hope of drawing upon the power of the Radiant Level."

?

"The Radiant Level—You have not forgotten the source of Your divine force?"

Wordless affirmation. The Father remembered.

"You will assist Your firstborn?"

Confusion. Irritable incomprehension.

"The westerners within our midst presume to hinder Your worship. They send spies to Your temple, they outlaw Your rites, they would abolish the Renewal itself. You remember this?"

Protracted pause, and then the Father remembered. Huge rage boiled the ebon air.

"Yes. Hate them, Father."

Incoherent, seething indignation.

"And help me to expel them from Aveshq."

?

"The power. Let it flow into me, let it fill me." KhriNayd spoke rapidly, for he sensed the waning of the other's inconstant interest. Once, the Father's intellect had been vast beyond reckoning. But that was long ago. "Irradiate my mind, that I may perform Your will."

There was another pause, during which it seemed that the Father strove to focus His diffuse consciousness. He must have succeeded, for there followed the familiar, unmistakable sensation of mental warmth and expansion, signaling the transfer of supradimensional power. KhriNayd-Son luxuriated, briefly drowning his purpose in pleasure. This, he recognized for the ten thousandth time, was what it was to be a Presence, of the Radiant Level's Aware. This strength, this certainty, this clarity and singleness of mind. His by right of birth, or so it should have been.

It should have been.

Little point or hope in questioning the Father, whose attention span of late had gone the way of His memory. Useless and foolish, to continue repeating the same question, throughout the endless, degrading centuries of Nether existence. And surely not the moment for it now, not with the power of the Radiant Level charging his mind and his hybrid body, kindling the light of the supradimensional artifacts that decked his robe.

The white light waxed in hard brilliance, illuminating a portion of the Holiest chamber. KhriNayd-Son stood at the edge of a dank stone room bare of furnishings and devoid of ornamentation. Here in this place, he had laid aside his mask, revealing a face never glimpsed by mortal man within the span of human recollection, never glimpsed by any save the vast entity inhabiting the darkness. The otherworldly luminescence barely touched the prominences of an impossible form, motionless at the center of the room; all else lost itself in shadow.

KhriNayd-Son, momentarily blind to the Holiest and its contents, sent his enhanced intellect questing far from JiPhaindru. Through the twisting streets of ZuLaysa ranged his disembodied vision, lighting at last upon the object of his desire.

A pool, the sacred pool of ReshDur, on the outskirts of the city, where the water was scented with sulfur, and always warm. Such waters, obviously imbued with magical virtue, were known to possess the favor of the gods.

Thus it was that the pilgrims journeyed to this spot from all the surrounding provinces, here to perform their annual rites of purification. Such rites were now in progress. Not less than a hundred bathers stood waist-deep in the yellow-brown water.

All that the Father required.

The intellect of KhriNayd-Son viewed the scene as if through a lens, and then, through that same lens, projected the focused power of the Radiant Level upon the pool of ReshDur.

The effect was immediate and spectacular.

For a moment only, KhriNayd lingered to view the success of his efforts. Then, withdrawing his mind from the altered site, he returned in his entirety to the Holiest beneath JiPhaindru.

"It is done," he announced, perhaps unnecessarily. In ages past, the Father would have known, would have seen. These days, however, the state of divine omniscience was problematic.

No response, spoken or voiceless, from the Father. Perhaps He heard, and was content, or perhaps He remained unaware.

The luminescence was fading fast from KhriNayd's supradimensional artifacts. The light in his mind was similarly on the wane. Now, as always, the sense of loss was profound and torturous. Now, as always, he clutched almost desperately at the ebbing force; and now, as always, failed to hold it. No effort of will, no mental contortion acquired in all his centuries of existence would serve to trap that light, and no accretion of experience would ever reconcile him to its loss.

Done. Gone. Dead. The Holiest was dark again. KhriNayd-Son, resuming his customary state of being, sensed himself unbearably impaired. And the frustration, the bitter disappointment that never diminished throughout the ages, prompted him to inquire, like the greenest of neophytes, 'Aoun-Father, when shall I take my place among the Aware of the Radiant Level?"

The ignorant among the Filial served Aoun-Father in fond hope of ultimate reward—eternal life among the gods, in Irriule. Delusions, of course, for gross Nether substance could never sustain the consuming virtue of Radiant atmosphere. But KhriNayd-Son, firstborn to the Presence Aoun Himself, bearing upon his person the clear personal marks of divine ancestry, might reasonably expect eventual transfiguration. Or so the First Priest chose to believe. But he required reassurance, from time to time.

None was vouchsafed now.

The space occupied by the Father might have been a vacuum.

"Father, hear me." How feeble it sounded. How small, and plaintive, and human. Almost, he was ashamed to hear himself, and yet he could not repress the words. "Favor Your Firstborn. Cleanse him of Nether imperfection, that he may take his true place at Your side."

?

"Father, give me hope. Answer."

The wordless response conveyed vast incomprehension, irritability, boredom. Nothing to suggest the smallest hint of recognition, or interest, or even sentience inhabiting the shadows.

"You remember me. You know Your son."

Silence, absolute as death. The Father remembered nothing. Perhaps He slept, or perhaps His consciousness strayed. For even a god, it seemed, was vulnerable to time.

KhriNayd stopped his own voice. Further pleas were worse than useless. Matters had altered sadly in recent years. Aoun's deterioration had been slow, but remorseless. There had been other, similar episodes of mental decline in earlier epochs—always reversible. But never before, in all His span of Nether divinity, had the Father sunk to such levels, and never before had the certainty of His full recovery ever opened itself to question. But this time—was there a way back? If there was not—if divine senility proved truly incurable—why then, KhriNayd-Son perceived in an instant, reality had lost all meaning, all value.

"Change." The First Priest spoke aloud into black nothingness. "This must change, or end."

There was no reply, no sign that his words had been heard. And KhriNayd-Son's face, veiled in darkness, assumed an expression not readily identifiable as grief.

• • •

The incident at the pool of ReshDur riveted public attention, less by reason of its abruptness and severity than by the indisputably supernatural character of the disaster. There was no lightning, no seismic upheaval, conflagration, or large rocks falling out of the sky—nothing, indeed, that might clearly explain the sudden, terrible incandescence of the water. The accounts of the numerous eyewitnesses to the scene, while varying widely, coincided in certain particulars. Beyond doubt, the waters of the pool swirled and rushed as if stirred by powerful, hitherto-nonexistent currents. A host of tiny, violent whirlpools briefly pocked the surface, and from those watery funnels arose an aromatic vapor, characterized by some as "celestial fragrance," by others as "abominable fetor." The vapor, either green or yellow in color, dissipated quickly, and when it was gone, the waters of ReshDur began to glow. The light, initially faint, intensified swiftly, and with it waxed the temperature of the pool. Within seconds, the waters boiled vigorously.

A number of favored faithful standing in the shallows near the bank managed to scramble clear of ReshDur, sustaining no worse injuries than severely scalded shanks. Those standing or floating in the deeper water were less fortunate. Almost before they recognized their own peril, the heat was killing them. Some few of the most resolute struck out for the shore, but the furious agitation of the water thwarted such efforts. The struggling bodies thrashed and floundered. The screams of mortal pain arose, continued for a little while, and then ceased. Presently the dead bobbed limp and flaccid in the water, helplessly acrobatic, like scraps of meat in a pot of simmering soup.

The luminosity faded. The heat subsided, and the water stilled itself. All was as it had been, save for the collection of cooked corpses polluting or perhaps sanctifying ReshDur's rapidly cooling waters.

Where had it come from, and what did it mean? As the sorrowful task of pool purification proceeded, devout ZuLaysans pondered. An answer was not long in presenting itself. Within hours of the catastrophe, the word—of unknown origin—was circulating through the streets. ReshDur's destructive incandescence communicated divine displeasure. The myriad impieties of the disOrdered resident westerners offended the gods, who had finally chosen to make Their dissatisfaction known.

Shortly thereafter, the angry Aveshquian crowds were rioting throughout ZuLaysa.

6

"What is going on out there?"

"Noise, you mean?" Greenface asked.

Renille nodded. It was late afternoon, approaching sunset. The shadows were long, and the heat was murderous. The shade of the lean-to roof provided some relief, but not enough. From the street beyond the tall fence surrounding the Nameless enclosure came the sound of shouting. "They've been at it for hours."

"Angry. Want to kill Esteemeds, all Esteemeds. Lucky you are safe in here, where nobody comes."

"Why do they wish to kill all Esteemeds this particular day, as opposed to any other day?"

"Priests stir them up. Tell them Aoun-Father angry at Vonahrish."

"There's nothing new in that."

"Aeh, but this time, there is proof, clear for all to see."

"What proof, this time?"

"Boiled bathers." Greenface appeared matter-of-fact. "At ReshDur pool, the waters glow, and boil like soup. The pilgrims at their rites are properly cooked."

"Nonsense."

"He is knowing so much, lying here on his backside for days."

"What you claim is absurd."

"You say so! Then why are so many seeing it? *Hundreds* see it!"

"Mass hysteria."

"What is this?"

"They are deluded."

"All of them? All are wrong, and only the poison-pate lizard-bait Esteemed is right?"

"You describe impossibilities."

"Nothing impossible to gods."

"Let us say that's true." *The Thing at the bottom of Jiphaindru. A god?* "If the gods are angry at the Vonahrish, why boil good Aveshquian pilgrims? Is that reasonable? Why not turn their wrath directly upon the Vonharish Residency?"

"Who fathoms the ways of the gods?"

"That's no answer."

"Aoun-Father desires proof of Aveshquian faith. We must justify ourselves in His eyes. This is what Filial say. Only—you can tell me—maybe—?"

"Tell you—?"

"What is this 'justify' meaning?"

"It has several possible meanings. In this case, I suspect it means that ZuLaysans are required by the Filial to provide Aoun-Father with some good reason to refrain from squashing them all like bugs."

"This is unfair!"

"Who fathoms the ways of the gods? Never mind, Greenface. Perhaps the priests are wrong, or perhaps I am wrong. You'll be fit to decide for yourself when you've learned more. Let's get back to the alphabet. But first, my throat is dry again—"

"You talk so much. Here." Greenface handed over the water bottle.

Renille drank freely. No need to stint himself, with Greenface ever swift to replenish supplies. The water was tepid and cloudy but, in the midst of the hot season, deeply satisfying. He hadn't gulped but a few mouthfuls, however, before a triumphant juvenile lisp assailed his ears.

"I thee you! I thee what you do!" Oozie, his approach

unnoticed, stood at the edge of the shelter. A pointing sausage finger dripped accusation.

Renille and Greenface traded uneasy glances.

"You give water to wethtern dithOrdered! I tell Mama! Then your backthide thmoke! You jutht wait, Greenfathe!"

"One word to her, and I wring your neck, you little slug," Greenface promised serenely.

"You do not thcare me!"

"One word."

"You thtay away from me! I tell Mama!"

"Have you ever wondered how it feels to be flayed alive, Oozie? Very *slowly*, Oozie?"

"Mama! MAMA!" Howling, Oozie fled.

"This is just what I feared," Renille said. "I've got you in trouble with Knobs."

"Pah, who is afraid of that shriveled thing?" Greenface's bravado was patently false.

"She has the power to make your life miserable."

"I spit at her. I do not care."

"But I care. It is time for me to go."

"You cannot go. You are weak, you cannot walk, you cannot even stand."

"Certainly I can, if I must."

"You must not! It is too soon! I do not know how to read, yet!"

"But you are very close to it."

"Close is not good enough! You must not leave! I will not allow it." Greenface folded his arms. "You hear? I will not allow."

"Yes you will. Listen. It is over. Knobs will no longer permit you near me—"

"She cannot stop me."

"She can, and she will. We both know this. Time for me to go. But I tell you this. You will read. I'll see to that. I will come back when I can, or send someone in my place, to finish the job."

"Pretty stories."

"Believe them. Now. Help me to my feet."

"Help yourself! Where do you think you go?"

"Out."

"Just try it. Priests with wivoors hanging about the street, outside the gate, for days. They see you, and you are finished. Best stay here, teach me to read."

"Are you telling me the truth?"

"Would I lie to the Esteemed?"

"Listen, Greenface—" Renille broke off abruptly, for Knobs, livid as any stormcloud, was advancing upon them. Oozie, waddling in her wake, could scarcely keep pace.

"Aeh, but Greenface never listens." Knobs had evidently overheard the last words. She bared her teeth in a smile. "Greenface does not need to listen, for he is so very clever. Only, sometimes he makes mistakes. He goes behind my back. He disobeys, he lies, he hinders me. These are all mistakes."

"He callth me a thlug!" Oozie interjected. "He thay he kill me, Mama!"

"Another mistake, my own. A big one."

"You are all talk," Greenface essayed.

"Yet another mistake. The biggest yet." Her right hand, grasping a rock the size of a fist, emerged from her pocket. She threw hard and straight at his head.

Greenface, caught in the act of rising, took the flying missile full in the chest. The boy staggered, but stayed on his feet. No sound escaped him, but a deep sun-bronzing could not disguise his change in color.

Advancing a couple of long strides, Knobs drove her clenched fist into his face, felling him to the ground.

"Now, who is all talk?" she inquired.

No answer.

"What, no clever words, for once? Get up."

Greenface lay still, and Knobs kicked him.

"Stop that," Renille told her.

Knobs turned to him, surprised. "It is good for him," she explained. "Teach him nice manners."

"Nevertheless, you will stop it."

"Why?" She appeared genuinely uncomprehending.

"Because I've asked you to."

"This is no concern of yours!" Knobs was becoming annoyed at him. "No one asks for your words!"

"You shall have them, however. Leave the boy alone, or—"

"Or what? What do you do about it? Sick lizard-leavings, cannot even stand up. What will you do?"

"I'll inform the Vonahrish authorities that you starve and abuse the children in your care. There are laws against that, you know."

"What of it?" Knobs flipped a dismissive hand. "You think Vonahrish authorities care what happens here, among Nameless? You think *anyone* cares? Go on, you tell them! Any time you like!"

She was absolutely right, of course. No intimidating her with that one. Renille thought. "I shall tell them," he decided, "that you and your husband are thieves and extortionists. I assure you, they'll care about that."

"Where is the proof? Aeh?"

"I can describe the stolen letters you hold in your possession. And, I think, my word will carry some weight."

"Ingrate!" Knobs was outraged. "Soulless western ingrate! I save your life, and this is how you repay me!"

Throughout the exchange, Greenface had lain motionless, silently collecting his faculties. Now, more or less recovered, he scrambled to his feet.

"Mama!" Oozie's shrill alarm split the air. "MAMA!"

"Big hole under back fence," Greenface informed Renille in a whisper, and bolted. Knobs made a belated grab at him, and missed. Seconds later, he had vanished.

"You will never eat again!" Knobs called after the fleeing culprit. No response, and her attention returned to Renille. "And that is true of you, as well! No one left to bring you food or water. You dry up like raisin. Unless you read for us. Do it soon, Esteemed—before you lose your voice."

"I will notify—"

"Nobody. For I will not allow it. You understand me? I will defend myself, and my Oozie. I will do what I must do. Whatever it may be. You think about it."

He thought about it. The possibilities were disquieting. The woman was a monomaniac, capable of anything.

"I am ashamed for the Esteemed." Knobs had re-

sumed her dignity. "He has abused my hospitality. It is up
to him to make amends. Until he is willing to do so, he
may lie here alone, wallowing in his own filth. He deserves
no better, for he is nothing but a—"

"Thlug!" Oozie crowed.

"Truly. Come, my own."

Mother and son marched off, hand in hand.

Renille lay watching them go. The maternal monster
had pretty unequivocally threatened his life, and he didn't
want to spend another night in this place. Fortunately, no
such necessity existed. He was well enough to stand and
walk, albeit unsteadily. And the means of exit? Had
Greenface told the truth about the wivoori lurking outside
the gate? Probably. Why else mention the big hole under
the back fence? An alternate escape route? He'd find out
soon enough, when darkness came. Best make a discreet
departure; best not disturb Mother Tigress.

The sun was setting. Renille watched the sky blaze,
then char to black. Darkness brought no relief from the
heat. The furnace breezes smelled of smoke, and dung, and
spice. A half-moon rose, and Nuumahni Heaven-Dancer
commenced cavorting overhead. The shouting in the street
continued. About the Nameless enclosure, the cookfires
glowed, the cookpots bubbled, the voices hummed. Time
passed, the moon traveled, and the voices gradually subsided. Now it was deep night, and most of the Nameless
slept, their snores hardly muffled by the thin canvas walls
of makeshift shelters.

Moonlight washed into the lean-to. The way was
clear. Renille drew a deep breath, and rose to his feet. Not
as hard as he'd expected. Wobbly, but workable, thanks to
Greenface, with his gifts of food and water. He'd liked to
have said good-bye to the boy. But Greenface was long
gone, probably for good.

He'll be back. Where else can he go?

No one accosted him as he made his way through the
enclosure. There was no sign of Knobs or her consort, and
silently he thanked the gods. He reached the back fence,
and located the promised hole without difficulty.

Ample size for Greenface, but a tight squeeze for an
adult. Renille squirmed through on his stomach. He

emerged into an unfamiliar walkway somewhere in the Old City. He was miles away from Little Sherreen, miles from Vonahrish aid, debilitated, and destitute. Not a fhozhee in sight, at this time of night, and not a single zinnu on him to pay a hurrier. No help for it, he'd have to walk.

It cost him time and precious strength to find his bearings. His lost wanderings ceased at last, when he stumbled upon a wakeful snake-shimmy, tending a sick viper by lamplight. The shimmy furnished directions to the Python Gates. Long minutes later, Renille exited the tangle of twisting alleys that was the Old City. He now knew where he was—still miles from Little Sherreen, and already dead tired.

He set off at a slow walk, pausing often to rest, but even such leisurely progress soon exhausted him. Presently he thirsted, his mouth gummed up, and this fresh misery monopolized his attention, for a time. Salvation presented itself in the form of a public pump, standing deserted in an open square some two miles south of Central Station.

Vonahrish officials awake at the station? Possibility of a loan, or a ride back to the Residency? Filthy, stinking, unshaven, clad scruffy native-style, as he was? Not a chance. They'd boot him out of there the moment he set foot over the threshold, and the most Exalted accent east of Sherreen itself wouldn't help him. No good.

He drank a great quantity of rusty water, and splashed a quantity more over his face, his neck and wrists. He rested a while, and then he drank again, before resuming the trek.

Better, now. Still tired, and a long way left to go, but better.

Or so he assumed, until he reached Nabarqui Obelisk, and found the insomniac citizens gathered there. Another mock-cremation in progress? Not this time. No faggots, no flames, no effigy. Only a makeshift platform of wooden crates, a row of lanterns, and a tired firebrand haranguing a tired crowd. He paused, and the zealous phrases hammered his ears.

". . . *Offense to the gods . . . Western pollution . . . Foreign infection . . . Cleanse Kahnderule . . .*"

The usual bitter litany, the customary call to rebellion, nothing new, but tonight's popular response was particularly fervent. The faces in that assemblage were drawn with fatigue, but unremittingly intent. How long had they stood here, listening to the Filial fanatic? All through the night? And how long before their skillfully stoked rage turned itself upon the foreigners in their midst? When that happened—and surely, it was inevitable—the bloodletting would be immense. The Vonahrish would be slaughtered, down to the last infant.

The Father would be pleased. He was partial to infants, after all.

And He was real, quite real. Not that the Vonahrish would ever believe it—not until they confronted Him directly. And then?

What do you do about it? Knobs's jeering challenge echoed. What *could* be done about it? Bad enough to deal with an enraged native population, goaded by the immoderately pious. Worse by far to encounter a hostile god.

God? Ridiculous.

What is It, then?

No answer, at present.

Perhaps the Vonahrish had best depart Aveshq, while they still could.

Good trick to convince the Protector of that. To convince anyone, for that matter.

What to tell vo Trouniere, when he reached the Residency? Enough to sic the Second Kahnderulese upon JiPhaindru? And how should human soldiers deal with It? Was It vulnerable to ordinary weapons? Might a god be wounded, or killed?

Unknown.

In any case, was attacking It the wisest course? Who was to say that Aoun-Father might not prove communicative, rational, capable of negotiation?

Possible. But somehow, Renille doubted it.

He moved on. He had left Nabarqui Obelisk behind him, and now he was trudging unnoticed along posh JaiPheel Street, with its clipped shrubbery, and its big houses owned by the affluent ZuLaysan merchants and brokers. Beyond that, Luruleanni Street, lined with pleasant boarding houses, occupied by native clerks and low-level bureaucrats. Another brief pause to rest, followed by another interminable interval of movement, and at long last he was nearing the Gates of Twilight, entrance to Little Sherreen.

It must have been close to dawn, but the skies had not yet begun to pale. It was very late, or else very early, but either way, the streets should have been nearly empty, which they were not. Clumps of purposeful Aveshquian pedestrians, and even the occasional fhozhee, hurried to and fro. Conversation buzzed everywhere, and as he approached the boundary of the Vonahrish enclave, the human clumps thickened and the noise swelled.

He passed through the Gates of Twilight into Havillac Boulevard, which was relatively quiet, at its bottom. Farther along the street, the citizens swarmed, and the way was torchlit as if for a celebration. But the mood of the crowd was far from festive. The angry voices rose, and rocks pelted the shutters of the Vonahrish-style brick dwellings, each and every one of which was closed up tight. Behind certain shutters, flickering dim lights suggested the presence of fearfully discreet spectators. Only one town house stood wide open, its interior ablaze with light. Literally ablaze, with flames chewing the brocade curtains, the upholstered western furnishings, the paintings in their gilt frames. Against that fiery backdrop, the animated forms of the native invaders were visible in silhouette. Deputy Assistant Secretary vo Doliet's house. (The late vo Doliet?) The Deputy Assistant Secretary had prized a collection of rare manuscripts, Renille recalled. Excellent tinder.

Where were the Second Kahnderulese?

The matter clarified itself as he turned into Avenue of the Republic, site of the Vonahrish Residency. The lamplit street before the compound contained a crowd poisonously inflamed as some monster ulcer. Upon the occasion of his last visit, the irate citizens had flung rocks and screamed insults. Now, they did neither, and their uncharacteristic restraint was more ominous by far than the bloodiest of verbal threats. The majority of them were armed, he noted. They carried knives, antique swords, heavy sticks, a motley collection of firearms. Between the ZuLaysans and the closed gate stood ranged a double company of the Second Kahnderulese Regiment of Foot. The remainder of the regiment was doubtless deployed about the courtyard behind the wall, and within the Residency itself.

This is it. He realized he'd been expecting cataclysm for days, weeks, forever. Tonight?

There was remarkably little sound, or movement. All stood quiet, awaiting the crucial spark destined to set off the explosion. Renille could feel the imminence of it tingling along his spine. He thought of hydrogen gas, and of lighted matches.

But the minutes passed, and the match remained unlighted. Perhaps the absence of organization or effective leadership among the ZuLaysans accounted for their hesitation. It might have been the disciplined forbearance of the soldiers, who stood preternaturally motionless. Time held its breath, eternity ensued, and nothing happened.

Then someone in the crowd flung an obscenity, scatological and commonplace. Others took the cue, and the howling taunts arose. A rock flew, and a shower of rocks followed. The din was appalling, and the whizzing missiles dangerous enough, but somehow the atmosphere had changed in an instant. The intense, almost uncanny pressure of hatred palpably dwindled, dissipating itself in comparatively minor acts of banal violence. The rioting was furious, and Aveshquian anger was hot, but it wouldn't culminate in a massacre.

This time.

The soldiers of the Second Kahnderulese were familiar with this sort of demonstration. Their lightweight riottarges, designed for city use, warded off the rocks and refuse. Presently a command was issued, and the troops advanced. The ZuLaysan mob sundered, retreated several yards, then regrouped and stood shriekingly firm.

As the citizens fell back from the Residency gates, Renille allowed the ebbing human tide to carry him. When independent movement again became possible, he detached himself, pushing his way through densely packed bodies to the side of the street, where he sought refuge in a dark recessed doorway. There would be no return to the Residency tonight; no return until the mob dispersed, hours or possibly days hence. In the meantime, what to do, and where to go? He realized then how drained and exhausted he was. In the heat of the moment, he'd forgotten his own fatigue, but now it was back, worse than ever. It would be a weary while before the effects of the wivoor venom completely left him.

Rest. Sleep. Preferably in his own bed.

And why not? Havillac Boulevard, at its bottom end, near the Gates of Twilight, was comparatively quiet. His lodging house was doubtless shut tight as a clam, like every other dwelling in Little Sherreen; but the concierge, if properly bullied, would admit him. He could have a bath. Decent meal. Sleep.

An extraordinarily invigorating thought. Once more, the fatigue seemed to drop away from him. Only a few short blocks to walk. He stepped forth from the doorway, only to shrink back into the shadows, as a familiar silent form glided by on outstretched leathern wings. Almost anyone catching so brief a glimpse would have taken it for a bat, but Renille knew better, almost upon instinct. His heart accelerated, as if he'd been running.

He scanned the street. Not far away, a hooded figure stood observing the wivoor's flight. No doubt there were others of his ilk present in that crowd, for the priest-assassins rarely traveled alone.

How had they managed to pick up his trail? And how had their pursuit escaped his notice throughout the past hours?

They didn't need to follow. They simply came straight here, anticipating your return.

No clairvoyance required; not after he'd so obligingly spoken his name aloud at the Renewal.

Impossible. He had only dreamed of doing that. Delirium.

Real. They know your name.

And his address?

Designs on the Vonahrish Residency at least momentarily thwarted, the crowd in the street was turning its angry attention upon the neighboring structures. The soldiers, maintaining their defensive stance before the gate, attempted no interference.

Wivoor and human henchman were lost in the midst of that tumult.

Breath quick, Renille slipped from his refuge, and hurried away down the street. He covered the distance between the Residency and his lodging house in a matter of minutes. Nobody harassed or heeded him en route, but he paused well short of his destination, and took some time to survey the scene. The streetlamps burned along Havillac Boulevard, great lanterns flanked the Gates of Twilight, and the view was clear. The building, as he had expected, was firmly closed and shuttered. Dim light glowed at a couple of windows. His own apartment wasn't visible from his present vantage point; no telling if his sole, ancient servant was at home, and awake. Here, at the border of Little Sherreen, reigned neither madness nor mayhem. And yet, the quiet figure loitering in the shadows, a few yards from the front door—did it bear a small, winged burden upon its shoulder? And another, still as a statue, at the edge of the light—waiting for what? And the dark blot clinging to the pediment above the front door—a bat? No.

No haven there. Or anywhere else, for the moment.

Renille stood motionless as the wivoori. His mind spun, swiftly considering and rejecting options, of which there were few.

He could sell Ziloor's Irriulen artifact, the only article of value left in his possession. Use the money to purchase food and refuge until such time as the rioting ended and the Residency was again accessible.

The crowd might disperse, but the wivoori would remain.

Send a message?

Which would probably land in the wrong in-basket, there to lie unread for days, weeks, months, or years.

No good. In any event, these plans demanded the sale of Ziloor's gift, a sacrifice of last resort.

What else?

Go back to the Nameless? Decipher their stolen letters, in exchange for gruel and a lean-to roof? No. Pointless and perilous. That maddened mama, Knobs, was downright homicidal.

Go somewhere else. Go—?

It seemed to spring from nowhere, but there in his mind was the recollection of JiPhaindru's Wisdom, with its huge central pillar, and its luminously alien images, detailed and complete as if he had returned in spirit to look upon them again. He was there, dank subterranean air heavy upon his skin, brittle old scroll crumbling in his hands.

Account of Events following upon construction of JiPhaindru, Fastness of the Gods, in the city of ZuLaysa.

Old Churdishu writings, legible after a fashion. Penned by the hand of Fahjeed, Scribe of the Temple. The characters, clear and immediate in his mind's eye. Certain phrases, all but disregarded upon first reading, but now— post-Renewal epiphany—immensely significant.

The banished lesser gods and goddesses—Hrushiiki, Nuumahni, Ahrattah, Ubhyadesh, and the others—withdrew to the hills beyond ZuLaysa's walls, where the human sorcerer/ruler known as Shirardhir the Superb oversaw construction of the palace called OodPray.

. . . finally locating the vital weakness in the atmosphere, proceeded to enlarge upon it, eventually blasting open the path to Irriule. For this feat of magic, Shirardhir the Superb won the gratitude of the lesser gods . . .

Then the lesser gods returned to their own world . . . the doorway closed behind them.

It is said that the locked portal between the worlds stands waiting to this day, its location known to Shirardhir's descendants . . . who yet retain the friendship of the gods . . . who yet retain the power to open the door and to call, once in a generation, upon the gods of Irriule.

Lesser gods—others like It? What a thought. Banished lesser gods—why banished? Had They quarreled with Aoun? Had They perhaps deplored His excesses?

And OodPray Palace. Occupied by the descendants of Shirardhir the Superb. Embittered Ghochalla Xundunisse, and her beautiful daughter. Direct descendants. What did they know of the—for want of a better word—gods? And more to the point, what would they be willing to tell him?

At least, they might believe his story. Nobody else outside of Aoun's cult would.

How do you know they're outside the cult?

That girl must be.

Because she's pretty?

Because she's got some sense.

What reckless assumptions.

To OodPray he would go. There was information to be had there, not to mention shelter, provided they were willing to grant either.

More reckless assumptions.

No better alternative, however. The palace occupied the low hills, some twelve miles north of ZuLaysa's limits. Ordinarily, he would walk such distance in about three hours. But now, weakened as he was—?

No matter. If he started off at once, before the sun was up, he might yet make good time.

He stepped out into Havillac Boulevard. A whisper of wings snagged his notice, and he looked up. A quick form glided overhead. He heard the thing hiss. A hooded form emerged from the shade of a portico, directly across the street. He'd missed that one altogether.

Unclear whether they'd spotted him.

Get out. Don't run.

He made for the Gates of Twilight. The eastern skies were starting to lighten. The streets beyond the gates were already busy, and soon they'd be thronged. Once clear of Little Sherreen, he might easily lose himself in ZuLaysa's teeming tangle. When he'd shaken pursuit, if such there was, he'd be free to turn his steps toward the foothills, and OodPray.

The skin between his shoulder blades was prickling. Chancing a backward glance, he saw three wivoori flowing toward him; amorphous and anonymously lethal figures, hardly human. They'd recognized him, and the presence of numerous witnesses meant nothing. Abandoning pretense, Renille filled his lungs and dashed for the gates.

• • • •

The sun rose, gilding the turrets of OodPray Palace. Viewed at some distance, from the dusty plain below the hills, OodPray seemed untouched by time—its complex delicate symmetry still perfect, white marble walls dazzling as ever, violet-tiled central dome gleamingly intact. Closer inspection, however, revealed extensive deterioration; corrosion of the polished façade, broken fretwork, holes in the roof, crumbling spires and balconies.

Inside the palace, the decay of magnificence was conspicuous, for here the dampness had entered and found a home, remaining to rot fabric, to stain frescoes, to undermine tile, mosaic, paint and gold leaf. Lingering moisture fostered the growth of the fungi whose odor was pervasive, the worms that devoured wood, the insects that fed the resident bats and lizards. Dirt and worse lay everywhere; unavoidably so, for vast OodPray required the attention of countless slaves or servants, whose numbers had long since dwindled to one.

Throughout the gorgeous, moldering structure, only two suites remained clean and pleasantly fragrant. One of them, comprising a small portion of the apartment originally designed to house the ruler of Kahnderule and troops of personal attendants, was presently occupied by the Ghochalla Xundunisse. The other—consisting of nothing more than bedchamber, bath, and tiny sitting room once used as a clothes closet—belonged to the Ghochanna Jathondi.

The dawn's earliest light witnessed the delivery of a summons from the larger apartment to the smaller. Around mid-morning, Jathondi presented herself at her mother's door. In accordance with the formal tone of the communication, she had arrayed herself in her best violet-gray, silver-embroidered silks, whose worn spots were well-nigh invisible to all but the sharpest eyes. Her mass of wavy, blue-black hair was smoothed into a decorous chignon. Silver and amethyst jewelry of negligible value completed her costume.

For some moments the young woman stood hesitating in the corridor. At last, reluctantly, she knocked. The door opened at once. The household's sole remaining, all-purpose servant ushered her in with a silent bow. His silence was perpetual, for the gigantic Paro—tallest, strongest mortal in all Kahnderule, and probably in all Aveshq—rendered voiceless within days of his birth, lacked the power to utter a single syllable. His duties, which went unremunerated, were varied and burdensome. Any number of wealthy establishments would have paid handsomely to secure his services, but he never sought employment elsewhere, for he was a slave, bound by law and custom to his present owner, the Ghochalla of Kahnderule. The Vonahrish abolition of slavery, legislated some decades earlier, was one of the many realities of modern existence that Xundunisse chose to overlook. Paro evidently chose to overlook it as well, if indeed he was aware. Impossible to judge what Paro knew or didn't know.

He led her to the left, toward the Ghochalla's private audience chamber, and Jathondi breathed a sigh. Her mother's choice of a formal setting for their meeting suggested a subject matter of some importance. She could guess what was coming, and she wasn't looking forward to it.

Upon the threshold of the chamber, Jathondi prostrated herself in traditional style. The multihued marble floor on which her forehead rested was clean enough, but many of its component colored lozenges were missing.

"Rise, Ghochanna," Xundunisse commanded.

Jathondi rose lightly to her feet. Her mother occupied a throne of wondrously carven ivory, surmounting a low platform of golden scrollwork. Above the platform hung a canopy of gold brocade, once splendid, now plentifully frayed. Xundunisse wore unbecoming black, whose starkness emphasized the sallowness of aging skin. At her throat, ears, and wrists shone rubies of the largest size and deepest color; all but priceless heirloom gems whose sale would easily have financed the purchase of a fine, amply staffed house anywhere in Aveshq—or out of it, for that matter. But the exchange of family treasures for cash was a concept alien to the current owner.

Xundunisse snapped her fingers, and Paro retired to a corner, there to assume the role of niibhoy. The gilded fans began to swing overhead.

An exchange of ritual courtesies followed. Concealing her impatience as best she could, Jathondi mouthed the requisite elaborate phrases. Inwardly, she wondered for the ten thousandth time why her mother attached such inordinate importance to archaic courtly form. Perhaps to compensate for the utter lack of courtly substance?

The verbal pavane concluded. Xundunisse motioned her daughter to the gilded chair at the foot of the platform, a level below her own elevated throne. A signal mark of favor, this. A Kahnderulese subject, or even a visiting dignitary, might expect to remain standing throughout an interview with the Ghochalla. Jathondi bowed deeply, and seated herself. The chair was comfortable enough, but her insides refused to unknot. Only the training of a lifetime enabled her to suppress all outward signs of uneasiness.

Xundunisse let the silence expand. Perhaps she deliberately sought to unnerve her daughter, or perhaps she simply didn't know how to begin. At last, taking up a document of some sort from the low ivory table beside the throne, she announced, "This arrived yesterday evening. I want you to read it."

Jathondi eyed the document with caution. Noting the ushtra marked in red at the top of the page, her worst, selfish fears abated. She accepted the missive, and read swiftly. Not what she'd expected, not at all; and yet, not really surprising.

To the Beloved Daughter of the Gods, the Most Effulgent Ghochalla of Kahnderule, Vessel of Divine Light—

A string of decorative titles followed.

Mother would probably love them.

Greetings from the Sons of the Father—

The Filial. Their own words, straight from the heart of JiPhaindru. Their purpose? Jathondi read on. The flowery phrases blossomed.

. . . We look upon you, Beloved of the Gods, True Daughter of the Father, to lead your subjects along the path of truth and reality. We look upon you to resist the darkness of alien incursion, the evil of godless barbarism. We look upon you, an enlightened one, to resist the tyranny of foreign rule . . .

More along these lines, an outpouring of patriotism and piety, and then:

Effulgent Ghochalla, we call upon you now to ally yourself openly with the Sons of Aoun; for the union of secular and holy powers, so pleasing in the sight of the Father, must surely prove unopposable. Thus bonded in righteous purpose, secure in divine favor, we shall drive the Vonahrish predators from our shores . . .

Jathondi read to the end, then handed the letter back to her mother. "How will you answer them?" she asked.

"To a great extent, the answer depends upon you, Ghochanna."

"Upon me, Effulgent Ghochalla?" Jathondi concealed her surprise.

"Truly. Before I tell you why, however, I will ask you this—what do you think of the Filial suggestion? Speak freely."

"I think they wish to use you, Ghochalla—to turn the love and loyalty that your people bear you to their own advantage."

"That goes without saying. The question remains, shall Ghochalla and VaiPradh find use for one another? Do you believe it possible that a union of our forces may indeed serve to cleanse Kahnderule of Vonahrish filth?"

"Perhaps, but at what cost? VaiPradh is rife with murderous fanatics. Aoun-Father is the cruelest of the gods, and His cultists are guilty of atrocity. Owning no loyalty to country, kin, or human law, they are altogether worse than the Vonahrish."

"Take care, Ghochanna. The Filial, at least, are our own."

"I am ashamed to acknowledge them as such—and I fear the consequences of the alliance they suggest. Should you join with them, and your combined efforts prove successful, their influence must increase."

"And—?"

"And VaiPradh will reign supreme in Kahnderule." Jathondi shot her mother a wary glance. No sign of storm clouds so far, so she continued. "Your Effulgence will lack the means to curb them, and their deeds of blood will dishonor us all in the eyes of the world. So much I believe. Forgive me if my words displease you."

"I am not displeased. I commend your honesty. As for your sentiments, they are not entirely dissimilar to my own. Does that surprise you?"

"It is as I hoped, Ghochalla." Jathondi's tension did not diminish. The discussion, she surmised, was far from over.

"Good. Let it be clear that I do not love the Filial. For all their excesses, however, the AounSons remain Aveshquian, and therefore preferable to the Vonahrish beasts, whom I hate above all others. Given the sad choice between VaiPradh and Vonahrish, I must cleave to my own kind."

"The Filial are not of our kind, Ghochalla. They are of our land, perhaps, but foreign in mind, and heart, and soul—more alien by far than the westerners."

"There our opinions differ, and there is little to be gained in arguing the point. I would, if forced to it, choose what I perceive as the lesser of two evils. Happily for all, however, a third alternative has presented itself."

"A third?" Jathondi's tension was heightening dread.

"Indeed. As of this morning, I received a communication from our royal neighbor, the Effulgent NiraDhar, Ghochallon of Darahule. His Effulgence requests the hand of my daughter, the Ghochanna Jathondi, in marriage. In his magnanimity, he demands no dowry beyond the beauty of the young Ghochanna, and the friendship of Kahnderule. You recognize the significance of this offer?" Xundunisse waited in vain for a reply. Her daughter sat silent and motionless. After a moment, she resumed, "You understand, do you not, the magnitude of our good fortune? Thanks to the Ghochallon NiraDhar, we are relieved of a choice too difficult. Only consider. The state of Darahule is wealthy, armed, and independent—strong enough to resist the power of Vonahr. The western wolves have gained no foothold *there*. Do you not see what this means?"

No reply. Her worst suspicions confirmed, Jathondi was momentarily mute.

"His Effulgence desires the friendship of Kahnderule,"

Xundunisse continued, a touch impatient of the other's dullness. "Implicit in that request is the offer of reciprocity. When you become the wife of NiraDhar, then all the military might of Darahule must be placed at the service of the new Ghochalla's native land. Thus supported, we shall drive the Vonahrish from Kahnderule, forever. We shall rule ourselves, in our own place, as Nature intended. The old ways, the true ways, will return. I shall be Ghochalla again, in fact as well as name, and after me you will rule here, my daughter. Your own children will follow, and then your children's children. This is the gift we are offered. Well?" Twin spots of deep color burned in her narrow, fierce face. "Have you nothing to say? Speak, Ghochanna, speak of your gratitude and joy. I give you leave to answer."

Jathondi met her mother's exultant eyes. The last thing in the world she wanted was to change their expression, but the Ghochalla had commanded.

"You are deceived," she said levelly. Taking a deep breath, she forced herself to continue, almost without pause, "Here is no offer of freedom. We are merely granted opportunity to exchange one set of overlords for another. Do you take the Ghochallon NiraDhar for an altruist? Be certain he will commit his resources to our cause in expectation of substantial reward."

"Your hand is his reward, Ghochanna."

"Ghochalla, we both know better. Should the armies of Darahule expel our Vonahrish masters, then the Darahulese simply become our new masters. In our present impoverished state, there is little we could do to oppose them. Your Effulgence might perhaps retain an empty royal title, for the term of your existence, but you would not survive to enjoy it long. Upon your death, the Ghochallon would lose no time in declaring himself administrator of his wife's inheritance. The ghochallates of Darahule and Kahnderule, melded into a single realm, would then be ruled by NiraDhar and his Darahulese successors. I see little benefit to us in that."

"You see only your own groundless fears." The color in Xundunisse's face had darkened, and her breath had quickened, but still she kept her voice even. "You impugn the honor of NiraDhar, you defame and accuse him, and all without a shred of proof. He is of the oldest blood, the purest Effulgence. How dare you?"

"Easily. All his past life accuses him. His rapacity is legendary, his treacheries and betrayals, too numerous to count. Consider the fall of JiraZeen. Remember the innocent blood that flowed at LeshNar. Should we commit the blunder of dealing with this man, we shall doubtless share the fate of his former dupes. But"—Jathondi met her mother's flaming gaze squarely—"in your heart, Ghochalla, you already know this."

For an endless moment Xundunisse stared back. A vein in her forehead throbbed visibly. "Do not presume to tell me what I know," she advised at last. "Who are you, a pampered chit, to judge?"

"Ghochalla, I—"

"Silence. You have said too much as it is. Now it is time for you to listen. There is, to begin with, no just cause to question the good faith of the Effulgent NiraDhar, who is willing to take you without dowry. Have you received another such offer elsewhere? If so, I do not recall it. No, do not speak. It is small in mind, and even ignoble, to assume the worst of a fellow Effulgent, in the absence of conclusive proof."

"Conclu—"

"Hold your tongue. You try my patience. Do not provoke me to anger. It is also time you learned that I am not quite the doddering fool you take me for. Do you think me unaware of the Ghochallon NiraDhar's reputation? Think again. Like you, I have heard the tales. Unlike you, I do not unquestioningly accept their truth. Again unlike you, I am a ruling Ghochalla, both sovereign and slave of the state. I must look, above all other things, to the best interests of Kahnderule. In the present case, it is clear what those interests demand. First and foremost, we must free ourselves of Vonahrish pollution, at any cost."

"At any cost? There is the real question. Ghochalla, do you not see—"

"Speak again, before I give you leave, and I shall command Paro to silence you by force," Xundunisse promised, and her daughter subsided. "Let us imagine, for the sake of argument, that all you most fear comes to pass, and the Darahulese are made our overlords. I say it will never come to that, but if it should—why then, better Darahule than Vonahr, or VaiPradh. You see, Ghochanna, it is time to accept reality."

"Ghochalla, may I speak?"

Xundunisse inclined her head.

"Our perceptions of reality differ greatly, and yet I wish to point out certain undeniable realities that Your Effulgence has chosen to overlook. It is real, for example, that the Ghochallon NiraDhar, some forty years my senior, is a depraved, diseased, disgusting old satyr—"

"What foolery is this?"

"Twisted, and by all reports, unnatural—"

"Do I hear correctly? You are complaining that he does not *please* you?"

"Whose previous eight wives have all died under unpleasant circumstances—"

"These are trifling, idle tales."

"And I do not wish to become number nine," Jathondi concluded.

"You do not wish! You speak like a foolish, spoiled child. Your wishes are of no consequence. Forget your vain desires, and recall your responsibilities. I am astonished that you require instruction. Remember your duty to Kahnderule, to your sovereign, and to your mother."

"My duty does not include pointless martyrdom."

"Your duty, as a Ghochanna of Kahnderule, includes absolute obedience. Your duty includes willing self-sacrifice, in the service of your country."

Xundunisse's hands were clenched on the arms of her ivory throne, and the vein in her forehead bulged. Jathondi noted the warning signs, steeled herself, and answered. "I should throw myself upon a blazing pyre, and do so joyously, if I thought my torture and death might serve Kahnderule. I should even welcome the diseased embrace of the Ghochallon NiraDhar, were Kahnderule to gain thereby. But Ghochalla, I don't believe our country would profit by this exchange. Better NiraDhar than VaiPradh, I grant. And yet"—she noted her mother's sharp intake of breath, but didn't allow herself to stop—"and yet, the

Vonahrish, for all their greed and arrogance, at least permit us to retain our own name. Under Vonahr, we are still Kahnderule, a nation. Once absorbed into Darahule, we are reduced to the level of a province. Moreover, Darahulese law is archaic and vengeful, while the Vonahrish Republican code is liberal, just, and worthy of study. Beyond that, the westerners are ingenious, offering much by way of medicine, machinery, scientific marvels, improved means of farming, general progress—"

"You call it that!"

"And truly, if we must be ruled—and there seems no help for that, at present—then I think the Vonahrish better masters than NiraDhar's Darahulese warriors." There, she had actually said it.

Really necessary to say it?

Yes, Jathondi decided.

"That decision is not yours." Xundunisse was striving hard to maintain control, but hers was a losing fight. The furious color suffused her entire face. "I am ruler here, and I decide the fate of my people. I, alone. And I tell you, the Vonahrish infection must be purged. How could you think otherwise? How could you, an Aveshquian of the Effulgent Order, a Ghochanna of Kahnderule, called upon to serve your people, hesitate for a single instant? I do not understand."

"I will serve the people gladly. I will serve Kahnderule as best I may."

"You are my daughter, after all. You will wed the Effulgent NiraDhar."

"No, Mother. I will not."

"I did not hear you."

"I said I will not."

White-hot silence, and then, "You will obey your sovereign's commands. The matter admits of no discussion."

"Then we will not discuss it." Jathondi hated herself, at that moment.

At that moment, her mother hated her more.

"You are not of my universe," Xundunisse declared in a voice that burned. "You are no part of me, you are no part of Kahnderule. You have no home, no family, no place. You are nothing. You hear me? Nothing. You do not exist."

"Please listen to me, Mother—"

"Do not address me by that title. I am not your mother, you have no mother."

"Effulgence, hear me. I beg you to consider. The Vonahrish—"

"Are your masters! Your schooling in their cursed land has flooded your veins with foreign poison, and now you are their slave, their fawning bitch! Yes—they own you!" All vestige of restraint had left her. Her face contorted, and her voice rose to a hoarse shout. "You are all theirs! You are surely none of mine—I despise you! You are unworthy of Effulgence, unworthy of Shirardhir's sorcerous legacy, which I had thought one day to share with you! You are unfit to wed Ghochallon NiraDhar, he is too high for you! You are base, you are vile, you are Nameless—yes, Nameless!"

"Ghochalla, please, you will make yourself ill—"

"I sicken in the presence of Nameless stench! Take yourself from my sight, let me not look upon your face, or hear your voice! Traitor, leave me! Go, before I order you whipped!"

Jathondi bowed low, and backed from the audience chamber. Her face was respectfully blank, but her heart was hammering. Once clear of the Ghochalla's apartment, she hurried straight back to her own rooms. Mother's anger was always intense. So long as it lasted, there was no hope of rational conversation. Moreover, her threats were far from empty. She was, at the moment, perfectly capable of ordering Paro to whip the erring Ghochanna. Paro would do it, too.

Mother's eyes—they had burned with such contempt and hatred.

Jathondi found that her hands were shaking.

She couldn't have meant all that she'd said. Mother was passionate, and she'd spoken at the height of her rage. She would doubtless cool down, but for now, best to give her wide berth. In a palace so vast and labyrinthine as OodPray, it shouldn't be difficult to stay out of sight, for a time.

How long? Difficult to say. She'd never seen the Ghochalla so angry before—at least, never so angry at *her*. But then, she'd never dared open defiance before, either. Never needed to, until today. What if Mother never forgave her—what if the break was permanent?

Impossible.

There were tears on her cheeks. Jathondi brushed them away. She took a deep breath. Mother would come around, eventually. She'd have to.

Mother's grudges were ironclad.

Not this one. She'd relent, certainly she would, in the end.

But it might take a while.

Jathondi stuffed a few essentials into a sack. Thus burdened, she made her way along the endless corridors to the deserted west wing, originally designed to house the wives and multitudinous concubines of Shirardhir the Superb. There, the chamber once occupied by Shirardhir's favorite remained tolerably dry, reasonably fauna-free, and, beneath its accumulated layers of dirt, still beautiful. Best of all, the room opened directly out into a walled garden, where the long-gone women had wandered among roses, lilies, and fountains. The fountains were dry, and the flower beds choked with weeds, but the little vine-covered belvedere poised atop its man-made rise was exquisite still, a perfect place to linger in the mornings.

Setting her silver-embroidered draperies aside, Jathondi donned serviceable garments of sand-colored qunne. The nearest bath contained a functional pump. She filled a bucket with water, and toted it back to her new lodgings. The contents of her sack included rags, brushes, and soap. Eyeing the magnificent, filthy chamber, she sighed. Cleaning it would take hours, but the labor might help keep her mind off the recent, appalling scene. Pushing back her sleeves, she began to scrub.

7

 Renille spent half an hour or more threading a complex path through the alleyways. When he was certain he'd shaken pursuit, he turned his footsteps north. Another forty minutes of walking brought him to the edge of ZuLaysa, where exhaustion reasserted itself. Grudging every lost minute, he seated himself in the dust of the roadside, back pressed to a wall of warm clay brick. The sun was up, and already scorching. He had no hat to shade his face, nor even a zhupur to wind turban-fashion about his head. He'd regret that lack soon enough—he was regretting it already. His mouth was dry—how would it be in another two hours?

There was bound to be water, somewhere along the way.

You hope.

Before him stretched the colorless plain, shimmering in the matinal heat. Beyond the plain rose the foothills, veiled in dusty haze. The palace of OodPray, visible from ZuLaysa on a clear day, was presently hidden from view. The glare of sunlight on the great, parched expanse was painful to the eyes. Renille allowed his lids to drop. When he lifted them again, the shadows were short. He had slept at least an hour, probably more.

Stupid. Dangerous. He glanced around him. No sign
·of priest-assassins, no winged lizards. Stupid, nevertheless.
The air temperature had risen while he slept. The heat
would increase as the day wore on, and he couldn't afford
to waste any more time. He hauled himself to his feet, and
found that the rest had served him well. He was still tired,
and the weakness hadn't left him, but for now it was manageable.

He looked around again, quickly scanning the few
small, nondescript dwellings that stood here at the shabby
verge of the city. There was little to see, but some happy
instinct prompted him to check around the corner of the
wall, where he found a wooden gate, unlocked. He went
through into a small, private courtyard, apparently deserted. In one corner of the courtyard stood a pump. He
wasn't about to ask permission.

He drank liberally, as much as he could hold, then
pumped the rusty water over his head and face, heedless of
the hair dye. Better. Much better. He was wide awake
again. His garments were sopping, and that was all to the
good—evaporation would mitigate the heat for a few minutes, which he'd better not waste. Exiting the courtyard,
he set off along a dry, colorless road almost indistinguishable from the surrounding terrain. Once, the busy traffic
had flowed between ZuLaysa and OodPray Palace. Now
the carts, wagons, and gorgeous fhozhees were so long
gone that the mark of their wheels had all but disappeared.
Likewise gone—the gaily painted markers once edging the
way, the flagpoles, and the little stands vending water to
thirsty travelers, their draft animals, and their hurriers. No
one went to OodPray any more, and the plain below the
hills was empty.

At first, the walking wasn't so bad. The air was thick
with dust, and heavy in his lungs, but not unbearable. He
held himself to a steady pace, and for a while he made
good progress. Ordinarily, he might have reached his destination by noon, but not now. He was tired again, damnably tired, much too soon. He fought fatigue until his
vision blurred, and then he halted to rest again. Not too
long, this time. No more sleeping.

He had come to the ruins of one of the abandoned

water stands. No water or food to be found there, any-more. Nothing remained but an empty wooden shack with a caved-in roof, but at least the place offered a modicum of shade. He sat in the hot dimness, knuckling the rheum from his eyes, and his sight cleared, but the fatigue still weighted his limbs, and the temptation to lie down was overwhelming. He'd fall asleep again if he did that, and then his thirst would increase insensibly, as the heat dried him out like a—

Raisin. Knobs's simile. Mundane, but expressive.

He shouldn't have allowed himself to think of thirst, for suddenly it was with him again—minor as yet, but present, and growing like a cancer. Dawdling in the shade wouldn't help matters.

He resumed the trek, arriving an hour later at a famous relic that marked the midpoint of his journey. Halfway between ZuLaysa and OodPray stood the remains of Pirramahbi's, most glorified of water stands, where the wealthiest travelers once paused amidst elegance to refresh themselves with fruit, sherbet, pastry, and iced drinks, sold at exorbitant prices. There they had sat at jade-inlaid tables, beneath jade-green ceiling fans, watching the play of fountains fed by an underground spring. Tables, fans, and fountains were doubtless long gone, but the spring probably remained.

He needed to rest again. He was dangerously parched, growing light-headed and queasy. The sunlight beat at his eyes. Not a good time for heat exhaustion. He walked into Pirramahbi's, and the photic assault ceased. Inside, it was breathless, but blessedly crepuscular. The furnishings were gone, along with the fans, and most of the green marble flooring. The fountain at the center of the room was bone-dry.

At the rear, a door hung ajar on its hinges. Behind the door, he discovered another room, much smaller, probably once a kitchen of sorts. Empty now, but in one corner stood a broken-handled pump. Still functional? He pumped, and the old apparatus coughed out brown water. A sigh escaped him. Crouching, he sent the water spurting into his open mouth, over his head and face, then into his mouth again. When he could drink no more, he paused,

but stayed where he was. In a minute or so, he'd be ready
to do it all again.

His head was wet and extraordinarily heavy. He could
no longer hold it up. He sagged, and his cheek pressed the
clay floor. His eyes closed, and time ceased.

It was evening when he woke. He was lying in a pud-
dle, and his clothes were soaked. Ruddy light slanted in
through the kitchen windows. The air was shot with small
flying things. Renille sat up slowly. For a moment he was
disoriented, and then he remembered where he was, and
why. He'd slept the entire afternoon away—he must have
slept for seven hours or more. Unplanned, unwise. No denying, however, that the rest had helped. He was no longer
dizzy, and the miserable weakness had abated. Perhaps not
so unwise after all.

Provided he hadn't been followed.

His eyes traveled. The empty kitchen offered no
threat. Rising, he stepped to a window, and looked out
upon nothing but sunset.

His fears had been groundless, and now he would finish the journey in relative comfort. And when he reached
OodPray?

He'd never stopped to think about that. How should
he, a Vonahrishman of sorts, present himself and his purpose to the Ghochalla Xundunisse? She lacked her ancestors' power to order his slow death, but such would be her
inclination, and who could blame her?

He'd tell her what he'd witnessed. When she heard of
the Renewal—the pregnant adolescents, the sacrificial infants—she'd surely succumb. She was a woman, after all.

A woman detesting all things Vonahrish. She'd never
assist him in any way, never grant him an audience, never
admit him to the palace at all.

Would she remember him from vo Trouniere's office?
Would it make any difference if she did?

Xundunisse was probably unapproachable. But her
daughter, the Vonahrish-educated young Ghochanna
Jathondi, might prove more accessible, and infinitely more
reasonable.

She looked intelligent.

Wishful thinking.

What could a girl like that know of the lesser gods?

He drank again at the pump, then rose and left Pirramahbi's. As he stepped through the doorway, a dark form clinging to the lintel detached itself with a drumming of wings. He looked up quickly. A small creature, black against the fiery sky, glided overhead, circled once, and flew away. A bat, almost certainly. Bats would naturally haunt the quiet ruins.

If only he'd had a better look . . .

For a few moments, he stood straining his eyes in vain, then shrugged, and resumed walking. It was easier, now. Sleep and plentiful hydration had restored depleted vitality. The sun was sinking out of sight, and the dying light was easy on the eyes. The heat had lost its blistering ferocity, and hatlessness was now bearable. In the hills rising before him, he could now discern the white façade of OodPray Palace, the slender turrets, and the distinctive contour of the Violet Dome. He trudged on toward them, and the world darkened around him. Night swallowed the palace and the hills. The stars sparked overhead, and a full moon rose in glory.

He had thought to complete the journey without further interruption, but his footsteps were dragging again. When he came upon the dry wreck of another water stand, he paused once more. Shelter was redundant, but the wooden walls were something to lean against. He sat. His weariness and thirst were moderate. The foothills, bathed in moonlight, rose but a few miles distant. The whiteness of OodPray shone through the night. Another hour or so, and he would be there. He could afford a moment's respite.

Or so he believed, until a diving, gliding form split the air above his head, and a sharp reptilian hiss singed his ears.

Shrinking back into the darkness of the ruins, he flung a protective arm across his face, bracing against the attack that never came. The soaring form was there and gone again, swift as troubled imagination.

When his racing heart began to slow, he applied his eye to a chink in a ramshackle wall. Moonlight bleached the surrounding emptiness. He caught no sign of life, animal or human. Cautiously he stuck his head out, swiftly surveying the roof and doorframe. Nothing there. Had he dreamed that saurian hiss? No.

They had followed him from ZuLaysa. Somehow they had picked up the trail, and now they were out there, behind him in the dark. The reconnoitering lizard that might easily have killed him, minutes earlier, had proved oddly forbearing. He considered. Perhaps these reptiles had been trained to attack only upon direct command of their human masters. The wivoori were swift, however, and the reprieve would be brief.

He might find refuge at OodPray, if he reached it, and if the occupants let him in.

He moved north, energized by fresh fear.

Only a couple of miles left to go, and they were flowing smoothly; his pace was good. The way was harder now, for the road angled up into the hills, its sharp grade recalling his fatigue. But he thought nothing of that, for he had come at last to the great gates of lacy wrought iron that marked the entrance to the vast palace grounds. Those gates—once gilded, once plentifully studded with semiprecious stones, once defended by magnificent human peacocks of the Guard Ghochalliir—now loomed, sad mementos of vanished royal splendor. The gold leaf had been stripped away, the stones prized from their settings, and the guardsmen were long gone. Likewise gone was the iron paling formerly girdling the property. The gates—attached to nothing, nonfunctional as their current owner—stood closed and ridiculously locked. He stepped around them.

On he marched, and now the road beneath his feet was paved with blocks of pale stone, still level and perfectly fitted. The ornamental shrubs lining the way were dead, but still upright as skeletal soldiers. Evidently, the system of irrigation maintaining their vitality had failed. The ground here was dry as the plain below, all but devoid of cultivated vegetation. These things he saw but scarcely registered, for his attention fixed on the palace rising before him, and it was a sight to take the breath away, even yet. The dirt and dilapidation, so evident by day, scarcely manifested themselves by moonlight. But the splendors of OodPray—the Violet Dome, the fanciful towers, the Crystal Archways of Shirardhir, and above all, the miraculous combination of immense size and apparent fragility—showed to superb advantage. Renille halted to stare. He hadn't viewed OodPray in years, and never before at such close range. Now, in an instant, he understood the depth of the Ghochalla Xundunisse's feeling for this place.

His reverie was broken by a stirring of air, a sense of fleeting movement, the ghost of a hiss. He glanced up. Nothing there. Turning about, he strove to pierce the shadows with his eyes. Nothing to be seen, nothing at all. Imagination?

He shivered a little, despite the heat, and his mind resumed functioning. The windows of OodPray were uniformly dark, he noted. The inhabitants slept, else occupied northside rooms. How many inhabitants? He wondered for the first time. The Ghochalla, her daughter, and at least one servant—the huge hurrier he'd glimpsed from vo Trouniere's office. Anyone else? Xundunisse had described conditions of squalor and misery, doubtless exaggerated for the sake of dramatic effect. A palace the size of Ood-Pray, dwelling of an Effulgent ghochalla, probably housed a battalion of servants.

But none standing guard, nobody alert to an intruder's presence. He stood practically upon the threshold, and no one had challenged him, or raised an alarm. A thief or assassin would have an easy time of it.

The place could be picked bare of its disintegrating treasures in a matter of hours. It was perhaps a measure of the veneration yet accorded the Ghochalla that her home remained unpillaged.

Someone was surely awake, in there. He'd find a lighted window at the back.

He moved left, circling clockwise about the building. Several minutes of walking brought him to the western extremity of OodPray, where he came upon a wall of white marble, enclosing a sizable outdoor plot. The wall was cracked and crumbling, affording many a foothold. He climbed it with ease, then paused at the top to look down into a garden, overgrown and choked with weeds.

At the center of the garden, topping a slight rise, glistened a golden-roofed fantasy of a belvedere, upon whose white steps sat the Ghochanna Jathondi. She hardly resembled the young princess he'd met in vo Trouniere's office, weeks earlier. Gone were the voluminous silken draperies, the gauzy hat, the polite chignon. She wore a low-necked shift of some weightless, neutral-colored stuff—so plain it might have been taken for a nightgown, but for the wide, fringed zhupur knotted about her waist. Her slender arms were bare, and her black hair hung loose down her back. In another setting, he might not readily have recognized her. But her profile, with its clarity and delicate chiseling, was as he remembered, quite unmistakable.

It didn't occur to him at that moment to wonder at his fortune in meeting her thus. Bemused, he simply stared. Within seconds, she must have felt the pressure of his regard, for her head swiveled sharply toward him, her slight body jerked, and the air hissed down into her lungs.

Another woman would probably have screamed. High marks for the Ghochanna.

Then she was on her feet, right hand darting to her waist, and suddenly she was grasping a knife—a tiny sash bodkin, drawn from the folds of her zhupur. The doll-sized weapon was needle-pointed and double-edged. The girl looked ready and able to use it.

If he took it from her, there was bound to be an outcry.

And, in his present state, it might not be that easy to take it from her. He was likely to lose an eye or two in the process.

Before he reached any decision, Jathondi spoke, with creditable composure.

"You are trespassing upon private property," she told him, voice courteously even, as if she imagined he had blundered upon her by accident. "You will leave, and the incident is forgotten."

"Ghochanna, I regret the intrusion," he answered in Vonahrish, and saw her face change at the sound of the western tongue. "Forgive me, and allow me the honor of an audience. I have come upon a matter of some urgency."

She was staring at him, quite expressionlessly, but he could divine her astonishment. The contrast between his speech and his wretched appearance was bizarre.

"I am not a stranger to you, Ghochanna," he continued. "I am Deputy Assistant Secretary Renille vo Chaumelle, whom you met in Protector vo Trouniere's office. Do you remember?"

No reply. Her eyes fastened intently upon his face, as if she strove to see beyond the dirt, the sweat, and days' growth of beard.

When he launched himself from the wall down into the garden, she stood her ground, but her hand tightened on the miniature dagger. He landed clumsily, but managed to stay on his feet. Her eyes shifted for a split second, and then returned to his face. Some yards to her right, a doorway offered entry to the palace. Another moment, he suspected, and she'd make a run for it.

"The Ghochalla Xundunisse was present at that meeting," Renille persisted. "Her Effulgence described the deterioration of OodPray, and I promised such assistance as I could provide. Ghochanna, do you remember?"

"The westerner in Aveshquian dress." She answered slowly, in her perfect Sherreenian Vonahrish. "The Vonahrishman speaking Kahnderulese like one of ourselves. I recall it. How should I forget a sight so unusual? Your courtesy pleased Mother, and pleased me, as well. Indeed, I do remember." She looked him up and down, taking in the rags, the filth, the haggard unshaven face. "But I should not have recognized you now, Master vo Chaumelle."

"I've been ill for some days, and unable to reach my countrymen," he answered the implied question.

"Why unable?"

"For a while, I couldn't travel, or send word to them. Then, as of last night, the Vonahrish Residency was surrounded and inaccessible."

"Surrounded? What do you mean?"

"The ZuLaysan mob, incensed by the recent death of the pilgrims at ReshDur, riots in the street before the Residency gates. The Second Kahnderulese defend the compound. Nobody enters or leaves, until it is over."

"I see. And this is the urgent matter you spoke of? You have come to entreat the Ghochalla's assistance. You wish her to disperse the crowd."

"That is an interesting idea. Actually, I hadn't thought of it."

"Just as well. You'll scarcely find her Effulgence sympathetic to your people's plight."

"Shall I find her daughter sympathetic?"

"State your errand, and we shall see. While you are at it, you might also explain your rather unconventional entrance."

"I'll explain willingly, should the Ghochanna grant me a small favor."

"Which is—?"

"Put away the knife. I assure you, I'm harmless."

"Are you, Deputy Assistant Secretary?" The tiny blade disappeared into the folds of her zhupar. "You may approach."

The incongruous formality of the invitation recalled him to the hollow reality of her royal status. Poverty notwithstanding, she was a princess born and bred, and it showed in every word and gesture. He bowed, ironically aware of his own scarecrow appearance, advanced to confront her, bowed again, and straightened. She inclined her head. Her expression was carefully gracious, but her nostrils flared, and he recalled then that he hadn't bathed in days, and that he stank like yahdeen breath. Doubtless he repelled her. He drew back a little.

"Ghochanna, accept my apologies, and know that I do not willingly offer disrespect—"

"No apologies are necessary, other than my own, for failing in hospitality. Your journey has surely wearied you. Perhaps you would like to rest yourself, before we speak? Sleep if you wish, refresh yourself, and eat?"

Eat. He hadn't tasted food since the previous morning. His stomach woke at the very word. She had a low-pitched, musical voice, he noted for the first time. Or perhaps any voice speaking of food at that moment would have seemed musical.

"You are hungry, Master vo Chaumelle?"

"Very," was all he trusted himself to say.

"And your hurrier is likewise tired and famished?"

"My hurrier?"

"You left him at the front?"

"There is no hurrier. I came alone and on foot from ZuLaysa."

"On foot? The entire distance? A Vonahrishman has done this?"

"Yes."

"An Esteemed has walked from ZuLaysa. This is a truly original concept. It is a thing of rare beauty. Allow me a moment to marvel." Her smile expressed innocent pleasure.

"I am privileged to entertain the Ghochanna."

"Oh, perhaps I am unkind, but you must understand, it is not often that we Aveshquians witness even the minor discomfiture of our Esteemed western—residents. So delicious a novelty must be savored."

"You share your mother's views, then."

"If that were so, you would have scaled the wall of an empty garden." The smile quenched itself.

"How so?"

"At the moment, my mother and I are—well, but this is not the time to speak of it. You will want to come inside. In fact"—her glance traveled over his shoulder—"you had best come in at once. This instant."

He turned to follow her eyes. There on the wall behind him squatted a small, scaled form, its ribbed wings folded over its back.

"That is a wivoor," Jathondi observed quietly. "I have never before seen one up here in the hills. This isn't their place, and I can't imagine what that one is doing here. They are quite poisonous, you know."

"I know."

"Come inside."

They walked away, without obvious haste. The wivoor's red gaze followed them, but the animal did not move.

"I'll tell Paro to kill it." Jathondi seemed to speak more to herself than to him. "But no, he won't hear me, I don't exist."

Renille had no idea what she was talking about.

He trailed her into the palace, and she shut the door behind them. The open windows, screened with fine wire mesh designed to exclude insects, were proof against the wivoor.

Unless the mesh is rusted, or torn.

He stood in a colorfully fanciful chamber, lit with the glow of twin lamps of heavy wrought silver—matched antiques of obvious value. The atmosphere, though fresh enough, was heavy and still. Glancing up at the ceiling— lofty, dark blue verging on black, picked out with silver constellations—he noted the ceiling fans, festooned with cobwebs. Obviously, they hadn't stirred the air in years. Where was the niibhoy to clean and tend them? He looked around him. The blue-tiled floor gleamed. The priceless furnishings shone. The coverings upon the bed were spotless, if threadbare. Not all the palace servitors were as idle as the missing niibhoy.

"This way," Jathondi commanded. Taking up one of the lamps, she ushered him from the room.

They exited into a corridor, where the reek of mildew weighted the air, but he hardly noticed the smell, for the place seethed with swooping winged forms, and the fear flared at the base of his brain. Instantly, he grasped his guide's arm, intending to pull her back to the safety of the room they had left, then recognized his error, and released her. For this time, the winged creatures were bats—commonplace, ordinary bats—disconcerting, but harmless.

"Sorry," he said, feeling ridiculous.

"My fault. I should have warned you, but I am so accustomed to them, I forgot."

"The Ghochalla spoke of these bats, but I assumed she exaggerated."

"No. Mother always speaks the absolute truth, as she sees it."

"I believe it, now." The glow of lamplight revealed dirty walls, water-stained ceiling, algous archways, guano-encrusted floor; every bit as dreadful as the old girl had claimed. A shame, really.

When he was starting to wonder where she was leading him, Jathondi halted before a door of purple-veined wood, inlaid with twining vines and leaves of malachite, opened it, and went through. He followed, and found himself in a bathroom the size of a gymnasium. A mosaic-floored pool, large enough to swim in, yawned dry, grimy, and empty at the center of the room. In this, the multiple wives of Shirardhir and his successors had once disported themselves en masse. A tub, carved of porphyry—commodious, but obviously designed for individual use—stood off to one side. The tub, and the floor area around it, were clean. At the shadowy far end of the room, he descried a stove, pump, buckets, and a couple of tall cabinets.

Jathondi walked to the stove, whereon sat a box of lucifer matches. Striking one, she touched the flame to candles contained in mirror-backed sconces, and the humid murk lightened.

"You'll have to pump your own bathwater, I'm afraid," she announced, voice echoing oddly in that cavernous place. "Paro certainly won't do it, and there is no one else."

"They are asleep, I suppose."

"Who?"

"The other servants."

"There are no others, Master vo Chaumelle. There is only Paro, and he is instructed that I do not exist."

Renille was silent. He'd blundered, but never had he believed that a palace of such magnitude possessed but one servant. It was all but inconceivable. When the Ghochalla Xundunisse had complained of want, he had assumed she'd meant that her household staff was reduced to a niggardly dozen or so—a dire indignity, in the eyes of Aveshquian royalty. He'd never dreamed that she stated her case with such accuracy. *"Mother always speaks the absolute truth, as she sees it."* Evidently. One servant, and *"he is instructed that I do not exist."* What in the world did she mean by that?

"If you'd like to heat the water, there is coal in the stove," Jathondi told him. "You'll find soap and towels in the cabinet, and some old robes you're welcome to use. Come back to my room when you're done, and there will be something to eat."

"Ghochanna, I'm most grateful."

"And I am ashamed that OodPray offers no better welcome." Jathondi departed, taking the silver lamp with her.

He didn't bother to heat the water, but merely filled the porphyry tub as quickly as possible, grabbed some soap, stripped off his loathsome garments, and stepped in. The bath was cool as a forest pond, and as refreshing. He lathered, he scrubbed, and the accumulated filth came off in layers. The area of his forearm lately poulticed shed grayish sheets of dead matter. The new skin beneath was reddened, but healthy. He soaped his hair, rinsed, and the last remnants of black dye washed away.

When he was thoroughly clean and dry, he checked the larger cabinet and found the robes Jathondi had mentioned—several ancient but clean cotton caftans, hanging on pegs. Three or four of them were small, pastel-colored, embroidered with flowers and butterflies. One was white, unadorned, and cut large enough to accommodate his shoulders. He put it on. The caftan, floor-length on its original owner, flapped about his calves. On one of the shelves in the second cabinet, he discovered shaving implements, and he used them. Finally, he filled a bucket, washed his own clothes, and spread them out on the floor to dry. Removing one of the lighted candles from its sconce, he blew the others out, then made his way back along the bat-ridden corridor to the Ghochanna's door, where he paused, and knocked. She bade him enter, and he obeyed.

Jathondi sat at a small table of Pashirian workmanship, probably centuries old, its surface crowded with bowls and dishes that she must have set out herself. In the glow of the silver lamps, the flesh of her arms and shoulders shone. Her brows rose as he came in. She looked at his light hair, his clean-shaven face, and smiled.

"Now I recognize you," she said.

"And not before?"

"Let's say I reserved judgment. Please sit and eat, Master vo Chaumelle. I know you are hungry."

"The Ghochanna is gracious." He seated himself opposite her. Snuffing his candle, he set it aside, and then examined the food. Fresh fruit, of half a dozen different varieties; flat bread; rice salad, blue with tavril; cucumber relish; preserved chuppils; a bowl of sardines in oil, evidently from a tin; round slices of jellied beef, on a plate, but likewise recognizably tinned; a pitcher of lemon water, and a carafe of white wine, both unchilled. Simple, inexpensive fare that might safely be stored at room temperature.

To him, just then, it looked magnificent. For the moment, he couldn't even attempt polite conversation. Swiftly filling his plate—a translucent porcelain plate, fit for the sublimest of culinary creations—he began to eat, holding himself to a more or less civilized pace. Only when he had cleared his plate once, refilled it, and eaten halfway through the second helping, did his jaws begin to slow. He looked up to find her watching him steadily. In the low light, her eyes looked altogether black, but he wasn't deceived—he had spotted the blue sparks that afternoon in vo Trouniere's office. It was the shadow of her dense lashes, he decided, that now quelled the characteristically Aveshquian colored highlights.

Silly thing to be thinking of, when he ought to be considering the strength of her possible allegiance to VaiPradh. Should this girl and her mother belong to the cult of Aoun, he might as well have saved himself the trouble of the trip from ZuLaysa. He needed to know where her loyalties lay, and he needed to know at once, because she was going to start asking questions any second now.

"Ghochanna, indulge my curiosity. Tell me what you meant, out there in the garden, when you said that you do not exist," he suggested, partly through genuine interest, partly to buy a little time.

"It means I have earned the Ghochalla's displeasure," Jathondi explained. She spoke almost matter-of-factly. Only the slightest hint of a vocal tremor revealed distress. "She has banished me from her sight, which is why I am living alone in this abandoned wing. She has declared me Nameless."

Nameless. The ultimate denial of spiritual identity. The mother's fury must have been cataclysmic. Renille did not conceal his surprise. "Whatever possessed her?" he asked.

"Oh, I flouted her wishes—no, worse, I defied her direct command. I have never done so before. She could not endure the double offense of disobedience in a daughter and a subject, and who can blame her? So there you have it, Master vo Chaumelle. I am in disgrace, perhaps for life—"

"Surely not."

"And perhaps deservedly so."

"I cannot believe that. This command you disobeyed—something offensive to you?"

"Extremely."

"What did she want you to do?"

"Perhaps I shall tell you, one day. At the moment, however, your own situation is of far greater interest than mine. While you were out of the room, I gave some thought to the peculiar circumstances of your arrival—the lateness of the hour, your furtiveness, your disguise, and all the rest—and I must confess to unworthy suspicions. It even occurred to me that you had come here to steal. Then, I considered the wivoor in the garden, so very far from its natural habitat. Never have I seen such a creature at OodPray, until the night of your appearance. Coincidence? Perhaps. But I remembered the tales I've heard of these wivoors serving as implements of assassination, and an explanation suggested itself. Master vo Chaumelle, have you come here pursued by the agents of VaiPradh?"

Renille was silent, disconcerted by the verbal ambush. He'd thought she looked as if she had some sense, but he hadn't expected quite such sharpness, or directness.

"You may as well tell me," Jathondi urged. "Perhaps I can help. I've no love for the Filial—they are worse than all the foreigners combined. I wouldn't betray anyone to them."

Wouldn't you? He looked at her. She was very persuasive, with her earnest expression and her compelling eyes. It would be easy to believe her. In any case, there was little choice. At some point, he'd have to risk confiding in someone at OodPray, and the Ghochanna was as good a prospect as any.

"The wivoor—perhaps only one, perhaps more, I'm not sure—followed me from ZuLaysa," he told her. "I haven't spotted the human masters, but it's likely they're not far behind. It's only right that I warn you of this. Should the wivoori penetrate the palace, then you and the

Ghochalla are both endangered. You may wish, under the circumstances, to withdraw your offer of hospitality."

"Oh, no." Jathondi's expression was serene. "The wivoori will not presume to set foot within OodPray. Ours is an Effulgent house, inhabited by the friends of the gods. The sons of Aoun will respect our family's divine alliance."

"I wish I could be certain of that."

"Believe it. They will never cross our threshold, without invitation. Nor will they send their wivoors into our home. They may, however, hover about the grounds for a while, so I shouldn't count on strolling the garden in the near future, if I were you."

"The Ghochanna appears confident."

"She is."

"She never doubts the gods' favor?"

"Never. You look about you, noting our poverty, our decline in state, and you wonder at my assurance. To this I can only reply that we do not abuse our privileges. We should not lightly invoke the gods, but only in direst extremity."

"That is probably wise."

"You humor me, Chaumelle? Do you think I don't know how this must sound to you? A Vonahrishman will smile at the quaint native superstition. He will wonder how a woman of western education could possibly believe such twaddle. That is the current expression, is it not? Twaddle?"

"Ghochanna, even Vonahrish eyes may be opened. Experience has lately opened mine. Trust me, I don't discount your beliefs. Quite the contrary, in fact."

"Indeed." She studied his face. "You surprise me. Perhaps I was too quick to take offense, and I regret it, but my dealings with westerners have scarcely inspired confidence."

"Understandable, but we are not all the same."

"*You* are anything but typical, that's clear. But we digress, I think. Tell me why the wivoori hunt you."

"Because I saw what I should not, in JiPhaindru."

"There can't be that much to see, in the temple courtyard."

"Disguised as a neophyte from HinBhoor, I got inside, and lived among the AounSons for days."

"That is absolutely extraordinary. I've never heard the like. Were you there as a tourist, for a lark, or was there some purpose to this lunatic escapade?"

"I was there, to put it bluntly, as a spy."

"Ah, I can see how you might well prove useful as such. What did your people send you to look for?"

"Information of any sort, as we know so little of Aoun-Father's cult, or its leader. Specifically, I was to investigate the possible connection between VaiPradh and recent events inflaming the ZuLaysan populace against the Vonahrish."

"The ZuLaysan populace probably requires little encouragement. What events?"

"The murder of a prominent astromage, for one."

"Kydhrishu-in-Wings. Did you discover anything?"

"Yes. The Filial murdered him, and blamed it on us. But that was hardly the greatest of discoveries. What I saw in JiPhaindru is difficult to describe, and so improbable that I despair of finding a Vonahrishman willing to believe my story."

"Try it on me, then. You know how credulous we simple natives are."

"Ghochanna, please."

"Sorry. Tell me your story, Chaumelle. I'll listen, and I will try to keep an open mind."

"Thank you." Renille hesitated, frowning, then commenced, "During my first several days in the temple, I learned nothing at all beyond the regimented dreariness of a neophyte AounSon's life. Eventually, however, I was commanded to bear a lavish meal on a tray up to a certain locked chamber. Within the chamber, I discovered a pair of adolescent girls—children, really—bedizened like harlots, and each of them hugely pregnant. When I tried to talk to them—"

It took some minutes to tell the entire story, but she never interrupted him. From time to time her face changed a little—freezing into stillness when he described his discoveries in the Wisdom, tightening at the description of the alien infants and their fate—but he couldn't judge whether

she believed him or not. At last concluding, he fell silent,
and she was similarly speechless. The silence stretched,
and still he had no idea what was going on behind her
eyes, but his own were lead-lidded, and the fatigue that he
had held off for hours was asserting itself with a vengeance.

Jathondi looked at him. "You had better get some
sleep," she said.

"Ghochanna, I've told you all. Have you nothing to
say?"

"Not just now. Don't worry, I'll answer you soon
enough."

"Do you not wish to know my purpose in coming to
OodPray?"

"In light of all you've told me, your purpose becomes
self-evident."

"Really." *Too clever by half.* "And—?"

"And, I'm afraid you'll have to sleep on the floor in
here tonight."

"What?"

"This is the only remotely clean place in the entire
wing," Jathondi explained politely. "Except, of course, for
one small area of the bath, and I assume you'd rather not
sleep in the tub. Or in bat droppings."

"No, but—"

"Here." She tossed him a pillow lifted from her own
bed. "The rugs are thick, you shouldn't be too uncomfortable."

"But—"

"Sleep, Chaumelle. We'll talk tomorrow morning. In
the meantime, you have given me much to think about."

Argument seemed pointless, and in any case, he hadn't
the energy for it. *She must believe what I've told her—or
at least, regard me as harmless—else she'd never allow me
to sleep in her own room.*

A male stranger in her bedroom, and no servants or
attendants within earshot. No protection beyond that toy
dagger of hers. *Don't be too sure. She could have a howit-
zer stashed away in the closet, for all you know.* Nevertheless, extraordinarily reckless of her. Or trusting. Of course,

in his present state, he didn't pose much of a threat to anyone, and she knew it. Or did she?

He wished he could read her mind. Her face was unrevealing. Inscrutable and beautiful.

The rug he lay upon was soft, and deep enough to drown in. The pillow beneath his head wafted a faint lemon fragrance. His thoughts insensibly softened into dreams, but he never dreamed that the Ghochanna Jathondi sat up far into the night, watching him as he slept.

Once more, the Holiness at the bottom of JiPhaindru was occupied. Within that stygian space, Father and Firstborn communed. Or such was the son's intent, but the god was proving less than communicative.

"Aoun-Father." KhriNayd-Son spoke aloud into the tenanted dark. There was no response, but he sensed the psychic weight of his sire's huge presence. "Enormity, hear me."

No answer. Only days had elapsed since their last interview, but the deterioration in the Father's condition was unmistakable.

"*Acknowledge me.*" The intense metallic whisper sliced the air, and finally there came a voiceless response, of sorts.

?

Vague, irritable curiosity.

"I am KhriNayd, Your firstborn. The Father remembers."

A pause, a mental groping, and then the Father remembered.

"When last I came unto Your presence, I spoke to You of the westerners in our midst. The Father remembers."

Confusion. The Father did not remember.

"They hinder Your worship. Their spies invade JiPhaindru itself. The Father remembers."

Incomprehension. The Father did not remember. Boredom, impatience. The Father's interest was fading fast.

"I spoke of the foreigners' impieties, and Your anger shook JiPhaindru. The Father remembers His wrath."

Wrath.

The Father remembered at last.

"And now, the moment of His vengeance is at hand."

Vengeance.

Fierce joy blazed in the darkness.

"Yes, Father. The time has come. The legion of Your faithful long to cleanse the realm of pollution. They have received guidance, and they are ready. Eager to serve, they await but a sign from the heavens. When it comes, they will rise in fury, slaying the foreigners, purifying the land, and reconsecrating all of Kahnderule to Your worship. Order thus restored, Aoun-Father will reign supreme, as in ages past; unequaled, unrivaled, and eternal."

Eternal.

A kind of infantile greedy pleasure warmed the Father's response.

"Therefore I have come once more to implore divine assistance. Lend me the power of the Radiant Level, that Your firstborn may communicate the will of the Father unto the faithful of ZuLaysa. Irradiate my mind, and Your voice will thunder from the heavens, and the righteous will answer with holy deeds of blood."

?

The Father evinced a hot, febrile incomprehension.

"The Radiant Level, source of divine potency. The Father remembers?"

A long pause, terrible to KhriNayd-Son, and then, emphatic confirmation. The Father remembered.

"Lend me the power, Father. Kindle the fires of Irriule within me."

Firstborn.

Decrepit cogitation, and then, a clear assent.

An almost inaudible sigh breathed from the luminous cavity that was the mouth of KhriNayd-Son. For a moment just then, an endless moment, he had feared the Father's memory irretrievably lost; shattered, this time, beyond hope of repair. Never before had the First Priest truly considered such a possibility. It was all but unendurable to contemplate, for such a calamity, he realized, condemned him forever to the degradation of Nether existence. Without Aoun-Father, acting as conduit to the power of the Radiant Level, then he, KhriNayd-Son, was little better than human. He had his supradimensional longevity, of course. The passage of centuries could scarcely diminish, much less destroy him. He had his intellect, enhanced by the accumulated knowledge and experience of many human lifetimes. He had his strength, both physical and metaphysical, that granted ascendancy over men. He had his remarkable collection of Irriulen artifacts, imbued with the force of Radiance, and he had the ability to exploit that force in the manner of human sorcerers. But these things were trivial, even negligible, by comparison to the potency flowing directly to brain and hybrid body by means of the Father's intervention.

When the Father fed him, he owned the ability to perform wonders, and such ability was essential now. Without the Father, and His gifts—

Nothing. Netherness. Futility. Despair.

For he was never part and parcel of this dingy plane, he had never belonged to it. Nor did he want to belong, for he was made of altogether finer stuff. The bright substance of the supradimension informed his being, and Radiance was his rightful home. He was not a human, he never had been. He was Aware, a Presence.

Or nearly so.

With the help of the Father, he was almost whole. Someday, perhaps, he could dispense with such help, but not yet. Until such time as he achieved full Awareness, he was dependent. He needed Aoun-Father; and loved Him, of course. For who was more wholeheartedly Filial than the god's own firstborn?

KhriNayd-Son closed his lucent eyes and opened his mind, in anticipation of the familiar supradimensional influx. He stood motionless and waiting. The moments passed, and nothing happened. The artifacts decking his dark robes glowed, but he sensed no internal illumination. The inner darkness deepened, and doubt stirred to life in the shadows.

He opened his eyes. "Aoun-Father," he said.

No response.

"Enormity, favor Your firstborn."

No response.

"I have displeased the Father. Tell me my offense."

?

Pettish confusion from the Father.

"Aoun-Father, I implore you. Lend me the power of the Radiant Level. Fill me. Complete me."

?

A hot psychic swirl of impatient incomprehension from the Father. Palpable boredom.

The Father had forgotten, again.

"Enormity." KhriNayd-Son so far forgot himself as to raise his voice, but it didn't matter, for the Father never noticed. Divine attention had withdrawn itself.

It had never happened before. It had never been as bad as this. Perhaps, this time, the Father's intellect was truly gone. And perhaps KhriNayd-Son was trapped for endless life, here in the mud of Netherness—alone of his kind, a mongrel misfit belonging neither to one plane nor the other, solitary and lightless forever.

KhriNayd felt the fear rise up within him—a dreadful sensation, worse than anything he had experienced in all the joyless eons of Nether existence. For a moment, purely Netherly panic all but choked him. He trembled, and the light of his supradimensional artifacts died. Then his Aware component came to the fore, and his intellect functioned again.

"Change." KhriNayd-Son spoke aloud into nothingness, as he had spoken once upon an earlier occasion. Now, as then, there was no indication that his voice was heard, but this time, the matter waxed urgent.

Change. Restoration. A cure. Renewal.

"Renewal." His mind traveled back through the centuries, back to the days of his youth, when he had ventured forth into the outer world in search of human vessels fit to serve the Father's needs. His experiences had proved instructive and, in the end, he had returned to JiPhaindru equipped with twenty serviceable females. These fleshly containers had been filled, tended, and at last emptied of their contents. The restorative effect upon Aoun-Father had been spectacular. Since that time, the principle of Re-

208   ■   *Paula Volsky*

newal had never altered; but never, since that initial glorious orgy of consumption, had the Father enjoyed such a bountiful feast.

It was time for another such; a great Renewal, the largest and most lavish ever offered.

KhriNayd-Son considered. The acquisition of suitable vessels, impregnation, and subsequent cultivation to optimum ripeness was a project of many months' duration, and the Father required immediate assistance, for His condition was desperate, almost as desperate as that of His son. At the moment, the polychrome chamber on the second floor contained but a single Blessed Vessel, presently nearing term. There were several others, he recalled, recently Glorified, unripe and unready for harvesting; the potential supradimensional yield of each, relatively minor at this point.

But circumstances pressed. And low individual yield might be offset by a multiplicity of donors. There were several among the females of the Chosen, he recalled, daughters themselves of earlier Blessed Vessels, preserved and reared within JiPhaindru; marked as potential producers of extraordinary offspring, imbued with supradimensional virtue of their own. There were acolytes of similar pedigree, particularly among the upper priesthood and the wivoori. There were others yet, product of various experimental unions among hybrids. There was a considerable assortment of beings, mongrelized to greater or lesser degree. All of them, his own half-brothers and sisters, his nieces and nephews, his family. All of them, bearing the stuff of Radiance within themselves. But none enjoying an intimacy with the Father that rivaled the closeness existing between Aoun and His firstborn.

Those bodies, consumed in bulk, would render sufficient Radiance to restore and sustain the Father, for a time.

"All of them." KhriNayd spoke aloud. The Chosen of mixed ancestry, the acolytes, the corporeal treasure chests of every description. All of them.

"You will be Yourself, again," KhriNayd-Son assured the occupied void. "You will be as You were when the world was young. Victorious, incomparable, divine."

No response. The Father's consciousness was absent or dead.

"And afterward—" Dawning luminescence quickened KhriNayd's Irriuliana. "Your larders will require replenishment. I will venture forth again, I will forage, and return with fresh sustenance. You will be strong, stronger than ever before. No longer will You confine Yourself to the land of Aveshq. There is a world beyond, awaiting Your rule."

No response in words or images, but he thought to detect a faint ripple of awareness.

"I shall be there at Your side, and together, we shall begin afresh. Your mind will be active, agile, and hungry, and this Nether plane will furnish endless recreation. In all Your endeavors, I will be there to serve You, there to assist and obey. Father? Do you hear? I say I am with You. Father?"

The shadows were bare of intelligence, and KhriNayd-Son knew that he spoke to himself.

8

 Sunlight slanting in through the louvered shutters cast bright bars on the floor. Renille opened his eyes, and sat up. Late morning, he judged. He had slept long, and now he was better, stronger and more rested, than he had been in days. He rose without a trace of dizziness, and looked around. He was alone. There was no sign of the Ghochanna Jathondi, but her bed was neatly made, its clean mosquito netting furled. No telling if she had slept in it or not. The table was bare. She must have stored last night's leftover food somewhere, and washed the dishes herself. Extraordinary, to imagine an Aveshquian of her rank performing such menial tasks. Even the modestly prosperous in this land employed numerous servants.

He hadn't offered to help. It had never so much as occurred to him.

Where had she got to? Not out into the garden, he hoped—not with that wivoor lurking there. She'd displayed an alarming confidence in the protective power of her own hereditary Effulgence, and probably it was true that the priest-assassins of Aoun-Father would hesitate to harm her, but still—

Stepping to the window, he peered through the shutters. The golden roof of the fantasy belvedere glistened in

the sunshine. Vigorous weeds rioted. The garden, so far as
he could see, was empty of women and wivoors.

A dream setting, something spun in imagination.

She'd never told him what she thought of his story.
She'd told him to go to sleep. He'd been so tired, he'd
obeyed without argument. But now it was morning, and
time to settle matters.

Where was she?

Crossing to the door, he opened it, and looked out
into the corridor. Morning light played on filthy fretwork,
exquisitely proportioned archways black with mildew,
marble floor buried in guano. He looked up. Motionless
bats hung from the decorative ledges overhead.

He made his way along the hall, back to last night's
bathroom. She wasn't in there. He washed, shaved, and
resumed his own clean, dry garments. Returning to the
bedroom, he encountered the Ghochanna Jathondi, her
arms full of bundles, struggling with the door. She was
clothed in simple, stone-colored qunne, plain enough for a
laborer of Flow. The blue highlights in the black eyes were
very evident, by day.

"Let me take those." Renille relieved her of her bur-
dens. Food, he noted. Fruit, bread, a jug of some beverage,
a collection of tins. He was suddenly hungry again.

"Thank you."

She opened the door, and he followed her in.

"You've just come from the kitchen?"

"I visit discreetly. I've not been formally barred from
the pantry, so far, but I don't intend to tempt fate."

"Your mother wouldn't let you go hungry?"

"If I am a stranger, and Nameless, why should she
concern herself?"

"She's angry, but surely not that unnatural."

"You don't know the Ghochalla."

I don't think I want to. Aloud, he merely replied, "I'll
put these things on the table."

"Good. I'll set out the plates and jishtras."

"Anything I can do?"

"Sit. Eat," she commanded. "And then, we will talk."

He supposed she didn't mean it to sound like a threat.
Seating himself, he poured out cups of lathered soap-

fruit juice, while Jathondi opened the tins. They ate in a silence that was not uncomfortable.

He almost hoped she wouldn't break it, but eventually she did.

"I've thought a great deal about what you told me last night," Jathondi informed him. "I've considered your story, I've tried to weigh the evidence, such as it is, and I've done my best to keep an open mind. At last, after a great deal of mental wrestling, I found myself forced to conclude—"

I don't think I want to hear this.

"—that I believe you," she finished.

"You sound as if you'd rather not."

"I would rather not. It would be easier, and far more comfortable, to dismiss you as a random crackpot. Unfortunately, I don't think you are."

"What's convinced you otherwise?"

"Several things. To begin with, the content of the writings you discovered in JiPhaindru coincides in every respect with the beliefs and traditions of my own family. The legend you recounted isn't generally known outside my House, and most certainly not among westerners. We do not advertise our link with the gods, yet you learned of it. Then," she continued, "there's your account of the Renewal ceremony itself. It is gruesome, shocking—more ghastly than ever I imagined—and yet, your description confirms the worst of the old rumors; again, unfamiliar to most westerners. The presence in the garden of the wivoor—traditional instrument of the Filial, not indigenous to these hills—likewise supports your claim. And finally, there is the disaster at ReshDur pool—clearly miraculous in nature, highly suggestive of divine displeasure—and this, too, supports your story."

"Is the Ghochanna always so analytical?"

"The Ghochanna, theoretically heir to royal responsibilities, has been trained to use her mind. But our current national infestation of Deputy Assistant Secretary vo Chaumelle's countrymen perhaps obviates that necessity."

The subject was a sticky one. Renille said nothing.

"And so, I believe what you've told me," Jathondi conceded. "This established, the question arises—what, if anything, should be done about it? What *can* be done to resist the might of Aoun-Father?"

"You are an educated woman, yet you accept the doctrine of Triumph in Submission?"

"Triumph, no. Survival, yes. We are only mortals, and we must yield to the will of a god."

"Ghochanna, that thing I saw in the temple was no god."

"What was it, then?"

"I don't know."

"You don't know. Was the entity not vast, potent, capable of wonders and terrors?"

"Yes. So is an elephant, but I don't pray to it."

"You don't wantonly provoke it, either—not if you're wise. So that is what you discovered in JiPhaindru, Chaumelle—an elephant?"

"Nothing nearly so agreeable. I discovered a being—not of our world, I suspect—possessed of extraordinary powers, which we don't begin to understand. Yet I wouldn't regard it as a divinity, entitled by its nature to human worship and obedience."

"I don't quite understand the distinction you seek to draw. You describe an entity imbued with all the powers and attributes of a god, yet somehow, you are certain, it is something other than a god. Or at least, you prefer to call it by some other name, if you can manage to think of one. But really, wherein lies the vital difference?"

"If it looks like a god, and acts like a god, and smells like a god—yes, I see your point. In purely practical terms, you may be right. But I believe there is a difference. The thing at the bottom of Jiphaindru is vile, and contemptible, for all its power."

"Be careful."

"It consumes, it defiles and destroys, it feeds upon humanity. It's no god, but rather, a monster. Fearsome, certainly, but never worthy of allegiance, or of willing submission."

"Willing or unwilling, it is all the same." Jathondi shrugged. "Aveshq may submit to the power of Aoun-Father as willingly or unwillingly as she submits to the power of Vonahr, but in the end, one way or another—she submits."

"Perhaps, Ghochanna, had the inhabitants of Aveshq not so perfectly schooled themselves in submission to the gods, they might have refused submission to Vonahr."

"Well, we are not quite so submissive to Vonahr at the moment, now are we, Deputy Assistant Secretary?" The angry hot color darkened Jathondi's cheeks, but her voice remained cool. "And there's your true concern. You foreigners are like to find yourselves chased clear out of Kahnderule."

"Leaving the country in the hands of the Filial, and the thing that rules them."

"Ah, you won't credit the legitimacy of a god whose actions don't conform to your own little human code of morality. Such a deity outrages comfortable, childlike western notions of a benevolently ordered universe. That must be distressing."

"I'll tell you what's even more distressing—the spectacle of a monster battening upon human beings, who do nothing to resist. Worse, humans who embrace their own slavery. Well, if it's a god, perhaps there's no choice. But if I'm right, then this Aoun creature is neither sacred nor supernatural, and its power, though formidable, may be opposed."

"Not by men, Chaumelle. Not even by men armed with Vonahrish guns."

"How can you be so sure? Has anyone ever tried? But let's say you're right—I suspect that you are. The writings in the temple mentioned others of Aoun's kind, once inhabiting Aveshq."

"Once. They are gone, now—returned to Irriule. Having read of my family's ancient friendship with the lesser gods, you've come to OodPray in hopes that our intercession might secure divine attention and favor."

"Something like that. It's occurred to me that these beings, whatever they actually are, might sympathize with our plight. Perhaps, regretting the damage inflicted upon us by one of their own, they'll be willing to make amends."

"The gods—make amends? To us? I'm not certain, but I suspect that suggestion qualifies as major blasphemy."

"I'll brace for the arrival of heaven's thunderbolt. But truly, who better fit to deal with Aoun than his own kind?"

"Don't rely on it. Aoun was always the greatest among them."

"That may have changed, over the ages. Isn't the matter worthy of investigation?"

"Worthy or no, you ask the impossible."

"Ghochanna, I've glimpsed your pride and spirit. Surely such a woman won't allow her own people to serve as cattle to some hungry alien. Had you seen those pitiful girls in JiPhaindru, degraded and abused beyond expression—had you witnessed the consumption of the hybrid offspring by the cannibal that conceived them—had you seen all of this, then surely—"

"There's no need to repeat the catalogue of horrors. And in truth, my sentiments are closer to your own than you realize. But I can't help you, Chaumelle—literally can't, because I don't know how. You see, the power to call upon the gods isn't something innate. It must be learned. The learning, the knowledge that the ignorant call sorcery, is something traditionally handed down from one member of my family to the next. But the Ghochalla hasn't yet passed it on to me, and now, in view of my unworthiness, she never will. She has said as much. The secret presently rests in her hands alone, and will probably die with her."

"If her Effulgence is approached in the right way, if she heard the entire story—"

"From whom? Me? She won't hear a word from my mouth. I'm forbidden even to approach her. Or do you imagine that you'll persuade her yourself? Think again. Despite all your eloquence and audacity—despite your Aveshquian features and fluent Kahnderulese—you remain Vonahrish, and she holds you people to blame for all ills, both national and personal. But for the Vonahrish presence in Aveshq, the Ghochalla insists, all would be well. She oversimplifies, of course, but it's something she needs to believe."

"But I know I impressed her favorably upon our first meeting—"

"Even if she remembers, it will make no difference. You are Vonahrish, and if she knew you were prying into family secrets, she'd feed you to those wivoori out there. You don't begin to recognize the depth of her bitterness."

"If she hates us so greatly, then why doesn't she call upon her friends the lesser gods to expel the Vonahrish from Aveshq? It would seem the obvious course."

Jathondi's eyes widened a little. "I have never presumed to ask," she answered, in a low tone.

"But you've wondered? Yes, I think that you have."

"That is irrelevant."

"Does she believe the gods' power unequal to the task?" Renillé persisted. "Or does she simply fear that they won't answer?"

"Perhaps she doesn't want to know." Jathondi seemed almost to speak to herself.

"Do you want to know, Ghochanna?"

He caught the quick blue-black flash of her eyes. Yes, she wanted to know, all right. This one would always want to know.

"What I might want is beside the point. I have explained the situation."

"The knowledge you spoke of—the sorcery, for want of a better term—no one but your mother has it?"

"No one."

"She keeps it all in her memory? There's no written record?"

"If there is, I can't reach it. In any event, I don't really know." Jathondi reflected. "There is a room, called Shirardhir's Sanctum, that's thought to be the kernel of OodPray—first-built of the chambers, about which all the rest of the palace has accreted in layers. I don't know if that's true, but I can vouch for the fact that the Sanctum is indeed part of the oldest section of the building. Family tradition has it that this Sanctum was once the workroom wherein Shirardhir the Superb practiced his high art. It's said that magical devices, artifacts, and writings repose there yet. If the record of all that my ancestor learned of

Irriule and the gods still exists, there is where it will be found."

"Have you ever visited this room?"

"I've never set foot over the threshold. The door is always locked."

"Your mother keeps the key?"

"There is no key, in the sense that you mean. The Sanctum's door is secured with a listening lock."

"A what?"

"A lock yielding to a rhyming password. I don't know the password, by the way."

"You could obtain it from your mother, however."

"Never. She would strike my face if I dared to ask."

"Then don't ask."

"What are you suggesting?"

"For the sake of insurance, if nothing more, her Effulgence must have this password written down, somewhere. Perhaps she keeps it among her records, her correspondence, or her valuables."

"Do you—dare—advise me to steal from my mother?"

"No, never. You'd remove nothing. Only observe."

"That is stealing a secret, and every bit as despicable as stealing money."

"It's a secret to which you are entitled by right of birth—after all, you are as true a descendant of Shirardhir the Superb as the Ghochalla herself. It's as much your secret as hers."

"Feeble sophistry. It's contemptible, and you know it. I am amazed you would venture to propose such a thing."

"You are scarcely amazed, Ghochanna. My suggestion can't be altogether unexpected."

"What do you mean?" She was sitting up, very straight and stiff in her chair.

"What did *you* mean, by telling me of Shirardhir's Sanctum, and its probable contents? Why, if it's truly inaccessible, did you bother to mention it at all?"

"Only because our conversation led naturally to it. I certainly expected no counsel to sneak and to steal!"

"What did you expect, then? What, exactly, did you think would happen?"

"I didn't really *think* at all." Eyes downcast, she considered. "I suppose, if anything, I thought you might find your own way into the Sanctum."

"You want me to, then."

"I never dreamed you'd ask me to do the job for you." She didn't directly answer the implied question. "Breaking and entering is more your business than mine, isn't it? You are the self-confessed spy, after all."

"Only an amateur. I'm Deputy Assistant Secretary, remember—a mere civil servant."

"Not all that civil."

"Ghochanna, I wouldn't ask your help if there were any way that I could do without it. But I don't know my way around this maze of a palace. I can't move freely, and I can't afford to be seen. Whereas you—"

"Whereas I. Yes. A very different story. Very fortunate for you, you assume."

"I hope."

"I don't believe you begin to realize what it is that you ask of me. You urge me to deceive my mother, who is the reigning Ghochalla of Kahnderule—"

"You've crossed her once already, when you had sufficient reason. The reason now is even stronger."

"A westerner makes light of such a lapse. To him, the duties of filial respect and obedience are foolish little anachronisms. But we of Aveshq still value these things."

"I know."

"Then you must know, too, that my mother, already deeply offended, would never forgive a second betrayal."

"It's no betrayal."

"She would perceive it as such, and this time, she'd surely banish me from OodPray—even from Kahnderule itself—forever. I would live without a country."

"Her Effulgence lacks the means to enforce such a decree."

"All the more reason to respect her authority. I would obey without question, for such deference is her natural right and due, rendered freely, and without stint. The Ghochalla requires neither soldiers nor weapons to validate her sovereignty. Can you understand that?"

"I understand it. I admire it. But I don't ask you to

defy your mother, to betray or disobey her. I only ask your help in entering that Sanctum you spoke of, where I'll neither steal nor destroy, but only acquire a little information. The Ghochalla will never know, her sovereignty won't be slighted, and you will act, Ghochanna, for the good of all your countrymen."

"To you, this is all very simple, isn't it?"

"Not simple. Only necessary. But I think you know that already."

"I do not know. I only wish I did. The one thing I'm certain of at this moment is that I need very much to think. You may have to wait a bit for your answer, Chaumelle."

"Certainly."

"And you'd do well to take the opportunity to clean yourself out a room, somewhere. Because, I can promise, you'll not be sleeping in here again, tonight."

A pity.

"I left the bucket and brushes in the bathroom," Jathondi continued. "You'll find everything you need. Don't try to work too fast in this heat, and do be careful of snakes."

"I will." *Snakes?* "But first, let me wash these." His gesture took in the dishes on the table.

"No. Better save your energy. You'll need it," she advised him, not without malice. "Go get started, Deputy Assistant Secretary. And while you scrub and sweat, I'll consider the gods, and their relationship to elephants."

He chose an inner chamber opening off one of the huge ground-floor suites once occupied by a quintet of Shirardhir's women. His room—originally some servant's sleeping-closet—was plain, tiny, and therefore comparatively easy to clean. A pallet, ancient and indescribably filthy, still lay on the dirty tile floor. A small window offered a view of the walled garden.

He swept, he scrubbed, he washed the pallet, and spread it out on a patch of sunlit tile to dry. Her advice about saving energy had been sound. Long before he'd finished the job, he was drenched in sweat, and tired. Of course, a native Aveshquian would have known better than to toil in such temperatures—all of them napped through the hottest hours of the day. Only Vonahrish stubbornness kept him from doing the same.

In the middle of the afternoon, he took a break, seating himself on the floor beside the window, through which he glimpsed the Ghochanna Jathondi, wandering the garden in the portable shade of a wide waterfiber hat and a frilled parasol. Her pace was slow, her head was bent, her attitude suggestive of troubled cogitation.

She must have forgotten the presence of the venomous lizard. Or else, purblind in her Effulgence, she simply didn't believe that the creature would presume to attack her.

The window was stingy, but he could squeeze through it. A moment later, he stood in the sunstruck garden, quick gaze sweeping healthy weeds and moribund shrubberies, belvedere roof and railings, crumbling marble wall—

To light on the little winged form clinging to the white stone, dragon head and torso protruding from the darkness of a fissure.

He broke a heavy stick off one of the dead bushes. Approaching quietly, he took aim, and swung with all his strength.

The dead wood shattered on marble. Splinters flew in all directions. The wivoor vanished into the depth of the fissure. Thwarted, Renille poked at the crack, then ducked as his quarry exploded into the light, circled hissing overhead, glided over the wall, and out of the garden.

Gone, unscathed. But not for good.

The thwack of wood on stone drew the Ghochanna Jathondi's attention. Turning to observe the lizard's flight, she inquired, "Are you bent on suicide?"

"I was wondering the same of you."

"Don't worry on my account. The wivoor offers *me* no threat. I thought I'd explained—"

"You did explain, but I'm timid by nature. Humor me, and come inside."

"Oh, very well, if you wish. But really, you worry too much—"

She was still expostulating as they reentered the palace. The door shut behind them, and the tension ebbed from his brain and muscles, but doubt remained. She'd given him no answer. He had no idea what was going on inside her head, and it would be a mistake to ask. She'd talk when she was ready.

"Finished cleaning?" Jathondi asked.

"Nearly. Ghochanna, I know you don't agree, but I'm telling you that something must be done about that lizard. I don't think you quite understand how dangerous the damned thing really is—"

The lift of her brows rebuked his effrontery.

"I understand more than you think." A touch of acid sharpened her voice. "I understand, for example, that a wivoor dispatched by a Filial assassin blinds itself to all save its designated victim. And that is you, Deputy Assistant Secretary."

"You seem to place tremendous faith in a reptile's ability to distinguish among humans."

"Just so. Faith is the cornerstone of that serenity so conducive to personal comfort in a hot climate," she returned helpfully. "I appreciate your concern, but it is misplaced. I'd advise you to keep away from the garden. You really should stay indoors."

For how long? He stifled the question. *Don't push her.*

"You must be thirsty." Jathondi had evidently forgiven his earlier impertinence. "Would you like some soapfruit juice?"

"Very much."

"Unchilled, I'm afraid. We'll have to do something about finding you a pitcher and cup to keep in your own room."

She thinks I'll be here for a while.

"I can get them the next time I visit the pantry. That will probably be tomorrow morning."

The flow of inconsequential chatter continued as she led him along the corridor to her own room. She was resolved, it seemed, to speak of anything and everything other than the one matter that most concerned him. At first, he suspected deliberate perversity, in the style of Cisette v'Eriste. Then, noting the nervousness of her loquacity, the tension tightening the skin around her eyes, he recognized her uncertainty. She hadn't decided, yet. Her alternatives were uniformly unappealing, and she couldn't bring herself to choose. She'd had troubles enough before he'd ever shown his face, and now, he'd made it worse. His conscience twitched.

No choice.

He followed her into her room, where the two of them sat at the Pashirian table, sipping cups of juice.

As if OodPray were some Sherreenian café. So improbable.

She continued to manufacture polite chitchat. He responded in kind, but would have preferred silence.

At last, matching her tone, he asked, like any commonplace tourist, "The inhabited section of this palace, Ghochanna—what does it consist of?"

"There's a portion of the original master suite, occupied by the Ghochalla. There's my own bedroom, bath, and sitting room—closet, really," she confessed with a smile. "Yes—that is all. You needn't ask, I can see the question in your eyes. Remember, though, that we house countless bats, rats, reptiles, spiders, and insects—but only one servant. It's all Paro can do to keep the few rooms we use decent. Sometimes I do some cleaning in my own apartment, but only on the sly. Paro would be wounded, if he knew."

"Has it always been like this?"

"Not always. Years ago, when I was a child, things were quite different. There were servants, then, not as many as OodPray needed, but enough to keep the central portion of the building clean and sound. The various wings and annexes were already deteriorating, even then, and I was forbidden to visit them. Naturally, I explored every chance I got. Once, my chahsu"—she used the Aveshquian term for a nanny—"caught me playing in the fireplace in one of the baths in the east wing, and she gave me a spanking I still remember. So I learned, at a very early age, that Effulgence is less than perfectly sacrosanct—a fact my mother will never concede, to this day. Within a week of that episode, by the way, the chimney above that fireplace collapsed, raining several hundredweight of stone upon my erstwhile playground."

"And that put an end to illicit wandering?"

"You'd think so, wouldn't you? But it seemed that nothing could stop me. My father, the Ghochallon-consort, used to say that I had firestingers in my feet, and a hungry ghirao in my brain. By which he meant, of course, that I was nosy, and inclined to roam."

"You were close to your father?"

"Very." She smiled at the recollection. "To my mother, too, in those days, for she was—how shall I say—milder, softer, while he was still alive. Mild or no, she was always Ghochalla, though. She was hereditary sovereign, and he was but her consort, so Mother definitely ruled. They argued, sometimes—never in front of me, but I was a shameless little snoop, and I wasn't above eavesdropping, back then. They argued mostly about money, which was all but exhausted. My father was forever calling for thrift, while Mother always insisted upon the necessity of maintaining royal state in the eyes of the world. I think, in light of her own upbringing, that she simply didn't grasp the concept of financial ruin—it had no meaning or reality for her. To Mother, the conditions of Effulgence and poverty were mutually exclusive. She just didn't understand that the well could ever run dry, even for royalty. My father understood perfectly, but he never managed to convince her. I know of only one argument with her that he ever won, and she gave way only because he lay upon his deathbed. That was when he got her to promise to send me to school in Vonahr."

"I've sometimes wondered how you ever got there."

"Unlikely, isn't it? But Father regarded Vonahr, with its modern western ways, as the future, you see. Not always a palatable future; something often disturbing, even repellent, but also exciting, and genuinely progressive in so many ways, and above all—inevitable. He wanted his only child equipped to comprehend and deal with that future, and to him, that meant a Vonahrish education. Mother loathed the idea, as you might imagine. But her consort was ill and dying—he was still young, and that made it all the worse—and it was his last request. So at last she gave her word and that, for her, is written in stone. Father died, the family fortune failed altogether, the servants departed, our home decayed, and Mother's dislike of the Vonahrish intensified to unreasoning hatred. Six years passed, at the end of which, Mother sent me to Sherreen. I don't know where she found the money for tuition, and I don't know how she managed to overcome her own bitter prejudices, but she kept her promise. Thus I spent the next seven years in Vonahr, and came home at the end of that time, transformed into something that Mother finds—quite alien."

"How long have you been back in Kahnderule?"

"About three years, now."

"Things getting any better?"

"Not noticeably."

"Ever think of returning to Sherreen?"

"For what? Cloying patronage among the determinedly liberal? They are so very tolerant, you know. Broad-minded enough, in some cases, even to receive the member of a subject race as a guest into their own overfurnished, underheated homes. It makes me slightly ill."

"I can imagine."

"Can you? Somehow, I almost think you might. In any case, my place is here. The Ghochalla needs me."

"As what? A whipping girl?"

"You know nothing of my mother. You speak very much out of turn, Chaumelle."

"Forgive me, Ghochanna. I think it is time for me to return to work."

"Please stay. I didn't mean to chase you away. It's still too hot to work. Have some more juice and tell me—oh, you might tell me how you, a Vonahrishman, came to speak such perfect Kahnderulese."

He told her of Sohbi, who had taught him so much. Then he spoke of his boyhood at Beviairette Plantation, of his uncle and aunt, and the others he had known there. He talked a great deal of Ziloor, and the Palace of Light. He never intended to speak at such length, but somehow her queries and her air of intelligent interest drew him out, and the shadows were long by the time he found himself describing his latest visit to Beviairette, Ziloor's intensive course in Filial lore, and the gift of the crystalline aetheric conflation.

"And there it is." Drawing the artifact from his

pocket, Renille handed it to her. "What do you make of that?"

"Very little, I confess." She inspected the thing from all angles. "It looks authentic, but that's about all I can say. The Ghochalla could probably tell you a great deal about this object, its nature and its use, but I wouldn't advise you to ask her." She gave it back to him.

"Not today, at any rate." He returned the conflation to his pocket. After that, he meant to leave, but somehow remained to talk some more. Now he told her of the time his well-intentioned advice had earned the niibhoy at Beviairette a beating, and she described her schooldays in Sherreen, and presently it was twilight, and the blue sparks in her eyes drowned in darkness.

Time to light the silver lamps, and then, time for another meal. This evening, he helped her with the preparations. They ate, and afterward he carried the ridiculously valuable porcelain dishes to the bath, where he washed them under the pump, while she dried them off with one of the clean old towels stored in the cabinet. Through it all, the flow of conversation never ceased. When he'd carried the dishes back to her room, however, and she'd stored them away on their closet shelf, there was no further possible excuse to remain. He bowed and retired, surprised at his own disinclination to leave her.

Oddly bereft, he returned to the closet he'd chosen for his own use, and, having nothing better to do, finished cleaning it. When he was done, he went to the window, and through it beheld the Ghochanna Jathondi, slender and impossibly ethereal by moonlight, once again strolling the garden. She was frowning at the ground, her unhappy indecision unmistakable. If the wivoor had returned, she was unaware, or else indifferent. He curbed his impulse to drag her indoors by main force. She'd be outraged if he dared attempt it, and understandably so. He'd have to find some subtler means of dealing with Effulgent obstinacy.

Hours later, when the Ghochanna Jathondi had retired, and the moon sagged low and spent in the sky, he slipped out into the garden. The warm night air was heavy on his face, thick with the scent of victorious weeds, sharp with the shrilling of insects. Arming himself with a heavy stick, he commenced a silent search. His eyes had adjusted to pallid silvery beams, and he could see well enough. Within minutes, he'd spotted the wivoor, crouched upon the belvedere railing, watching him through idiot reptile eyes.

He wanted to run. He'd fully recovered from his dose of lizard poison, but the memory remained fresh.

She'd probably be wandering the garden again, tomorrow morning. Firestingers in her feet, a hungry ghirao in her brain.

He forced himself forward. The wivoor's eyes tilted in their sockets. He raised his stick, and heard a hiss. He swung, and the weapon came down on a vacant railing. The lizard was already aloft, circling tightly about him. He spun to keep the creature in view, and the silver garden whirled. He struck out wildly, and by some miracle, connected. The light little body broke under the blow, dropped to the ground, shuddered and twisted in spasms. A second blow killed it.

He nudged the still form with his foot. There was no response. Dead, beyond doubt. Lifting the corpse by the tip of one wing, he pitched it over the garden wall. Let the wivoori deal with their own casualties.

Nothing left to fear in the garden, either for himself, or for her.

Or so he believed, until the next morning, when he rose with the sun to discover a winged lizard perched on the ledge outside his own window, staring in at him through the screen. At first he thought it last night's adversary, impossibly returned to life. Then, noting the distinctive scarlet facial stripes, he recognized a new visitor.

If he killed this one, there would probably be another to take its place. The wivoori were no doubt well supplied. So much for gallantry.

An hour later, she was out there again, restless amongst the weeds. The lizard, ignoring her, clung to the window ledge.

She was barefoot, he noticed. There was something beguiling about that. Her hair was braided into a single, massive cable. He watched until she went back inside.

Later, he joined her for breakfast, after which she gave

him a guided tour of the wondrous, disintegrating west wing. The corridors were deserted, save for malodorous animal life. They walked without care, or fear of discovery, and he drank his fill of moldering marvels. Later, there was a visit to a playroom of sorts, still stocked with the carven puzzles, jeweled games, and cunning mechanical toys with which the women had whiled away those arid intervals stretching between the visits of the Superb. There, they engaged in a no-quarter bout of the ancient board game *rishmish,* concluding two hours later, mentally exhausted, the match a draw. Then, back to the Ghochanna's chamber, for lunch.

Conversation was continual and wide-ranging, touching on every conceivable topic, but one. She never spoke of Shirardhir's Sanctum, with its listening lock, and he never mentioned it himself. She hadn't forgotten, however. The frown he sometimes surprised upon her face, and her occasional selective reticences, suggested inner debate. Her mind clicked almost audibly in the infrequent lulls.

She'd decide in her own good time. Curiously enough, he found himself almost devoid of impatience. He slept on the freshly laundered pallet that night, in a closet tolerably clean, his slumbers unvisited by Aoun-Father. He slept deep and long, then awakened to another day, similar to the first. And then, another.

A rhythm established itself. Shared meals, shared diversion, work, and talk; separate sleep, separate intervals of cogitation. All congenial, natural, and easy, except for the blue glints in her dark eyes, the glow of sunlight or lamplight upon her, the music in her voice, and the urge to touch her.

He'd ruin everything if he tried it.

But maybe she wanted him to try.

Never any telling, with women. They were so inconsistent, so capricious and misleading. Not all of them, of course. The memory of Sohbi's face filled his mind for a moment. Unfair to tar them all with the same brush, but hard to avoid, in light of a lifetime's experience. The evidence suggested dishonesty, irrationality, petty manipulativeness. Some of them were free of it, but which ones?

This girl?

Irrelevant. An untimely distraction. He'd do well to dismiss all thought of the thoroughly Effulgent Ghochanna Jathondi, but she'd somehow sunk a hook into his mind. He didn't like it, but couldn't dislodge or ignore it.

Had she acted deliberately? She contrived to appear so unaware, but she couldn't be as unconscious as all that. He shouldn't have allowed the invasion.

He wondered how she'd managed it. What tricks of face, body, or voice had she employed? For the life of him, he couldn't recall just what she'd done, or when she'd done it, whatever "it" was. He was neither naïve nor unobservant; she must have been very clever. Unless he was imagining things, of course. Unless she was simply herself—gracious, beautiful, intelligent—and "it" was imaginary, entirely the product of his own wishful thinking.

Not entirely. Not possible.

Perhaps the puzzle would solve itself eventually, but in the meantime, his peace of mind, such as it had ever been, was gone.

Jathondi didn't know just when she'd made up her mind. Throughout the days of obsessive deliberation, possibility had gradually condensed to probability, then hardened to certainty, and she wakened one morning to find the process complete. It was a disturbing discovery, whose most troubling aspect involved the question of motivation. She preferred to believe her new resolution built upon the firmest possible foundations of logic and moral principle, but honesty compelled her to admit the existence of another, less exalted possibility—elemental response to the personal appeal of the visitor.

She wanted to think better of herself than that. There were sound reasons supporting a decision to investigate Shirardhir's Sanctum. Chaumelle had stated them clearly, and his case had been strong. She'd pondered his argument at length, finding it consistently resistant to assault. In the end, she'd accepted it, because she believed it right in the deepest sense of the word. She'd also welcomed, if truth be told, the chance to scratch the mental itch of curiosity, to learn the true nature of the gods Themselves; a piece of presumption perhaps verging upon hubris, but neither unworthy nor ignoble. Her choice had nothing to do with the warming effect of the first real companionship she'd known in years. Nothing to do with the sound of his voice, his smile, his lean height, or her own reactions to the expression she sometimes surprised in his eyes, when he thought she wasn't looking. Nothing at all to do with any of those things.

Otherwise, she was indeed contemptible, deserving of all the abuse her mother might heap upon her, and worse.

It was ridiculous, in any case. She was Ghochanna, heiress to Xundunisse's high, if empty, title. (Or was she still? Hadn't she been disinherited?) Chaumelle, on the other hand, wasn't Effulgent, wasn't Kahnderulese, wasn't even Aveshquian. He wasn't exactly Vonahrish either, not quite, but that only made it the more absurd. He really wasn't much of anything definite, other than a foreign spy and fugitive, who'd be gone the moment he'd succeeded in using her to get what he wanted.

But what he wanted—regarding VaiPradh, at least— was what she herself wanted, for the sake of which she'd dared the Ghochalla's worst anger. Dared, in fact, losing her mother altogether.

What would Mother say, and how would she react, should she discover her disowned daughter's present intentions?

It didn't bear thinking of. The connection between the two of them would be severed forever. Mother must never know.

And the Deputy Assistant Secretary? He didn't bear thinking of, either, for the distraction he offered was ultimately meaningless. He'd be gone soon enough, and he'd dismiss her from his thoughts the moment he turned his back on OodPray. The look in his eyes, that seemed to say so much, had probably lighted indiscriminately upon many women.

She had little direct experience of men. The Sherreenian academy she'd attended, designed to polish the daughters of wealth, had employed male tutors of the oldest and driest. Since her return to Aveshq, she had lived in near-total seclusion. But the recollection of long-ago conversations with more knowledgeable schoolmates, reinforced by her own extensive reading, had taught her that men were deceitful, selfish, and ruthless. No doubt exceptions existed, but dangerous folly to assume that Chaumelle qualified as such.

The memory of their days together would probably fade from her own mind, in time.

There would be a great deal of time. Many years, perhaps. Here in glorious, rotting OodPray, alone with angry Mother, and mute Paro. All the time in the world.

She'd start sinking in self-pity, if she weren't careful. Action would serve to divert her. She'd spent more than enough time brooding.

The task itself, simplified by her knowledge of the Ghochalla's habits, was almost too easy. Each day, around mid-morning, Xundunisse immersed herself in the vast onyx tub dominating the master suite's largest bath, sometimes soaking there for the space of half an hour or more. During this interval, Paro invariably withdrew to the kitchen garden, there to weed and water the homegrown pijhallies that were the staple of the sovereign's diet. The bedroom then stood empty and unguarded; the master bedroom, wherein reposed the Ghochalla's jewelry, favorite keepsakes, personal journal, letters, and documents.

It was mid-morning now.

She allowed herself no further time to reflect. If she paused to think, repugnance might overcome resolve, for the task she undertook was utterly unappetizing. Until now, she wouldn't have believed herself capable of stooping to it.

Jathondi exited her room at a nervously quick pace. The corridors were deserted, as always, and she encountered no one. Minutes later, she stood at the door of the master suite. She knocked lightly, and waited. There was no response. Paro was elsewhere; as expected.

Drawing a deep breath, she let herself in. The door was unlocked, of course, for never would it occur to Xundunisse that any mortal would presume to enter uninvited. Guilt stabbed Jathondi. Her heart galloped. Many times, throughout the course of the last three years, she'd steeled herself to step across her mother's threshold. Often, it had been difficult, but never like this, never remotely like this.

She stood in the vestibule, its walls lined with ten thousand painted peacock feathers, each touched with gold, each inset with lapis lazuli, turquoise, and malachite. To the left, a double set of gold-filigreed doors of peacock blue guarded the entrance to the Ghochalla's private audience chamber. To the right, behind a similar set of doors, lay a small reception chamber. Straight ahead rose a golden archway, and beyond it gleamed an azure-tiled hall, off which opened the various rooms and small suites belonging to the sovereign's apartment.

Through the archway and along the blue corridor, she hurried straight to her mother's bedchamber. The door was ajar. The room was empty. She slipped in, and paused to look about her. Mother's own chamber—silent, secret, sacrosanct—

Jathondi stood very still. She shouldn't be here, she had no right, she wasn't allowed, and Mother was always strict. She'd be punished, when she was found out—

She felt like a conscience-stricken child. But she wasn't a child; she was an adult, and a thief. A sneaking spy, a tool of the Vonahrish, their creature, and their dupe.

A traitor.

At least, that was how the Ghochalla would see it.

But she'd be wrong. Jathondi lifted her head. Mother was wrong, this was necessary, and there was no point in self-recrimination.

Her eyes roved. Bed, draped in cloth of gold. Hangings, ancient, all but leached of color by the sunlight of centuries. Rugs that were treasures, worn drab and threadbare. Furnishings, superb and worm-eaten. Magnificent luruleanni shrub, ensconced in its great tub of alabaster. Mother was curiously possessive of that plant, never allowing anyone to touch it. Motionless fans overhead. Still air, faint tickle of Mother's scent, sharp and cleanly bitter as mountain herbs. Mother's presence, invisible and pervasive. Mother's convictions, Mother's hopes and hatreds, charging the atmosphere. Not the time to think of them. Drawers and closet doors, built invisibly into the walls.

Tables, lamps, cushions. Gilt escritoire, a rare concession to western style.

She stepped to the writing desk. The drawers were unlocked. Searching them in quick succession, she discovered packets of old letters, tied with frayed old ribbon; account books, and small ledgers; paper, pens, and ink; guest lists dating back thirty years; an old miniature of her father, painted upon an ivory tablet; a coin-sized ivory box, containing a curl of black hair, and a curl of silver hair; and in the center drawer, the Ghochalla Xundunisse's diary, bound in gold-tooled black leather.

Jathondi slowly drew forth the volume. No lock upon it to safeguard the diarist's privacy, of course, for the Ghochalla Xundunisse would never dream that a member of her own household could be so base, so vile—could sink so inconceivably low—

Her hand twitched, moving almost of its own accord to replace the diary in its drawer. She checked the impulse. She'd no intention of perusing the entries. She meant only to leaf through the book, alert to the shape and spacing of verse. So she did, until the sight of her own name arrested her attention. Pausing without volition, she began to read. Her mother's hand was bold and very legible. The writing itself was recent.

Days pass, and the Ghochanna Jathondi remains obdurate, seeking neither her mother's blessing, nor her sovereign's pardon. The Ghochanna's rebellion, verging upon treason, warrants lifelong banishment, but I am weak and cannot bring myself to pronounce this sentence. Her disloyalty, together with her shameful indifference to the welfare of Kahnderule, have pierced my very soul with grief. Her blood is good, her Effulgence intense. I do not comprehend her moral decay. And yet, so soft and fond is a mother's heart that I confess I would forgive her—yes, forgive her freely, withholding all reproach—should she but acknowledge her error. Let her but kneel to me in submission, let her promise obedience, and I should once again embrace her. But she is made of stone, caring nothing for me, nothing for Kahnderule, and here alone in the refuge of my chamber, I weep tears of fire for her unworthiness . . .

Jathondi snapped the diary shut, guilty and ashamed as if she'd peeped through a keyhole, to glimpse her mother naked. A loose paper scrap, tucked between the pages, fluttered to the floor. She picked it up, noted the form of the written content, and read:

Exhortation to the Lock

Guard all secrets, guard the door,
Lock away the priceless store.
Ward the cache of cryptic lore,
Keep it safe forevermore.

Heed no menace, heed no plea,
Brave the world, defy the sea.
Never let the door swing free,
Ere you hear the verbal key.

Nursery rhymes. Shirardhir or one of his successors must have possessed a certain sense of whimsy. Jathondi took a minute or two to commit the singsong stuff to memory. Then, returning the scrap to its place, and the diary to its drawer, she departed.

When she got back to the west wing, Chaumelle was nowhere in evidence. She didn't know just where he'd gone, and for the moment, she didn't care. Hurrying down the hall to the bath, she locked herself in, filled the porphyry tub with water, undressed, and immersed herself. Presently taking up scented soap and soft brush, she began to wash. She lathered with care and great vigor, she scrubbed until her skin was raw, but still she did not feel clean.

• • •

". . . that the Vonahrissh profaner, vo Chaumelle, hass found refuge within the palace of OodPray, whither we may not follow. There he hass murdered another of our winged brethren, and yet the Ghochalla casstss him not forth from her housse. For now, we wait without the palace wall. One day or night, the impiouss one musst emerge."

The wivoori's oddly cadenced, hissing whisper died away. In the deep shadow of his black hood, his eyes glowed greenly.

KhriNayd-Son's wordless gesture enjoined the other's withdrawal. The priest-assassin bowed and backed from the room, luminous gaze fixed upon his master's masked face, until the closing of the door broke the ocular contact.

Those eyes, so inhumanly radiant, bespoke a generous measure of supradimensional essence—no rare thing within the confines of JiPhaindru, but now, precious as never before. The wivoori—anonymous, as all his kind— carried the substance of Irriule within him. He was a descendant of divine Aoun, KhriNayd's own hybrid kin, and as such, capable of rendering the greatest gift unto the Father.

. . . Thereby elevating himself unto the state of radiant tranquility that is the ultimate oneness with Infinity.

Supradimensional essence. Aoun's sustenance. Little veins and nodules of the stuff were scattered throughout the temple, like gold hitherto deemed too scarce to mine. But now, the need was great, and every lucent morsel mattered. The wivoori's contribution, though modest, would be welcome.

Less welcome, however, was his disclosure. For here was the Effulgent Xundunisse's response, eloquent though wordless, to VaiPradh's recent suit. The royalty of Kahnderule sheltered the Vonahrish spy. The Ghochalla's position was self-evident. She was no daughter of the Father, no friend to the Filial. She had cast her lot with the foreigners, whose meddling presence in Kahnderule had grown intolerable. The moment of national self-purification, so long awaited, was finally imminent, but the kindling of the glorious conflagration required the Father's intervention, and the Father was presently—preoccupied.

Wandering.

Temporarily inattentive.

Oblivious.

Contemptuous of tiny human concerns. Detached. Indifferent.

Senile.

Unknowable, ineffable, His vast consciousness surpassing Netherly comprehension.

Mad. Forever lost.

Such thoughts were sacrilegious. There was one certain means of excluding them. KhriNayd-Son removed his mask, and stood there motionless. Slowing his intellect almost to a halt, he opened his mind fully, freely, to the light that was the Father's consciousness. Such a state of receptivity served almost as a plea. Thus he was wont to draw the notice of Aoun, who flooded the mental vacuum with Himself.

Receptivity drew no divine attention now. KhriNayd waited in vain. The moments passed, and internal emptiness remained unfilled. The First Priest's fingers—long, snake-sinuous, impossibly luminous—rose to the greatest of the Irriulen artifacts decking his person. Ordinarily, the favored Firstborn, beloved of the Father, required no such artificial aid to achieve divine communion. Now, the world had altered, but the force of the Radiant Level would surely suffice to reestablish contact.

He spoke, both aloud and in silence. His mind performed the requisite contortions, and the familiar inner light dawned. Thus enhanced, he sent his awareness questing through various levels of reality, only to encounter—nothing. Nobody. A void, empty as despair.

Never before had his call gone unanswered—never. It was as if Aoun-Father had died, if such a thing were possible, which it was not.

Perhaps the Father slept. Perhaps He had returned to His supradimensional home, abandoning Netherness forever. Leaving His firstborn marooned alone in the muck of the lower plane.

No. The Father merely slept. Presently, He would awake, returning to Himself, and hungry for a great Renewal.

He would surely wake soon.

The supradimensional artifacts about the First Priest were waxing and waning in brilliance, an indication of imperfect mental focus, sometimes the result of strong emotion. But KhriNayd-Son, heir to Radiance, was sensible of no emotion. There was only a curious, shuddery coldness deep within him. He did not know what it was. Perhaps something inside was turning to stone.

9

 Renille stood in his clean closet, staring through the windowscreen into the eyes of a stripe-faced wivoor. The lizard, motionless upon the ledge, returned his regard. Mutual surveillance had continued for days, with no overtly aggressive action on either side, but the armistice could not last forever.

It was well past noon. According to recently established routine, he should have received the Ghochanna Jathondi's summons to the midday meal ere now. He was tempted to seek her out, but that would probably be a mistake.

He heard a knock at the door. The wivoor's tongue flicked vibrating air. Then, her voice:

"Renille, are you in there?"

She'd never before called him by his first name. He opened the door at once.

Her hair was damp, and her skin glowed, as if she'd just stepped from the bath. She stood quite still, her face unrevealing, but somehow, the air around her crackled. He knew what she was going to say.

"I did it. I've got it."

He felt a peculiar impulse to apologize to her. Instead, he asked, "When did you decide?"

"Not sure, exactly. I *did* it just now." She looked away.

"It" must refer to a search of her mother's belongings, which she'd obviously hated doing, and he'd hated asking of her.

"I know that must have been difficult." The words were awkward, inadequate.

"No, it was very easy. Everything was unlocked and unguarded, because she never expected—it never even occurred to her—"

Resisting the urge to put his arms around her, he spoke dispassionately. "Then teach me the password, and tell me the way to Shirardhir's Sanctum, and I'll trouble you no more."

"Teach you? Tell you? What for? Surely you've no thought of going there alone?"

"I wouldn't expect you to involve yourself any further. No one could demand that of you."

"Think again. You imagine, now I've served my purpose, that I'll obligingly vanish?"

"Nothing like that. You misunderstand—"

"No, *you* misunderstand, if you plan to use me, then set me aside. It's not so easy as that, Chaumelle."

"I never thought so. I only supposed you'd rather be quit of all this—"

"I've soiled and shamed myself," Jathondi continued, the words tumbling headlong, "and for that, I want compensation. Knowledge. Insight. Understanding of the gods, or elephants, as the case may be. I'll have it, too, after what I've done. Don't try to shut me out, not after this."

"I never intended to sh—"

"Because, if you can't endure my company, then you can bay at the moon for that password. You're the one that needs me, you know, not the other way around. Come to think of it, I can visit the Sanctum on my own, any time I like, without ever letting you—"

"Ghochanna, I only sought to spare you unhappiness."

"No, you sought to spare yourself inconvenience. You hope to accomplish your aim, expeditiously as possible.

You are Vonahrish, after all, and for every one of the Vonahrish—"

"Jathondi, I didn't think you'd want anything more to do with it!"

"Well, you were wrong! And don't raise your voice to me! I get enough of that from my mother!"

"I can well imagine."

"No, you can't, but that's not the point."

"What is the point, then?"

"Not the same for you as for me." Jathondi moderated her tone. "I suppose I feel, if I'm to live with myself, that such an act as I've committed must find some semblance of justification in its worthy purpose. Serving Vonahrish interests in Aveshq hardly qualifies as such. Enlightenment may, however. So I'll see for myself what Shirardhir learned of the gods."

"I understand." He could see there was no point in trying to change her mind. And who could blame her? There was, he had to admit to himself, a certain measure of truth to her accusations. He'd underestimated both her perceptiveness and her determination, an error he wouldn't repeat. "When shall we visit this Sanctum, then? Tonight?"

"Why wait? It's well past noon. The Ghochalla will already be napping. She always does, at this time of day. Paro's probably asleep, too, unless he hasn't finished in the garden. In any event, no one is likely to see us."

He suspected she feared a delay would undermine her resolve. Truth-hungry though she was, this entire furtive, prying business revolted her. He himself would be glad to finish with it, as quickly as possible.

And then? A return to ZuLaysa, on foot, unarmed, pursued by priest-assassins? Perhaps Jathondi might secure him a weapon of some sort?

Once he left OodPray, he might never meet her again.

Not the time to be thinking of it.

"Now, then," he acquiesced aloud, whereupon she conducted him from the west wing, along endless, filthy corridors, until they came to the massive bronze portals, once piercing an outer wall of the original palace, that marked the entrance to the oldest, central section of Ood-

Pray. Antiquity notwithstanding, the architecture here possessed subtlety, grace, and squalid splendor to equal the newer additions. The interior bathed itself in golden light. An array of immense, crystal-paned windows, astonishing even today, must have bordered upon the miraculous in Shirardhir's time.

A row of such windows, closely spaced and running nearly floor to ceiling, converted the salon through which she was leading him into something resembling a greenhouse. The heavy draperies once excluding the fierce afternoon sun had long since rotted away. The light poured in, and the heat was intense. Through the dirty panes, Renille glimpsed a stand of pijhalli bushes, homely utilitarian replacement to the ornamental shrubberies once bordering this wall of the palace. In the shade of the bushes reclined the Ghochalla's huge factotum, wide hat covering his face.

"He's asleep," Jathondi said.

If she's wrong, the damage is already done.

As the two of them traversed the long room, he kept his eyes fixed on the supine figure, but sleeping Paro never stirred.

The salon with its wall of windows lay behind them, and now she led him down a curving staircase, railed in silver black with tarnish, and he remembered another descent, another feminine guide—Chura, leading him through the bowels of JiPhaindru. His stomach tightened, and he listened for the drumming of leathern wings, but heard nothing beyond the tap of footsteps on marble, and the thin drone of unseen resident insects.

At the bottom of the stairs, the air was still, and comparatively cool. They had come to a small underground passage, dimly visible by the faint light filtering down through the ornamental grillwork set into the ceiling. The passage contained but a single door, secured with a curious device.

It looked something like the marriage of a padlock and a musical instrument, with polished steely coils, nodules, ivory buttons, and, in place of a keyhole, a trumpet-shaped projection. Jathondi knelt. Approaching her lips to the trumpet, she recited the rhyming password.

"Guard all secrets, guard the door—"

Eight lines of similar puerility, spoken very clearly. Jathondi concluded, and the mechanism whirred. Colored light glowed from its various orifices, an arpeggio of clicks sounded, and the listening lock snapped itself open.

Entertaining. But the device, possessing no particular advantage over a conventional padlock, seemed pointlessly flamboyant. On the other hand, the thing was genuinely mystifying. He couldn't begin to imagine its principle of operation, but obviously the inventor had possessed working knowledge, that some would call magical. Perhaps that in itself had been Shirardhir's point.

The door was extraordinarily heavy, built to withstand the attack of armies. Renille pushed it open, with effort. The room beyond was dark.

"I didn't realize there were no windows." Jathondi frowned.

"There's sure to be candles or a lamp."

He extended his hand. She took it without hesitation, and they entered together. The door behind them gaped wide, admitting a faint wash of weak light from the hall.

The air in Shirardhir's Sanctum was still, but comparatively fresh. There had to be ventilation shafts somewhere, but he couldn't see them, he couldn't see much of anything. Renille strained his senses. The walls were invisible, but somehow he knew that the room was large. No recognizable scent in his nostrils—no pungency of mold, rot, or droppings. The place was clean, and therefore, visited yet by the Ghochalla. For what purpose? He listened, caught the quick cadence of his companion's breathing, and nothing else, nothing at all. He turned to look back, and his eyes must have adjusted, for now the rectangle of gray light that was the doorway seemed much stronger, and beside it, he discerned a low stand, supporting a triple-armed candelabrum.

Loosing his hand from Jathondi's clasp, he moved to the stand. A box of matches lay beside the candelabrum. He lit one, touched flame to three candles, and the darkness lightened.

Shirardhir's Sanctum was immense, vaster than he had ever dreamed, and even now, in the light of three candles, its distant extremities drowned in shadow. The ceiling above was likewise invisible. Something about the size of the place, the quality of its air, reminded him of another chamber, likewise huge and uncanny—the Assembly, of JiPhaindru, where the god(?) Aoun manifested Himself, in all His might and hunger. The Sanctum was indefinably similar.

Aoun-Father, or others of His kind, might well visit this room.

Renille tried to drink it in at a glance. He saw a large pit-of-elements yawning at the center of the floor, a footbridge spanning the pit, and shelves lining the walls, shelves crammed with more strangeness than he could encompass in a year. There were ranks of written works, notebooks and folios, phalanxes of exotically filled glass vessels, stone jugs, mechanical enigmas, bone sculptures, spills of artificial water, braided clouds, petrified articulations, preserved oozies and wingbane eggs, three-dimensional maps, antique spirit-sympathizers, a collection of crystalline aetheric conflations, and more.

Intriguing though they were, the shelves and their contents hardly held his attention. Candelabrum in hand, he advanced to the center of the room, and when he stood upon the ebony footbridge above the pit-of-elements, the light found the rear wall of Shirardhir's Sanctum, illuminating a stone archway, beyond which lay a region of intense blackness.

He had to force himself toward it. For some reason, his instincts were screaming. He glanced down at the girl beside him, wondering if she shared his qualms. If so, her face showed no sign of it. The stones of the archway were crowded with glyphs, their meaning unknown to him. The semicircular section of flooring before the opening was spotless, and polished to a sober gleam. The darkness beyond the arch remained inviolate.

Advancing several long paces, to stand within touching distance of the carven stones, he raised the candelabrum, and beheld—nothing. Black nullity. The darkness he confronted was impossibly impervious to light.

There was always the option, of course, of walking through the archway, and straight into it.

Impossible.

He looked again at Jathondi. She met his eyes.

"The notebooks," she said firmly, and her voice was startling in that stillness.

They returned to the shelves. Jathondi's fingers lightly scanned successive leather spines, then halted upon an embossed circular design ornamenting one of the largest and oldest of the volumes.

"Shirardhir's seal," she said. "Shirardhir's own."

Drawing the folio from its place, she opened it. Renille lifted the candelabrum to spill light across pages crammed with spidery writing, text and lists, equations and formulae, diagrams and charts—

All meaningless to him. He wondered if the Ghochanna could make anything of it. She'd been born in this place, drinking its atmosphere from childhood, and although she lacked formal instruction, she might have developed some sort of feel for this kind of thing, some natural sorcerous sense—

Sorcerous? Absurd.

Not so absurd. Only another name for something real, but imperfectly comprehended.

He studied her face by candlelight. She was frowning over the text, lips compressed, wholly intent. He stifled his own urge to suggest another folio, another avenue. She didn't need his advice. For she saw something, quite invisible to him, or else she intuited; so much was unmistakable. This sinister lunacy was at least partially intelligible to her, and he could only assume—

Assumptions were interrupted by an alteration in the quality of the light, a fleeting shadow glimpsed obliquely.

Renille looked up in time to glimpse a huge form framed in the doorway. He saw it only for a moment, and then the door crashed shut. His hand tightened on the candelabrum, the flames jumped, and the shadows on the walls shuddered.

The folio dropped from Jathondi's hands. Running straight to the door, she strove uselessly to pull it open. Renille added his own, equally ineffectual efforts. The door was immovable, obviously locked from the outside.

"Paro! Open up!" Jathondi kicked furiously at the barrier. "Open it! Paro!"

No response. The Ghochanna subsided, breathing heavily.

"I do not exist," she muttered.

"Doesn't matter," Renille said.

She looked up at him, caught his meaning, and nodded. In tones painstakingly distinct, she recited the rhyming Exhortation to the Lock. Nothing happened. The door remained shut. She repeated the password, her voice louder.

No results. Either Paro had replaced the listening lock with another of less exotic character, or else, more likely, the Ghochanna's voice simply failed to penetrate the heavy barrier. She tried once more, practically screaming, and this time, he shouted the words along with her, but the lock was deaf.

Buried alive. Renille considered the eventual consumption of the candles. Crushing darkness, deadly hunger, deadlier thirst—

But no. The age of barbarism was over. Such punishments as premature entombment belonged to the past. *Didn't they?*

"What will Paro do?" He wasn't certain he wanted an answer.

"He will fetch Mother." Jathondi dealt the door a final, futile kick. "He'll lead her straight down here."

"And then?"

"Ever witness a volcano in full eruption?"

"Not up close. Think she'll listen to reason?"

"Perhaps, when she's cooled down. Eventually. Maybe."

"I'm sorry I involved you, Ghochanna."

"I chose to involve myself. But never mind about that. You know, if we're to look through those old notebooks, we'd better do it now. We're not likely to have another chance, after this."

"You're a cool-headed one, aren't you?"

"Product of a first-rate Vonahrish education."

"Much more than that."

"We've not much time." She wouldn't meet his eyes.

"The content of Shirardhir's book—you understood it?"

"Some of it." She frowned. "The subject was atmospheric instability, or weakness, the point at which a hole, a—doorway—might exist. According to Shirardhir, such an anomaly in the atmosphere exists here, exactly *here*. By 'atmosphere,' he didn't mean actual air, or gaseous elements, but rather—"

"Tell me later."

Jathondi nodded. Returning to the fallen volume, she scooped it up, and resumed reading. Renille followed, with the light. Selecting another notebook, he scanned the pages. Diagrams, lists, numbers. Gibberish. He put it back.

Before he had chosen another, Jathondi spoke, her whisper electric. "Now see there—this entire page—it explains a means of communication. By this method, if it is true, one might converse with those—er—over there, on the other side of the opening—"

Renille looked. To his eyes, the writings were meaningless.

"Is it something you yourself could do?" he asked. "Do you think you might contact—the—"

"The gods?"

"If that's what they are, which I doubt."

"I believe I could learn to follow this procedure, but it would take some time. I can see at a glance that the degree of mental discipline required is—"

She broke off as the door of Shirardhir's Sanctum yielded with a groan.

The Ghochalla Xundunisse entered. She was a little disheveled, black garments slightly disordered, wisps of hair escaping the coil at the back of her neck, eyelids swollen. Probably she had just risen from sleep. Behind her came Paro, bearing a lamp.

"Effulgence." Setting the book aside with care, Jathondi performed a ceremonious obeisance, straightened, and faced her mother squarely.

Renille likewise bowed. The Ghochalla ignored him. Her black gaze fixed on her daughter, as if the two of them were alone.

"It is true, then." Xundunisse's voice was husky with uncharacteristically repressed emotion. "I would not believe it until this moment. But it is surely true."

"I have entered this chamber without securing the Ghochalla's consent. I cannot deny it."

"Indeed. And what else can you not deny, Ghochanna? But no, I must not honor you with that title, for it is no longer yours. Can you deny that you have entered my bedchamber by stealth to filch the Exhortation to the Lock? For there is no other way you could have acquired it. Can you deny that you are a common thief? If so, then do it."

"I cannot," Jathondi replied tonelessly.

"Can you deny that you rifled my drawers, discovered my journal and read therein—probing the deepest secrets of my heart, violating my very soul? Can you deny that you have betrayed all trust, outraged all decency?"

"I cannot."

"Can you deny that you have revealed the high mysteries of Shirardhir's Sanctum to a foreigner, one of the Vonahrish enemy?"

"No."

"Can you deny that you have aided and sheltered this western spy?" The Ghochalla's contemptuous gaze flicked Renille for the barest fraction of an instant, the first indication that she had noted his existence.

"No."

"And what was the reward of treason, you Nameless? I hope the secrets of Aveshq sell at a good rate. What was your price?"

"Knowledge," Jathondi returned, expressionlessly. "I desired understanding."

"Of what?"

"The gods, and their nature."

"I see. Enlightenment was your sole aim."

"Effulgence, I wanted—"

"And if such was truly your heart's desire," Xundunisse continued, with the same unnatural self-restraint, "then perhaps you will explain the necessity of this westerner's presence. You might have come here by yourself. Why bring this mongrel dog of vo Trouniere's? There is, I am to understand, no insight possible without him?"

"This man," Jathondi returned steadily, "has walked

the corridors of JiPhaindru. He has witnessed the rite of Renewal, and he has looked upon the being we call Aoun."

"You believe this!"

"Ghochalla, it is the truth," Renille interjected. "And what I saw there—"

"You believe this," Xundunisse repeated, evidently deaf to his voice.

"I believe," Jathondi told her, "because he spoke of things he could not know unless his story contained some measure of truth. I believe, too, because I think him honorable. He was courteous, generous, and considerate, that day we met him in ZuLaysa. You said so yourself, Effulgence. Do you not recall it?"

"I recall with shame that I was taken in. My eyes are open now, belatedly."

"Hear him, Ghochalla. You will be moved, as I was."

"As you were. Ah." Xundunisse paused to consider. "I begin to understand, I think. It is all becoming clear."

"Listen to Master vo Chaumelle's account, and you will see—"

"I will see, perhaps, the depths to which the traitor once known as Ghochanna has sunk." The Ghochalla's restraint was beginning to fray. Her breath came fast, and her narrow face took on a curiously pinched look about the mouth and nostrils. "She has betrayed her nation and her House, she declares, for love of knowledge. Or was it, perhaps, just for love? This western spy, this thing—you have harbored him here within the palace, perhaps within your own chamber?"

"What does the Ghochalla imply?" Even by warm lamplight, Jathondi's sudden pallor was evident.

"He has a pleasing form and speech. He has come to you like a disguised prince in one of the old tales. It is all very romantic, very entertaining—and life at OodPray is dull for a worldly young woman, is it not?"

"You cannot truly believe—"

"That one I gave life to is whore to the Vonahrish? Their dupe and plaything, as well as their informant? You are right, it is harder to accept the stupidity than the venality."

248 ■ *Paula Volsky*

"Ghochalla, you wrong your daughter," Renille broke in. "She has offered kindness and hospitality to a stranger in need, but never has there been the slightest—"

"Silence," Xundunisse commanded, without troubling to glance in his direction. "I give you no leave to speak."

"Nevertheless, I must assure you—"

"Hold your peace, or I will instruct Paro to silence you." Her eyes never left her daughter's face.

Renille inspected Paro. Meeting the speculative regard, the servant lifted one hand to the butt of the ancient dueling pistol thrust through his zhupur.

Paro could silence him, all right. Renille subsided. In any event, his intervention seemed unlikely to benefit the Ghochanna.

"Ghochalla, I have confessed the truth of your accusations, but this last one is unfounded." Jathondi was standing very straight. "Master vo Chaumelle has accorded me all respect—"

"All that you deserve. That I do not doubt."

"He has attempted no liberties, no—questionable persuasions—"

"I am to take your word for that?"

"I have never lied to you."

"You have only stolen from me. Deceived, circumvented, and deliberately flouted me. Aside from that, you are honest as the sunlight."

"I am sorry and ashamed. But Effulgence, in all that I have done, the purpose has been worthy. You will see that for yourself, once you've heard what Chaumelle found in JiPhaindru—"

"I will hear nothing from that one's Vonahrish lips—nothing!"

"Then hear it from mine. Within JiPhaindru, the being Aoun begets hybrid offspring upon the bodies of human females. Prior to natural delivery, the infants are torn from their mothers' wombs, to be consumed by the entity that conceived them. Aoun's craving for such nourishment reveals much, for it suggests a need hardly consonant with the perfect, self-contained wholeness of divinity."

"These are nursery nightmares. This man has befooled you with his lies."

"It is the truth, Ghochalla," Renille insisted. "I was there, and I saw it."

"Paro." Xundunisse gestured. Her servant drew the pistol from his zhupur, and leveled it. "If he speaks again, without permission, shoot him."

"Mother, you cannot—"

"Never address me by that title!" The Ghochalla's self-control slipped, and her voice rose to a shout. *"You have no mother!"*

"Forgive me, Effulgence." Jathondi's lips quivered. She took a moment to compose herself, and then resumed. "The possibility exists that Aoun, though real and potent, is something less than a god."

"Take heed of blasphemy."

"It was in hope of learning the true character of these entities we call gods that I came to Shirardhir's Sanctum," Jathondi continued. "I brought Master vo Chaumelle with me, because he has dared so greatly that he has earned the right to knowledge."

"The right! You are his gull, and he is all deceit!"

"I do not think so. And I firmly believe, in light of all he's told me, that we owe it to ourselves to learn the truth. If it is a fact that we have worshiped false deities, then it is time to correct our error, and time to resist the rule of Aoun-Father. The aid of our family's friends, the lesser gods, might render such resistance possible. The Ghochalla possesses power to call upon them. Will she not use that power, to discover the nature of reality? Does she not wish to know?"

"She already knows." The Ghocalla seemed to speak through some constriction of the throat. Her voice rasped, and her chest heaved. "She knows that the miserable creature she once loved as a daughter is lost, forever lost to decency and honor. She knows that the beautiful child on whom she fixed her hopes is gone, and in that child's place remains but a foul and spoiled remnant. There is nothing left of the Ghochanna Jathondi. There is only a thieving harlot, who sells her country's secrets for no better price than the casual embrace of a mongrel western spy. And does this degraded wretch account the world well lost for love? What will the answer be, six months hence?"

"Ghochalla, I implore you to believe. I've told you nothing but the truth—"

"You have forgotten the meaning of truth!"

"If you'll only hear Renille's story—"

"Ah, 'Renille,' is it? What a pretty intimacy!"

"Only listen to him, that is all—"

"Silence! Not another word! I have listened long enough. Now you will listen, and so will your seducer, but do not fear tedium—I will be brief. It does not take very long to tell you that your rose-colored idyll has come to an end. Be thankful that we do not live in sterner times, for if it were so, I would order this man's death by torture. But we of Aveshq no longer rule ourselves, and even a Ghochalla must live by the law of our foreign overlords. Therefore, though it sears my heart to stay my hand, I will not harm him, but only expel him from OodPray. And he may well thank the gods for his escape. As for you, Nameless, I have not yet determined your fate. Until such time as I reach my decision, you will remain within your accustomed chamber. Go now to your confinement. Paro will escort the Vonahrishman to the gate. Bid him farewell if you wish, for you will never see him again."

"You cannot turn Chaumelle out," Jathondi said.

Her mother stared at her, astounded.

"He has come to this place pursued by VaiPradh's wivoori, with their poisonous winged lizards," the young woman continued. "Turn him out unarmed, and he'll be killed within sight of OodPray."

"I shall watch, with immense enjoyment," Xundunisse returned.

"Effulgence, that is equivalent to murder."

"I have said I will not harm him. If others hunt him to the death, that is none of my doing."

"It is beneath the Ghochalla to split moral hairs. Should her action result in a man's destruction, she is responsible. She knows this."

"Is it possible, this soiled rag dares school me? This wreck of virtue mouths high words at me? I have been temperate, mild, and soft, but patience finds its limit."

"The Ghochalla requires no instruction. Her conscience will guide her."

"Beware that her conscience does not demand the traitor-harlot's presence beside her at the window from which she will observe the Vonahrishman's expulsion."

"He will not depart unarmed. For the Ghochalla's own code will not permit the compromise of OodPray's integrity."

"What is this?"

"For days, Master vo Chaumelle has enjoyed the hospitality of this palace."

"I have offered no hospitality. And you—your offerings to him were yours alone."

"Truly. And yet, whatever the source of the invitation, the fact remains that Chaumelle has sheltered himself as a guest beneath the palace roof. That happening has woven itself into the fabric of OodPray's history. It cannot be excised. And now, should this guest die, by the will of its inhabitants, OodPray's character is forever stained."

Xundunisse was silent.

"OodPray crumbles," Jathondi observed. "But its soul has remained clean—until now."

"Serpent, you would use my love of this place as a tool to serve your ends?"

"I only direct certain truths to the Ghochalla's attention."

"I would hate you now, were you worthy." The Ghochalla's internal struggles concluded, and she conceded, "The Vonahrishman may carry a knife away with him."

It was far more than Renille had expected, but his defender wasn't satisfied.

"That won't do." Jathondi folded her arms. "He can't ward off AounSons and poisonous reptiles with a knife alone."

"He is fortunate beyond expression to have so much."

"It is not enough. But you might lend him Paro's gun. Or better yet, Paro can bear him by fhozhee back to the city."

"You dare suggest—oh, is there no limit to your insolence? How could I ever have thought that I knew you? You are a stranger!"

"OodPray's character—"

"Speak no more of that, it means nothing to you! Now hear me. Rather than lend him Paro's gun, or Paro's services as hurrier, I would see him cast into the lake of eternal flame—and you along with him—to burn forever. He may take a knife, or not, as he chooses, but there is no alternative."

There is one. Wordlessly, Renille drew Ziloor's gift from his pocket.

Xundunisse beheld the crystalline aetheric conflation. "He has stolen this," she stated.

"No, Effulgence. It is his by right, but he is untaught in its use. May it not furnish him protection? I ask the daughter of the gods, privileged in understanding." Her mother hesitated, and Jathondi added, "Here is a chance of acceptable compromise. The Ghochalla sacrifices nothing belonging to OodPray. She grants words, only."

Only?

"She preserves the honor of the palace, at no cost."

There was a protracted pause, and then the Ghochalla slowly extended her hand.

"Let me see it," she commanded.

He could scarcely bring himself to part with the thing. She was perfectly capable of smashing it underfoot. As things stood, however, that would mean little. Renille handed it over.

Xundunisse studied the artifact.

"Rare," she observed.

He didn't need the Ghochalla to tell him that.

What is it, then? He said nothing aloud. Paro stood ready to burn his brains at a syllable.

"It is a reflector," Xundunisse observed. For a moment, her anger lost itself in wonder, and the bitter years dropped away from her face. "I have seen only one other in my life. It is truly part of the substance of Irriule, its power intrinsic to its being. Properly used, it will reflect intelligence and observation back upon the point of origin. Or else, it can deflect consciousness in the direction of the user's choice."

Properly used?

"Teach him to use it," Jathondi said. "There is the

solution. Nothing is lost, for a mhuteez of the street might know as much."

The Ghochalla was silent, motionless, and flint-eyed. Eons elapsed, before she finally turned to face Renille.

"I have striven," she remarked quite calmly, "to devise the means whereby your destruction may be achieved, without compromise of OodPray's integrity. The answer eludes me, however, and I find myself trapped. Your paramour, though lacking true intelligence, possesses the cunning to turn my affections against me, thus preserving your miserable life."

Renille drew a deep breath, saw Paro's finger tighten on the trigger, and held his peace.

"I will not blemish OodPray's honor," Xundunisse continued. "Not for any man, and most certainly not for such a thing as you. Therefore, I will share my wisdom, and you shall have use of the amulet that you carry."

He met her eyes, and she curved a small, minatory smile.

"Do not presume to render thanks," she advised. "I will do this thing, but even as I teach you, I will inwardly entreat the gods. Should they favor me, then these secrets that this Nameless dupe of yours forces from my mind will never serve or save you. The power will fly your grasp at the moment of ultimate need, and the servants of the Filial will drink your blood. This I will pray for."

Fair enough, he thought. *Only teach me, and then pray all you like.*

The Ghochalla obliged. Very clearly, and no doubt precisely, she then explained how to tap the artifact's power, and it was all mental focus, and words, and internal intensification culminating in explosive release, linked with something inconceivably outside the self, and yet, recognizable.

It was alien, but familiar. He knew it, almost upon instinct.

He had it now, and he could use it. Never would he have imagined the skill so accessible to an ordinary human, just anyone. Accessible, of course, did not mean easy. His brain all but boiled inside his skull.

But he had it, the secret of a mental mirror.

He could use it, in a feeble sort of way. With practice, he might hope for greater proficiency.

"Now, conduct him from the palace," Xundunisse commanded. "I will no longer look upon him."

Paro's huge hand closed upon his shoulder.

"He must have some water, some food—" Jathondi attempted.

"He has his life. Let that content you."

"At least, a wide hat—"

"Enough. Leave my presence."

Renille looked into Jathondi's eyes, and before he knew he meant to speak, the words slipped out. "Come with me."

Her eyes widened, probably in simple surprise.

Paro's finger twitched, but he hesitated an instant, and his mistress lifted her hand.

"Do not fire," the Ghochalla directed. "But cleanse my vision of this western pollution. Take him away." She turned to her daughter. "And you, stay where you are. I see your soul in your eyes, but you will stay. You have brought shame enough upon an Effulgent house. There will be no more. Take but a single step to follow that man, and OodPray's honor notwithstanding, I will order Paro to shoot. Believe this."

Jathondi stood motionless, and Paro dragged Renille from the room.

Renille did not resist. The mute was twice his weight, and the gun was pressing his ribs. The Irriulen artifact that might have deflected unwelcome attention lay in his pocket, and Paro would probably break his arm if he reached for it. Pointless, in any case.

Through the corridors and galleries Paro propelled him, through the ballroom-sized foyer, out the door, and down the wide steps. Then, on along the drive of pale stone, between the rows of skeletal shrubs, straight on to the orphaned iron gates, still uselessly locked, and there the mute released him, with a firm shove to speed him on his way.

He stepped around the gate, and looked back to behold the Ghochalla's servant, pistol in hand, solidly planted in the middle of the drive.

With the aid of the artifact, Paro might be circumvented.

To what purpose? He'd only succeed in worsening matters for the luckless Ghochanna, and he'd already caused her trouble enough. That asinine suggestion that she accompany him—what had possessed him? He'd only inflamed her mother's rage, and it wasn't as if there had been any chance that she'd actually accept.

But what if she had?

Absurd.

What if she had? What if she stood beside him now, what if he brought her back to the city? What then?

Sisquine vo Chaumelle had married an Aveshquian princess, and the world hadn't ended.

His head was filled with idiot moonbeam fantasies. Time to discard them. As Xundunisse had rightly observed, the rose-colored idyll was over. He would probably never see the Ghochanna Jathondi again. And if he should by some chance meet her, he'd find she despised him for the misery he had caused her.

No point in lingering. *Hoping, somehow, for a last glimpse of her?* In the city, vo Trouniere awaited the news. *News he'll never believe.*

Paro still stood there watching him. Turning his back on OodPray, Renille set off for ZuLaysa.

The sun was high in a colorless sky. Yellowish heat haze shrouded the plain, and a furnace breeze sent clouds of powdery grit billowing along the road. A strip of qunne torn from his tunic furnished a makeshift dust-ward. A hat would have been welcome, but he could do without, for a while. Fortunate that he had drunk deeply, earlier in the day. Better yet that he had fully recovered from the wivoor poisoning. Head and vision were clear. He was healthy, vigorous, and fit to travel.

He made good time, without pushing himself. He rested briefly at the ruined water stand below the foothills, sitting there in the meager shade for no more than ten minutes. After that, he didn't stop again until he reached the remains of Pirramahbi's. There he paused at the kitchen pump to drink plentifully, and to wash the clinging dust from his eyes, face, and neck. A quarter hour's rest in this shaded, deserted spot, and he'd be ready to resume walking.

A far cry from his first visit—only days ago, but it seemed far distant, for the OodPray interval had somehow skewed time. On that occasion, he'd slept the entire afternoon away—and the place had not been deserted.

But was it now?

He sat listening. All about him, breathless silence. No human voice or step, no creak or rustle, no insectile twang, or avian squawk. No drumming of leathern wings, no reptilian hiss. He was alone. Or so he believed, until he chanced to glance up at the kitchen rafters, to one of which clung a small, winged form. The wivoor must have been watching him for minutes. Why didn't it attack? Because its priestly master was not present to command? Perhaps.

He forced himself to remain seated. When he drew Ziloor's conflation from his pocket, the wivoor's mindless ruby eyes tracked his moving hand. He sat very still; focused intellect and volition, reached inside his own being to find that element linking him to the universal substance of the Irriulen artifact, and then, as the Ghochalla had taught him, channeled his force to establish a fleeting connection. He felt the bond, tested it with his mind, found it firm, and exerted his will. The aetheric conflation began to glow, and his mind quaked with the wonder of it. A commonplace mhuteez might have done as much, to net a few small coins. But the beggar-magicians rarely comprehended the purpose or the true power of their own Irriuliana, else they wouldn't have remained beggars.

He knew the use of this mental mirror, however. Now he caught the tiny, concentrated beam of the wivoor's attention, bouncing it away from himself and out the kitchen window. The red eyes turned to follow. When Renille rose and walked from the room, the lizard's gaze never flickered.

No telling how long the effect would last. Perhaps only as long as the conflation in his hand continued to glow. Seconds? Minutes?

Outside again, blazingly victorious, profoundly triumphant, but breathing hard, and sweated, as if with tremendous physical exertion. For a few moments he stood motionless, looking back the way he had come, and waiting for the race of his heart to slow. The hills were blurred with haze, the outline of OodPray's Violet Dome barely visible. Down below, the dirty clouds thickened to obscure the plain. He thought for a moment to glimpse a dark figure gliding amidst the distant mists, but then it was gone.

The conflation was starting to dim. He put it back in his pocket, and left Pirramahbi's behind him.

The sun was sinking below the horizon by the time he reached the outskirts of ZuLaysa. He stopped to drink at the first well he found. Thirst assuaged, he was well enough. He walked on, and the city coalesced around him. The buildings sprouted thick and tall, the density of the pedestrian population waxed, the vocal volume swelled. The oven air began to press, weighty with heat, smoke, and a thousand odors.

ZuLaysa was always alive at twilight time, but this evening the streets seemed more than ordinarily populous, the mood of the crowd more than ordinarily volatile. There was a great deal of shouting, jostling, and cursing, together with some sort of visual anomaly that took Renille a moment to identify. Ushtras. Scores of them, chalked up or painted on buildings and vehicles everywhere. A number of the more assertively submissive of citizens flaunted outsized triskelion emblems upon their garments. The ushtra, always revered in Aveshq, had of late been all but annexed by the Filial.

The noise and pressure intensified, as the crowd sundered to permit passage of a clamorous troupe. There were some ten or twelve members, all displaying ushtras, all armed. They were howling or chanting something, their synchronization so faulty that the words of the Great Invocation to Aoun were nearly lost. Possibly a number of the faithful were drunk—their wild gestures and wobbling footsteps suggested inebriation, or perhaps an extremity of spiritual exaltation. A dapper young white-jacket, presumably a salary-man, too slow in clearing the path, was in-

stantly surrounded. At first, it seemed likely that the
zealots would beat him to death, for they were shaking
their truncheons in his face and yelling at the top of their
lungs. Presently, however, the tenor of the earsplitting demands resolved itself and the prisoner, waxen with fear,
dropped to his knees to gabble out a faltering oath of fe-
alty to the Source and Finality. Satisfied, the AounSons left
him, but for minutes thereafter, the white-jacket knelt
there in the street, trembling in every limb.

Renille walked on, and as he went, he heard the voices
of Filial preachers thundering in openly seditious exhortation. There were many such voices, for they were everywhere, in every street and square, urging the faithful to
cleanse Aveshq of western disOrder, crying out for revolt,
for blood, for fire, in the holy name of Aoun. And the
ZuLaysans answered with shouts of ravenous enthusiasm
that sent the chills along his spine, despite the heat of the
atmosphere. Inwardly, then, he blessed the luck that had
returned him to the city at dusk, when his light hair and
western complexion might pass unnoticed. There wasn't
another Vonahrishman to be seen upon the street.

As he neared the boundary of Little Sherreen, the roving bands of Filial fanatics proliferated, and just beneath
the Gates of Twilight, he came upon one such group beating a jukkha vendor with sticks, while the spectators
cheered, indifferent to the victim's screams.

They seemed to have gone mad, these ZuLaysans. The
Filial ruled them, and Aoun-Father ruled the Filial. It oc-
curred to him for the first time to wonder whether Aoun
Himself might not be mad.

He passed through the gate into Little Sherreen, and at
last encountered his first Vonahrish faces of the evening—
officers of the Second Kahnderulese, with their native
troops, patrolling the streets of the western sector. No
doubt the military presence damped devout ardor. Here
were no frenzied Filial preachers, no roving fanatic
troupes, no wildfire violence. Here, a semblance of nor-
mality maintained itself. He stood in Havillac Boulevard,
his own lodging house rising in the near distance. Days
ago, he had found the place guarded by wivoori, but they

were probably gone by now. If not, Ziloor's gift equipped him to deal with priests and lizards.

He'd bathe, eat, sleep in his own bed, and report to the Residency in the morning. He'd dress in proper Vonahrish style, adopt an impeccably Vonahrish demeanor, and relate findings all but certain to be dismissed as lies or lunacy . . .

He surveyed the house, from a careful distance. No lurking observers, no winged reptiles, that he could discern. No light leaking from the shuttered windows. The place appeared deserted, but couldn't be. The tenants were cautious, understandably so.

Approaching boldly, he tried the front door, and found it locked. His latchkey presumably still reposed where he had left it, weeks earlier, in his sitting room, within the mouth of the goddess Hrushiiki's sandstone image. No matter. At this early hour of the evening, the concierge would still be at his desk. He knocked. There was no answer. Again, harder. Nothing. The concierge was absent, or stubborn, or fearful, or deaf.

The back door was always locked. He couldn't afford to make himself conspicuous with shouting, or flinging of pebbles against the windows.

He wouldn't report to the Residency in the morning. He'd go tonight, in hopes of better luck than he'd had last time.

The intact dwellings along Havillac Boulevard were uniformly shuttered, and all but lightless. Only the occasional timid gleam seeping out into the evening betrayed the presence of self-effacing humanity. A charred and gutted ruin marked the site of Deputy Assistant vo Doliet's town house. Several of its neighbors were similarly blackened. As he turned into the Avenue of the Republic, the crowd thickened, its collective hostility crackling the heated air. Before the Residency compound itself, the citizens had gathered to jeer, and here he encountered a company of the Second Kahnderulese on guard at the gate.

He recognized one of the officers. Forcing his way to the front of the crowd, he made his presence known, and the soldiers let him in. As the light of the big lanterns flanking the entrance caught his sunstreaked brown hair, a shrieking storm arose.

The gate closed behind him, and the racket dwindled. He crossed the courtyard, and there were soldiers everywhere, as he would expect, and something more, that he couldn't immediately account for. Ranged about the yard stood an assortment of vehicles; several private carriages, together with a number of wagons, many of the latter loaded with cargo concealed beneath roped tarpaulins. Whose property?

He passed through the foyer without incident. The guards, recognizing Deputy Assistant Secretary vo Chaumelle despite the fantastic tatters, permitted him to pass unchallenged.

It wasn't until he reached the top of the central stairway that he recalled the rigid protocol of the Aveshquian Civil Service, compelling him to report first to his immediate superior, Assistant Secretary Shivaux. A miserable prospect, but unavoidable.

To his pleasure, he found Shivaux's office empty, a condition freeing him to seek out the Assistant Secretary's own sole superior.

The clerk was still on duty in Protector vo Trouniere's antechamber. Yes, the little man reported, the Protector was present, at the moment closeted with Assistant Secretary Shivaux. Yes, he would convey the Deputy Assistant Secretary vo Chaumelle's request for a meeting. The clerk vanished briefly, then reappeared to usher Renille into the office beyond.

The Protector and his Assistant Secretary, both seated, faced each other across the desk. Shivaux, sartorially splendid as ever, turned his head to inspect the newcomer's raggedly native-clad, travel-stained figure. One eyebrow rose.

"Never let it be said," the Assistant Secretary drawled, "that our Chaumelle is anything less than colorful."

"Been out there on the streets tonight in those checked trousers of yours, Shivaux?" Renille inquired. "No? Didn't think so."

"Quite right. I couldn't hope to blend with the yellow rabble, as you do. But surely"—the Assistant Secretary's nostrils flared—"an occasional bath wouldn't too greatly have marred the perfection of your disguise?"

"There's your first concern? The Assistant Secretary's choice of priorities is singular."

"Enough," vo Trouniere cut in. "Enough. You've been out of sight a good while, Chaumelle. We were starting to wonder if those Filial hadn't fed you to their god."

"Pretty nearly."

"Sit down, and deliver your report."

"To begin with"—Renille took possession of the nearest unoccupied chair—"since I saw you last, I've visited Beviairette, JiPhaindru, and OodPray Palace—"

"OodPray? Off on a pleasure jaunt, were you? A little sightseeing?" Shivaux inquired.

"Hardly."

"Why go sniffing around OodPray, then? What had that to do with your mission? Explain yourself."

"Presently."

"Now."

"He'll tell it in his own way, Shivaux," vo Trouniere said.

"Then let him get on with it."

Inwardly wondering at the Assistant Secretary's insistence, Renille resumed. It had come at last, the moment he'd been dreading for days. Now he must spin his preposterous yarn, and somehow make these two believe it, or at least, believe some of it. So he touched lightly upon his excursion upriver, then spoke at length of his pilgrim disguise, his prolonged obeisance in the temple courtyard, the manner of his eventual admission into JiPhaindru, his reception there, his dreary life as a neophyte AounSon. To all of this they listened attentively, displaying no sign of incredulity. Their interest sharpened when he told of the pregnant adolescents, of his meeting with Chura, of his sortie into JiPhaindru's Wisdom, and what he found there. So far, he'd held them. And when he spoke at last of the Renewal, he held them still, for a while.

Their eyes were intent as he described the gathering in the Assembly, the commencement of the ceremony, the introduction of the sacrificial Blessed Vessels, the entrance of the First Priest. Thereafter, he proceeded with caution, editing his own narrative, toning it down, omitting details of the most improbably bizarre. He deemed it safe enough to describe KhriNayd-Son as "an individual of remarkable abilities, exerting an almost mesmeric control over his followers." His listeners could accept such a description, and he did not attempt to enlarge upon it.

He had not witnessed the actual destruction of the Blessed Vessels, for his eyes had been shut against the unbearable light at that ultimate moment. Thus he remained honestly ignorant of the destructive method, and his suspicions on that score were best omitted from the narrative. In the matter of the infants, however, accuracy and plausibility were all but irreconcilable. He could only skirt the issue, describing them as "peculiarly deformed, almost inhuman in some respects, unnaturally advanced in development"; and even this dilute, pallid version of the truth sufficed to chill his listeners' eyes with doubt.

How could he speak of the infants' incandescent demise, or of the enormity that consumed them? He had to speak, however, for that impossible reality, with its implication of unknown forces charging unseen levels of existence, was the very essence of his discovery at the heart of JiPhaindru. There was no point in telling any of it, unless he told of Aoun.

He did his best to keep it marginally rational. He spoke with restraint, his language all but colorless, his demeanor detached, his story larded with possible explanations of all that he had witnessed.

No good. He could see the skepticism congealing upon their faces as he spoke, and that skepticism never altered as he went on to describe his own unmasking; his flight from the temple, pursued by wivoori; his sojourn among the Nameless; his excursion to OodPray, his ignominious expulsion therefrom, and his return to ZuLaysa.

Renille fell silent. He had talked uninterrupted for the better part of an hour, and now his mouth was dry. His two listeners were similarly speechless for a time, and into that lull rushed the angry voices of the citizens gathered in the street before the Residency.

Vo Trouniere finally cleared his throat. "This will take some sorting out," he said.

"What is there to sort, sir?" Renille inquired.

"Fact from—er—misapprehension."

"You don't actually suppose there are facts to be picked out of that fever dream?" Smiling, Shivaux shook his head.

"I do, and useful ones," vo Trouniere expertly forestalled Renille's retort. "He has, for example, confirmed the practice of outlawed rites within the temple. The possibility of human sacrifice appears to exist. Right there is all the justification required to send the Second Kahnderulese into JiPhaindru. He's told us of underage native females, detained, and forced into prostitution. There's another glaring illegality. He's verified the presence of the current KhriNayd-Son, and furnished grounds for prosecution. Such information is valuable."

"If accurate. And the rest of his story?"

"Easily explained. Drugs in the air during that infernal rite, and then the effects of wivoor venom. Enough to flummox anyone."

"Exactly so." Shivaux nodded. "But how are sober listeners to distinguish between fact and delusion, when the speaker himself cannot?"

"Sir, I can't wonder at your doubt." Ignoring Shivaux, Renille addressed the Protector alone. "I only ask that you keep an open mind. If you believe nothing else in all I've told you, then at least believe this—JiPhaindru contains a force unknown to us. It's real, it's aware, and the Aveshquians call it 'Aoun.' "

"Chaumelle, no one questions your honesty." Vo Trouniere stirred uncomfortably. "You've done your duty, at considerable personal risk, and you're to be commended for that. No doubt you witnessed extraordinary sights in that temple, and you've reported them to the best of your ability, but certain aspects of the situation remain unclear. That is not your fault. In view of your recent illness, a mild degree of confusion is only to be expected. You won't take it amiss, then, that I order you to go home. Take a few days to rest and recover. During that time, give some thought to JiPhaindru, and all that you saw there. When you've got the facts clear in your mind, and not before, come back and talk to me again."

"Protector, the facts are already clear in my mind." Renille held his temper strenuously in check. "My health is excellent. And much as I'd like to oblige you, I can't go home tonight. I've already tried it. My lodging house is locked, and apparently empty."

"Yours, and plenty of others. It's the rioting," vo Trouniere told him. "The arson, and the murders. The Second Kahnderulese keep pretty good order here in Little Sherreen, but they can't be everywhere, and several town houses have burned. Three or four mutilated western corpses have turned up in odd alleyways within the past weeks, and now our nervous countrymen are sending their wives and children home to Vonahr by the boatload. Can't say that I blame them. Little Sherreen is emptying like a leaky water jug. Of those remaining, about half have taken refuge here in the Residency, which accounts for the abandoned houses along Havillac Boulevard."

"And for the wagons in the courtyard?"

"Some of them, but most belong to the refugees coming in from the country. It's as hot out of the city as in it, and a number of the Gold Mandijhuur tavril planters have descended upon us, along with their families, favorite servants, pets, and household goods in tow. This place is starting to resemble a cross between a hotel and a warehouse, but we can't very well turn them away. Your uncle and aunt are here, by the way."

"Good. I advised them to leave Beviairette."

"You'll want to greet them, I suppose. They're probably at dinner, right now."

"He won't be admitted to the staff dining room, in that extraordinary costume," Shivaux observed. "There are limits."

"The limits may shortly alter," Renille suggested.

"Perhaps, but in the meantime, Shivaux's right," vo Trouniere countered. "You'll have to scrounge some decent clothes, Chaumelle. Borrow something from somebody. You can sleep in your office—it's still vacant, I believe. Perhaps it's just as well about your lodgings. All things considered, you're probably better off here."

The Protector fell silent and, once again, the voices in the street were audible, deep and ominous as the rumble of an approaching storm.

The lock snapped, and Jathondi turned to face the sound. It was late afternoon, not yet time for Paro to bring in her dinner. Throughout the days passing since the disaster in Shirardhir's Sanctum, the servant had never presented the evening meal prior to sunset.

The door opened, and the Ghochalla walked in. She wore her customary unbecoming black, above which her face looked more than ordinarily sallow. Her shadowed, bloodshot eyes bespoke sleepless nights.

Jathondi performed a deep obeisance, which her mother did not acknowledge.

"I promised you," the Ghochalla commenced without preamble, "that I would inform you of my decision concerning your fate. I have considered at length, and I have reached that decision. You are to be given in marriage to the Ghochallon NiraDhar of Dharahule. The match will effect Kahnderule's liberation from Vonahrish rule; mutually enhance the Effulgence of two royal Houses; and, at the same time, resolve a painful personal difficulty. By all standards, it is the best possible choice. I hope to find you suitably appreciative. If you are not, that is hardly my concern. Now that I have settled the issue, matters will proceed swiftly, and I would advise you to prepare for your transition."

By no means surprised, Jathondi returned steadily, "Ghochalla, we have discussed this, and you already know my position."

"Your caprices do not signify. Should your new husband choose to indulge your whims, that is his decision. Be warned, however. The Ghochallon NiraDhar is not renowned for his complaisance."

"No. He is renowned for far different qualities."

"He is master of his own house, that is certain. He will know how to deal with your self-will."

"He should, he's had plenty of practice with his former wives. He'll not be correcting my faults, though, because I will not marry him."

"It is not for you to choose."

"Pardon me, Effulgence, but it is. Under the present Vonahrish code governing Kahnderule, I cannot be compelled to wed."

"The commands of your sovereign and your mother count for nothing?"

"They carry great weight. I will not accept NiraDhar, however. Nobody can force me to it. I am sorry, but that is the current law."

"That is the law in Kahnderule. Fortunately, Dharahule resists such western decadence. There, the old ways rule yet. Once you stand upon Dharahulese soil, your designated male guardian may dispose of your hand, your body, and your belongings, at his own discretion. Your consent is not required. I have already written to the Ghochallon, conveying my acceptance of his proposal, together with my formal relinquishment of parental authority, in his favor."

"It does him little good. I do not stand upon Dharahulese soil."

"But you will, and shortly. I have urged the Ghochallon to dispatch an armed party to collect you, and I do not think he will hesitate. Until such time as your escort arrives, you will remain here in your chamber, under lock and key."

For the first time since the interview began, Jathondi's

apparent assurance flagged visibly. "Effulgence, you cannot mean to do this. You would not sell me into foreign slavery?" she appealed.

"Fool, who speaks of slavery? I arrange a brilliant match for you. You will occupy the gilded hassock at the foot of NiraDhar's Sunrise Throne."

"He may keep his gilded hassock, I want none of it! I beg you, Mother—"

"Never call me that!"

"Please, don't force this on me."

"Ingrate, it is better than you deserve. If I've any regret, it is only for my sharp trading with the Ghochallon. He thinks to acquire an Effulgent Ghochanna of Kahnderule, but receives from me only cheap and damaged goods. I pray that he will make the best of a poor bargain, and govern you, as I cannot."

"Ghochalla, if you have ever cared for me, if a single spark of affection remains alive within you, then listen to me now. If you recall the child that I was—"

"That child is enshrined within my memory. But she is dead."

"Not unless her mother consigns her to a living death. Mother—and pardon me, but I will call you that, for that is what you are—do my happiness and peace of mind mean nothing at all to you?"

"Far more than mine mean to you." The Ghochalla looked away. Her face, stiff and brittle as plaster, appeared to crack in places. "You have betrayed me, and you have—greatly injured me, but never have you asked my pardon, or shed a single tear."

"I have shed many."

"I am to believe that!"

"Yes, and you may believe this, as well—that I am truly, deeply sorry for the pain I've caused you. I never meant any harm in this, never thought that you would suffer, or that you would even know. Now I am sorry, and ashamed, and I will beg forgiveness upon my knees, if that will move your heart. Effulgence, will you not accept my repentance and my love?"

"If you are in earnest—" The Ghochalla wavered briefly, then rallied. "Oh, what an actress you are, when it suits you. What feeling you project, what sincerity, and all of it lies. I am weak, and you know too well how to play upon my frailty. But this time, your motives are transparent, and I will not be deceived."

"You've every right to be angry. But surely your anger will not drive you to sacrifice my freedom, my health, my very life?"

"Always you think of yourself, nothing but yourself!"

"No, I think of you, as well. Someday, your rage will cool, and then you will wish this thing undone. But then it will be too late, and you will spend your life in vain regrets. Now, while there is still time, I beg you reconsider, Mother—for your own sake, as well as mine."

"Not another word!" The Ghochalla was shaking. Drawing a deep breath, she paused a moment to steel herself, and resumed more calmly, "These complaints you make are typically peevish. Your personal satisfaction is not the issue. It is the good of Kahnderule that must outweigh all other considerations. But why do I trouble to speak of that to you? Patriotism is a concept exceeding your mental grasp."

For a moment, Jathondi stared at her mother, and then she spoke, in a different tone. "Very well, Effulgence. Let us speak of Kahnderule, whose welfare means so much to you that you cannot wait to welcome the rule of Dharahule. Let us speak of Kahnderule, which must change, one way or another. The Ghochalla would cling to the old ways, because she truly believes them best, but she sets herself an impossible task. The world has altered. The old ways are gone, and there is no bringing them back. The days of unthinking submission to a hereditary ruler are over."

"There are still those remembering their duty."

"What duty? Duty to abase themselves before a Ghochalla, or a god?"

"That is the great truth of the world, our eternal foundation. What else have we to cling to? Without that, what is there?"

"The hope of better things."

"A false hope. You are ignorant and shallow as you are faithless. The 'better things' you value are counterfeit baubles. For these glistering toys, you would cast away treasures."

"The old treasures have outlived their usefulness, Mother. That which cannot adapt to a changing world must sink into decay, even as OodPray itself decays around us. Father knew that. You remember. Father was determined to send me into Vonahr, because he saw the face of the future, and he knew that the western ways—"

"Do not speak of him, you have no right!"

"—that the western ways are overspreading the world. Good or bad, these foreign ideas have taken firm root, and things will never again be as they were in Kahnderule. The gods no longer walk among us. They have withdrawn to their own place. A sovereign is no longer a god or goddess among humans—"

"I do not hear you!"

"And she who will not bow to inevitability must be crushed."

There was silence for some seconds. Jathondi watched her mother's face, while the Ghochalla stared straight ahead at the wall.

"You have shown me once and for all what stuff you are made of," Xundunisse said at last, and her voice was dry as drought season, but her eyes were wet. "I see you clearly, now. These brilliant, modern insights of yours— perhaps you will enjoy discussing them with your new lord, NiraDhar. No doubt he will appreciate the instruction, and I pray that you will find his conversation equally agreeable, as you shall have no more of mine. I will never speak to you again."

The Ghochalla exited, locking the door behind her.

Twilight time. The last colored splash of sunset had faded from the sky. Paro brought her dinner, lighted the lamps in her chamber, and withdrew. Eyes fixed upon the window, Jathondi spooned her stewed pijhallies mechanically. Outside, the air was darkening, and the stars were smeared with heat-haze.

Not much left of this, Jathondi reflected. Not very much time before the rains came to wash the world clean.

Not much time at all.

Almost before she knew what she was about, she was packing. Clothes, modest jewelry, hairbrush, toothbrush, nail file, a few keepsakes, all went hurriedly into a light valise. Water bottle, filled from her carafe, on top. A few morsels of bread, a couple of ripe fhurshibs from dinner, and the valise was full, but not heavy.

She looked down at herself. Her clothes were all right, she decided. Plain, inconspicuous garments. Simple, striped zhupur, knotted about her waist. The folds of the sash concealed her tiny dagger, and a couple of zinnus, all the money she had. Her shoes, however—not so good. Quickly, she exchanged the delicate, thin-soled slippers for a pair of sturdy sandals and then she was ready to go, but knew it would be safest to wait until Mother and Paro slept. Fortunately, the servant retired early. And Mother, though often insomniac, shuttered her front-side windows at dusk . . .

An hour passed, the night deepened, the insect chorus swelled, and the thick air cooled a little. The moon rose, and Jathondi tossed her valise from her third-story window, then climbed down along a rope fashioned of knotted bedsheets, coverlet, and curtains. The rope terminated some eight or nine feet above the ground. She let herself drop the remaining distance, hit the cultivated garden soil, and sat down hard. Rising unhurt, she took up her valise, and cast a quick glance around her. Save for the light shining from her own bedroom, the windows of OodPray were dark. She saw no sign of life, but heard and felt the insects. From her present vantage point, she could look out over the dusty, moonlit plain stretching below the hills, to the lights of ZuLaysa, golden in the distance. She looked back one last time at the palace, then squared her shoulders, and walked away from it.

The trek to the city was long and taxing. Jathondi was unused to walking. Often she thought longingly of the royal fhozhee, antique but still grand, and quite comfortable, with its springs, and its upholstered seats. Paro was capable of hurrying that fhozhee all the way from Ood-Pray to ZuLaysa in three hours or less, even in the hottest weather. At her present pace, the trip would take longer, but at least she'd be spared the merciless sun.

The weight of the valise slowed her, and yet she made reasonable time. She stopped once at Pirramahbi's, to rest and to drink from her water bottle, but never set foot within the ruins bulking dark and oddly sinister under the moon. She did not care to linger there for long.

The moon was setting, by the time she reached the outskirts of ZuLaysa. It was the dead of night, and though the city never truly slept, the streets were customarily quiescent at such an hour. Not tonight, however.

There were lights, there were people, there was agitation that quickened noticeably as she made her way deeper into the heart of the human hive. There was noise, a lot of noise, madhouse shouting that resolved itself into overlapping litanies of bitterest complaint. They were inveighing against the Vonahrish, she noted. The Filial were preaching revolt, in the name of Aoun. Ordinarily, she might have expected the soldiers of the Second Kahnderulese to be there, ready to suppress native unrest, as they had suppressed it so many times in the past. But not now; the population was too large, the fervor too intense. She recognized that, almost at a glance, and realized that the local fanatics were rampaging out of control, beyond the bounds of the commonplace discontent.

On such a night, the Vonahrish Residency would be shut up tight, and heavily guarded. When she got there, Jathondi reflected, she would certainly be stopped at the gate. They'd let her in, however, when she revealed her identity. And when vo Trouniere heard her reason for seeking asylum, he'd doubtless offer assistance.

She tried not to let herself wonder too hard if she'd encounter Renille at the Residency. He worked there, after all. They would certainly run into each other, at some point. Perhaps he'd be embarrassed to face her. She'd served her purpose; he might have nothing left to say to her.

He'd asked her to come with him.

Probably he hadn't meant it.

But then, why had he said it? He'd had nothing to

gain. Quite the contrary, in fact—he'd come within an ace of taking a bullet between the eyes.

But for Paro, and his pistol, would she have accepted the invitation, then and there? Before the threat of enforced marriage had driven her from OodPray? Would she have chosen to go with a Vonahrishman?

Maybe.

And now? What if he asked her again?

Unlikely.

But what if he did? How would she answer?

The questions fully occupied her attention. She scarcely noted, as she made her way through the city, that the crowds were thickening as she neared the boundary of Little Sherreen. Voices were louder, collective rage hotter, almost volcanic; perhaps stoked by the presence of the buff and gray soldiery at the Gates of Twilight. She certainly never noticed keen eyes in the crowd fasten upon the golden wreath, emblem of Effulgence, depending from her zhupur; never noticed the same eyes travel to her face, and narrow in recognition; never noticed the signals passing among a number of robed figures, out there upon the street.

She never dreamed that she was being followed. Never thought of danger, until it was upon her, and then it was too late.

As she passed the shadowed mouth of an alley, an arm emerged to yank her backward into darkness. The valise dropped from her grasp, a cry escaped her, and a hand closed on her mouth. Then there were other hands upon her, and they were fearfully strong, and struggle though she might, there was no escaping them. Someone tall and powerful was gripping her from behind, one of his hands clamping her mouth and nose, cutting off voice and breath, his other arm locked across her chest. The force of the hold lifted her off her feet. Her head pressed a shoulder clothed in rough fabric. She couldn't scream, and she couldn't see. No chance of elbow-jabbing her captor, with both arms pinned to her sides, but her legs were free, and she kicked wildly, kicked until she felt both ankles caught in the grasp of a second attacker, and then there was nothing but ridiculously ineffectual wriggling, and equally ineffectual efforts to breathe. Her lungs were bursting, and fireworks flared behind her closed eyes. The red light dimmed, the pain diminished, and then she was sliding down some psychic chute into darkness, where only one sensation remained—astonishment. She was Effulgent, of the Order of royalty and priests, and correspondingly sacrosanct of person. What Aveshquian of lower Order would dare lay hands upon her? It was unthinkable, impossible. Astonishment was all she carried with her into the void.

The world gradually resumed existence. There was sensation—hard surface beneath her, odorous warm air about her, pain within her. There was thought, most of it confused, and there was astounded alarm.

Jathondi opened her eyes. Her head ached, and her throat burned. Her cheek pressed body-temperature hardness. Her hairpins had loosed themselves at some point, and now the long, blue-black locks streamed everywhere. Sitting up slowly, she tossed the hair back from her face. Her surroundings dimmed, then brightened. There was something wrong with her eyes, they must have been injured. The fear leaped, then sank as she looked up to behold faintly green glass globes hanging on chains from the ceiling. Within the globes crawled glowing, flickering forms.

Heedri, with their erratic luminosity. An all but obsolete form of illumination, now that the Vonahrish had come with their modern kerosene lanterns, and their astonishing gaslight. Here, however, the old ways still ruled.

But where and what was "here"?

She had never in her life encountered such a room, with walls, floor, and ceiling of some smoothly undulant, highly polished substance—glass? porcelain? stone?—like a frozen black sea, with motionless ripples reflecting the greenish light in tremulous gleams. She could see her own face endlessly mirrored in those billows, each tiny image unobtrusively warped, the distortions so varied and subtle, that the recollection of reality would soon lose itself among them, if she made the mistake of looking too closely or too long. Jathondi blinked, and the small movement repeated itself a thousand times, around and above and below her, each reflection individual, each somehow wrong.

Bewildering, dizzying, and nowhere to turn for relief. She could only close her eyes to blot out the madness, and when she did that, she could think clearly again. The questions swarmed through her mind.

Who would dare lay violent hands upon an Effulgent? A westerner, indifferent to Order, wouldn't hesitate. But somehow, it was her distinct impression that her kidnappers hadn't been foreign. Fellow Effulgents, royal or priestly, were the only Aveshquians free of the prohibition.

Priests.

She knew where she was, then. They had carried her to JiPhaindru, beyond doubt. It could hardly be anything else, but the Filial purpose was unclear. Only weeks earlier, they had written to the Ghochalla Xundunisse, urging an alliance. Mother had disliked the idea, but she wouldn't have rejected it outright; at least, not yet. So far as VaiPradh knew, the possibility remained viable. In which case, an attack upon the Ghochalla's sole heir seemed inexplicably premature.

Unless, of course, the presence of the Vonahrish spy Renille vo Chaumelle within the palace of OodPray had been perceived as the Ghochalla's wordless response. The Filial wouldn't realize that Mother had never admitted Renille, that she hadn't even known he was there. They would assume she had thrown her support to the Vonahrish. What sad irony.

Should the AounSons harbor any such delusion, her own kidnapping became comprehensible. They intended coercion, or vengeance, or both. Little did they dream that Xundunisse would only welcome her despised daughter's removal. VaiPradh had simply done Mother a favor.

Jathondi's breath came quick and shallow, while the pain throbbed in her head and her heart. Not the time to give way to emotion. She needed to think. She probably wasn't in much immediate danger, for they'd surely attempt negotiation with the Ghochalla, before inflicting any significant damage; but somewhere, the clock was ticking.

Could she reason with them? Bargain with them? Make them understand that she held none of the value they'd expected? Would they release her, once they realized there was nothing to gain by holding her, and nothing to gain by killing her? Perhaps, but she needed to talk to someone in authority, and it wasn't clear when that opportunity was apt to arise. Sooner or later, however, the door would open, and someone would walk through—

Door? Where?

Jathondi's eyes opened of their own accord. The flickering, dizzying light was back again, along with the myriad distorted miniature images. Everywhere, she confronted her own face, endlessly warped in countless curving mirrors, but nowhere did she see a door, or anything remotely resembling an exit. The black walls were seamless, there was no way out—

Ridiculous. The place was oddly designed, that was all. Her eyes traveled the undulating walls. No visible door. All right. Invisible, then.

She couldn't see it, so she'd have to feel for it. But she couldn't stand up to finger the walls; she was still far too giddy, her ears were buzzing, and the door was sure to be locked, anyway. She needed to rest a bit before moving, and therefore she stayed where she was, slumped in a corner, back pressing knobby protrusions. The multiplicity of self-images mocked her, but this time she didn't turn away, for somehow the mouths seemed to be moving, while her own lips, as far as she knew, were not. Rubbing her eyes, she looked again, and the mirrored mouths remained indisputably active. Words were emerging, words *she* never spoke; at least, she didn't think she did.

"The Chosen is beloved of Aoun-Father, she is His cherished, and His bride. She is the wife of Totality, the mother of Forever, honored and favored above all mortals. Here in this place of Glorification, she knows the radiance that is Infinity, which is the mind of the Father. His splendor transforms her, His divinity makes her whole, and she is a vessel, filled with His eternal light."

There was more, and she didn't know exactly what it

meant, but she could guess, and the terror welled inside her. It took a few moments to regain her composure, and she had to close her eyes again to do it, for the spectacle of those multitudinous subtly misshapen faces, jabbering at her from every direction, precluded rational thought.

With her eyes closed, she could concentrate on the whispering voices—men's voices (or were they?), probably AounSons, but peculiarly sibilant. Persistent, relentlessly loquacious voices, that never ceased. Probably, the lunatic litany was designed to soothe and reassure the listener, but on her it produced the opposite effect, and very soon she'd heard enough. She pressed her palms to her ears, and that helped, but didn't exclude all sound. The voices receded, and she could distance them still further by focusing her mind on other things. Had she but learned her way through the Palace of Light, she might have sent her consciousness winging across time and space. As it was, she could rely only upon her natural powers of concentration.

The implications of her present position, she did not wish to consider. Instead, she thought hard about what she would say, when she finally faced her captors. There were several possibilities, none of them particularly promising. Still, she meant to prepare as best she could; but it wasn't easy, not with a mind so clouded and slow. Her thoughts strayed, drifting about inside her head, and she could only suspect that her confusion had something to do with the perfume weighting the warm atmosphere. Strange that she hadn't noticed it before—a smothering, sleepy fragrance, its sweetness indefinably unclean. She coughed and shook her head, but the scent lingered. The taste of sour milk filled her mouth, and her stomach churned. She opened her eyes, and the countless self-distortions were with her again, mirrored tongues still clacking.

"The Chosen is bride of Aoun-Father. In the unspeakable moment of Glorification, she knows rapture transcending mortal comprehension, for therein lies the perfection of absolute self-renunciation."

They never shut up, it seemed.

She diverted herself as best she could with thoughts of books, and plays, and poems; with memories, and dreams and hopes. Somewhere in the midst of her mental wanderings, the sickly soporific poisoning the atmosphere took effect, and she sank into unquiet slumber. When she awoke, unrested and unwell, she found a tray sitting on the floor beside her. The location of the doorway or aperture through which it had entered remained unknown to her. Worse, she had missed her chance of confronting her gaolers.

Jathondi's eyes stung briefly. She fought down incipient tears, then turned her attention back to the tray, lifting a silver dome to discover a meal grand enough to satisfy the Ghochallon NiraDhar of Dharahule himself. There were at least eight different dishes, each rich and rare, sparked with priceless spices, brave with silver leaf and luruleanni blossoms. Odd fare for a prisoner. She sampled a mouthful of Jade Rainbird, its white flesh dyed green with a mixture of saffron and tavril. Well cooked, so far as she could judge, and of course, wildly extravagant, but she couldn't eat it—she couldn't eat anything. She'd be sick, if she tried.

They had given her three carafes of assorted beverages. One of them brimmed with cool tartwater, faintly lime-flavored. She drank deeply, then stroked a little sour wetness over her face, her neck, and wrists.

"The Chosen encompasses perpetuity. She is conduit of the life-force that conquers illimitable darkness. Within her body, past and future merge. Through her, the Father expresses His principle of life and death everlasting."

Still at it.

Jathondi choked the sobs back down her throat. She needed distraction, major distraction, and therefore she allowed herself an indulgence—she let herself think of Renille. His face, his voice, their time together; a thousand details filled her mind.

There was much to remember, but the fuel was not unlimited. She didn't want to burn it too quickly. Best to play the miser, spending one detail, one moment, at a time.

The last moment—his expulsion from OodPray—she remembered all too well. There had been wivoori, waiting to destroy him the moment he abandoned sanctuary. He'd possessed magical fortification, but had he really learned to use it? Renille, divided though he might be, was

Vonahrish more than anything else, and the Vonahrish never truly grasped Aveshquian magic.

He might or might not have made it safely back to ZuLaysa.

If he'd made it back, then what would he be doing now? She could afford the luxury of speculation. Assuming his good health, what was he doing now?

Not thinking of her.

Maybe he was.

She let herself wallow in that possibility, for there was nothing better to do. Probably, he'd reached the city. Probably. If so, he'd have an angry population to deal with.

They'd rip a Vonahrishman apart in seconds, these days.

She wondered if she'd ever see him again. Or anyone else, for that matter.

The excavation was going too slowly. At the present rate, it would never be finished by nightfall. Renille frowned. A few well-placed threats would doubtless spur the native laborers he oversaw to greater speed, but he couldn't bring himself to utter them. The poor wretches had been toiling since early morning, and now it was past noon, an hour when all sensible creatures sought shelter from the Aveshquian sun. He himself, while relatively inactive, and comfortably attired in borrowed khakis and pith helmet, was drenched in sweat. The coolies, engaged in digging to a depth of several feet, suffered visibly.

They had performed prodigies over the course of the last couple of days—strengthening walls, blocking up windows, placing guns, storing ammunition in makeshift magazines, stowing provisions, digging trenches and latrines. They had completed the wooden stockade edging the perimeter of the Residency compound, dug a ditch behind the stockade, heaped a mound behind the ditch to a height of five feet, and now they dug an inner ditch, to be furnished with upright sharpened redtooth stakes. They had worked night and day, under miserable conditions, at a time when Aveshquians were deserting their Vonahrish masters in droves. Renille made his decision then, decreeing a half hour break, and the coolies instantly fled for the shade.

He contemplated the burgeoning fortifications. Primitive, but probably effective enough. Better if vo Trouniere had begun the work earlier, but the Protector, regarding the defenses as a precaution against an attack unlikely to materialize, had delayed. Not to the point of disaster, however—vo Trouniere was too careful and canny for that.

But how long could even the best of fortifications exclude an inflamed population?

"ReNILLE!"

The familiar feminine soprano poked at his back, and he turned reluctantly to behold Tifftif vo Chaumelle bearing down upon him, her hands outstretched, her aspect sweetly plaintive. Behind her came Cisette v'Eriste, cradling her loathsome Forest Baby, Momu the Magnificent. Both women had shaded their white skins with wide hats and filmy veils of improbable elegance, and Tifftif bore a ruffled frivolity of a parasol. Renille suppressed a sigh. His uncle's wife and her niece, accustomed to indulgence, displayed a tiresome, noisy intolerance of anything resembling privation. This boded ill, for conditions within the Residency were certain to deteriorate before they improved again. *If* they improved again.

"ReNILLE, dearest boy, I appeal to you—"

Not in the least, Tifftif.

"I invoke your gallantry. Help us. Rescue a pair of damsels in distress. We are—" She broke off, surveyed the scene, and observed in an altered tone, "How these yellows slack their labors! See how they idle in the shade! You allow this?"

"I encourage it, for the moment."

"What folly. You should take a whip to them."

I'd rather take one to you. Aloud, he merely replied, in terms she might hope to understand, "We'll do best by husbanding our resources."

"You hope to gain their gratitude with this softness? Perhaps you dream they will love you for it? They'll only think you a fool." For the moment, she was the woman he remembered from his childhood. "Bah, you couldn't hope to run a plantation, that's clear."

"What can I do for you, Tifftif?" He smiled pleasantly.

"Help us, darling boy. Save us."

"That's our intention. In the event of attack—"

"We are running mad, in this place," Tifftif told him. "Conditions are intolerable, quite insane. We cannot endure it. You must use your influence on our behalf, Renille. We are family, after all."

"What's the trouble?"

"Suffocation," Cisette fluted dolefully. "Heat and overcrowding. You cannot imagine, Renille. It is quite dreadful. Auntie and Momu and I are packed into one little room along with fourteen other women and children! I am not making this up—I have counted them. We cannot live like that, it is not even *healthy*."

"I daresay it isn't," he admitted. "I'm sorry for the discomfort and the inconvenience, but you must understand, the Residency is packed to the rafters. We're sheltering hundreds of Vonahrish refugees. They've been arriving by the score these past few days, and they—"

"They are not your *family*," Tifftif reminded him. "You owe them nothing. Whereas we—"

"We are suffering terribly," Cisette broke in. "There's no privacy, and no rest. Women are always coming and going, they chatter and weep all night long, and the children—oh, they are dreadful, with their squalling, and their continual scampering about underfoot. The noise, the heat, the *smells*—they are quite unbearable, and I cannot *sleep*. That loud, overbearing Madame Zhouville insists on leaving the windows open, and the flies come in by the million. My beautiful Momu is growing fat upon them, but even he cannot consume them all, and they are into everything. They get all over the *food*, and it is disgusting beyond description, but there are almost no servants about to shoo them away, not even a proper niibhoy, for most of the servants have deserted, and some of those yellows have *robbed* us, too. We weren't brought up to live this way! Oh, Renille, you must help us, you are the only one who can!" Floating near to lay a hand upon his arm, she lifted blue eyes that had lost none of their luster. "Please, please, Renille, you *will* help us—won't you?"

Momu the Magnificent's proximity spoiled the effect.

"I would if possible," he assured her, truthfully enough. "But there's really nothing I can do. The Residency is filled, and all of the rooms are crowded."

"But not your office, I'll wager," Tifftif observed at once. "You've a very decent little office that would suit us perfectly well. I trust, my dear, we may rely upon your chivalry?" She essayed a coaxing simper.

"I only wish you might." He repressed a smile of his own. "But Uncle Nienne is in there with me, now. So are Quisse v'Ieque and two of his sons, along with Faquenz Zhouville and his valet, a couple of Deputy Assistant Secretaries, and, as of yesterday, a clerk from the counting house. So you see, the suggestion is hardly practical."

"Perhaps not. We shouldn't wish to appear selfish." Tifftif reflected. "Here is what you must do, then. Order some of these coolies here to take a bit of wood, and partition off a corner of one of the great salons for me and my niece. Preferably, a corner containing a window, one that has not been boarded up. Place two beds, a wardrobe, and washstand in there, and we shall do famously. There, now, Renille—surely that is not too much for your foster mother to ask of you?"

Foster mother? He swallowed laughter. Expression scrupulously grave, he answered, "Unfortunately, I couldn't hope to justify such a command. You see, the coolies' first concern is to complete the Residency defenses. They can't be spared from that task before it's finished. And the wood itself is a precious commodity—needed now for the stockade, the windows, the barricades and traps. Presently, needed for cooking fires. You understand that."

"Then you actually believe that the yellows might attack us here—that they would dare?" Alarm darkened her eyes.

"Yes." All inclination to laugh abandoned him.

"In that case, why has vo Trouniere not brought in the Second Kahnderulese?"

"He fears to precipitate crisis. The troops are all about Little Sherreen, however."

"Pooh." Cisette tossed her head. "You are only trying to frighten us, Renille, but I am not deceived. You will not trouble to help me, and Auntie, and Momu, but there are others who might care for us! Others, with hearts much larger than yours! That man, with the beautiful whiskers—what is his name, again?"

"Whiskers?"

"Lovely auburn hair, whiskers and imperial, wonderfully curled. Tall, imposing, and *so* splendidly dressed, as if he'd stepped off a Sherreenian boulevard. I dote upon men who care for their appearance, I think it is a sign of self-respect. And discipline, too. I admire men who maintain the true Vonahrish standards of elegance, for not everyone does, or can. The man I speak of—I'm sure you know him. What is his name?"

"Assistant Secretary Phesque Shivaux," Renille told her, bleakly.

"Phesque Shivaux. That is a very distinguished name, suitable to such a man. And Assistant Secretary—that sounds terribly high and grand." Her wide eyes rounded. "Why, that is above you, isn't it, Renille? Pardon me, for I know nothing of such things, but couldn't this Assistant Secretary Shivaux be called your superior?"

"Immediate supervisor, within the civil service."

"To be sure." She nodded earnestly. "And he is wonderfully important, then?"

"Far more important than I."

"He seems a very *nice* man." Cisette planted a kiss upon the flat brown spot between her Forest Baby's bulging eyes. "I'm sure that Momu thinks so, too."

"No doubt."

"I am convinced this Phesque has a beautiful soul. It shines through. Momu and I will appeal to his generosity."

"Who could hope to resist you? Who could resist Momu?"

"You could, you brute."

"Don't judge by my reaction—I haven't a beautiful soul."

"You know something, Renille?" Cisette's lips thinned. "I am sorry for you. Anyone else would be angry. But I am only sorry for you."

He had no immediate reply. Tifftif and Cisette wheeled and marched away, veils indignantly aflutter. Renille watched until they disappeared into the Residency, and then consulted his borrowed watch. The half hour was more than up. He signaled, and the coolies resumed their labors.

On the other side of the wall, the hot city growled.

Within the perpetual darkness of JiPhaindru's Holiest, day and night merged indistinguishably. Alone in the humid shadows, KhriNayd-Son scarcely noted, much less counted, the passing hours and days. His solitary pilgrimage through the great void was not to be quantified, or circumscribed. It would end in success, or else in the utter annihilation that was the essence of self-renunciation.

The totality of his protracted life had distilled itself to a single concentration of purpose. He would locate the Father, who could never abandon him here in Netherness. He would reestablish contact, he would tap the limitless power of the Radiant Level and then, at last, this empty impotent interval would conclude. The world would right itself, and this time he would allow no resumption of the insidious deterioration that had begun long ago, he realized, with the first appearance of the Vonahrish upon Aveshquian shores.

The arrival of the initial boatload of paste-faced dis-Ordered, some two hundred years earlier, had posed no obvious threat. Merchants, those first ones had been, ordinary money-grubbers seeking only to open trade between their own western land and Aveshq. So few of them, in the beginning, that nobody—not even an Awareness of the Radiant Level—could possibly have foreseen the eventual consequences. And then, in the years that followed—the gradual increase of foreign influence and control—so slow at first that it had progressed all but unnoticed. Later, additional significant incursions, with the shortsighted collaboration of weak or venal local rulers. At last, the introduction of foreign troops, and the final transformation of the Vonahrish from resident aliens to acknowledged overlords.

All through those years, the First Priest had rested quiescent at the heart of JiPhaindru, scarcely deigning to mark the murky ripples in surrounding Netherness. Absorbed in obsessive contemplation of Radiant virtue, he might never have noted mundane alteration, had not the effects begun to make themselves felt within the temple itself. The Vonahrish interlopers presumed to meddle in purely Filial affairs, and now the flow of adulation and worship, so essential to the Father's well-being, was significantly reduced. And this great loss, above all other factors, accounted for the Father's shocking decline.

The First Priest should have been more vigilant. He should have recognized and dealt with the western menace a century ago. He had been remiss, even irresponsible, but it was not too late to correct his error. He intended to do so at the very earliest opportunity. It was only a question of catching the Father's errant attention.

Not easily accomplished, these days.

So long had he searched through black nothingness, vainly entreating the Father's response, that he was almost taken by surprise when it finally came.

One moment, he was alone in the Holiest; the next, the darkness was occupied. The air tingled with awareness. The Father was awake, and very near. Not fully Himself—but present. KhriNayd-Son, floundering in the quicksand that was Netherness, seized upon that tenuous psychic lifeline with all the force of desperation; as if by sheer intensity of determination, he might bond himself forever to his sire.

"Enormity." His voice, just then, was nearly human. He paused a moment to master himself, and resumed in more appropriately reverberant tones, "Hear me, Aoun-Father."

Firstborn.

The Father remembered. KhriNayd's sensations were almost painful.

"I entreat you, Father—" He spoke rapidly, for there was no telling how long the other's lucidity might continue. "Fill me with the power of Radiance. Grant me Awareness. Make me whole, that I may perform Your will."

Explain.

Astonishing. So great was KhriNayd-Son's amazement, that the luminous artifacts decking his person flickered, waning briefly. The Father was conscious, unwontedly coherent, His incomparable faculties restored. For this one moment, at least, He seemed almost Himself again—victorious, omnipotent, divine.

The god Aoun was not lost.

KhriNayd resisted the tide of emotion that threatened to swamp his concentration. Later, Father and son might share in rejoicing, but the precious present instant was a gift not to be wasted.

"The time has come to expel the impious Vonahrish, whom Your heart hates, from this Nether land of Aveshq. The human population, Your worshipers and Your slaves, stand ready to serve You. They await but a sign, clear to their understanding, and they will rise up to slay the westerners in their midst. Fill me with power, Father, fire me with sublime Radiance, and the very heavens will thunder forth Your commands."

Now?

"This very hour."

Kill?

"Down to the last pallid infant, sucking poisoned nourishment at its dam's disOrdered breast. Then, when they are gone, and this land is clean again, we shall begin afresh. In the great Renewal that follows, You will resume Your full majesty. You will sire a new and greater race of sons to carry Your splendor and worship across the borders of Aveshq, and into the great world beyond. The first of the human vessels has already been selected. It is a female of ancient lineage and high degree, fitting container to the first of Your new children. Even now, she awaits Glorification." KhriNayd paused. The Father's intellect, comparatively clear though it was at the moment, might drown in such a flood of words.

His concern was unfounded, however.

Kill.

The Father had grasped the essential point. He acted.

KhriNayd-Son opened himself, and the power of the supradimension filled him, huge and consuming as he remembered, and once again he was whole. Now he was complete, ablaze with internal light, as he was meant to be. Anything less, and he was barely alive.

His vision encompassed all the city, and beyond. He saw its present and its past, its living and its dead, its reality and its shadow, all clear and distinct in his mind's eye. He focused his intellect, his will, and the invisible Radiance flowed through and from him, gushed away through the night, straight to the destination of his choice.

The substance of Netherness was ridiculously malleable. He molded it with his thoughts, shaping unnecessary elaborations for the sheer joy of it, and during that unmeasured span, knew peace.

It was early evening, when the sky above Little Sherreen appeared to catch fire. The conflagration commenced with a single spark of red, no larger than some distant, angry star. For a time, the spark passed unnoticed by all save the most astronomically acute of ZuLaysans. The entire brotherhood of professional astromages spied it at once. The Birthwitnesses were almost equally alert. But the majority of citizens marked nothing, at first.

Over the course of an hour or so, the speck enlarged to a disk like a miniature red moon, by which time, hardly a soul in ZuLaysa remained unaware of its presence. Thereafter, miraculous events proceeded swiftly. The disk swelled, its edges blurred and swam, while sharp coruscations livened its face. There followed an abrupt, almost explosive expansion, that sent a host of brilliant flares shooting across the sky. The crimson streaks diffused through the night air, smudged and softened to a luminous cloud, burning like an advertisement of divine wrath directly above the Vonahrish Residency. From the fiery heart of the cloud issued the brazen strokes of a gong, audible throughout the city.

The celestial phenomenon required no explanation. All of ZuLaysa recognized the long-awaited signal. The pent rage of years flamed at the sight and sound of it, and a collective roar of savage exultation briefly suppressed the clangor of the gong.

Weapons of every description, plucked from countless hiding places, materialized as if by magic. The torchlit streets and alleys suddenly teemed with armed insurgents; undisciplined, disorganized, but wholly united in purpose. They turned first upon the isolated Vonahrish dwellings and Vonahrish-owned businesses scattered throughout the city, and these were swiftly demolished. A few westerners, discovered cowering in closets and storerooms, were zestfully slaughtered, along with their misguidedly loyal native servants. Central Station, that western oasis in the heart of an Aveshquian quarter, with its brick walls, marble floors, and tile roofing, refused to burn. Its wooden furnishings, however, together with its wicker ceiling fans and paper records, provided fuel for a splendid bonfire. Into this fire was tossed an industrious Vonahrish manager, found working late in his office, and the Esteemed's extravagant contortions were exquisite to witness.

But these were minor targets, their destruction affording only limited satisfaction. The true object of divine dissatisfaction was glaringly apparent, and soon the disparate human clumps and clots were moving through the streets, converging from all directions upon Little Sherreen. They marched by the thousand, under standards bearing the ushtra, and as they walked, they called aloud upon the gods of Irriule.

Nothing at all impeded progress. They flowed, hot and inexorable as lava, as far as the edge of the western enclave, and only then encountered resistance. The half-dozen avenues offering access to Little Sherreen were blocked with slapdash makeshift barricades, behind which crouched soldiers of the Second Kahnderulese. A double-sized contingent defended the principal point of entry, at the Gates of Twilight.

Beyond the gate, Havillac Boulevard swarmed with pedestrians, fhozhees, and carts, all making for the shelter of the Residency. The sight of their fleeing prey galvanized the faithful. A howling outcry arose, and some anonymous zealot fired a pistol. The nervous soldiers returned fire, and the clamor rose to a hurricane roar. The mob fell back, amidst shrieks, imprecations, flying rocks and bullets. A number of citizens armed with muskets sought the nearest recessed doorways, and from that shelter, poured steady, accurate gunfire upon the gate.

Similar scenes enacted themselves on a smaller scale about the perimeter of Little Sherreen, and, for a time, the soldiers of the Second Kahnderulese thwarted a multitude. They might have held the enclave for hours or days to come, had the native troops proved uniformly steadfast.

At the barricades on Constitution Avenue, however, morale lapsed. There, the Kahnderulese—all of that particular company ZuLaysans born and bred, the majority belonging to the mettlesome Order of Divergence—defied their Vonahrish captain's command to fire upon the crowd. For some moments, the motionless soldiers maintained stony silence, while their captain spewed threats, and the delighted citizens cheered. The cheering crescendoed, the mob surged forward, and the barricades went down in an instant. The Vonahrish captain and a couple of his subordinate officers vanished screaming into the human sea, and then the riotous citizens were pouring along Constitution Avenue, past the Nirienne Gardens, into the Avenue of the Republic, and on toward the Vonahrish Residency.

The Residency gate still stood open, to admit the tardiest of refugees. The last of the fhozhees were hurrying in between two long files of armed guards. The soldiers stood like statues, bathed in the red glare of the impossible cloud burning overhead. As the insurgent mob roared into the Avenue of the Republic, the statues came to life. Upon the command of their officer, the soldiers opened fire, and the advancing chaos slowed, but did not halt. Wildly irregular musket, carbine, and pistol fire pelted the men of the Second Kahnderulese, and several soldiers fell, but the survivors never faltered.

Only when the final straggle of terrified civilians had made it through into the courtyard was retreat ordered, but already it was too late, for the vast tide was crashing at the base of the wall, the soldiers were engulfed, and the Residency gates were swinging shut.

The gate closed with a final crash audible above the shouting, the gunfire, and the strokes of the gong from on high. The guards trapped in the Avenue of the Republic swiftly died. ZuLaysan detachments then sped to aid their compatriots at the Gates of Twilight, at Sevagne Street, and Equality Arch. The soldiers at the barricades, attacked front and rear, were almost effortlessly crushed. The citizens gushed into Little Sherreen and, barely pausing to loot, streamed through the streets, straight on to the Residency.

The massive gate was shut and firmly barred. The girdling wall was high, and solidly constructed. The crowd seethed about the barrier, its armed members peppering the stone face with useless musket fire. Presently the big guns placed atop the ramparts spoke in reply, forcing the ZuLaysans to fall back.

Thereafter, the cooler and wiser among them took control, and, under such direction, surrounding buildings were occupied, loopholes drilled, and guns sited. Long before the rising sun reduced the clangorous crimson cloud to silently smoldering haze, the Residency was under siege.

11

"Assistant Secretary Shivaux has visited Sherreen within the last twelvemonth," Cisette v'Eriste informed the table at large. "He has driven about the Girdle, heard Guidissercio sing *The Unfortunate Ulor* at the Opera, attended performances at the National Theater, and dined at Nezhille. He has done *everything*!"

Her listeners strove to appear suitably impressed.

"He has inspected the paintings at the Academy," Cisette added, for their edification, "and he has visited the tailors in Riquenoir Street."

"Ah, Sherreen." Tifftif vo Chaumelle sighed. "The art—the culture—the gentility!"

"Civilization," Nienne vo Chaumelle summed it up.

Quisse v'Ieque and his wife nodded dutifully, while Renille addressed himself to his reconstituted cress-rabbit soup. The seven of them sat at one of the many small tables placed about the staff dining room. Every place at every table in the room was filled, and this was only the second shift of three. Such were the exigencies of the woefully overcrowded Residency. The fare was plain, and distinctly meager, eked out among the happy few with tinned or otherwise preserved delicacies, carted in by the more farsighted among the refugees. Uncle Nienne and Tifftif had been farsighted; so much had to be granted.

"How difficult it must be, for a man of the world to exist in such a dreary backwater vacuum as ZuLaysa!" Cisette's sweet soprano pierced the dining room babble of conversation. "How galling to endure, when one is used to better things! Even I, foolish little colonial that I am, can appreciate the hardship. Assistant Secretary Shivaux, you are surely a patriot."

She had been wooing him assiduously throughout the meal, and not without some success, to judge by the Assistant Secretary's gratified expression. A year ago, the spectacle would have heated Renille to an internal simmer, and doubtless Cisette imagined that it still did. This evening, however, he looked on with a wintry amusement that quickly gave way to boredom. Her excessive animation, her gestures, smiles, and moues wearied him. The pink and white, dimpled little face faded from his awareness, and he saw another, ivory-skinned and finely chiseled. Jathondi. Miles from ZuLaysa, safe at OodPray. By this time, with any luck, she'd have made peace with her gorgon mother, and the troubles he'd brought her were at an end.

But what if they weren't? The Ghochalla had been furious. Angry enough to punish her daughter, even to harm her? Angry enough to whip her, starve her, or turn her out, penniless, into the streets?

If so, perhaps she'd have come here.

Unworthy thought. Would he have wanted her here at the Residency, at such a time? She was far better off where she was. And the Ghochalla's wrath? Well, the old girl would come around, in the end. She might scream, threaten, denounce, and foam at the mouth, but she'd never go so far as to hurt Jathondi. Underneath the anger and bluster, she still—unwillingly, no doubt—loved her daughter.

You hope.

Jathondi was safe and well; an article of faith, perhaps never to be verified. Should the ZuLaysans actually rise in revolt, the possibly shaky loyalty of the Second Kahnderulese Regiment of Foot would be put to the ultimate test. Some of the component companies were rock-solid, of course; others, distinctly less so. The Residency itself was capable of withstanding a siege, for a time. But that period, already limited, would be further reduced by the unexpectedly massive influx of the refugee planters, their families and retainers.

How long could they hold out against all of ZuLaysa? Long enough for one of the messengers that vo Trouniere had planted about the city, with instructions to ride hell-for-leather at the first sign of concerted revolt, to reach Bhishuul and the Eighteenth Aveshquian Division stationed there? Bhishuul was over a hundred miles away, and all the territory in between might be up in arms, should the villagers, farmers, and plantation pickers follow the lead of their urban brethren. A relief column from Bhishuul might have to fight its way over each and every mile. In which case, how long would it take the Eighteenth to reach the Residency?

And if relief arrived too late, or not at all?

Thank all the powers of the cosmos that Jathondi was not in the city.

"*I* have visited Sherreen just once, in all my life! And *that* was when I was scarcely more than a child! Only think of it!"

Cisette's voice penetrated his reverie.

"I am terribly backward, nearly uncivilized, I must confess it," Cisette lamented musically. "Quite the untutored little barbarian! But where is the remedy? How shall I, marooned in such a place, render myself fit for society?"

"Sherreenian society might well consider itself much brightened by Miss v'Eriste's presence," Shivaux hastened to assure her. The Assistant Secretary's reddish imperial had been petted to an exquisite point. He was wearing his finest ivory moiré waistcoat, and he smelled strongly of expensive cologne.

"Oh, I know I am altogether hopeless!" Cisette lifted helpless blue eyes.

"Quite the contrary. The sophisticates of Sherreen would view Miss v'Eriste as an exotic of the rarest type. The discriminating among them would surrender without struggle." Shivaux appeared much concerned for her peace of mind.

"Ah, but I am so terribly rustic, so unpolished! I have been nowhere, seen nothing!"

"Scarcely true, Miss v'Eriste. You cannot begin to imagine the Sherreenian hunger for tales of Aveshq, a land regarded as colorful, exciting, and mysterious beyond expression."

"What—*this* dreary, primitive oven of a place?"

"I assure you, it is all the rage. The ladies in their boxes at the Opera wear gowns trimmed in the mode 'Aveshquienne.' At Nezhille, one dines upon Chicken Kahnderulese. The strolling musicians in Fraternity Park fiddle Aveshquian airs. The Rivennier Cup was taken this year by vo Crev's two-year-old, Ghochallon. I tell you, there's no end to it. In Sherreen, you would find yourself besieged, for the sake of your Aveshquian anecdotes no less than your inherent charm."

"Oh, I hope not, for I have no Aveshquian anecdotes! There is nothing in the least interesting here!"

"Come now, ZuLaysa is hardly devoid of diverting oddity," Shivaux suggested. "In Sherreen, at the Strellian Embassy, the Ambassador's dinner guests were quite enthralled with my account of OodPray Palace and its curious contents. The Urshoun Poison Chalice—the Infinity Throne—the Crystal Archways of Shirardhir—the ZuLaysan Globe—the golden bed of Ghochallon NiShi-iri—the astonishing Thousand-Year Automaton—I was beseeched to describe them all, at length. It is no boast to observe that I was given no peace until I obeyed."

Renille's interest stirred faintly. He would not have expected to find the Assistant Secretary so conversant with OodPray's marvels.

"Miss v'Eriste has lived through the native uprisings along the Gold Mandijhuur. Not all were so fortunate," Quisse v'Ieque observed dryly. "That might furnish her an anecdote or two."

"We missed the yellow frolics," Nienne vo Chaumelle informed him. "I took my nephew's advice, ordered my affairs at Beviairette, and pulled out early. We've had a fairly quiet time of it."

Not for much longer, Renille thought.

"Wish I could say the same," v'Ieque replied. "At

JewelLeaf, naïvely confident in the loyalty of our yellows, we dawdled until the pickers murdered the overseer, fired the barns, and started potting away at the house. At that point, we ran with only what we could carry in a couple of carpetbags. But for the generosity of our neighbors, we'd be living now on stringy mutton, lentils, and flatbread, like so many others." His gesture encompassed the surrounding tables. V'Ieque himself, and the others seated about him, dined upon soup, truffled pâté, preserved goose, pickled lorbers, brandied Vonahrish peaches, and excellent wine, all from the Beviairette stores.

"We are happy to share with our fellow unfortunates," Tifftif declared warmly. "There is not enough for all, of course, certainly not for these little tradesmen they've let in here. But there's nothing Nienne and I wouldn't do for our *friends.*"

"We should hardly consider ourselves unfortunate," observed v'Ieque's mouse-faced wife, Euline. "We are safe and well, after all—"

Safe? Renille wondered in silence.

"We are among the lucky ones," Euline continued. "Think of some of the others. Laillie—poor Laillie Bozire. Slaughtered by her pickers, and Azurenne torched. Gerin and Ouenne Millain, the three children, all killed, and Blue Refuge up in flames. The same story at Jerundiere. And at Mandijhuur Star. So many gone—" She broke off abruptly.

There was silence about the table, until Renille asked, "And at Beviairette? What was the mood of the pickers when you left, Uncle?"

"I did not trouble to observe their *mood.*" Nienne elevated his chin. "Who can judge such things? In the days preceding our departure, there were—some few, small incidents. At the time we left, however, the yellows continued orderly and dutiful, most of them. They had best remain so, else answer to the military, upon our return."

What makes you think there'll be anything to return to? Aloud, Renille inquired, "Any injuries, or desertions?"

"Seven or eight, more or less."

"Ziloor?"

"That superannuated pet of yours, Nephew? Behind bars, I believe."

"What have you done, Uncle?" Renille carefully kept his voice even.

"My duty, as always. The old Ziloor—he's been shamefully indulged, by the way. He's spoiled as any fashionable belle. At any rate, as you know, Ziloor had been warned time and again to abandon that Palace of Light claptrap, or at least, to keep it to himself. The old man persisted in his folly, however—continued pouring his antiquated nonsense into the ears of any yellow whelp willing to sit still for it—and that sort of deliberate defiance is quite unacceptable, as I'm sure even you will agree. Sets an impossible example. So I felt I had no choice but to notify the County Board, and shortly thereafter, your umuri friend was brought up on charges. He didn't trouble to deny them—you've no conception of that old yellow's insolence, Nephew—and so, naturally, he was convicted."

"Naturally." Renille curbed his impulse to strike the other. "And?"

"And he was sentenced to six months in gaol."

"I see. So Ziloor is now locked up in AfaHaal?"

"No. For a term exceeding ninety days, the felon is transferred to ZuLaysa Correctional Facility."

"No doubt the proper abode of so hardened a criminal." Actually, it wasn't such bad news. Here in the city, Renille reflected, his own influence as Deputy Assistant Secretary would probably suffice to effect Ziloor's immediate release. Assuming, of course, that Secretarial influence survived the impending attack. Assuming, too, that the umuri himself—elderly and frail—survived even brief incarceration. How pleasant it would be to drive a fist straight into Uncle's smug, self-righteous face.

"I feel it only fair to inform you, Nephew. When the old man is released, I do not intend to permit his return to Beviairette."

I doubt he'd go back there again if you paid him.

"Perhaps you will think my decision harsh, but I am convinced it is just." Nienne folded his arms. "I must consider the general welfare."

"Truly, Uncle. It is a moral obligation. You cannot

allow this corruptor of youth—this vessel of villainy—this senescent serpent—to spread his poison at Beviairette."

"Very amusing. You would reward him for his obstinacy, I suppose. Probably build the old loon a white marble schoolhouse, and pay him a stipend."

"As a matter of fact—"

"Oh, please, this is all so grim!" Cisette complained, patently bored. "May we not speak of something *agreeable*?"

"I second my niece's request," Tifftif declared. "We are at table, and I want to hear something *pleasant*."

At that moment, the clang of an immense gong resounded through the staff dining room. All conversation ceased, and the noise repeated itself. It seemed to originate directly overhead, presumably upon the roof.

"What is *that*?" Cisette v'Eriste clutched Assistant Secretary Shivaux's arm.

Shivaux's answering gesture enjoined silence—needlessly so. The plangent clanging triumphed over vocal competition. For several moments, the astonished Vonahrish sat listening, and then, almost with one accord, rose from their chairs and rushed to the windows.

The sky overhead burned crimson. From the fiery cloud anchored directly above the Residency boomed the inexorable strokes of the gong.

"What is it?" Tifftif sank her nails into Renille's arm. *The Filial. Their nightmare First Priest. The Thing in the temple.* Aloud, Renille merely replied, "It is an atmospheric disturbance of some sort, Tifftif. Electrical discharge irradiating a dust cloud—a swarm of luminous insects—aurora australis—or perhaps—"

"Don't insult my intelligence with such nonsense, you liar! What is it?" Her voice went shrill. *"And what is that noise?"*

Gunfire in the streets, audible between the strokes of the gong, precluded reply. The sound of distant shouting reached their ears. The courtyard below was stirring to life, as armed humanity erupted from the Residency.

"Take Cisette and any other women you can round up, and go down to the cellar," he told her. "That's the safest place in the event of attack."

"Attack—they wouldn't dare! And *what is that noise?*"

"The cellar, Tifftif. Step lively." He disengaged his arm from her grasp.

Minutes later, rifle in hand, he stood with his compatriots upon the wall. From that vantage point, he could look down on the Avenue of the Republic, along which scurried the last of the refugees, making for the shelter of the Residency, their belated retreat covered by a contingent of the Second Kahnderulese. Presently, the roaring ZuLaysan mob swept into Little Sherreen, and the soldiers died in the street.

Rifle and musket fire from the ramparts scarcely discouraged the attackers, but artillery proved effective. The crowd grudgingly drew back. Thereafter, the Residency suffered no direct assault, but the ominous preparations for a siege continued throughout the night.

At dawn, the strokes of the gong ceased, the crimson vapors faded, and the bombardment began. Grapeshot, together with a variety of alternate missiles fired from mortars, battered the Residency compound. Flying chunks of iron, blocks of wood, bundles of wire, carriage springs, and assorted stinkpots rained upon the roofs and courtyard, while musket balls whistled continually overhead. Through the leaden hail, a pair of carrier pigeons, bearing urgent appeals, winged for Bhishuul. Should human messengers fail or flee, the avians might yet succeed.

The outer walls and earthworks resisted the assault. The buildings edging the enclosure, however, were vulnerable; a reality manifesting itself around noon, when a shell crashed through a boarded upper-story window, to explode at the feet of Euline v'Ieque, killing her instantly. Thereafter, the besieged shunned the upper levels, but learned within hours that no place in all the compound offered real safety. Round shot from the outside could smash its way through brick walls, but far more lethal was the accurate, incessant musketfire, which, by the end of the first day, had accounted for ten Vonahrish deaths.

Defense, for the most part, consisted of similar sharp-shooting, directed from the ramparts at infrequently glimpsed, quick-moving targets. Success was all but impossible to gauge, save by the absence of concerted assault. The ZuLaysans, as yet, displayed little inclination to storm their target. Perhaps they feared the defenders, or perhaps they meant to erode western morale prior to attack.

The sun set, and the defenders breathed a collective sigh of relief, for it was not in the nature of their light-loving enemies to launch a nocturnal assault, or so they assumed. But the waning of the day brought the waxing of the red cloud above. The strokes of the gong did not resume, but the fires in the sky heated ZuLaysan blood. Activity continued. The big guns periodically flashed and roared through the night. Under cover of darkness, the native sappers commenced their excavations. Few among the Vonahrish slept that night.

Morning witnessed the resumption of musketfire, together with a new and ominous development. Aveshquian archers, armed with flaming arrows, were shooting with great accuracy at the grain stacks and wood stores placed about the courtyard. Where the arrows struck, fire flared; and, although the flames were quickly extinguished, the heavy demands upon the Residency water supply boded ill. Water became an even more pressing issue when the motley assortment of missiles clearing the wall began to include putrescent meat and ordure, some of which reached the well. The offending matter was promptly cleared away—all that was retrievable. An improvised shield of boards and tarpaulins was stretched across the mouth of the well, but there was ample reason to fear contamination, and thereafter all water used for drinking and cooking was thoroughly boiled.

"I believe they'll attack some time tonight, or else at dawn," Renille informed Protector vo Trouniere. The crash of round shot striking the nearby stables underscored his words, but neither man so much as started. Artillery fire had been fairly constant throughout the past three days, and the occupants of the besieged compound were largely inured to the sound.

"What makes you think so?" Vo Trouniere's unshaven face was haggard, even by soft candlelight. It was only late afternoon, but the boarded office windows excluded all sunlight, as well as every breath of fresh air, and lanterns burned throughout the Residency all day long. Since the siege began, the Protector had permitted himself no more than four hours of sleep a night. His efforts had transformed a heterogeneous band of civilian defenders into a fairly effective force, but the strain took its toll on health and temper.

"NuuMahni Heaven-Dancer," Renille told him.

"Eh?"

"Tonight, NuuMahni partners the moon—that is, enjoys exceptional lunar proximity, which—"

"What is this drivel you're spouting, Chaumelle?"

"The Aveshquians regard NuuMahni's moon-dance as a signal of celestial approbation and encouragement. It marks the promising commencement of hazardous endeavor."

"They take this nonsense seriously?"

"Very much so."

"I'll assume you know what you're talking about, and I'll double the watch. In the meantime, while the daylight holds, I want you to take a few men and commence an inspection of the cellars."

Renille nodded. The ZuLaysan sappers, at work under the walls for days, surely verged upon a breakthrough into the lowest level of one or more of the buildings contained within the compound. The Protector had posted sentries in every cellar, but sentries were fallible, and additional surveillance a sound precaution.

"I'll take v'Ieque, Zhouville, and the Zhouville servants, if they're available," Renille said.

"The valet—what's his name again—?"

"NaiVook."

"That's right. The valet was on the wall all night, he'll be no good now. One of that gang—the cook, I think—is in B.H., and out of commission."

The Banqueting Hall, or "B.H." as it was now known, converted to infirmary at the commencement of the siege, was rapidly filling with the wounded. Already, the supplies of bandages and painkillers were running short.

"Amputation?" Renille inquired.

Vo Trouniere shrugged. In the intense heat of Aveshquian summer, and the primitive conditions of the makeshift hospital, a wound necessitating amputation amounted to a death sentence. Already, the shallow graves proliferated in the new cemetery adjacent to the Banqueting Hall.

"What about your uncle?" The Protector suggested.

"Unsuited to the job," Renille returned. "Put him on guard, let him spot an unfamiliar Aveshquian face, and he bawls at the top of his lungs, 'Boy! Here you, boy! Over here to me, and explain yourself, this instant!' I've seen him do it."

"He'll learn." Vo Trouniere allowed himself an arid smile. "Give him a chance. I want you to start off with the Residency cellars. It's a maze down below, and the likeliest target."

"Right. Any word from the Eighteenth, yet?"

"No."

"Think the message reached Bhishuul?"

"Good chance. One of the runners probably made it. We might see some relief, in a few days."

If we can hold out that long. Aloud, Renille replied, "I'll see to the cellars. Aside from that, Madame Zhouville wants your permission for the formation of a Women's B.H. Relief Team—"

"Infirmary nurses? Excellent."

"A Nursery-Tutorage for the children—"

"Fine."

"And a Ladies' Long Rifle League."

"A what?"

"Madame Zhouville declares that she and a number of her friends are accomplished markswomen, qualified to assist in the Residency defense."

"What a charming picture."

"Madame Zhouville expresses herself rather forcefully on the subject."

"You don't mean to tell me the woman actually imagines it possible?"

"She does."

"We've no time for this nonsense."

"I'm inclined to respect her logic."

"Then you've abandoned your own common sense. She may be a dead shot, for all I know—that's not impossible. But she doesn't seem to realize that skeet shooting, or bird hunting on a pleasant morning along the Gold Mandijhuur, is a far cry from firing at a human target who happens to be firing right back at her. Zhouville's wife is no fool—she ought to understand that women, even of the modern masculine type, simply aren't suited to combat. If she doesn't grasp that, then you'll have to make it clear to her."

"I doubt that I could convince her, Protector. She'll want to talk to you personally."

"I've neither the time nor the inclination."

"She is likely to insist. The lady is renowned for her tenacity of character."

"Deliver us from amazons, from fire-breathing viragos, from all unsexed women! We've more important concerns."

"I'll convey your response to Madame, Protector. No doubt you'll hear from her soon."

"No doubt. That will do, Chaumelle. Find some men, and get started."

Renille withdrew. Down in the relative coolness of the foyer, he discovered Zhouville and the recently bereaved v'Ieque, both of whom were impressed into service. A couple of newly armed clerks from the counting house completed the party, which descended first to the Residency cellars—a labyrinthine complex of storage chambers, cubbies, and closets, already patrolled by three sentries. None of the guards had seen or heard anything noteworthy. None of the walls displayed any telltale sign of damage.

From the Residency, they proceeded across the cluttered and scarred courtyard, baking under the vicious afternoon sun, to the Banqueting Hall/hospital. The windows here were boarded, and the interior mercifully dim, but the heat was torturous. The motionless air stank abominably of blood, sweat, excrement, vomit, dirty linen, dirty bodies, and gangrene. One of the clerks retched violently. Renille gagged, and his stomach roiled. For a moment he stood still, breathing shallowly, then the qualm passed. His eyes adjusted to the noisome gloom, and he gazed unwillingly about him.

The vast table and countless chairs formerly occupying the hall were gone, their varnished mahogany doubtless incorporated into the barricades, or consumed in the nightly watch fires. The space was crowded with cots, sofas, mattresses, and featherbeds, upon which lay the wounded and the diseased.

So many of them.

Only a few days into the siege, and the hospital was already filled with scores of unfortunates, too many of them clearly doomed. How many would lie here, days hence?

Not a one, should the Aveshquians manage to break in.

Only two doctors within the compound, to tend the entire resident population. Not enough.

A handful of amateur nurses. Inadequate medical supplies. Heat. Filth. Flies.

Thousands of flies, everywhere, their dull buzz underscoring the moans of pain and the feeble pleas for water, for assistance, or for death. Here and there knelt volunteers, armed with whisks to shoo the insects from helpless bodies; but not enough to serve all the patients, never enough. Fearless vermin—rats, fleshbores, snakes, and worse—were everywhere, snatching food from the plates of the prostrate, and growing fat on it.

Soon the influx of patients and outflow of corpses would equalize. And after that?

The inspectors descended to the cellar, which proved well guarded, and unbreached. Satisfied, they proceeded from the Banqueting Hall to one of the storehouses, and then on to the "Blockhouse," a three-story heap of offices and archives. In the Blockhouse cellar, they found the sentry dead upon the floor, a brace of very live native sappers, and a shoulder-width hole in the wall, beyond which lay the profound darkness of a tunnel.

A couple of pistol shots, deafening in that low-ceilinged place, dispatched the sappers. One of the clerks ran to fetch a workman, who soon arrived, armed with trowel and mortar. The displaced stones of the wall were soon restored to their original positions, the repair reinforced with boards and braces. But the tunnel still existed, a perpetual threat; and thenceforth, an armed detachment would have to guard the cellar day and night.

Inspection that afternoon uncovered no further evidence of enemy incursion. But the compound perimeter offered many possible points of entry. The attackers were energetically determined, and it was only a matter of time before they would break through again.

Evening came, and the sultry darkness overwhelmed ZuLaysa. The moon rose to embrace NuuMahni Heaven-Dancer, and the celestial spin commenced. Rhythmic human voices lifted from streets to skies and, alone among the attentive Vonahrish, Renille vo Chaumelle recognized the Celebration of the Goddess, customarily chanted throughout the two days of the Festival of Dance.

The night deepened, and the voices faded. The sentries' cries of "All's well!" periodically pierced the dark, and the song of mosquitoes never ceased.

They attacked at dawn, without warning. One moment, there was pregnant peace; the next, the streets about the compound were alive and the silent dark figures were swarming toward the wall.

The guards on the ramparts opened fire, and the sentries yelled an alert. Seconds later, a straggle of bleary-eyed, rifle-carrying civilians came hurrying from all directions. Even the wounded, those that could move, rose from their beds in the Banqueting Hall.

A sea of heads and glittering weapons surrounded the Residency. The Aveshquian bugles sounded an advance, and the artillery bullocks dragged forward the heavy guns. Musket balls flew over the compound in showers, and grapeshot battered the fortifications, while a reckless band attacked the front gate with stones, axes, fire, and steel.

The defenders on the wall, under the command of Protector vo Trouniere, poured steady, rapid rifle fire down upon the ZuLaysans. The Vonahrish bullets took their toll, and the natives dropped by the score. Those at the front gate were killed or driven off and, at length, the attack ceased. The fire dwindled and the Aveshquian force withdrew, leaving a corpse-littered street behind them.

At least a dozen of the defenders had been hit—either killed outright, or dealt wounds that would in several cases bring death in hours or days. Those with life left in them were assisted to the Banqueting Hall, and the dead were promptly buried; for the climate admitted of no delay.

In the days that followed, the besieged grew accustomed to the boom of the big guns outside the compound, the whiz of missiles, and the explosion of shells. Children played or studied in the Nursery-Tutorage, women changed bandages and fanned patients in the hospital, or gathered firewood in the courtyard, undisturbed by the continual whistling of musket balls overhead. Although a shot occasionally found its mark, there was little point in trying to hide indoors, for even brick walls succumbed to the force of artillery.

The ZuLaysans launched concerted attacks at irregular, unpredictable intervals, and such assaults were similar in character to the first; each beaten off by the gunfire of the defenders, with plentiful loss of life on both sides. In between attacks, there was a restless quiescence, monotony broken by numerous funerals, personal inconveniences, and privations that worsened with every passing day.

The little graveyard beside the Banqueting Hall was rapidly expanding, and the hospital was crammed to bursting. Beds were in short supply, and numbers of wounded lay upon cloaks spread out on the stone floor.

By the end of the first week, food supplies remained adequate, but the incessant dousing of fires set by flaming arrows had lowered the water level in the well to an alarming degree, and Protector vo Trouniere decreed rationing. Thereafter, bathing became an infrequent luxury, and the discomforts of the siege, already considerable, increased a hundredfold.

The heat continued unabated, the red cloud burned overhead every night, and Vonahrish tempers began to fray. The shortage of water, combined with varied fears

and miseries, drove some to alcoholic recourse, for there
was no dearth of wine. Incidents of minor violence, already on the rise, took a sharp upward turn at the end of
the week, when individual stores of tobacco began to fail
and certain habitual smokers, deprived of their customary
solace, grew frantic. When two refugee railroad employees
were beaten senseless within the space of a single afternoon, vo Trouniere declared the imposition of heavy fines
upon all brawlers, but this measure proved ineffectual, and
the quarrels increased in frequency, even among the
women. Madame vo Losieux was known to have
scratched the face of Madame Myette when the latter deliberately ignored a request to cease cracking her knuckles.
And when Miss v'Eriste encouraged her pet Forest Baby to
stroll about the tabletop during the evening meal, Madame
Jumalle openly threatened sylvan infanticide.

Such difficulties, galling though they were, paled to
insignificance, however, upon the day that three children,
admitted to the Banqueting Hall within hours of one another, were found to display unmistakable signs of cholera.

The Ghochalla Xundunisse sat at the writing desk in her
bedchamber at OodPray. Her journal lay open before her,
with a pen beside it, but she never glanced down at them.
Her burning blind gaze aimed itself at the wall. She neither
stirred nor blinked. So had she sat for the last two hours or
more, and a stranger seeing her thus might well have
doubted her awareness, or else her sanity. Her mind, however, was furiously and fruitlessly active. The maddening
thoughts, recollections, and speculations spun through her
head, repeating themselves relentlessly. So it had been
since the night she'd learned of her daughter's flight. And
so, perhaps, it would continue, at ever-increasing speed,
until her fevered brain finally broke under the strain.

A knock upon the door roused the Ghochalla from
her miserable trance.

She has returned. She has come back to me.

"Come," she said, in a voice a statue might have
owned.

The door opened. Paro stood there, bearing a letter upon a salver.

She has written. She repents. She longs for reconciliation. She is unworthy, but if I find her truly contrite, I shall not withhold forgiveness.

"That is from the Ghochanna," she observed aloud. "Did you receive it from her hand? Is she here at Ood-Pray?"

Paro signaled a negative. His gestures described the arrival and prompt departure of a messenger from the city.

Xundunisse accepted the missive without visible eagerness.

"Leave me," she commanded, and Paro withdrew. The Ghochalla was alone, and now her face blazed with emotion. Her fingers were trembling as they broke the seal. Black wax, she noted, imprinted with an ushtra. The Ghochanna Jathondi possessed no such sigil. There was coldness now, where there had been heat. She unfolded the letter, and her eyes flew at once to the bottom of the page, where she found no signature, but only another ushtra, and the number twenty-two; symbolic of the letter *ahv*, twenty-second in the Aveshquian alphabet, and first letter of Aoun-Father's name. The letter had come straight from JiPhaindru.

Not from Jathondi.

She should have learned, by now. She should have known better than to hope. The Ghochalla drew a breath from the bottom of her lungs, and commenced reading:

To the Effulgent Ghochalla of Kahnderule—

A simple salutation, unadorned with compliments and titles. Very different from VaiPradh's last communication.

This to you from the Sons of the Father.

Tersely civil. They weren't out to court her, this time.

*Be it known to you that your daughter the
Ghochanna presently resides at JiPhaindru,
Fastness of the Gods. It is the desire of the
Effulgent lady's virgin heart that she should
serve the high purposes of Aoun-Father, bending
her spirit to His will in all things. To this end
she has dedicated her young life, in pursuit of
perfect self-renunciation.*

*There can be no doubting the Ghochanna's
worthiness of soul. Her devotion finds favor in
the eye of the Father, her offering is pure, and
now it remains only to determine the form and
substance of her service.*

*In this matter, the Filial strive to fulfill the
desires of the Father, but many paths lead to
the same destination, and the choices are varied.*

*It is our hope and fervent prayer that the
Ghochanna's spiritual awakening and elevation
shall serve to inspire a similar resurgence of
piety within the bosom of her Effulgent mother;
a divine enlightenment manifesting itself in the
renewed and loving alliance between the royal
House of Kahnderule and the Sons of the
Father.*

*Even now, the faithful of ZuLaysa, inspired
by fiery skies, rise to smite the godless
disOrdered in our midst. The Vonahrish
Residency resists, but must soon fall, and the
final destruction of the western tyrants marks
the commencement of Aveshquian renewal. The
ancient forms of worship shall restore
themselves, and our happy land will bask in the
warmth of the Father's love.*

*In this great endeavor, the approval and
public support of the Effulgent Ghochalla—
whose word is golden in the ears of her
subjects, whose image is enshrined within their
hearts—will greatly aid the Filial cause, thereby
revealing the Father's ultimate purpose in
leading the young Ghochanna Jathondi to
JiPhaindru.*

*Should her Effulgence oppose the Sons of the
Father, we shall mourn her inner emptiness, and
we shall search elsewhere for the truth of Aoun-
Father's intentions regarding the Ghochanna.*

*Prayer and meditation sharpen spiritual
vision. We shall entreat guidance.*

*It may come to pass that the very highest
and holiest of honors awaits the Ghochalla's
daughter. Should she prove worthy, perhaps she
will know the glory of the Father's most
intimate favor. Thus Chosen, privileged above
all other women, she will feed and renew divine
vitality and, in the consuming agonies of
corporeal dissolution, achieve the perfection of
self-renunciation that is Eternity.*

*The future is cloaked in shadow, and the
young Ghochanna's destiny remains as yet
unknown. But the great principle of mortal
interdependency never alters, and the Effulgent
Ghochalla may rest assured that immense
consequences hinge upon her decision.*

May the Father grant her wisdom.

The Ghochalla Xundunisse set the letter aside, with
care. She would not need to glance at it again, for every
word was engraved upon her memory. One phrase above
all others proved particularly persistent:

*. . . in the consuming agonies of corporeal dissolu-
tion, achieve the perfection of self-renunciation that is
Eternity . . .*

Consuming agonies.

Jathondi would die in torment, should her mother refuse to support VaiPradh.

They meant to rule, in the name of their hungry god.
Kahnderule would serve as Aoun's great larder, and His
playground. The feast would continue as long as humans
remained to furnish nourishment. When the supply failed,
if not before, the Father would doubtless turn His attention outward, upon fresh and plentiful populations.

The Filial were all that she had feared, and more.

As Ghochalla, stripped of real power, yet venerated by her subjects, she might urge rejection of VaiPradh, and her words would carry some weight. Weight to reinforce Vonahrish domination of Aveshq, weight to destroy Jathondi.

. . . *in the consuming agonies of corporeal dissolution* . . .

Head thrown back, eyes squeezed shut, and face contorted, the Ghochalla Xundunisse voiced an animal howl of grief and fury.

12

"Going once—going twice—sold! To Serchine Merlagne, for the sum of forty biquins. Serchine, come on up and collect your property!"

Amidst laughter and a spattering of applause, Serchine Merlagne—visibly the worse for drink—lurched to the makeshift auctioneer's podium set up in the Residency's grand ballroom, and took possession of his purchase; a suit of formal evening wear, complete with white cravat, embroidered black waistcoat, tall silk hat, and patent pumps. The laughter swelled, as Serchine donned the hat and coat. Their former owner, the merchant Bergue Foisont, recently dead of cholera, had been a small and slight man, nearly bald of pate. The purchaser was burly and long-limbed. The coat stretched to the breaking across his shoulders, and the hat perched ridiculously atop his large, wiry-haired head.

Arms outspread, Serchine strutted from podium back to his seat, and the laughter persisted for a few moments, but soon gave way to expectant silence.

The auctioneer, Touveel vo Faybrieuse—youthful master of Sapphire Plantation, no more than twenty-six years of age, and looking even younger than that, with his slim frame and baby face—was finally bringing forth the true jewel among the dead man's effects, the real prize of the afternoon. Vo Faybrieuse, canny behind his boyish smile, possessed a natural dramatic sense suitable to his present avocation. He had forced the audience to wait for the past two hours and more; to wait while the clothes, the soap, the shaving implements, the preserved meats, the weapons, ammunition, games, knickknacks, and cooking utensils were vended; to wait until anticipation had climbed to feverish levels.

And now at last—

"Lot Twenty. An unopened tin of Llavanese tobacco, top grade, two trets in weight," vo Faybrieuse announced. "A box of Ubourion cheroots, first quality, one hundred eight in quantity. Probably the last Ubourions left within the Residency. Consider that, gentlemen—the very last. One tret of Goldenheart tea, exquisitely fragrant, a sonnet to the senses. A standard of Risarou coffee beans, dark roast. There's nothing so sinfully lush as Risarou coffee— but I need hardly remind you of that. One case of champagne, v'Isseroi vineyards. Bubbling paradise, dry as true wit. Six bottles of old Fabeque apple brandy, Derrivalle Commune label, dating back to the Revolution. Words fail me. I shall auction these items one at a time, beginning with the tobacco. Ladies and gentlemen, two trets of prime Llavanese. What am I bid?"

"The promise of all I possess, up to and including my firstborn child," offered one of the young Civil Interns, and his listeners chuckled politely.

That joke had been funny, the first few dozen times it had been uttered.

"My soul," someone suggested, and the response was perfunctory.

Another old one, and it was getting harder to laugh in the midst of the sickening heat, and the dangers, the discomforts, the cumulative miseries eroding collective morale. Hard to laugh with the bullets flying night and day, the red cloud above and the sappers below, the cholera raging, and the graveyard expanding. Getting harder every day, but decency demanded the effort, and therefore, occasions such as this one witnessed displays of exaggerated jocularity, of which Serchine Merlagne's performance was a typical example. As for the limp jokes, and clichéd sallies, senescence notwithstanding, they touched a universal chord. For there was no one among the defenders who didn't feel the shortage of certain small indulgences, and an auction of some dead Vonahrishman's personal property was now the sole source of supplies once considered necessities, and now regarded as rare luxuries. Fortunately for the survivors, such auctions—or "ZuLaysan Probate," as they were waggishly known—occurred often.

"Who'll start?" vo Faybrieuse demanded.

"Ten New-rekkoes." Assistant Secretary Phesque Shivaux spoke up clearly, and not so much as a raised eyebrow greeted this bid, a figure ordinarily sufficient to purchase three times the quantity of tobacco offered. But prices within the literally hothouse atmosphere of the Vonahrish Residency scarcely reflected market values in the outer world.

Bidding proceeded apace, appetite stimulated by young vo Faybrieuse's skillful theatrics, until Phesque Shivaux finally secured the tobacco for the sum of twenty-two New-rekkoes. Shivaux then proceeded to purchase, at similarly inflated prices, the cheroots, the tea, and the champagne. His pockets were deep, and yet he might have curtailed such extravagance had not Miss v'Eriste's musical exclamations greeted each successive acquisition.

Cisette, it was clear, admired the Assistant Secretary's taste; just as she admired his intellect, his accomplishments, his gentility, his whiskers, and the beauty of his soul. No doubt, for modesty's sake, she strove to disguise her sentiments, but they revealed themselves in every languishing glance, every soft smile, and prettily confiding gesture. Certainly Shivaux himself was neither unaware, nor indifferent. He'd made no overt declaration as yet, but his newfound gallantry was nauseating to behold.

Social convention obliged Renille to observe the performance at close range. Even in the midst of a siege, the young and unmarried Cisette v'Eriste was all but bound to her guardians, Nienne and Tifftif vo Chaumelle. Tifftif's hypertrophied sense of fitness demanded the constant attendance of her husband's nephew, no matter how much she disliked him, and Renille found it less wearisome to humor her than to argue the point. Much of the time, his duties offered him legitimate escape, but all too often, he found himself chained to her side. The present instance was a typical example. Given free choice, he would have shunned the auction, for the public sale of a dead compatriot's belongings, while sensible under the circumstances, struck him as faintly ghoulish. This time, however, Tifftif had managed to capture him, and he'd tried to make the best of it. Overcoming his own distaste, he'd even made a couple of small purchases, paying out of the back wages reluctantly disgorged by the bursar. No one had bid against him for Bergue Foisont's razor, strop, soap, and brushes, so he could now stop borrowing Quisse v'Ieque's implements. Similarly easy to secure were Foisont's service revolver, and a stack of books that included Shorvi Nirienne's seminal *Todaytomorrow;* a pile of amusingly awful verse-dramas; and *Northern Star,* yet another biography of Dref Zeenoson, brilliant third president of the Vonahrish Republic. These transactions complete, he was ready and eager to withdraw, but Tifftif remained clamped to his arm, and there was nothing for it but to stay where he was, watching Cisette v'Eriste mesmerize Phesque Shivaux.

"They call Goldenheart tea the perfect restorative," Cisette fluted. "Master Shivaux, you must tell me if it is true. I ask only on behalf of my sweet baby Momu. As for myself, the cause is hopeless, as you can plainly see. I am ancient, tired, blasted, ruined—a penance upon the eyes of all. I should do the world a favor, to bury my head in the sand. Perhaps, however, it is not too late for Momu the Magnificent. Tell me, how shall I serve him? I entreat you—guide me."

"Fortunate Momu, to bask in the light of so radiant a mistress. Miss v'Eriste's youth and beauty defy all privation. She is a hope and an inspiration to every beholder." A killing smile accompanied this verbal bouquet.

"Oh, shame on you, Master Shivaux, for telling such fibs! I know I am an eyesore."

He spent the next few minutes assuring her otherwise.

Renille's attention soon wandered. Hyperbole notwithstanding, he reflected, Shivaux's point was well taken.

Cisette was indeed fresh, rose-cheeked, and immaculate as ever—a considerable accomplishment, under the present water-straitened circumstances. Equipped with a large wardrobe, countless clean white shirts, substantial supplies of hair pomade and perfume, the Assistant Secretary likewise contrived to keep himself comparatively spruce.

Others hadn't fared so well. Uncle Nienne was yellow-pale, grubby, and, like so many of the besieged these days, troubled with persistent skin rashes. And Tifftif vo Chaumelle—gray roots betraying her artificially colored hair, dark pockets bagging beneath her eyes—seemed to have aged ten years since the day of her arrival. Renille himself, reduced to three or four hours of sleep a night, was haggard and perpetually fatigued, a condition he usually managed to ignore. The faces about him, in repose, reflected exhaustion, deprivation, tension, depression. Even the debonaire vo Faybrieuse was visibly tired and worn, behind the smiling façade.

Vo Faybrieuse believed, however, in playing the game. The pace of his spirited patter never slackened, and his gestures retained their vivacity.

"Ladies and gentlemen, I present for your consideration the final bottle of Fabequais apple brandy. Last call, last bottle, last chance to capture the very distillation of northern Vonahr. The sun, scents, and fragrant orchards of Fabeque Province dwell in this brandy. One sip to banish your present surroundings—two to transport you home. Who can fix a price upon the priceless? Who can name the value in money of Vonahr-in-a-bottle, the last bottle? It is impossible, it cannot be done. However, I advise you to try. Ladies and gentlemen, what am I bid?"

No doubt some enterprising party would have attempted the impossible, had not a shell come crashing through the boarded window into the grand ballroom, to explode with a roar at the very feet of the auctioneer. Masonry and debris flew in all directions. For long moments thereafter, the air was full of smoke, brick dust, and screams. When the dust began to settle, and the smoke to clear, the survivors discovered Touveel vo Faybrieuse's body parts scattered amidst the wreckage of the podium. Several spectators standing in vo Faybrieuse's immediate vicinity had likewise died, though none so spectacularly. Injuries of variable severity abounded among the living.

It took a dazed instant for Renille to register that he had not been touched. He was still on his feet, unhurt, and the pressure upon his chest was only the weight of Tifftif vo Chaumelle, who was clutching him convulsively, and keening at the top of her lungs. But no, those shrill, abandoned shrieks that were sending the knives through his skull didn't come from Tifftif, they originated somewhere else, very close, low down, near the floor—

He shook his head, drew a deep breath, and looked around him. Through the drifting, choking clouds, he discerned Cisette v'Eriste, down on her knees, and screaming—screaming—

He thought for a moment she must have been hit, but then perceived that she knelt beside a supine, motionless figure. Shivaux was down and seriously wounded, no doubt caught by whizzing debris; unconscious but still alive, as the powerful arterial jet of blood from his leg attested. Cisette hadn't the faintest notion what to do about it. Both her little hands covered the wound, but the blood continued to spurt through her fingers.

Shaking himself free of Tifftif, Renille knelt beside the fallen man, applied pressure at the appropriate point, but found something wrong, some sort of impediment.

"Cisette. Hush," he commanded sharply, and to his surprise, she obeyed. The screeching gave way to muted sobs. "He's got something in his pocket. Get it out of the way."

"I don't want to touch him! He's going to die!"

"Not if you do as you're told." She gaped at him, and his voice lashed. *"Now."*

She flinched, and then gingerly slid her hand into Phesque Shivaux's hip pocket to bring forth a blood-splotched paper packet, which she handled with extreme reluctance.

"Oh—*oh*!" Cisette grimaced. "Please, *you* look after this for him!" Hurriedly, she stuffed the paper into Renille's shirt pocket.

He barely noticed. Without shifting his eyes from the prostrate Assistant Secretary, he commanded, "Tear me a strip off your petticoat, then hand me a fragment of wood, about the thickness of your finger."

She did as she was told, and with these items he quickly improvised a tourniquet. Shivaux's bleeding was more or less under control, but the man needed immediate medical attention.

"Now, we must get him to B.H."

"But *I* haven't the strength to carry him, Renille!"

"No." *But I'll wager Jathondi would, and she's considerably smaller than you.* An absurdly irrelevant thought to enter his mind at such a time. "Hurry and fetch an able-bodied man."

This task lay well within the scope of her abilities. Rising, she cast her eyes about the devastated ballroom, fixed upon a promising target, and launched herself. Moments later she was back, with an unwounded Faquenz Zhouville in tow.

They bore Shivaux from the ballroom, along the corridor, down the central staircase, and out into the courtyard, where the sudden blinding intensity of sunlight struck like a blow. Cisette was hovering hummingbird-fashion about the victim, dabbing at a cut on his forehead with her handkerchief, maintaining a steady flow of soprano sympathy. Renille scarcely heard her. The ground beneath his feet was scarred and pocked with the recollection of countless explosions, crisscrossed with trenches, cluttered with a thousand obstacles, and a misstep was likely to land Shivaux in a ditch. Not that he would personally mourn the Assistant Secretary's loss, but these days, within the Residency, all Vonahrish life held value. The courtyard stank abominably, for the latrines dug at the commencement of the siege were full, their stench augmented by the nauseous decay of several animal carcasses, but he had learned how to ignore all that. In any case, his attention was otherwise engaged, focused on the noise arising in the street outside the wall.

The Aveshquian voices blended and rose, no doubt in celebration of the successful strike upon the ballroom. He recognized the cadences even before he distinguished the words of the Great Invocation to Aoun. The Filial ruled that crowd out there.

He glanced at Zhouville, who appeared unaware. And Cisette, of course, would never recognize the chant, for she spoke no word of Kahnderulese.

They crossed the baking, stinking courtyard to the threshold of the Banqueting Hall, and there Cisette halted.

"I cannot go in there," she murmured. "I am sorry, but I cannot. Do not think too ill of me, Renille."

"No point in risking your own health, and I'm sure Shivaux wouldn't want you to," he assured her briskly.

"That's just the way I see it! Only—only—somehow it seems—I don't know, but it seems— Oh, Renille, perhaps you'll understand me, and all my odd feelings, because you're so much older than I, so much wiser, and so peculiar. Maybe you can explain me to myself—"

"Some other time."

Into the fetid dimness of the Banqueting Hall they carried Shivaux, and, to Renille's surprise, Cisette followed.

The atmosphere of the infirmary reduced the courtyard stench to nothingness. It might have been different, had they dared to open the doors and boarded windows. As it was, the noisome vapors reinforced one another, intensifying at geometric rates.

"Faugh!" Cisette coughed.

They'd fumigated recently. So much was obvious, for the acrid nasal assault of chemicals rose above the deeper, primal odors of disease, death, and decay.

One of Madame Zouville's B.H. Relief Team ran to them, took a look at Shivaux, and ordered, "Put him there."

She indicated an empty pallet on the floor between a couple of cholera-ridden wretches. Probably, the space had been vacated no more than hours, or perhaps minutes, earlier.

They set Shivaux down upon the pallet, and the nurse withdrew. Cisette gagged.

"I cannot—I cannot—" she choked.

Renille found himself almost interested in her decision.

"There's nothing I can do for him here," she observed, not without justice. "Nothing! What do you expect of me?"

"Nothing more," he responded, truthfully enough.

"Oh, you think so little of me! You always did!"

"Nobody judges you. Calm yourself, and consider—"

"I will consider your disapproval, and your contempt! I don't deserve it from you, Renille, it isn't fair! Who are you to judge—just who are you?"

"I never claimed—"

"You didn't have to! It comes through in every word and look! You are so perfect, the rest of us aren't fit to wipe your shoes! Or so you think. You've always been like that!"

"Cisette, I never said—"

"You never said anything! That is your custom! You say nothing, but you look everything! You look *down* on everything, and everybody, and most of all, on me! That is your specialty!"

"Ridiculous. Would you please lower your voice?"

"Oh, now I'm supposed to pretend that I have no feelings?"

"*That will do.*" Madame Zhouville's disciple was back, accompanied by an exhausted doctor. "This is a hospital, not a tavern. If you must quarrel, do it elsewhere."

"Very well, I'll go!" Cisette declared. "You see, Renille—I'm only leaving because I have been *told* to, not because I *want* to! But I suppose you'll hold it against me, all the same!" Without awaiting his reply, she rushed from the Banqueting Hall.

"Shivaux going to make it?" Renille inquired of the doctor.

"Under ordinary circumstances, with adequate supplies, almost certainly. As it is—" The doctor's shrug was eloquent. His attention returned to the patient.

"My wife anywhere about?" Faquenz Zhouville asked the nurse.

"Not here," the woman replied. "Right now, she's up on the wall with the Ladies' Long Rifle League."

"Typical. Haven't seen her in days," observed Zhouville.

"She's a remarkable woman, your wife."

"Indeed. I believe she's discovered her true métier in

this place. Sometimes I suspect she'll be positively sorry when the siege ends."

"If it ever ends," the nurse mused.

"It must, Madame," Zhouville assured her. "One day, one way or another."

Perhaps rather sooner than you expect, Renille thought. He said nothing aloud.

"Very well, what is it you wanted to see me about?" vo Trouniere demanded, with more than a touch of impatience. The Protector was unshaven, unkempt, unrested, and unhealthy. His temper, always short, was sharper than ever, these days.

He would, no doubt, appreciate brevity.

"In the first place, to ask if you've had any word of the Eighteenth," Renille returned.

"Message arrived by carrier pigeon, just this morning, and the news is good. The Eighteenth is on the move, its advance periodically impeded by native insurgents. Nevertheless, the regiment progresses, and there's good reason to hope for relief within the next three days or so—perhaps even less."

"That is likely to be too late, Protector."

"How so?"

"I've reason to believe the ZuLaysans will attack at dawn, if not before."

"Why do you think so? Last time, it was some sort of astrological mumbo jumbo, which sounded absurd, but your prediction was absolutely correct. What is it, this time around?"

"The Great Invocation," Renille told him.

"The what?"

"The Great Invocation to the god Aoun. They're chanting it, out there in the street, which means that VaiPradh governs the crowd. It's the usual method of the Filial to spend some hours rousing their followers to suitable heights of pious homicidal enthusiasm, prior to an assault."

"I see. Then our artillery will disperse that mob, before things get out of hand. We have the capability."

"We have the capability to force their temporary withdrawal."

"That should suffice to break the collective native trance, or ecstasy, or whatever you want to call it."

"Not this time, Protector. They'll merely regroup elsewhere, and the process will continue. Moreover, we are now so depleted, so diminished in strength and numbers, that a full-scale attack by Aveshquians prepared to die in the service of their god is all but certain to overwhelm us. But you already know that."

"This isn't the kind of defeatist talk I want to hear, Chaumelle. I don't want anyone else hearing it, either, so keep your opinions to yourself. I won't have you undermining Vonahrish morale. If you're right about this attack, then we shall resist it with all our strength and will, as we've resisted the others. Or are you suggesting that we give up without a fight—is that your sage advice?"

"No. My advice is that we strike directly at the Filial, where the stroke will inflict real damage. Sever the head, and the body will eventually regenerate a new one, but I suspect it will take some time, which we can sorely use."

"What are you talking about?"

"You recall the account of my findings within JiPhaindru."

"Yes. Very colorful, very fanciful."

"Entirely accurate. I told you of the First Priest, the present KhriNayd-Son. Whatever you accept or don't accept in all that I described, you may at the very least believe this—that the KhriNayd-Son I encountered there is an extraordinary individual, possessed of remarkable abilities, and enjoying an absolute ascendancy over his followers. His is, I believe, the guiding intelligence, the very mind of VaiPradh. Eliminate KhriNayd-Son, and the Filial may find a new leader, but not immediately, for this First Priest is not to be readily replaced."

"Well, and what of it, if this KhriNayd-Son is safely holed up in JiPhaindru?"

"I got in once, Protector. I will get in again, and this time, I'll do what I should have done in the first place—eliminate the First Priest, once and for all." He hoped he looked and sounded convincingly confident.

"That is the greatest nonsense I've ever heard. You propose, I take it, to stroll out through the front gate, under the noses of several thousand yellows, who will no doubt courteously clear passage for you through their ranks?"

"The latest breakthrough into the Residency cellar isn't yet bricked up. Tonight, disguised as an Aveshquian, I will exit the cellar by way of the sappers' tunnel, emerging somewhere on the far side of the compound wall. I will then make my way to the temple."

"No you won't."

"It's not an infeasible plan, Protector."

"It is absolutely absurd. In the first place, you'd probably be spotted and butchered before you'd proceeded fifteen feet along that tunnel. If by chance you were lucky enough to make it through, you'd most likely never reach JiPhaindru. If you did reach JiPhaindru, you probably couldn't get in—didn't you claim that they made you wait a day or two in the courtyard before admitting you the first time?"

"Yes, but this time I have a—"

"And if, by some strange freak of fortune, you actually succeeded in reentering the temple," vo Trouniere continued remorselessly, "what makes you think yourself capable of dealing with the First Priest, what with those 'remarkable abilities' of his that you so often speak of?"

That is the real question. Renille was silent.

"Didn't this KhriNayd-Son manage to hypnotize you, or drug you, or somehow befuddle you, last time? Didn't that teach you?"

It taught me caution. Astonishment. Fear.

"So I'm ordering you to abandon all such harebrained schemes," the Protector concluded. "You're not a half-bad shot, and you usually know what the yellows are up to, and you are useful here. We can hardly afford to throw away a Vonahrish life for nothing. You'll stay, and do your duty here."

Duty, again.

"Protector, I don't think you've fully considered the potential benefits—"

"I've granted the suggestion all the consideration it

deserves, and more. You aren't about to go jumping down
some rabbit hole, Chaumelle. That's my decision, and
there's nothing more to be said."

Nothing more to be said.

He could agree with that.

Renille spent the next couple of hours standing watch
on the wall, and during that time, the devout chanting in
the street below never ceased, but not a single bullet flew;
this last variation from the norm, disquieting in the extreme. Once, a member of Madame Zhouville's Sentry
Support Squad came by with cool, mint-flavored tea for
him, but no other incident broke the monotony. He was
relieved in the late afternoon, and thereafter, free to proceed with his preparations, which were simple and few. It
wasn't hard to procure Aveshquian clothing. The storeroom adjacent to the Banqueting Hall contained scores of
qunne garments, property of native servants dying during
the siege. Not the cholera victims, of course—their belongings were burned, down to the last scrap of gauzy dust-
ward. But the others, when washed and thoroughly boiled,
could be cut into strips and used as bandages, for which
there was a constant demand. Even such delicate flowers
as Tifftif and Cisette were willing to roll clean bandages
upon occasion, in the fond belief that this restful activity
represented their fair contribution to the general defense
effort.

The storeroom was vacant, save for a couple of the
refugee houseboys from Sapphire Plantation, asleep on the
floor in the corner. Renille appropriated tunic and baggy
trousers, bronze insignia of Flow, zhupur, and hat, without need of manufactured explanation. Rolling his acquisi-
tions into an anonymous bundle, he returned to his dim
and suffocating office, crowded with the cots and pallets of
the various tenants, but presently empty of humanity. The
bundle disappeared into one of the desk drawers. With it
went Bergue Foisont's service revolver, a pouch of ammunition, and Ziloor's aetheric conflation. Locking the
drawer, he pocketed the key, then stepped to the boarded
window and looked out through the chinks; warm light,

long shadows, two hours at least until darkness. How best
to fill the empty time?

Write a letter to her.

A silly notion. No way of sending a letter from this
place, and even if there were, it would never reach her. The
Ghochalla would somehow intercept it.

Don't underestimate Jathondi.

If she received a letter from him, she might answer.

Sillier by the moment. He'd brought her nothing but
trouble, and she'd doubtless prefer to forget his existence.

Write to say good-bye.

That one had slipped through his mental guard. No
profit in contemplating prospects of failure and death; or,
for that matter, of success and death. And yet, there was
no denying that the probability of surviving JiPhaindru a
second time was low; the probability of surviving the siege,
lower yet. Usually, he didn't let himself consider the ultimate fate of the Residency and its defenders; for alcohol-
ism, opium addiction, or suicide was all too often the lot
of the overly contemplative. Nevertheless, the black
thoughts couldn't always be staved off, particularly of late.

Seating himself at the desk, he lit a candle, took up a
pen, dipped it, and began to write—slowly at first, and
then with increasing speed, until it seemed that his hand
moved of its own accord. He had filled four sheets before
the hurrying pen slowed to a halt. He signed his name,
then settled back to read the missive, surprised and almost
unnerved, to discover what had come pouring out of him.

And now? He wanted her to see it. He wanted her,
somehow, to see *him*. But let this thing fall into the wrong
hands—Filial hands—and Jathondi was dangerously compromised. He'd done her enough harm already, and he
wasn't about to do more, through indulgence of his own
newly awakened appetite for self-expression.

He touched one corner of the letter to the candle
flame, and the fire leapt. After a moment, he dropped what
was left into somebody's ashtray, watching in oddly keen
regret as the paper dwindled to blackened crisps. The blaze
sank and expired. So much for that. He wondered what
she would have thought, had she read it.

Probably she'd have thought him an awful fool.

Once again he stepped to the window, squinting out to discover that his labors had eaten time. While he'd written, the sun had set, and now, the luminous cloud unnaturally anchored above the Vonahrish compound was brightening to sullen red life.

Nienne vo Chaumelle came in, changed his clothes, and went out again, without a word. Nienne was looking wretched—disheveled, dyspeptic, and unutterably depressed. For the first time in his life, Renille was sorry for his uncle; a little sorry.

Alone again, and now, time to change his own clothes. He retrieved the bundle of native garments, began to unbutton his shirt, encountered an alien object in the pocket, and drew it forth. He held a stained and sticky paper packet. Unfolding the sheets, he saw unfamiliar script, and automatically began to read, before he realized what it was that he held. Assistant Secretary Phesque Shivaux's correspondence, stuffed into his pocket by Cisette v'Eriste earlier that day, and forgotten. By then, a well-known name or two had already caught his eye, and he read on. A low whistle escaped him. He read to the end, then read it all again, from start to finish.

Interesting information contained herein; interesting indeed, but of no immediate utility. Nevertheless, if he survived this evening's venture, and if Shivaux survived this afternoon's wound—if any westerner survived the Residency siege—there would be much to discuss with the Assistant Secretary, upon their next meeting.

Too many ifs.

Consigning the bloodstained documents to the desk drawer, Renille resumed his interrupted self-transformation, swiftly exchanging western garments for Aveshquian garb. The revolver and ammunition disappeared beneath the layers of qunne. The aetheric conflation vanished into the folds of his zhupur. The dust-warded hat concealed his undyed hair and shaded his pale western face.

The corridors were populous, and the tall Aveshquian hurrying down from the second story attracted little attention. Certainly nobody recognized a disguised Vonahrishman.

The storage cellar that he sought, occupying the deep-

est of the Residency sublevels, was well illuminated and
well guarded. A number of lanterns placed about the room
cast their light upon damp stone walls and floor, alive with
insects; low ceiling, veiled in spiderwebs; piles of broken
glass, a mound of rotten straw, and a sedan chair, doubtless dating back to the last century, that had somehow
escaped destruction. The packing crates and old barrels
ordinarily reposing here had long since fed the watch fires.
Close to the northwest corner of the room, yawned a black
hole in the wall. The aperture was roughly circular, and
quite small, barely wide enough to admit passage of a single adult body. Certainly, had their luck held, its engineers
would have enlarged it.

On the floor, close beside the hole, a group of men sat
playing at Antislez with a wilted deck of Obranese cards.
Some of the faces were familiar, some weren't. A couple of
the guards, uniformed in buff and gray, must have survived the massacre of the Second Kahnderulese. All of the
cardplayers were Vonahrish. The only native visage in
sight belonged to Preeay v'Azay's valet, who sat a little off
to the side, silently polishing a pair of his master's boots.

The loud conversation and immoderate laughter were
unmistakably designed to carry along the sappers' tunnel,
advertising Vonahrish vigilance to those within.

As he entered the cellar, Renille wisely removed his
hat.

"Gentlemen," he intoned, and was recognized at once.

"On your way to a masquerade, Chaumelle?" was the
predictable greeting.

"Pantomime?"

"Pissie wedding?"

"Filial festival, perhaps?"

"You have guessed it," Renille returned.

"I'll tell you what," announced one of the soldiers,
"Chaumelle here means to play the terrier."

"Oh, he's too civilized and sedate for that."

"Nevertheless."

"That explains the costume. Gives the terrier an advantage."

"Just what's wrong with it. Makes things too easy for
him. I'd say it bends the rules."

"But not to breaking. I call it creative."

"And I call it slippery. Creative, bah! Raw courage is the hallmark of a terrier."

"Wrong. Skill. Skill and cunning. Both are required."

"Full Pissie rig-out, though. That may be a bit too cunning. There's something demeaning about it, something a bit—slimy."

"You're narrow. Me, I see nothing wrong with a crafty terrier."

"If terrier's what he aims to play at all."

The recently coined term "playing the terrier" described the pastime, popular among certain adventurously bloodthirsty Residency defenders, of combing the sappers' tunnels in search of Aveshquian prey, who were, ideally, to be dispatched in absolute silence, by means of a blade or garrote. The stealthy crawl through the dark, the degree of skill required, the mortal peril, combined with the luscious satisfaction of the reward, were accounted incomparable by devotees of the sport; but their numbers were few, and attrition was continual.

"Well, enlighten us, Chaumelle," v'Azay urged. "Are you for the tunnels?"

"Wouldn't miss the chance," Renille assured him.

"Shouldn't have thought it your style."

"I've decided to expand my mental horizons."

"Better hurry, then. They'll have this rat hole plugged by midnight. If you're not out by the time the bricklayers come, we'll assume you're dead, and tell them to proceed."

"I intend to be out of the tunnel long before midnight."

"In that case, good hunting. Bag a big one."

Amidst general expressions of encouragement, Renille approached the hole.

"Esteemed. A word."

The quiet voice of v'Azay's valet halted him, and he turned, mildly surprised that an Aveshquian in that western company would presume to speak without leave.

"Beware the exit. It is well guarded by the AounSons. Shun the exit, Esteemed. For your life."

Renille nodded, then knelt to squeeze himself through the hole, into a narrow burrow, too low to stand upright

in. He, like the Aveshquian miners, and the Vonahrish terriers, would have to crawl. Unlike the terriers, he hoped to
meet nobody.

For the first several feet, the faint light filtering in from
the Residency cellar illuminated stout wooden supports,
shoring up the tunnel wall at regular intervals. After he
had passed the second such support, the light was fading,
and by the third, it was gone. The darkness was absolute,
and he found himself curiously reluctant to draw the
blackness down into his lungs. His breath came quick and
shallow. A few matches lay in the folds of his zhupur, but
nothing short of desperation would justify lighting one.
Pausing, he listened intently. The talk and laughter of the
cellar guards filled the passageway. He could hear nothing
above that racket. If Aveshquian sappers, cautious as himself, lurked in the darkness ahead, they were invisible and
inaudible.

He advanced slowly, often touching the tunnel wall to
count the wooden supports, whose growing sum measured
his progress. The black air was dead, and just barely
breathable. The passage ran straight and unequivocal for
the first twenty-five supports, and then it forked. He
halted, considering. The Vonahrish voices behind him
were faint and distant, but there was nothing else to be
heard.

And some human terriers considered this enjoyable.

He struck off to the right, inching his way along with
caution, but he didn't get far. The offshoot terminated
abruptly, widening into a tiny chamber. His groping outstretched hand encountered a curved wooden surface. His
fingers explored, quickly recognizing the familiar contour
of a small powder keg. Beside the first keg stood a second.
And a third. There were half a dozen stored there in the
dark, below the Residency wall, buried too deep at present
to achieve maximum destructive effect. Presumably, the
sappers intended excavation of a vertical shaft.

He crawled back the way he had come, but halted
short of the tunnel divide, for a mutter of Kahnderulese
was stirring the dead air. Then there was light, tiny red
points glowing through the holes in a pierced metal container, and it seemed to shout in the midst of that dark-

ness. Two native miners were approaching. Evidently, the depredations of the Vonahrish terriers had taught the Zu-Laysans the wisdom of traveling in pairs.

He waited, scarcely breathing, until they had passed him by, then slipped in silence from the tributary shaft, out into the fork again, and up the left-hand passageway, scuttling along on hands and knees at his best speed, for he was inexpressibly eager to be free of this place which seemed, like a nightmare version of Infinity's Closet, to enclose timeless immensity.

He passed a couple more offshoots without pausing to explore them, and then the quality of the air changed, and his lungs, sensing the difference, expanded accordingly. The atmosphere was coming to life again. There was an almost imperceptible stirring, and he caught a whiff of smoke. The tunnel curved slightly, angled sharply upward, and he spied the exit—a sizable hole framing a patch of starlit sky. He crawled toward the light, and well before he reached it, a silhouetted head appeared in the opening. He heard the click of a cocked pistol, and then an imperative ZuLaysan voice.

"Who is there? Speak or die."

"NaiVook." Where had that name sprung from? Oh yes—Faquenz Zhouville's valet. Took a bullet in the stomach. Died in B.H., five days ago.

"You are none of ours."

"I am NaiVook, Order of Flow, former valet to Esteemed planter Zhouville. I was a worm, toiling in the sty of a Vonahrish pig. I was a fool, feeble, and a slave. But the gods, pitying my wretchedness, granted me wisdom at last. They came to me in my dreams, They showed me the path. Then I took my knife, and I cut the throat of my master, who now lies dead in a red pool. His wife I likewise slaughtered like a sow, nor did his children escape my vengeance. I spat into my Esteemed master's face, I fingered the breasts of his wife, I drank the blood of his oldest son, and then I came away, purified in spirit and burning to serve the Sons of the Father."

There was a low-voiced colloquy, outside the tunnel. Renille waited, and soon his interlocutor spoke again.

"Utter surrender to the will of Finality offers—"

"The only true freedom." Renille effortlessly took up the phrases of the First Self-Renunciation. *"Self bars the way to the Source. Nonentity is Infinity, which is the mind of the Father."*

He might have continued to the end, had not the other cut him off.

"You are Filial. Praise the gods for your salvation. Come forth." The silhouetted head disappeared. The colloquy outside resumed.

He wondered if someone would blow his brains out, the moment he emerged. He crawled up the grade, climbed through the hole, and found himself in the walled garden of a private property separated from the northern boundary of the Residency compound only by the width of a single street. The town house, once the dwelling of a ridiculously wealthy Vonahrish banker, had been spared serious damage, for obvious reasons. Its proximity to the compound, together with its unusual height, offered every advantage to the native snipers.

A small watchfire burned in the garden, surely kindled for its light alone, for no heat was needed in the sultry night. Yet the heavy air was glorious, by contrast to the tunnel atmosphere, or by contrast to the stench of death and disease overhanging the Residency, and he drew hungry gulps of it. Half a dozen ZuLaysans sat about the fire, and they were unabashedly inspecting him.

Let them gawk all they pleased, they'd find no revealing anomaly in his appearance. So long as he kept his hat on.

"Welcome, Brother," one of them remarked at last. He, too, wore the insignia of Flow, and this commonality of Order established instant fraternity, of sorts. "Will you join us?"

"I have tasted Vonahrish blood, and relished it," returned Renille. "I am eager to drink again. Where shall I go to quench my thirst?"

"Join the force of Bhansattu-in-Wings before the great front gates of the Vonahrish House," advised his fellow Flowman. "There, you will shortly find ample refreshment. And may the gods grant you good hunting."

Just about what Preeay v'Azay had said.

Thanking them profusely, he departed, ostensibly in search of Bhansattu.

He stood once more upon the streets of a Little Sherreen transformed, its Vonahrish-style buildings plundered and gutted, its parks and gardens torn, its barricaded boulevards ruled by native Aveshquians. He blended perfectly with them. He would never be recognized as an Esteemed, and he might go anywhere, dare anything.

Vo Trouniere would be livid when he found out. He wouldn't believe that "playing the terrier" nonsense for a moment. If by any remote chance the two of them survived all this, the Protector might even be angry enough to trot out that insubordination charge he'd threatened. It carried a possible two-year prison term, Renille recalled.

Good thing we're not in the military. He could have me shot for mutiny, or desertion, or something.

Desertion. It was the first time the thought had occurred to him, and suddenly it seemed to fill every corner of his mind. Desertion.

Against all odds, he alone among the Vonahrish had escaped the doomed Residency, and now he was free, quite free. Nothing compelled his return to JiPhaindru and its uncanny horrors. He was only just beginning to realize how much he dreaded the place, with its nightmare First Priest, and the Thing lurking at its center.

He didn't have to go back. He had the power to choose otherwise.

Almost without volition, his gaze swung north, toward the foothills, and OodPray. Invisible, of course, at the moment. But it was still early, and if he started walking now, he could reach that crumbling heap of wonder well before dawn. They'd still be sleeping when he arrived. He'd scale the garden wall, enter through a ground-floor window, and make his way through the endless corridors to the Ghochanna's chamber—

He didn't know where that was.

No matter, he'd find it, he'd find her. He'd wake her gently, hoping she wouldn't scream at sight of him—

Jathondi doesn't scream.

He'd wake her, and they'd talk, as they hadn't been permitted to talk when they'd parted. And maybe this time she'd choose to go with him, and they could go—anywhere in all the world. Lanthi Ume, perhaps. Travorn. Strell. Anywhere they chose.

The Vonahrish Residency would fall, its occupants would be massacred, and the westerners would be driven first from Kahnderule, and then from the surrounding states.

We've no right to be here, anyway.

Foreign influence purged, the Filial would rule in Aveshq. The Filial, with their pathetic Blessed Vessels, and their obscene, pitiable hybrid infants, and their assassins, and their poisonous lizards, and their drugged, mindless, fanatical priesthood, and their god, that consumed and destroyed, their god that blighted the world, their monstrous and horrifying Father—

He might turn his back on all that, but it would always be with him.

"He's Vonahrish. He'll do his duty."

Curious that vo Trouniere's simplism should come back to haunt him now.

"Anyone with an ounce of decency knows his duty on instinct."

Vo Trouniere, again. Hardly contemplative, and thus, free of doubt.

"You have the vo Chaumelle name, but what sort of stuff are you actually made of? Is it sound, or rotten at core? Are you one of us at all?"

Not entirely, now or ever.

The Great Invocation to Aoun rose, strong in the night. The sound spurred him, and he began walking. Nobody heeded or hindered him. Unmeasured time passed, the riotous streets streamed by, and he hardly noted his own progress, until at last he passed beneath writhing stone serpents, through the Python Gates and into the crooked alleyways of the Old City. The world was narrow and dim for a while, then it suddenly expanded, for he had reached the open expanse of Jaya, the Heart. There he halted, to gaze once more upon the Fastness of the Gods.

13

The gates stood wide open, as always. Crossing Jaya, he walked beneath the carven ushtra to discover the temple courtyard thronged as he had never seen it. Hordes of the faithful had gathered in this place to worship at the foot of Aoun-Father's great sculpted image. The crimson light of the temple lamps washed hundreds of crouching figures, and the air buzzed with pious chants.

Upon the occasion of his first visit, weeks earlier, he had crawled to the base of the statue, pausing often en route to press the pavement with his lips. Tonight, the crowd's density relieved him of that necessity. The area about the marble Father was solidly carpeted with humanity. He could stay where he was, or lose himself in the restless tide of new arrivals circling the courtyard in search of unoccupied space.

He joined the wanderers, edging slowly along the inner face of the wall, working his way by gradual degrees to the quiet southwest corner of the courtyard, where the stink of rotten refuse discouraged loitering. And there was the door he remembered so well, the one whereby he had last exited, pursued by wivoori. The door would be locked now, but an AounSon probably stood guard within.

Drawing the aetheric conflation from his zhupur, he

exercised his mind, as he had been taught, and the artifact began to glow. When its light waxed strong and steady, he commenced tapping his fingernails upon the closed portal, communicating in the voiceless language of the temple. The sequence of clicks, requesting admittance, was standard among the neophytes of JiPhaindru, and would, with any luck, snag the unseen guard's interest.

The door opened. A massive AounSon towered upon the threshold. Catching the beam of the other's attention within the Irriulen mirror, Renille bounced the mental energy back upon its source, and the guard was instantly transfixed, lost in rapt self-contemplation.

Sidestepping the petrified obstacle, Renille entered JiPhaindru. He was sweat-soaked and breathing hard. A human mind, even of the dullest, offered considerable resistance to magical manipulation, and the effort had drained him. But the sense of wonder, the thrill of almost savage triumph, were as he remembered—even better than he remembered—and the eternal lure of sorcery was at that moment utterly comprehensible.

Sorcery was only a word, of course. A term designed to overawe the ignorant. There was nothing supernatural under the sun, or so he assured himself.

And—It?

There was a rational explanation. Somewhere.

He stood once more within the infernally lit stone corridors of nightmare recollection, and realized then that some part of him had deeply hoped to find the place impregnable. But he was in, and now it remained to locate and eliminate KhriNayd-Son, if possible.

He did not want to locate KhriNayd-Son. The First Priest was something other than human, and the memory of that alien intellect dominant in his own mind, however briefly, was enough to shrivel resolve. Too well, he recalled his own impotence and fear. Above all other things, he remembered his clear sense of KhriNayd-Son's amusement.

Yes, he feared the First Priest, almost as much as he wanted to kill him.

The tranced guard would soon regain his senses. He'd better wake to find himself alone. Renille hurried on along the corridor, and his feet seemed to remember the way, for they carried him unerringly downward; down the galleries, down the tiny, slime-slicked stairways where red lamplight gave way to tremulous green *heedrishe;* through the gaping mouth of Aoun-Father's gigantic mask, and down, down to the region of undulant passageways that poor Chura had called "below."

This, the very core of JiPhaindru, was his hunting ground, KhriNayd-Son's natural habitat.

Natural?

He did not greatly fear discovery, for his disguise would protect him through such chance encounters likely to occur within the space of a single night. But it was never put to the test, for he met nobody. Other than the guard at the door, he had glimpsed not a single AounSon.

Curious. At night, the robed priests customarily roamed JiPhaindru, but they were invisible now. Only once had he found the corridors so deserted—upon the evening that the temple population had gathered in the Assembly to witness the Renewal. Were they there again tonight?

Images of that ceremony burned in his mind. Try as he would, he couldn't exclude them. For a time he walked, blind to his immediate surroundings.

It passed. He found himself facing the door that Chura had called "Chosen." Beyond, presumably, lay the communal prison of the wretched girl-children, ripening to serviceable puberty. No sound within. This time, the door was unbarred. Upon impulse, he cracked it open, and applied his eye to the gap. He saw a large, dim chamber, something like a barracks or one of the more ascetic of boarding schools, with sleeping pallets lined up in rows along the walls. The pallets were unoccupied, the room empty of tenants. Strange. It had been his impression that the Filial kept this preserve well stocked.

Closing the door, he walked on until he reached the Assembly, where he paused again. The door was shut, but through it he could hear the drone of the Great Invocation; a sound to stir the hairs at the back of his neck. For a moment reality slipped, and he was back in the past, about to witness the ceremony of Renewal, and this time he knew what was to come but was helpless as a ghost to prevent it. The chant was strong, the voices numerous. Except for the few AounSons assigned guard duty, they must all be in there. Within him twitched some lunatic inclination to join them.

To get one clear shot at KhriNayd, when he appears. Suicidal, but effective.

Possibly. But that was hardly the basis of his urge, he realized. Should he enter the Assembly, taking his place among the self-renouncing faithful, he would never fire that shot at KhriNayd-Son. This time he would be absorbed, his identity annihilated. Worse, the Filial might well permit him to live on, afterward.

KhriNayd-Son's image filled his mental vision, and he recalled the brilliant Irriuliana decking the priestly robes. His own recent mastery of Ziloor's aetheric conflation had taught him the power of such artifacts. KhriNayd must be permitted no opportunity to invoke—for want of a better word—magic.

The First Priest had to be close at hand. In the Assembly? Not yet. The Renewal was still in its early phase.

Renille forced his feet to move. The Assembly was behind him now, and the Great Invocation was losing its sinister immediacy. He turned a corner, and the sound died. Then there was another of those innumerable doors before him, and this one was distinctive, with its shaky outline and its wavy, mal-de-mer surface. A hint of luminosity teased the edges. "Glorification," Chura had called this one.

He paused to look, and caught the sound of sobbing. Child's voice? No, a woman's; some pathetic, mentally stunted Chosen, awaiting divine visitation. Best to ignore her, no time for her now—

But somehow his hands were moving, to lift the bar and open the door. He glimpsed green *heedrishe* flickering upon a frozen expanse of black waves, and then the Ghochanna Jathondi stumbled forth and fell into his arms. A puff of poisonously sweet air followed her.

For a moment he thought himself dreaming, drugged by the very atmosphere of this place. But the slight, shaking form pressed against him was substantial, the tears were wet, and she was certainly real. Holding her tightly, he blurted the first words that entered his mind.

"Your mother handed you over to these people?"

"No, of course not. She wouldn't." She looked up at him. Her breathing was distressed, but already, the sobs were subsiding. " 'These people?' Is it VaiPradh? Are we in JiPhaindru?"

"Yes."

"Thought so. Wasn't sure, though."

"Are you all right?"

"Frightened. Otherwise well enough."

"How did you come here?"

"They just plucked me up off the street, almost within sight of the Vonahrish Residency, and carried me to this place. It was night, nobody noticed. I never saw them. Must have been priests, nobody else would have dared."

"You were alone?"

She nodded.

"Why? What were you doing out on the streets of ZuLaysa by yourself?"

"I ran from OodPray. I had to. Mother had locked me up, you know. She was threatening to marry me off to NiraDhar of Dharahule."

"The Merry Multiple-Marriage Monarch."

"I don't find it funny."

"Neither do I. So you escaped?"

"Yes. Let myself down from the window on knotted sheets."

"When?"

"When—" She briefly pressed both hands to her eyes. "I'm not sure, exactly. When did you leave? Not long after that."

"That was a while. You've been in here all that time?"

"I suppose I must. I've been in this room—it's very confusing."

"Has anyone hurt you?"

"Not physically. Nobody's touched me, or even threatened harm. In fact, I haven't even seen anyone, or talked to anyone—although I've heard them, heard their voices all the time. They're never still, it's enough to drive you mad. It *would* have driven me mad, I think, if I hadn't torn cloth off my skirt and made myself some earplugs. Not very good ones, but they helped. Even with the plugs, though, there were still all those distorted faces, all around me, everywhere, and—and—you're looking at me strangely. You think I'm demented, don't you?"

"No."

"Yes, you do. I know all this is coming out in a jumble, I know it sounds mad, but—"

"Jathondi. I don't think you're demented, although it wouldn't be surprising if you were, after all they've done to you. I think that you're exhausted and distraught, and I think I'd like to kill those responsible. Perhaps I might manage a little something along those lines," he added in an undertone.

She relaxed a little, drew a couple of deep breaths, and her trembling ceased. "When the door opened and I saw you, I thought my mind *had* snapped," she confessed. "I had dreamt of it so often, that I thought I must be dreaming again, while awake."

It will be all right, he wanted to tell her, but did not, for she deserved better than lies.

"And I've done a fair job of driving myself mad," she continued, "what with wondering endlessly what might have happened if I'd been more clever and alert that night—wondering if I might not have made it to the Residency—"

"You were headed for the Residency?"

"Seemed best. For political asylum, you understand."

"Then you didn't know that the place is under siege? Surrounded by an angry mob, and shut up tight as a clam."

"So, when you returned from OodPray, you couldn't enter there."

"I returned before the siege started, and got in easily. I've been serving the defense since the night of the first attack."

"My mind is not working properly. It's that room—" She gestured, but did not turn her head to look back into the Glorification. "I don't seem to understand how or why you could be here now."

"Because I can pass myself off as an Aveshquian, I was

able to leave the Residency tonight by way of the sappers' tunnels. As for the reason—I've come here to kill the Filial's First Priest. It's the single act, most destructive to the entire cult, that I can conceive. I hope you aren't shocked."

"It only shocks me that you've thrown away so much for so little. You escaped the Residency. You could have got clean out of ZuLaysa, and you could have been safe. Instead, you've chosen to come back here—and all to kill a single man?"

"You haven't encountered KhriNayd-Son, I see. He's something remarkable, and his loss will cripple VaiPradh."

"It is still a poor bargain. Go ahead and kill their leader, if you can. But what good will that do, as long as the god—or elephant, or whatever It really is—remains among us? You'll only anger Aoun-Father, to no purpose."

"There is a purpose. I've looked upon the being called Aoun. He exists. But in all these years that we Vonahrish have dwelled in Aveshq, Aoun has never personally manifested Himself. Perhaps He's been somnolent, or inattentive, or simply indifferent. But He has never shown Himself outside this temple, and His work is performed by human agency. Lately, His human servants have proved too zealous for comfort. Remove their leader, and Filial activity subsides, for a time. Perhaps Aoun-Father will then resume His interrupted sleep."

"Or perhaps you'll call divine wrath down upon all of Aveshq."

"Half dead with fright and fatigue, and you can still debate."

"On the other hand," Jathondi continued, "the two of us might still escape JiPhaindru, escape ZuLaysa altogether. It isn't too late for that."

"I'm afraid it is, for me," he told her. "I used the Irriulen reflector to daze the guard at the door, when I came in. He'll have recovered by now, alerted others, and they'll be looking for me."

"You still have the reflector?"

"Won't have the chance to use it, a second time. And wouldn't if I could. But I can give the thing to you. You heard your mother's instructions. You might escape the temple, on your own. And then, when you're out, you can—" He paused.

"Yes? I can—? Marry NiraDhar of Dharahule, perhaps? Trot on over to Little Sherreen, to watch the mob obliterate the Vonahrish Residency? Seek employment as a chahsu?"

"You might go anywhere, do anything you want."

"Without a zinnu to my name?"

"Impossible. You must have resources—family, friends. You are a Ghochanna of Kahnderule, and Effulgent, after all."

"Not if Mother disinherits me. As my parent, and head of our House, she has the traditional right to withdraw name and Order."

She was a pauper and an outcast, he realized, because of him. She had fled OodPray, fallen into the hands of the Filial, also because of him. Her chances of survival were slight. Should she somehow manage to flee the temple, her young life was nonetheless blasted, because of him. There was a pressure inside his chest, but no chance to dwell on it, because she was still talking.

"But this is all beside the point," observed Jathondi. "I hate the Filial for what they have done to me, to my mother, and my country. While I have been held in that room there, the hatred has kept my mind from crumbling into a million fragments. If the loss of their First Priest is devastating as you believe, then I welcome the chance to assist in his destruction. And now, I am the one to hope that you are not shocked."

"A little." *That slip of a girl is made of steel.*

"Beyond that," she continued, "there is you. Above all things, I would wish for your safety. But you will not abandon your plan. I cannot change your mind, it is useless to go on trying, and therefore I am free to answer a question you once asked of me."

"I recall the question."

"Probably, at such a moment, you spoke without thought."

"Entirely without thought, but very much from the heart. Afterward, I was astonished at my own presumption. Is this the time for discussion?"

"When else?" Receiving no reply, she went on, "My answer to your question is yes. I will go with you now."

Too late, he thought, and yet an inappropriate happiness momentarily warmed him.

"We will be together as long as we may be," Jathondi went on. "Our lives will be as one, and together we will kill this KhriNayd-Son."

"What?"

"Together we will kill—"

"No. It's unthinkable."

"You do not want my help?"

"No."

"But you won't come away from JiPhaindru with me now?"

"I can't."

"Then it is clear that I misinterpreted your question."

"You misinterpreted nothing. 'We will be together as long as we may be.' That is what I want, but you can't join me in this."

"We are together, and yet I may not join you. That is logic I do not comprehend. I am Effulgent, and the offer of my life is not to be mocked."

"That's the last thing I'd do. Do you think I'd expect you to soil your hands with blood?"

"Ah, Renille." She actually smiled. "This is western naïveté."

"Have you considered what could happen to you?"

"Nothing insupportable. I am quite safe. Look—" Her hand dropped to her zhupur, and the tiny sash bodkin materialized. "There is my release and escape, any time I choose to avail myself of it. You are welcome to share, should the need arise. So, you see, there is nothing to fear."

"I see." Remorse and admiration warred within him. "Put it away. You win. Your mother was wrong, by the way. Vonahrish education notwithstanding, you are still Aveshquian."

"Always." The blade returned to its resting place. "Mother wouldn't see it that way, but she's unlikely to give the matter any further thought. She has set me from her, and buried my memory. By now, Mother has surely forgotten that I ever existed."

"Vile." The Ghochalla Xundunisse's hands clenched on the arms of her chair. Her gaze charred the blank wall before her. "Vile. Unspeakably vile."

She was not aware that she spoke aloud. She did not know whether she had eaten, or drunk, or slept, throughout the last several days. She supposed she must have done these things, else she would be sick, but the recollection was gone and, in any case, irrelevant. There was no room in her mind for anything beyond the image of her daughter's face, the vision of her daughter's horrific destruction, and the terror of it.

VaiPradh's letter lay open on the desk before her, but she did not glance down at it. Every word was branded upon her memory.

They would torture Jathondi to death. They had promised as much. Her own compliance would purchase her daughter's life, perhaps, but not her freedom. They would never part with so valuable a hostage. Jathondi would live on, imprisoned somewhere within JiPhaindru's stony depths, her existence forever contingent upon her mother's obedience to Filial dictates. The Ghochalla of Kahnderule, already deprived of all wealth and glory by the Vonahrish invaders, would sacrifice the last remaining rag of sovereignty—the moral authority accorded her by her subjects, and the freedom to wield it—and thereafter, VaiPradh would rule in all things.

"Vile," she muttered again, unconsciously.

Savages, butchers, merciless fanatics. Worse even than the Vonahrish, if such a thing were possible. Aveshquian, yet scarcely human. And worse—yes, it was true—worse even than the Vonahrish. Jathondi had been right about that.

Murderers, madmen, demons—and would the Ghochalla of Kahnderule submit to them?

In a heartbeat. There was nothing she wouldn't do, Xundunisse had come to realize over the course of these lost days—nothing she wouldn't sacrifice, no humiliation she wouldn't endure—to save her daughter's life.

Only her daughter wouldn't want her to.

She could picture Jathondi's face so clearly, almost hear her voice:

"I should throw myself upon a blazing pyre, and do so joyously, if I thought my torture and death might serve Kahnderule."

She had spoken those very words, and meant them. Jathondi detested the Filial, would rather die than see them rule her country, would rather die under torture than serve their interests.

She would despise a life purchased at such a price. And what a life it would be—mewed up forever in the Fastness of the Gods. Imprisoned, exploited, abused, perhaps for decades to come. She would not want it.

What would she want?

If she were here, if she could express an opinion, she'd beg her mother on bended knee to fire off a white-hot refusal. A dozen times at least, Xundunisse had taken up her pen, had even written out a sentence or two—only to halt, her hand incapable of tracing the phrases of Jathondi's death sentence. She found herself equally incapable of penning an assent to the implied demands. Thus, the days passed, and she did nothing.

Under other circumstances, she would have sought assistance of the Vonahrish. Yes, the Ghochalla reflected, she would actually have gone to her enemies, and no consideration of personal dignity or self-respect would have stopped her from pleading humbly, even abjectly, for the Ghochanna's rescue. She would have kissed vo Trouniere's feet, or the floor beneath his feet, if necessary.

An ironic thing it was, now that she was finally willing to abase herself, that option no longer existed. The besieged Vonahrish Residency, and all its inhabitants, were clearly doomed. And if the western soldiers should come at some future date to avenge the massacre of their countrymen, they should find all of ZuLaysa, and perhaps all of Kahnderule, up in arms.

No, the Vonahrish could not help Jathondi now.

But there were Others who might, should They prove

willing. Others, whose power infinitely exceeded human force, either Vonahrish or Aveshquian. The royal House of Kahnderule had enjoyed the favor of the lesser gods since the days of Shirardhir the Superb. Shirardhir's descendants possessed the right to call upon their divine allies, in the name of ancient friendship, once in a human generation. It was not a right to be invoked lightly, for the temper of Irriule was unpredictable at best, and a frivolous or unworthy summons might well sever the connection, once and for all. Certainly, in all these years, the family members had never abused their privilege. Quite the contrary; through extreme respect, or caution, or downright fear, they'd habitually eschewed magical meddling.

They had shunned it so consistently that all recollection of Irriulen contact had long since faded, and therein lay the trouble. Xundunisse herself, having received appropriate instruction from her own sire, decades earlier, had never in her life made practical use of it. Nor had her father, in his day; nor yet her father's father. In fact, Ood-Pray Palace contained no evidence verifying an occurrence of divine communication subsequent to the day that Shirardhir the Superb had closed the portal behind his radiant departing visitors.

No one had ever dared to call upon Them.

Perhaps the royal claim upon Their friendship had died unnoticed, long ago. Perhaps the feeble importunings of humanity would weary Them. Perhaps the mortal presumption would even rouse Their wrath. But worse, far worse to contemplate, was the possibility of silence.

There was always the chance that a royal salutation and summons, ostensibly winging straight to Irriule, would encounter—nothingness. Silence, emptiness, a limitless void. That, in the depths of her heart, was what she had always feared.

If nothing was there, and there was nothing—no gods, or else, gods so unreachably remote that They might just as well not exist—then she did not want to know. If the structure of her beliefs was founded upon delusion—if life was devoid of cosmic purpose, and utterly meaningless— she most certainly did not want to know. So long as she did not know, hope persisted. Perhaps her ancestors had felt the same, for none of them had ever tested their power. Not even with the advent of the Vonahrish invasion; not even with the decline of the family fortunes; not even with the decay of the incomparable OodPray.

She had never intended to disturb that equilibrium. She had shied away from the very thought of it. But now, with Jathondi dead or worse, unless her paralyzed mother intervened, there could be no further evasion.

Time to move. More than time.

She stood. Her joints were stiff, she had not stirred in many hours. She looked around. Outside, it was dark. Several lamps illumined her chamber. Paro must have come in to light them, at dusk. She hadn't been aware of his presence. A tray of food sat on the desk before her. It was the first time she had noticed it there. She wasn't hungry, but her mouth was parched. She drank deeply of cool lemon-water, then rose, took up a lamp, and walked from the room.

Through the corridors she hurried, through the moldering chambers of state and down the stairs, down to Shirardhir's Sanctum. She recited the rhyming password, and the Listening Lock yielded. She hesitated, then tightened her jaw and went in, shutting the door behind her. She hadn't entered this room since the dreadful afternoon of her daughter's exposure. She had thought never to come here again.

Immense, silent, uncanny—Shirardhir's Sanctum never changed, throughout the ages. For a moment she stood drinking the shadowy atmosphere, and then she set to work. Her movements were precise and swift, for there was much to do. Never once did she pause to consult the notebooks and folios lining the shelves, for the entire complex procedure was engraved upon her mind, so deeply and sharply that each successive detail seemed obvious, and all but inevitable.

It was all so natural, so effortless, she could hardly believe she had never done it before. And it was beautiful, in its way. Another time, another world, and she would have been enjoying herself.

Now, the instruments and substances were assembled. Now, the mind-enhancing potion had been mixed and ingested. Now, the dawning light within signaled her readiness to set consciousness against ordinary physical limitation. Now, the hellish fires kindled within the pit-of-elements were heating the substance of the human plane to the requisite level of instability.

The preparations were complete, the preliminaries concluded. The Ghochalla drew a deep breath, and then she began to speak, almost singing the words designed to facilitate those mental contortions that freed awareness of material bondage, the words that cleared the lens through which consciousness focused to a single incandescent point, the words she had thought to teach one day to her child, as her father had taught them to her—

No time now for regrets.

Her mind encountered resistance, and attacked. It was good to express the pent anger of so many years. The rage lent power, and she smashed through all obstacles in a matter of seconds. The weakened substance of the human dimension gave way before her. She felt something rip, knew the anguish of a metaphysical wound, and then there was new space, never there before, and it was boundless. There was infinity around her and within her, and the Ghochalla Xundunisse knew that the door had opened.

She opened her eyes. At the rear of the room, the glyphs marking the stones of the archway glowed. Beyond the archway, within the region of impenetrable darkness dawned—Radiance. Before her yawned the gateway to Irriule, land of the gods.

She narrowed her eyes against the light, but never averted her gaze. The ancient words of salutation and of summons burst from her lips.

Her voice died away. There was silence, and insupportable brilliance, and more silence. The ensuing interval defied quantification. To the Ghochalla Xundunisse, it was an eternity; perhaps, by other standards, it was more.

She waited, and the light beyond the archway fed the hope inside her. She waited and then, at last, the light or some component of it started to move, flooding in luminous waves through the open doorway. Terror filled her, but she stood her ground. Motionless, she watched as the formless waves began to resolve themselves into discrete, dazzling forms. Impossible to look straight at them for more than a moment—they were too brilliant for human eyes, too alien for human minds. The Ghochalla blinked, and caught her breath in a sob. But the tears that wet her face blended pain and joy, for now, at last, she knew beyond all doubt that They existed, to fill the universe with meaning. They were here, They were real, They were with her. She could even recognize several of Them. There was Hrushiiki—Nuumahni Heaven-Dancer—Ahrattah—and others, but she couldn't quite make Them out; the forms were too diverse, and too bewildering.

Shirardhir's Sanctum, spacious though it was, could not possibly contain such vastness; and yet, somehow, it did. The substance of the gods, clearly transcending the limitations of natural law, seemed capable of altering worldly space, time, energy, and matter as required. The resulting distortions all but confounded human perception.

The Ghochalla Xundunisse was forced to lower her eyes. She could no longer bear to look upon Them, but she felt Their presence, more strongly than ever; felt Their detached graciousness, and Their mild, impersonal curiosity.

She dropped to her knees. For a moment, her voice stuck in her throat, and then the words fought their way out.

"Divinities of Irriule, I implore you. Save my daughter."

They had left the Glorification behind. They were descending a short flight of stairs, and Renille remembered this place, the weight and smell of its dim air. At the bottom, they emerged into a small gallery to confront an ancient wooden door, sunk deep in polished stone. Jathondi pushed the door open, and they looked in upon an empty Wisdom.

The far end of the gallery cloaked itself in darkness. There yawned the deeper concentration of shadow marking the entrance to the place that Chura had called Holiest. Chura, he recalled, had been scared to death of it.

He took Jathondi's hand, and they advanced. The

darkness swallowed them, and then it spoke. Its voice was ancient, metallic, and reverberant. The voice of the darkness was the voice of KhriNayd-Son.

"They are gathered, in readiness," declared the First Priest. He spoke in Old Churdishu.

The hairs rose at the back of Renille's neck.

There was no audible reply.

"They await Your coming."

Still no reply. Renille glanced at his companion. No good. She was invisible, lost in shadow. But her hand in his was warm and steady.

"Every priest-of-the-light, every female flesh-vessel. All of them await You," KhriNayd promised. "Their inner radiance will nourish and restore You. Their sacrifice will make You whole. Enormity, will you accept the offering?"

Silence.

"Hear me, Aoun-Father."

Silence.

"*Hear me.*"

Oddly, Renille fancied to catch a note of human emotion—urgency or even fear—in the First Priest's impossible voice. Present only for an instant. When next KhriNayd spoke, his tones were characteristically assured.

"Enormity. Tonight's Renewal marks the full resurgence of Your splendor, and the first of the female vessels destined to contain Your rekindled light cannot restrain her eagerness. Hungry for her Glorification, she has come unto Your presence—even now, she waits upon the threshold. With her waits another, likewise yearning to lose himself in You. I pray you, grant their desires.

"You two who stand in darkness are welcome here." KhriNayd-Son now spoke in Vonahrish. "Enter."

14

Renille heard the hiss of Jathondi's sharply indrawn breath, and felt the startled tightening of her hand. His own heart accelerated, and he drew the revolver. He could see nothing, but the weight of the weapon in his grasp reassured.

Together they advanced through unrelieved blackness. There seemed to be no solid doorway into the Holiest, but only an intense distillation of shadow, guarding the entrance. The density of the air was extraordinary, its weight a burden upon his lungs. Then the darkness relented a little, and he descried the outline of Jathondi's profile. They walked on, and the light strengthened, and at length they came upon its source.

The First Priest KhriNayd-Son stood motionless, tall figure swathed in voluminous robes, face concealed behind a mask of beaten gold. A dozen glowing Irriulen artifacts decked his chest and shoulders, while greenish light glared from the apertures in his mask. The pale nimbus revealed the priest, a small patch of the dank stone floor beneath him, and nothing more. Beyond the radius of that strange luminescence, the Holiest vanished in darkness.

Renille and Jathondi stood in shadow, yet obviously visible and exposed to their host.

Exposed, inside and out. Energy crackled the atmosphere, power blazed from the First Priest's amulets, and Renille sensed the pressure of alien consciousness impinging upon his own, as he had felt it once before, upon the nightmarish occasion of the Renewal. Somehow, despite his vigilance, that awareness had slipped straight through his mental guard, lodging itself deep within. An intolerable invasion. Internally, he burned, but passion wouldn't help him. Now, as then, a perfect mastery of self was the key to self-defense. Upon that night, his recollection of Ziloor's teachings had served him, but now, face to face with KhriNayd-Son in the very heart of JiPhaindru, the Palace of Light seemed unreachably distant. Perhaps he might remember the way back, if only he could focus his thoughts, but KhriNayd was speaking again—inside his head?—and concentration was impossible.

"We have long expected your return," observed KhriNayd, metallic tones at once human and inhuman.

Unthinkable to disbelieve him. The words, the voice, flew straight to his center. Or else, originated there.

"There was no need of secrecy."

Beyond question, the voice spoke inside his head. His alarm and resistance ebbed. The sense of mental contact had frightened him with its unfamiliarity, but he was growing used to it. He had been like a child, terrified of the unknown, but now he was learning, his mind was expanding. Clearly the First Priest intended no harm, and never had.

"You have always been welcome here. There is no limitation to your welcome."

Renille was a little ashamed. He had assumed the worst of Filial and Father. All of the Vonahrish did so, without just cause. They had been narrow, deeply prejudiced, ignorant, and blind. But it wasn't too late to change.

"Never too late," KhriNayd assured him.

How could he ever have thought that thrilling voice anything less than symphonic?

"The Father's love embraces all mankind. His love will make you whole. In losing yourself to Him, you find yourself at last."

There was, some shred of his mind suspected, something wrong with this, but he didn't know what. Probably nothing, a remnant of his groundless fears.

"Here, you will find the unity you seek." The voice lodged deeper yet, delving below surface layers of intellect. "Here, you will know the Source and Finality. Here, is your Father, offering purpose, certainty, peace, belonging. Here, vo Chaumelle, is your home."

He could have wept at the beauty of it. KhriNayd-Son and he were part of one another, the two of them in turn part of something infinitely larger, deeper, and older. The link was strong and mutual, and somewhere behind the First Priest's benevolence he sensed something—unquiet— but he couldn't identify it, couldn't glimpse it clearly, because there was some sort of external disturbance, something distracting him—

The girl beside him was shaking him, tugging at his arm, even poking his ribs. She wanted his attention. She seemed upset. He had no idea why. She was very intrusive, and he wished she'd disappear.

"Renille. Renille." She pinched him, hard.

She was annoyingly persistent, quite impossible to ignore.

"Renille, what's the matter with you? Wake up! Renille!" She had her hand up under his hat, and she was pulling at his hair.

"Renille, *please!*"

She thought there was something wrong, that was her trouble. Obviously her intentions were good, but she just didn't understand. Perhaps, if he explained things to her, she'd shut up and leave him alone.

"Say something!" This time, she slapped his face stingingly.

It was too much. She went too far. He gasped, and the anger rose in him, to crack the contact with KhriNayd-Son. He was isolated and incomplete again, and she—this meddlesome, blundering girl—was responsible. The rage flashed, and he came within an ace of slapping her back, but managed to restrain himself. She'd meant well, after all, and obviously hadn't the faintest idea of the harm she'd done. He grew conscious, then, of a faint surprise. Strike a woman? And not just any woman—Jathondi.

Strike Jathondi? Where had that foreign impulse, those thoughts, come from? They weren't his. Fear quelled the heat in his blood, and he was more or less himself again. She was still pulling his hair.

"Stop it," he told her dully, and she obeyed at once.

"What happened?"

"Nothing."

"You've been standing here, mumbling to yourself!"

"I was listening."

"To what? To what?"

"The female flesh-vessels do not experience oneness," KhriNayd stated, and this time there could be no doubt that he spoke aloud, for Jathondi gasped at the sound. "Their minds are not sufficiently evolved. Nevertheless, their bodies are of use."

"Remember why we are here," Jathondi urged in a whisper.

Why we are here. Something violent, something dark, but he didn't quite recall it.

"Remember the peace of self-renunciation," Khri-Nayd counseled. "Remember the beauty."

He did remember. The voice no longer spoke inside his head, but its power was not broken, and he remembered. There was something more, however; something he had sensed in KhriNayd's mind, moments earlier, but he couldn't quite grasp it. He was advancing toward the light, and the still figure at its center. The figure seemed to grow as he approached, until it towered before him, immense, and dazzling, and semidivine.

"Renille, what are you doing?" Jathondi was still beside him.

What *was* he doing? Confused, he halted. The Palace of Light was continents away, far beyond his reach. Vonahrish logic similarly offered no refuge. There was no support, and no anchor. The hand that grasped the gun shook.

"Renille. Give the revolver to me." Jathondi spoke very calmly. "Can you hear? Give the revolver to me."

"He will not obey you." For the first time, KhriNayd-Son addressed her directly, and she started as if electricity shot through her. "He will not be led astray, he will not be corrupted by you, for he has found his truest self."

The First Priest's voice held absolute certainty, along with the note of subtle amusement that Renille had encountered once before. No hint now of the doubt, the urgency verging on desperation, audible moments earlier.

"He has discovered infinity," KhriNayd concluded. "He has found the Father."

That final word—so recently pronounced in very different accents—echoing in his mind—

And the elusive perception was recaptured. This time, he did not let it escape.

"You called upon the Father, when you were alone," Renille heard himself observe slowly. "And He did not answer."

The glare behind the mask intensified. There was no other reply.

"He did not hear you," Renille continued, recalling those fleeting revelations of shared awareness. "Or else, He did not care. Perhaps He has forgotten you."

The Irriulen artifacts burning upon the black robes flickered like guttering candles. Some slight measure of mutual sympathy between himself and the First Priest must have persisted, for a winter gust of fearful desolation briefly chilled him. For a moment, he sensed a bitterly solitary pain amounting to despair. Then the flickering of the Irriuliana gave way to a renewed and concentrated brilliance, while desolation yielded to an elemental anger that blasted the last remnant of connection, once and for all.

Renille found himself autonomous again, whole and mentally intact, though drained. Before him loomed the First Priest, ablaze with otherworldly light. He could feel the heat of it across the space that separated the two of them.

"You are unworthy." Never had KhriNayd's voice sounded less human. Anger whetted the metallic tones to a knife edge. "And unwise."

Renille was silent.

"The world has finished with you, and your fellow interlopers. Your time is done. Tonight, the sleeping Father awakens to the greatest of all Renewals. The light and lives of hundreds will restore Him to His former splendor."

"Perhaps He will only sleep on," Renille suggested, recognizing the other's sole weakness. His own voice gathered strength. "Perhaps He will never awaken."

"Tonight He resumes His full glory. Thus renewed, He will mold this Nether plane to His liking."

"But will He consent to remain here? Perhaps He will choose to withdraw."

"He will create a new and vital order of AounSons, their bodies and minds replete with the essence of Radiance, that humans call Irriule. These new priests-of-the-light, His children and His servants, born of human females, shall lead His armies, here in Netherness."

"Has He not already abandoned you, First Priest? Are you not alone here?"

KhriNayd's Irriuliana wavered once more, and steadied. When he spoke again, the note of amusement, or mockery, had returned. "The flesh-vessel at your side, graced with royal blood regarded by humans as pure, will serve as container to the first of a remarkable new generation. Her Glorification is imminent. The substance of Radiance, implanted within her, will flourish and expand. In the consuming agonies of her final dissolution, the vessel may take comfort in the knowledge that her male offspring, son of the god Aoun, will live on, to serve the Father's will throughout the ages. Thus, fortunate and blessed above all others of her kind, her name will be honored forever among the faithful."

Renille was speechless, but Jathondi never hesitated.

"I will not allow that to happen," she replied evenly.

KhriNayd ignored her as if she had not spoken. The greenish glare that was his gaze remained fixed on Renille alone, as he resumed, "The dawning age will witness the Father's ultimate triumph. His worship will grow and spread across this land known as Aveshq, and then, into the world beyond. In the immediate future, those insolent foreigners presuming to meddle in the holiest of mysteries will flee Aveshq, or die. For you, vo Chaumelle, that choice has already been made."

KhriNayd-Son was motionless and silent for the moment or two required to focus the power of his glowing artifacts. He neither gestured, nor spoke aloud. Evidently, such an intellect functioned effectively without recourse to the hoary trappings of traditional sorcery. Or so Renille inferred, as he watched the First Priest's already lucent Irriuliana flare to a new and overwhelming brilliance.

The atmosphere ignited, and the Holiest was suddenly a furnace, filled with lightless flame. He was burning in it, dying in it. He gulped lethal air, and the fires shot down his throat, and the scream of pain that sought utterance found no outlet, yet there were shrill cries, echoing wildly—

Jathondi's. She was calling his name, she was reaching out to him—his eyes, miraculously, hadn't been seared, yet—but she couldn't touch him, couldn't even get close. An outstretched hand approached, recoiled, and he heard her wordless shriek. But she herself appeared uninjured. The invisible flames lapped him alone, and she was still safe—

Safe?

He could see the backs of his hands blistering. His lightweight garments were starting to smolder. His lungs labored vainly. But somehow, perhaps through some refinement of the First Priest's malice, he remained fully conscious.

Conscious of the gun, still clasped in one hand. Raising the weapon, he fired. At such range, even in his agony, he could scarcely miss. The bullet took KhriNayd-Son full in the chest.

The robed figure rocked slightly under the impact, and the amulets dimmed for a fraction of a second. The wound should have been fatal, but the First Priest stood firm, apparently untroubled, Irriuliana blindingly alight.

Renille squeezed off a second accurate shot, and this time, his enemy did not so much as flinch, nor did the brilliance of the amulets abate in the slightest. Perhaps the First Priest wore some sort of bulletproof armor beneath his robes, but his head could not be similarly protected. Renille fired again, straight into the golden mask, and again, his aim was good. The thin beaten gold yielded easily, and a new aperture appeared between the eyeholes.

Light beamed from the orifice, but KhriNayd-Son never faltered.

Impossible. Hallucinations, fever dreams. Almost spasmodically, he yanked the trigger, and the shot went wide. His blistered hand was quivering. With effort, he managed to steady it, before loosing another bullet. A fresh, inconsequential hole appeared in the mask. Thereafter, he fired mechanically, until the repeated futile click of the trigger alerted him to an empty cylinder. The useless revolver dropped from his grasp. He stumbled a few paces, vainly seeking escape from the heat, and then collapsed to his knees. He couldn't breathe, for his lungs rejected such air, and the still, impossible figure of the First Priest was starting to soften and blur before his eyes.

He could still see, however. There was room in his mind for a flash of horrified admiration, as he beheld the Ghochanna Jathondi launch herself like some small, infuriated gazelle upon the First Priest KhriNayd-Son. She was wielding that ridiculously tiny sash bodkin of hers, and she had to be mad, or suicidal. Did she imagine for one moment that a blade not much larger than a corsage pin would damage a being capable of withstanding bullets fired at point-blank range?

Out! Run! Mentally he shouted at her, but no sound emerged.

She'd better be going for the throat. It was the only possible point of vulnerability to such a weapon as hers, but she'd never succeed, she hadn't a chance, she'd only get herself killed—

Perhaps that was just her intention.

Helplessly he watched as she flung herself forward, to ply her bodkin once, very swiftly, nowhere near KhriNayd's throat. A single short, almost horizontal slash, and the silken cord binding one of the brightest of the Irriulen artifacts to the black robes gave way. A great aetheric conflation fell to the floor. No sooner had it slipped from its owner's person, than its radiance died.

She managed to detach and darken a second conflation, before KhriNayd-Son immobilized her wrist. Without haste, he twisted the bodkin from her hand. Effortlessly he lifted her, holding her at arm's length as if she were all but weightless. For a moment she squirmed and kicked in his grasp, before he hurled her from him. Jathondi flew through the air, and hit the stone floor hard.

The attack and its repulsion lasted no more than seconds, but they were enough to reveal the nature of her intentions, which were desperate, but neither mad nor suicidal. The disposal of two large artifacts of power had brought a distinct diminution in the atmospheric heat that was killing him, and the means of self-preservation was apparent.

Too bad that little knife lay out of reach. And to think he'd considered it a toy.

The air was still torturous, but now he could breathe it. Rising, he lunged at KhriNayd-Son, managed to catch hold of an amulet glowing upon the black-clad shoulder, and yanked sharply. The cord broke, and the bright thing came away in his hand. Its light died even before he'd flung it from him. Then a fleshless hand closed upon his wrist, and he was caught in a grip unbreakable, and indefinably inhuman. He could visualize a skeleton claw beneath the dark glove. The golden mask was too close, the greenish light glaring from the eye holes, the mouth hole, the bullet holes, intense and insupportable. That light would capture his mind again, if he looked too long.

"He does not answer you," Renille struck back in a whisper, and felt the other's free hand close upon his throat.

His struggles were useless at best, and weakening by the moment, but he could still see. A flash of motion behind KhriNayd, and there was Jathondi, back again and plucking Irriuliana from the First Priest's back like a picker stripping forbidden fruit from a poisonous tree. Her speeding hands blurred. She'd got four or five before he spun to face her, whereupon she backed away hastily.

The strangling pressure was gone. Renille staggered, but stayed on his feet. The air about him had resumed its normal state. His throat and lungs ached fiercely, but functioned. His eyes were burning, his vision dimming—Something the matter with his eyes—

He blinked, and the problem resolved itself. There was nothing wrong with his eyes. The First Priest's radiant adornment, sole source of illumination in this place, was much reduced, its luminosity fluctuating wildly.

KhriNayd might have suffered a loss, but he was deadly yet. Jathondi's retreat wasn't fast enough. A couple of long paces, and the First Priest easily overtook her. A backhanded blow of one gloved hand struck her to the floor. And then, it wasn't clear what he was doing, but his remaining amulets blazed like miniature suns, and Jathondi was screaming, her body twisting in spasms.

Scooping the empty revolver from the floor, Renille smashed the butt down on KhriNayd's hooded head, striking again and again, until the lights waned, and Jathondi's outcry ceased. And still, the First Priest seemed unhurt, when he should have been dead a dozen times over. Unhurt, but momentarily slowed—too slow to evade his enemy's darting hand, too slow to guard the source of his power.

Twice, Renille grabbed and pulled. Twice, he came away with an amulet, and now there were only two of them left, burning upon KhriNayd's breast, above his heart, assuming the First Priest possessed such a mundane organ. Only two, their light greatly weakened, but no more extinct than their owner's life-force.

Why doesn't he die? What is he made of?

Steel and smoke, it seemed. Certainly not worldly flesh. Perhaps he couldn't die. Perhaps he was immortal, and invulnerable.

Not altogether.

"He has abandoned you," Renille essayed.

The greenish fire flared behind the mask. He was caught, overpowered, and engulfed in an instant. The flames were licking at his mind, consuming all defenses—

Cognizant of danger, Renille pulled his gaze from the other's eyes. And found himself held fast, two gloved implements of steel gripping his face, turning it back to confront the golden mask, and the greenish glare. The hands were too strong to resist, and perhaps he didn't really want to resist—

The light devoured him, he was lost in it, and the voice was speaking inside his head, again.

"He is here. The Father is with us."

There was something comforting in that. Oddly, some small fragment of his mind rejected such comfort. He couldn't imagine why.

"We are His sons."

It was a beautiful thought. A beautiful voice, that would not lie. How inexplicable, that he had feared and loathed it. A part of him feared and loathed it still, but that part could be disregarded.

Newfound peace was short-lived, however. There was disturbance, disruption, and Jathondi was there again. She'd reclaimed her sash bodkin, and now the tiny blade flashed twice, and the last two amulets fell from KhriNayd's robe. They hit the floor, and the brilliance bled out of them.

For a moment only, the First Priest's sense of piercing loss suffused Renille's consciousness. He stiffened, shuddered, and then his mind was his own again. Only the light glowing from the apertures in the golden mask illumined the Holiest, but it was enough. A snarl escaped him, and he swung the empty revolver at the light with all his strength. The butt struck gold, and KhriNayd lurched. A second blow to the face, fatal to an ordinary mortal, drove him backward a couple of paces. A third staggered him, but failed to conquer monstrous vitality.

"Aoun-Father." KhriNayd-Son spoke aloud, and both listeners jumped. His voice, though much weakened, retained its alien resonance. "Enormity. Hear Your first-born."

"He has abandoned you." Renille struck again. The golden mask shifted under the blow, and KhriNayd sank to his knees.

"Aoun-Father. Answer."

"He does not hear you." The revolver swung in a violent arc.

The mask crumpled and fell away, exposing the face of KhriNayd-Son.

It was an indescribably ancient version of the doomed infants torn from the wombs of Blessed Vessel and Chosen. There were the nightmare eyes, and the luminous teeth. There, the phosphorescent flesh, the misshapen skull, the subtle distortion of lineament shouting of inhuman parentage. So might the sacrificial infants have appeared in suffering maturity, save for one conspicuous divergence. At the center of KhriNayd-Son's forehead, embedded deep in flesh and bone, shone the last and largest of the Irriulen artifacts.

"Enormity." The plea was barely audible. The First Priest slid to the floor. "Enormity."

"Gone forever." Renille turned to Jathondi, and she handed him the knife. "Look away," he told her.

"No."

She watched without flinching as he knelt to pry the luminous object from its impossibly bloodless setting. He tossed it aside, and the artifact flew like a shooting star, to extinguish itself in the shadows.

A faint light shone yet from the First Priest's eyes and mouth. He was smiling. He spoke, in Old Churdishu, but his voice was extinct.

They read his lips.

"Aoun-Father. You are with me. You are here."

He died, and the last light died with him, plunging the Holiest into absolute darkness.

Renille's hand found Jathondi's. For a moment, the two of them were motionless. The surrounding blackness pressed, and the silence ached. Perhaps it was the intensity of darkness that fostered his burgeoning sense of terror. Strange that he should feel it so strongly, now that the greatest of dangers was past. But feel it he did; a sickly flutter in the pit of his stomach, ice in his veins. Jathondi's hand in his was cold and damp. She felt it, too.

It?

He knew then what he feared. Absurd. Save for Jathondi and himself, the Holiest was empty.

Get her out of here.

He rose, senses questing for the exit. But he had no idea where it was, they'd have to feel their way along the walls—

Cogitation was interrupted by Jathondi's gasp, and the convulsive tightening of her hand. His own heart hammered, he was shivering, and he knew the cause even before he turned to confront a vast radiance dawning at the center of the room.

KhriNayd-Son had spoken truly. Aoun-Father was here.

He petrified, gazing in wonder, as he might have stood to observe an approaching tidal wave. But here was no force of mundane nature, nothing of humanity's world. The Father was alien beyond comprehension, huge beyond conception, lucent beyond endurance. No wonder He had been taken for a god.

Renille looked away, unable to support the light or the sight. The form before him, defying physical possibility, warped perception. He'd lose his bearings altogether if he tried to watch It. His eyes were burning and tearing, and still the light intensified, exposing every corner of the Holiest, exposing everything inside him. He heard Jathondi cry out in fear or pain, pulled her to him, and held tight.

It had something roughly akin to a face, a shield-shaped plane of light, marked with greenish regions of concentrated incandescence. That brilliance was focused upon the corpse of KhriNayd-Son.

Aoun's silent howl exploded in Renille's brain, filling him with anguish and madness. It seemed an eternity before the soundless onslaught ceased, leaving him dizzy and dazed, still rocked with internal echoes of the Father's grief. He swayed, and the tears ran down his cheeks. Jathondi was sobbing.

It could not be said that Aoun advanced. Rather, he expanded, substanceless substance swelling to fill the chamber. The two humans stumbled from His path, but He seemed hardly to note their terrified presence. The mask of light that was His face shone on KhriNayd alone. The atmosphere glowed, bathing the corpse in radiance that kindled no responsive light in that dead mind and heart. Energy irradiated the body, enveloped it, and abolished every trace of its existence. The light faded. Nothing remained. The First Priest KhriNayd-Son was gone.

A second soundless primal howl quaked the Holiest. This time, grief gave way to gigantic rage. The elemental force of it battered intellect, smashed reason. The Father's boundless dementia roared.

The stone walls of the Holiest trembled, softened, and

started to flow. The floor quivered, and pitched. Great winds buffeted the chamber.

The Father's attention fixed upon the humans.

To the left, a dark gap in the rippling granite. The exit. Renille flung himself through it. He still had Jathondi's hand, but didn't need to drag her—she'd moved as quickly as he.

There was darkness about them for a moment or two, and then, a flicker of *heedrishe*. But the corridor, the stairway? Nowhere in evidence.

Wrong exit. He didn't know where they were. Jathondi followed him trustingly. She'd no idea that they were lost in a maze of dim and branching passageways.

Behind them, the air shuddered, and he felt the vibrations of the Father's wrath shake his heart. The furious bellows resounded noiselessly. The gales that chased them along the passage were hot, and the walls were starting to glow, but that was all right, for this constricted space offered a kind of refuge. Immense as He was, Aoun-Father could never follow them here.

The little stone capillaries twisted in all directions. He chose one at random, followed it to a fork, and chose again. No sign of the Filial; they were all gathered in the Assembly, awaiting the First Priest who would never appear.

He needed to find a stairway, any stairway, to bring them up out of the depths of JiPhaindru. So far, no sign of one, and the desert winds were gathering strength, the floor was pitching, and bits of masonry rained from the ceiling. Behind them, Aoun-Father's raging efforts to force Himself into a space too small to hold Him were shaking the temple. How long before He shook His Fastness from its foundations?

There ahead of them, at last—a narrow flight of stairs. They raced up it, and he thought to catch the chanting of priestly voices near at hand, but the whistle of scorching winds muted the sound.

Up the stairway, stumbling upon the shuddery treads, through the open trapdoor at the top, and together they emerged onto the dais at the front of the Assembly. Behind them rose the semicircle of twisted columns. Before them,

the cushioned altar, crowded with garishly garbed Chosen.
At least a couple of dozen girl-children waited there—too
many for the altar to accommodate, and several reclined
on cushions deployed about the dais. They ranged in age
from blank-faced adolescents, displaying signs of well-
advanced pregnancy, down to moppets years short of fertility. This explained the emptiness of their dormitory. The
entire reserve of Chosen had been brought here, tonight.
All of them.

Beyond the altar, stretched the great, torchlit chamber, crowded with JiPhaindru's resident priests. The air
was sweetly foul with scented smoke, whose soporific
quality perhaps accounted for the sluggishness of Filial reaction. As the two trespassers came up onto the dais, the
Great Invocation broke off confusedly, but nobody
moved. Glass-eyed priests and slack-jawed neophytes
gawked. Several wivoors rose from the shoulders of their
masters, circled aloft, but received no command to attack.
Seconds stretched elastically. In the midst of that stunned
silence, the muffled shriek of an underground gale made
itself heard. Subterranean rumblings shook the temple,
and the vibrations of a tremendous hatred set sympathetic
human nerves aquiver.

The walls of the Assembly incandesced, assuming an
impossible transparency. Beyond those luminous veils
loomed a being clothed in fiercer light, and He was approaching.

The Father, evidently recalling His divine powers, dal-
lied no longer with trivial impediments.

The grinding crunch of granite devouring itself signaled the dissolution of JiPhaindru's substance. Walls, ceilings, and floors began to crumble, reducing themselves to a
fine, gray dust. Choking clouds billowed everywhere. Behind the clouds, Aoun-Father blazed like the sun at noon,
His great light diffusing through the atmospheric pollution
to fill the room with swirling whiteness.

The faithful emerged from their drugged torpor to
find themselves strangling upon unbreathable air. The
most devout among them, sinking facedown to the floor in
the presence of their god, were swiftly cloaked with powdered stone, and most of them suffocated in mid-

obeisance. Others, advancing to greet the Father in pious ecstasy, were caught in the heat of His passionate glare, and instantly incinerated. The majority, retaining some remnant of self-preserving instinct, fled for the exits. The Chosen girl-children, grouped atop and around the altar, converged upon the trapdoor through which they had been introduced to the Assembly. No doubt, instinct drove them in search of their dormitory, sole familiar refuge in their dwarfed universe, but that sanctuary lay beyond reach. As the coughing Chosen descended, the stairway crumbled beneath them, pitching the group into the dark and airless trap of the passage below, where heat, dust, and terror swiftly overcame them.

Most of the AounSons streamed for the door at the rear of the room. The first several to reach it passed through safely into the relatively clear air of the corridor beyond. Within moments, however, the narrow doorway was clogged with frantic Filial. Those who fell were trampled underfoot, and several died there, their bodies blocking the exit. Within moments, the rush of fleeing priests was effectively dammed. Shortly thereafter, the disintegration of the Assembly's back wall resolved the difficulty, but clouds and showers of pulverized rock hid the escape route from the remaining faithful.

The crazed advance of Aoun-Father sent Renille sprinting for the rear exit. He retained Jathondi's hand, and she easily kept pace. Straight through the ranks of astounded AounSons they sped, the full length of the Assembly, and cries arose about them and there were clutching hands, but nothing to hinder their flight. The sole clear-headed individuals present, they were among the first to reach the door. They were through it in a flash, into the corridor, and then running for the stairs at the far end.

Behind them came Aoun-Father. The temple was crumbling to dust around Him, the Filial were falling in droves, but He never paused. His progress was unrelenting, and the luckless faithful failing to clear His path perished in His light.

Renille resisted the impulse to look back. The stairs rose before him, but not for long. Soon they would collapse, along with the rest of JiPhaindru, leaving him and

Jathondi trapped below ground level. He accelerated, and still she kept pace.

Halfway up the stairs now, the furnace air scorching his flesh, the reverberations of Aoun-Father's fury shaking his insides. The stone beneath his feet was starting to go. His feet kicked up powdery billows, each step driving deep into erstwhile solidity.

They reached the top, and would have been lost in the stone maze, but for the panic-stricken Filial, whose flight pointed the way from the temple. The hurrying AounSons guided them straight to the great front door, and they emerged into a courtyard crammed with consternated Zu-Laysans.

There was no forcing a passage through that crowd. Renille's assault on the densely packed human mass rebounded uselessly. He turned back to behold JiPhaindru, luminous from foundation to roof, crumbling away to powder, reducing itself to dust. Through the clouds of destruction surged Aoun-Father, immense and terrible, the greenish conflagration that was His gaze sweeping left and right. The mob drew in on itself, cringing. Perhaps the fawning cheeps of His worshipers offended the Father, or perhaps He simply vented emotion. In any event, His hostile will transformed worldly substance, creating a region of measureless atmospheric pressure that smashed down on the courtyard with the force of an invisible piston. Some dozen or so of the faithful were squashed, and the chorus of praise splintered to screams. The survivors stampeded for the open gate as the piston crashed again upon them.

A gigantic silent howl of frustration charged the air with lightning. A couple of petulant thunderbolts leveled a sizable section of the outer courtyard wall. Then, the Father's shifting gaze arrested, fixing at last upon the two objects of His particular detestation. Renille shoved and battered surrounding bodies in vain. He and Jathondi were immovably mired. Her arms were around him, her face pressed to his chest. He gazed up at Aoun-Father looming over them, towering to the black heavens, and turned his eyes away.

A change in the quality of the light bathing the terrified crowd drew his involuntary attention. He looked up, and his breath caught. The sky above was alive with refulgent beings. They resembled Aoun in radiance and dizzying plasticity of impossible form, but They were perceptibly smaller than He, Their light of an inferior intensity. Impossible to count visitors so diverse and bewildering, but one or two Renille recognized. Ahrattah was there, and the implacably rational Ubhyadesh, and there was Hrushiiki, whose sandstone image graced his lodgings, and others, many others. He could not imagine where They had come from, how They had appeared so suddenly, or what had brought Them. He could, at that moment, scarcely think at all.

Perhaps Aoun-Father was similarly astounded, as He lifted His gaze to behold His brethren. No telling what ancient recollections the sight awakened, but the rapid, almost fluttering fluctuations in His radiance bespoke strong emotion, as They descended upon Him in a glowing tide.

The awed faithful dropped to their knees. Renille and Jathondi alone remained standing as the lesser gods enfolded Aoun-Father. Jathondi turned to watch, and only Renille caught her tiny whisper:

"Mother. What have you done?"

It is held in the common memory of the Aware that the confrontation between the Presence Aoun and his former followers, occurring in the tenth revolution of the Muted Epoch, amidst the tumultuous vapors of the Nether plane, was an occasion marked by the coarsest of disharmonies.

The Radiant Presences, streaming into Netherness through the portal opened by the human female, were struck at once by the alteration in their erstwhile leader's demeanor. Aoun, once so brilliant, retained considerable energy. Yet his light was shockingly diminished, his pulsations arrhythmic, his colors sullied and impure. The effects of prolonged immersion in Netherly murk were only too apparent, and it was clear to all that their ailing compatriot starved for the virtue of the Radiant Level.

Unhappily, this reality eluded the understanding of

Aoun himself, who seemed destructively bent upon the cultivation of his own grossest Anomalies. His reply to the telepathic greeting of his fellow Aware was ungracious, and his response to their collective urgings, abusively incoherent.

Evidently, the impaired Presence was capable no longer of rational autonomy. It was the duty of clearer intellects to judge on Aoun's behalf, and, if necessary, to effect such decisions by means of communal force—a feat impossible, in earlier epochs.

But now, circumstances had changed. The Presence Aoun, though formidable yet, was no longer invincible, and the combined luminescence of his old disciples more than exceeded his light.

Decay notwithstanding, he had lost none of his native intensity, and his struggles were ferocious. The visiting Presences, for all their numerical superiority, barely managed to contain him. And when he broke free to mount skyward, unendurably bright as a dying star above the pulverized ruins of his temple, almost it seemed that Aoun was himself again, lucid and lucent, as in revolutions past. For that brief span, the dull heavens of Netherness burned, lighting the upturned faces of countless humans watching from the city below. Aoun's light flared superbly, momentarily surpassing the brilliance of his fellow Presences, and for a time they were helpless against him.

It could not continue for long. Aoun's Netherly-polluted intelligence, no longer capable of sustained exertion, soon exhausted itself. The disciplined will of his Radiant adversaries prevailed, and gradually they wrapped him once again in cocoons of light. His resistance subsided to a hostile telepathic simmer, and they drew him from that spot, bearing him across the sky of Netherness, back to the open portal and through it into Radiance.

Contrary to communal expectation, the virtue of supradimensional aether failed to restore the Presence Aoun. Time passed, the revolutions spun in their eternal cycles, yet Aoun continued mentally clouded, disturbingly erratic in his pulsations, forever dulled and dirtied by his Netherly sojourn. At last abandoning all hope, the Aware resigned themselves, thereafter tending and guarding their ruined compatriot, as befit his former glory.

The fiery gash in the black sky closed itself, and the night resumed its customary complexion. The gods had departed, leaving behind Them a city of overwhelmed witnesses to Their passing.

Renille glanced around him. The red lamps still glowing along the standing section of the outer wall illumined an enormous mound of fine powder, all that remained of JiPhaindru. Scattered through and around the mound were the dead bodies of the Father's faithful—crushed, burned, trampled, suffocated, or otherwise dispatched. Scores of wounded bled and moaned upon the shattered pavement, while the ambulatory injured, and the terrified uninjured, streamed from the site in droves. Nobody paid the slightest attention to the lean young man and the seemingly delicate young woman, motionless in each other's arms.

He looked down at Jathondi. She was disheveled and dirty, but unhurt, as he was. The strength of her grip on him revealed terror, but she neither cried nor trembled.

"We had better get out of here." His voice was steady, to his surprise. She looked up to meet his eyes. "If they should return—"

"No." She shook her head. "They will not be back. She has surely closed the portal behind them."

"She?"

"Mother."

"You think—"

"I know. She summoned them, with the old magic, as we could not. She did it—" Jathondi swallowed, and now the tears did rise to fill her eyes. "She did it for me."

He did not attempt to argue the point. She could be right. He suspected that she was. Aloud, he merely observed, "The surviving AounSons may seek vengeance. In any case, we can't stay here."

"Where can we go?"

He thought. The immediate possibilities flashed through his mind, each to be rejected in turn. Only one alternative seemed remotely feasible, and remote was the word.

"I have a friend," he told her. "Not far from here. We might find shelter, but only of the very meanest sort."

"I don't care if it's mean."

"You may care that it's shelter among the Nameless."

Her eyes widened. She was silent.

"They're people like any others, but for their exceptional poverty," he continued. "Some of them are admirable, others unspeakable, most somewhere in between, as in any other group. I'd never venture to suggest such a thing to most Aveshquians. But you are fair-minded and generous. Beyond that you're Effulgent, and your Order stands above all accidental taint."

"And beyond even my Effulgence, there is my progressive Vonahrish education," she returned dryly. "Very well. Lead us. I will breathe Nameless air."

He contained his surprise. He had never actually expected her to consent. Now that she had, he could only hope he might remember his way through the tangle of Old City streets, back to the rickety gate and the blank tin disk marking the entrance to the Nameless enclosure.

He conducted her from the ruins of JiPhaindru's courtyard, straight across the open expanse of Jaya, and into the shadow of alleyways alive with awed and whispering Aveshquians. The citizens were out in force, electrified, yet curiously subdued. Everywhere, they gathered, and the air hummed with verbal exchange, and the gestures were expansive yet constrained, as if the speakers imagined themselves subject to divine scrutiny.

Somehow, he remembered the path. The gleam of weak lantern light on a blank tin disk arrested his eye, and he halted. The door was unlocked, as always. He led her in, and his nostrils flared at the well-remembered scents.

Lean-tos, tents, huts, cooking fires, garbage heaps; just as he recalled.

He hurried toward one familiar shelter, and before he reached it, a small figure came running to meet him.

Slight little body, shaggy black locks, great dark eyes.

"The Esteemed has returned, as he promised," Greenface observed. "He has come to finish teaching me to read."

"I'm afraid that's not—"

"I know the Esteemed would never break his word."

"I don't intend to break my word, but—"

"He would never make excuses, delay, deceive, or mislead," Greenface confided. "He is Vonahrish, after all. He will keep his solemn vow to the one who saved his life. Vonahrish honor demands no less."

"I haven't forgotten my promise, Greenface—"

"There is justice in the world."

"But that's not why I'm here tonight."

"I knew it! Vonahrish honor! Pah!" Greenface spat.

"Tonight, I need shelter—"

"Again!"

"And afterward, there's someone I know who will teach you to read. A far better teacher than I."

"Words!"

"True ones. Believe. Help me one more time, and you won't be sorry. Assuming that Knobs knows nothing of it. She's here?"

"Knobs!" Greenface grinned. "She has got her reward, that one. After you go, she is caught with stolen writings in her hand, and the Stick-fellows"—he used the popular term for the local military police—"drag her ugly bones off to gaol, where she rots. With her goes Itch, who is also a thief. I am staying here, collecting the monthly fees from all the families, including my own, and all of us are eating fine. Rice and spikkij, pijhallies, nutsweeties—all very fine."

"What about Oozie?"

"What about him?" Greenface laughed evilly. "He eats. But I make the little slug draw water, scrounge kindling, scrub pots, like everyone else. He yaps, but he works."

"Tonight, however—"

"Tonight is amazing!" The boy's eyes lit. "Did you see what happened? Did you see? *I* saw, and all my life I must remember, for always men will beg me to tell of the night that the lesser gods carry Aoun-Father back into Irriule."

"Very likely."

"They are gone, the gods have gone! All of ZuLaysa witnessed their going. It is changed, now, everything is changed. And *I* saw it!"

"Indeed."

"And they say in the streets that JiPhaindru is fallen. Can this be true?"

"It is. Greenface, you must understand that we are very tired—"

"Old people are always tired! The world somersaults, but old people want to sleep! Well, Esteemed brother, there is room in Knobs's shack for you, and for this fine slice of pastry you bring with you. She is no blanched Vonahrishwoman, that is clear. She is one of us, and Nameless, else she wouldn't come here. My sister"—the boy addressed Jathondi directly—"for the sake of my brother the Esteemed, you are welcome. Come, let us clasp hands."

She froze, and her eyes shifted for an instant to Renille's face. As if in a dream, she extended her hand. Seizing it in both of his, Greenface pumped enthusiastically. Then his gaze sank to the golden insignia of Effulgence at her waist, and his jaw dropped.

The portal closed, and the great light faded from Shirardhir's Sanctum. For several moments, the Ghochalla Xundunisse stood staring at the archway where it had glowed. They were gone, all of Them. Before They withdrew, she had been made to understand, by some mysterious agency, that They had granted her request. Now, inexpressibly tired and drained, she wanted only to rest, to sleep.

It was not yet time to rest.

Taking up the lamp, Xundunisse departed. She paused briefly upon the threshold to look back once at the dim and empty chamber, then closed the door behind her.

Through the corridors she dragged her listless way, until she came again to her own apartment. It seemed an age since she had left it, and almost she expected alteration, but all was as it had been. Lamps still burning, luruleanni shrub gloriously abloom in its great alabaster tub, tray of food still sitting untouched upon the escritoire, soft bed awaiting her. Her gaze lingered on the bed.

Not yet.

Seating herself at the desk, the Ghochalla dipped a pen, and began to write. Composition proved easier than anticipated. She had thought that the phrases of a royal proclamation commanding the restive ZuLaysans to lay down their arms would kink in her brain, but in fact, they flowed. She wrote swiftly, without hesitation. She wrote concisely, expressing her desires in a minimum of clearly worded sentences, and very soon, the work was done. She read it over. Quite unequivocal, it was. The Ghochalla of Kahnderule called for peace. She lacked the means to enforce her will, and yet, such a proclamation, carried by the highly recognizable Paro and read aloud in the shadow of Nabarqui Obelisk by the public Vociferist, would carry considerable weight. Many, if not all, of her subjects would obey.

Those Vonahrish yet surviving in the besieged Residency would be saved, together with their western brethren scattered throughout Kahnderule. Thousands of them saved, the Ghochalla reflected. Thousands to occupy Aveshq, to dominate, to exploit, to spread their modern, soulless ways across the land.

There was nothing to stop them now.

"Good or bad, these foreign ideas have taken firm root, and things will never again be as they were in Kahnderule."

The Ghochanna Jathondi's words. Fortunately, the Ghochanna's mother was not obliged to remain and watch.

Xundunisse scrawled her signature, then folded and sealed the decree, stamping the golden wax with the elaborate royal insignia of Kahnderule. She twitched the bellpull beside the desk, and moments later, Paro entered. She gave him the paper, a little money, a carpetbag, and instructions. The slave bowed and withdrew. Paro didn't know it yet, but his freedom was imminent.

Alone again.

Now Xundunisse extinguished all but one of the lamps. Crossing the room to the flowering luruleanni, she tapped a certain rhythm upon the trunk of the shrub. At once, a narrow, polychrome form emerged from its burrow amongst the roots. The creature was nearly the length of her forearm, its crimson body splotched with vivid purple, and fringed with countless legs. The Kahnderulese name of this gigantic, notoriously venomous centipede was "Bhijas Xunesh," or Jeweled Destroyer. Despite the sinister hiss of its name, the death that Bhijas brought was kindly, wreathed in dreams widely regarded as prophetic.

The Ghochalla took the centipede up in her left hand. Its myriad legs tickled her flesh. She pinched a crimson segment sharply, and felt the lethal pincers stab her wrist. The pain was nothing, no more than a pinprick.

"Thank you," she said, and gently returned Bhijas to the tub of soil that was its home.

She went to her bed, and lay down upon it. She was tired, very tired, but comfortable enough. The air was hot, but an unfamiliar coldness was stealing along her veins. The sensation was odd, but not altogether unpleasant.

Presently her eyes closed, and the dreams came to fill her mind with movement and color.

She dreamed first, as she would have wished, of her daughter. Jathondi was well, beautiful, very alive. She was walking hand in hand with a man recognizable as the foreigner, vo Chaumelle. Curiously, this sight failed to incense Xundunisse. The two of them strolled in brilliant sunshine, but the dreamer failed to recognize the setting. Not ZuLaysa, not OodPray. She caught the sparkle of light on water—a canal?—and she saw marvelous palaces. Not so marvelous as OodPray, but wondrous, nevertheless. Such architecture never rose beneath the Aveshquian sun. Jathondi and Chaumelle walked some foreign city. In Vonahr? Somehow the Ghochalla doubted it. She couldn't identify the locale, and it didn't matter, for her daughter was smiling.

The dream changed, and now she could see all of ZuLaysa, all the surrounding land of Kahnderule, and the territories beyond, stretching on to the borders of Aveshq. And it was as she had feared, for the Vonahrish ruled over all. The land was changing, just as Jathondi had threatened. The temples were falling, the sacred rituals were fading from memory, the gods of old were gone, and with them vanished the ancient magic. The land was webbed with western-style railroad tracks, and elevated wires whose purpose she couldn't guess. Everywhere loomed great, hideous buildings housing hospitals, schools, libraries, factories. These eyesores were governed by Vonahrishmen—arrogant men, contemptuous men—and her mind burned at the sight of her countrymen groveling before them. Yet it seemed that her vision encompassed time as well as space, and she could gaze down the tunnel of the years to see a generation of young Aveshquians—the healthy, well-nourished, well-educated recipients of patronizing Vonahrish largesse—maturing to reclaim their country, and to do it without bloodshed. She saw the divisions among the old principalities and ghochallates vanish, and she saw a united, wholly autonomous state. That altered Aveshq was not a place that she understood, or wished to inhabit, but she could take pleasure in its strength, its pride, and its hope.

The dream changed again, and she beheld OodPray Palace—an OodPray transformed. Gone was every trace of damage, dirt, and decay. Peacocks strutted the manicured grounds, the fountains played, while sunlight wrought wonders upon the Crystal Archways and the Violet Dome. The palace glittered, its original splendor fully restored, and her heart almost broke with the beauty of it. Roaming the gorgeous halls within were children, many children, of both sexes and all ages. She didn't recognize any of their faces, nor understand their presence in her home, but she saw at a glance that they were Aveshquian, brimming with health and spirit. Their voices reached her across a vast gulf, and she caught the echo of laughter.

The voices faded. The darkness embraced her, and at last it was time to rest.

15

"You are reckless, Ren," observed Ziloor. "Some would call it insolence."

"Umuri, that is no news," Renille returned.

"You will damage your own standing among your fellow Esteemeds."

"I'll survive that tragedy."

"They will think it outrageous that you bring a native other than a servant here, to their lily-white Residency."

"Probably."

"You may feel the repercussions. Of course, that difficulty is forestalled, if we are simply refused entry."

"We won't be." Renille spoke with unfeigned assurance.

The two of them approached the Vonahrish Residency. Renille's huge umbrella shielded them both against the torrential downpour that hammered the world at frequent intervals, now that the rains had come. The Avenue of the Republic was thick with soldiers of the Eighteenth Aveshquian Division, but nobody had troubled them, which was not surprising in view of Renille's present well-tailored western respectability. Even had he been otherwise attired, however, the probability of hindrance would have remained low. The presence of the Eighteenth within

ZuLaysa throughout the past month had proved largely
redundant. The force summoned to the relief of the Residency weeks earlier had arrived to confront a quiescent
city, its unruly inhabitants stunned by the departure of
their deities, and disarmed by the command of their self-
slaughtered sovereign. Thereafter, but for some few out-
breaks of bloodless looting in a couple of damaged neigh-
borhoods, ZuLaysa had continued reassuringly pacific.

The signs of struggle were still everywhere to be seen.
Little Sherreen stood in ruins, its handsome brick town
houses razed and pillaged, its gardens ravaged. The devastation was all but complete along the streets surrounding
the Residency. Here even the pavement was cracked, broken, and virtually impossible to repair in the rains. Rivulets rushed in the fissures, and the mud was all but boiling
up from beneath to create a swamp, certain to persist for
weeks or months to come.

The outer wall of the Residency was a miserable sight,
its surface pocked with gunfire, blackened and battered.
The guards on duty at the scorched and scarred front gate
were equally miserable, standing ankle-deep in mud with
the rainwater streaming off the visors of their sodden
dhurlies.

Recognizing the Deputy Assistant Secretary vo
Chaumelle, so greatly distinguishing himself throughout
the late unpleasantness, they admitted him without hesitation. The ragged old Pissie accompanying the Deputy
Assistant Secretary was likewise permitted to pass unchallenged.

The courtyard was a wilderness of mud, dangerously
dimpled with softening potholes and trenches. A month
ago, the place had been crammed with wagons and
fhozhees. Now most of them were gone. The owners, assured of safety, had departed for their Mandijhuur plantations, once more deemed habitable. A number of less
fortunate Little Sherreenians, their homes leveled, remained yet; their soggy conveyances sinking swiftly into
the seasonal bog.

The two of them entered the foyer, and Renille folded
his umbrella, loosing rivers upon the dirty marble tile.

Crossing the great open space, they mounted the central staircase.

"So. Here is where our poor Aveshquian fate is cast by the wise Vonahrish." Ziloor's black eyes roamed.

"Only enacted. It is cast in Century Hall, in Sherreen, on the other side of the world."

"Nevertheless, I have often longed to see this place."

"And does it live up to your expectations?"

"Indeed. But fresh from the ZuLaysa Correctional Facility, I am easily pleased."

"You're sharp as ever, Umuri. Incarceration must agree with you."

"Quite so. Two helpings of execrable slop a day, very sound stone walls to keep the weather out, and all the vermin one could possibly desire. I rather liked it."

Slop and vermin notwithstanding, his sojourn in gaol seemed not to have damaged Ziloor. He had weathered the recent storms, safe behind bars. When Renille had gone to effect his teacher's early release, he'd discovered the old man, hale and spry, conducting guards and fellow prisoners through the First Antechamber of the Palace of Light.

Ziloor, barred forever from Beviairette and regretting it not in the least, had agreed at once to his former student's proposal; though maintaining some sardonic reservation as to the likelihood of securing official consent.

"Leave that to me, Umuri," Renille had counseled. "After all, do you yourself not teach that 'the hungry spirit finds sustenance in smoke and shadow'?"

"What a clever boy."

Now they were walking the second-story hallway, its carpeting in rags, its remaining pier glasses cracked and dim. Halting before one of the anonymous wooden doors, Renille knocked, then ushered his companion into Assistant Secretary Phesque Shivaux's office.

Shivaux was seated at his desk, head bent over a daunting spread of paperwork. As the door opened, he looked up, and his eyes narrowed. Laying his pen aside, he leaned back in his chair, to observe indolently, "Ah, Chaumelle. I do not recall sending for you."

"Pestilence couldn't keep me away, Shivaux. Speaking of which, how is your health, these days?"

"Quite recovered." No doubt Shivaux spoke the truth. His eyes were clear, if wary, and his complexion once again florid.

"Delighted to hear it. I understand, too, that congratulations are in order."

"Yes. Miss v'Eriste has done me the honor of consenting to become my wife."

"Making you the happiest of men. I cannot conceive of two souls more perfectly suited." Renille's satisfaction was deep and genuine. "A most fortunate match."

His subordinate spoke with the most guileless amiability, but Shivaux must have scented a taunt, for he smiled, and replied, "I gather you've had a bit of good luck yourself. That little yellow piece of yours is altogether delicious."

"The Ghochanna and I are to marry next month." Renille's eyes never flickered.

"Ah?" Shivaux stroked his moustache. "I see. I see. Another most fortunate and suitable match."

"We think so. But pardon me, I am remiss, I've failed to introduce my distinguished companion. Assistant Secretary Shivaux, allow me to present the Umuri Ziloor—preeminent scholar, teacher, explorer, and guide through the Palace of Light."

"Assistant Secretary." Ziloor inclined his head courteously, but without subservience.

Shivaux ignored him. "What can I do for you, Chaumelle?" he inquired.

"I have brought the Umuri," Renille told him, "because I think it only appropriate that you meet the future principal of the first state-supported Aveshquian public school, whose establishment you so enthusiastically endorse."

"I so enthusiastically—? What school? What are you chattering about?"

"I apologize. I run ahead of myself, it is one of my faults." Renille shook his head. An inner pocket yielded a paper packet, which he carefully placed upon the other's desk. "There. That's a rough draft of the proposal. You may wish to read it at once. The finished copy will reach you in a couple of days, but it won't contain anything not already there before you."

"What is this foolery?" Shivaux prodded the packet.

"It is a proposal for the establishment of a state-supported Aveshquian public school," Renille repeated patiently. "No doubt the first of many. The Umuri Ziloor, acting as principal, will design the curriculum and select the instructors. All qualified Aveshquian students, of both sexes, will be eligible for admission, and the campus will include a well-isolated facility housing the resident Nameless scholars."

"This is utter nonsense." Shivaux brushed the packet from his desk.

"Not at all, Assistant Secretary," Ziloor remarked serenely. "There are many among the youthful Nameless gifted with mental quickness. I will consent to instruct such youngsters and, no doubt, there are others willing to do the same."

Shivaux appeared unaware of Aveshquian presence.

"Nor do I believe," Renille continued, "that we shall lack for acceptable Nameless applicants. I know of one already, living right here in ZuLaysa, whose candidacy I myself will sponsor. He is clever, courageous, determined, and very eager to learn how to read."

"This is a sweet little vision, worthy of an adolescent girl," observed Shivaux.

"Isn't it, though? And only to think, there's even more," Renille informed him. "No doubt the inevitable expense attaching to such a project alarms you, and understandably so. Construction costs alone could run to the hundreds of thousands of New-rekkoes, but I offer a comparatively economical alternative. The new school will be housed in OodPray Palace. I'm happy to convey the Ghochanna Jathondi's assent to the rental of her family property at an almost nominal sum."

"Very good of her." Shivaux did not trouble to conceal his boredom.

"The greatest expense," Renille continued, "covers the cleaning, restoration, and renovation of OodPray. A substantial sum is called for, but far less than new construction would demand. Fortunately for all concerned, the Assistant Secretary's influence with the Protector is such that a single recommendation will serve to secure the required allocation of funds."

"Chaumelle, I always thought you a trifle unstable. Mental byproduct, no doubt, of impure blood. Not really your fault, I suppose." Shivaux's frown expressed concern. "But now, I perceive that the trouble exceeds mere temperament. You are deeply confused. I would strongly advise you to seek medical assistance. And you had best do it quickly, before those about you find themselves obliged to act on your behalf."

"I thank you for the good wishes, and the good advice. Here is my reply." Dipping into his pocket, Renille produced a second document, which he deposited upon the desk.

"What is this thing?" Without awaiting reply, Shivaux unfolded the paper, and read. His face froze.

"It is a communication from the commercial establishment Zouq's Transactions, Ltd., in Sherreen. The proprietors of Zouq's offer the Assistant Secretary Shivaux a recompense of two hundred fifty thousand New-rekkoes, upon delivery to them of the Thousand Year Automaton, currently ornamenting OodPray Palace, where it has stood for the last half-millenium."

"Am I responsible for some tradesman's presumption?" Shivaux was no longer ruddy.

"I'd venture to think so, in view of the fact that the letter refers to your offer, by date, conveying the buyers' acceptance, in accordance, it is clearly noted, with the terms of your original correspondence."

"Fine. And now, nothing is clearly noted." Shivaux shredded the paper.

"Oh, come." Renille wasted no glance upon the white fragments. "You know better."

Shivaux was very still in his chair.

"You recall the contents of your pocket-folder."

"Pilfered—"

"Acquired by chance, upon the day of your admission to the infirmary."

"Stolen. I always knew you were the thief. Who but a

mongrel would rifle the pockets of a wounded man? There was no proof, but I knew."

"You consider yourself ill-used."

"I won't debate the issue with you. I won't trouble to defend the concept of decency, you wouldn't grasp it."

"Perhaps not, but there's a good deal else that's easy to grasp. I hold some dozen letters, dispatched by various commercial enterprises in Sherreen, and elsewhere. They vary somewhat in their content, but the tenor is clear. Within the coming months, it's your intention to strip OodPray Palace of its treasures, sell them, and pocket the profits—which will, it appears, amount to some ten million New-rekkoes, or more. A small fraction of their real worth, but impressive all the same."

"There is nothing in those documents supporting the accusation that I planned to pocket the profits," Shivaux returned slowly. "How like you, to spew calumny. Do you hold anything resembling written expression of intent to deposit those funds in any account belonging to me? I think not."

"Very well. What did you intend to do with them, then?"

"What should I intend, but to turn them over to the Vonahrish government? But that is hardly a matter I would choose to discuss with you."

"You would rather discuss it with vo Trouniere?"

"The Protector's time is too valuable to waste upon trivialities."

"I'd regard the sum of ten millions as anything but trivial. The difficulty lies, however, in the means of acquisition. If you'll recall, the Treaty of Mandijhuur prohibits Vonahrish appropriation of Aveshquian personal property."

"Does it? Ah, well. I'm not at all certain that the contents of OodPray Palace qualify as personal property. Are they not chattel of the Kahnderulese Ghochallate? Given the recent death of the hereditary Ghochalla, and the current debate regarding the advisability, in these troubled times, of permitting continuation of titular native sovereignty, it would appear to me that the legal status of the OodPray art treasures is quite unclear."

"Chops logic like a champion, this one." Ziloor looked entertained.

"That may be. I should think the fact that your correspondence predates the Ghochalla's death, some of it by as much as a year, suggestive of questionable motives, but then, I am no lawyer," Renille conceded pensively. His supervisor stared in silence at the shredded paper littering the desk, and he added, "Vo Trouniere may judge for himself, when he sees the remaining letters."

"These days, the Protector is all but buried in work." Shivaux found his voice again. His expression was tolerant, but his face remained colorless. "Overtaxed as he is, our leader should never be called upon to waste precious time on this tradesmen's twaddle, with which you would quite unnecessarily force my assent to a suggestion clearly full of merit. Establishment of an Aveshquian public school is a worthy project, entirely deserving, I daresay, of my endorsement and full support."

"Delighted to hear you say so. I shall submit the proposal to vo Trouniere in a couple of days. With your backing, success is all but assured."

"That is best, no doubt, for all concerned. And now that we have arrived at a mutual understanding, I trust I may expect the prompt return of my property."

"The correspondence, you mean? I don't think I can bear to part with it," Renille told him.

"Come, this is absurd. You shall have your school at OodPray. You have my word."

"I'm relying on it."

"Then you'll return what belongs to me. Are we not gentlemen?"

"One of us is."

"Ah. I might have expected as much, of you." Shivaux kept his tone negligent, but couldn't control the rush of angry blood to his face. "The dashing, brilliant vo Chaumelle. So ingenious. Such an original. Perhaps this shining paragon will discover, before very long, that he is not quite as invulnerable as he imagines."

"Vague threats depress me, Shivaux."

"I have uttered no threat. I merely state possibilities."

"In that case—"

"Ren." Ziloor laid a hand upon his former pupil's shoulder. "Enough. We have what we came for. It has been a most enjoyable and enlightening experience, but all good things must come to an end."

Renille nodded, and the two of them departed.

Three days later, Renille answered a summons to vo Trouniere's office. He found the Protector at his desk, entombed in paperwork; a little grayer, a little wearier, and a bit testier than ever but, on the whole, surprisingly unaffected by recent events.

"Sit down, Chaumelle." Vo Trouniere was smoking, his elaborate manipulations of a meerschaum pipe suggesting uncharacteristic uneasiness. He fiddled with the bowl for a moment, then looked up to meet his subordinate's eyes squarely. "I won't beat about the bush. Do you know why I've called you in here?"

"I assume, Protector, that it has something to do with my proposed establishment of an Aveshquian school at OodPray. There are areas requiring clarification, additional explanation, or justification?"

"Not at all. It's perfectly clear, and strongly reasoned. You did a good job."

"Thank you, sir."

"Shivaux thinks so, too. You'd be flattered at the speed with which he passed on his endorsement. He's even suggested a feasible means of financing. I've rarely, if ever, seen him so wholeheartedly enthusiastic."

"I'm delighted to hear it, sir."

"I think it safe to tell you, at this point, that approval is assured. I'm glad of it. I believe this is something that would have pleased the poor old Ghochalla. You remember what a burr under her saddle that crumbling palace was."

"You liked her, didn't you?"

"Thought she was quite a woman. She was no friend of ours, but in the end, she commanded her subjects to lay down their arms. We owe her for that."

Vo Trouniere pondered, frowning.

The comfortless silence lengthened, and Renille, disagreeably mystified, at last essayed, "You're considering approval of the funding required for an investigation of the phenomena accompanying JiPhaindru's destruction?"

"You already know my opinion. Nice work for those scientific eccentrics well versed in the ways of lightning storms, electrical disturbances, and seismic tremors, but who's to pay them? With Little Sherreen in ruins about us, and ZuLaysa still simmering, we can't afford the luxury of academic self-indulgence."

"It can't be regarded as luxury, Protector, if those so-called lightning storms were in fact—"

"Spare me. We've been through all this at least twice. I know your views, and sometimes I suspect you're suggestible as any of these yellows. These people—" Vo Trouniere's nostrils widened. "You've heard the tales the loonier among them have concocted. There's some sort of absurd twilight-of-the-gods scenario they've cooked up, and I wonder if you haven't swallowed it whole."

"I think we'd be remiss if—"

"We'd be remiss if we squandered our inadequate funds upon inessentials. Listen, I share your curiosity. It was a most striking celestial manifestation we all witnessed that night. Perhaps, someday, when our fortunes are brighter—"

"When the portal has been closed for years, and it's far too late. Won't you even consider—"

"Portal. Such expressions. Be reasonable, and govern your tongue. For your own sake."

"Be reasonable? I couldn't agree more. By all means, let's be reasonable. Reason dictates the closest scrutiny of physical evidence, does it not? An examination of JiPhaindru's dust—"

"Forget the dust, Chaumelle. It doesn't concern you now."

"It concerns—"

"You aren't here about dust, or collapsing temples, or wayward gods."

"What, then? Let's hear it."

There was another unpleasant pause, and then the Protector resumed, with obvious reluctance. "We find ourselves forced at this juncture to confront a situation of some delicacy."

Renille suspected that the last sentence had been rehearsed. He waited.

"I allude, Chaumelle, to your open liaison with the Ghochanna Jathondi."

"It is an engagement, Protector."

"Very well. An engagement. That doesn't improve matters." His subordinate did not respond, and vo Trouniere continued, with some discomfort, "Surely I needn't point out the drawbacks of this connection. Mind you, I've no personal objection to offer. I've met the Ghochanna, and find her admirable. Were it left to me, the two of you might do as you please. But there are others to think of, many of whom consider it a very shocking thing—a very repugnant, even unnatural thing—that a Vonahrishman would form such an attachment. Frankly, I've been bombarded with complaints, some of them remarkably vehement."

"I can guess the source."

"The sources are varied. You don't seem to understand what a nerve you've touched. There are many among us regarding miscegenation as but one step removed from bestiality."

"That is extraordinarily ugly, Protector."

"I agree. But there it is. Face facts. In such a situation as ours, relations with native women are bound to occur. It may be self-indulgent, but we're mortal men, and these things will happen. And certainly, there's no great harm in that, provided such affairs are conducted discreetly. A secluded little house for the woman—quiet visits—no blatant offense to anyone's standards of decency."

"The Ghochanna and I are to marry next month." Nothing in Renille's face or voice revealed the storm of rage swirling to life inside him.

"Then I fear you'll lose all credibility as a representative of Vonahrish interests, here in Kahnderule. Your actions reflect, you see, upon the entire Aveshquian Civil Service. Too many will feel that you bring disgrace upon us all."

"I see." Renille spoke very calmly. "And is it of no

importance whatever that the Aveshquian woman in question is royalty, who lowers herself immeasurably in consenting to accept me? That she is, but for the ceremony of investiture, the new Ghochalla of Kahnderule?"

"The young lady may perhaps insist upon regarding herself as such." The Protector gazed studiously out the window. "In point of fact, I have it upon good authority that Congress in Sherreen hovers upon the verge of declaring Kahnderule a Vonarhish Territory. Once this decision is ratified, and native rule officially abolished, the lady's title is invalidated. She will receive generous treatment, of course. No doubt there are various properties and perquisites that she'll be permitted to retain."

"Permitted? Vonahrish Congress hasn't the right to—"

"And so you perceive, I'm certain, the alarming political ramifications possible here—the conflict of interest, the divided loyalties, the sheer incongruity of it all. I'm certain you also see why a marriage, or even an open association, between a Deputy Assistant Secretary of the Aveshquian Civil Service, and a native woman, most particularly *this* native woman, is quite unacceptable. Believe me, Chaumelle, I am sorry to place you in this position. In light of your splendid service during the siege, I regret it all the more. There comes a time, however, when a Vonahrishman must place his duty ahead of all personal concerns. I appreciate the significance of the sacrifice that duty now demands of you, and I'm willing to grant such time as you want to think it over."

Renille stood. "I don't need to think it over," he said.

There came one of those brief, intermittent lulls in the pounding rain. Renille lowered his umbrella, and, in the near distance, saw Jathondi do the same. She was easy to spot; a graceful figure, clad in the violet that was the Aveshquian color of the mourning she wore for her mother, waiting for him beneath the Gates of Twilight archway. Tall chopines lifted her above the mud, and in one hand she gripped the carpetbag that lately, for reasons best known to herself, she kept with her at all times.

They met, embraced, and kissed in the shade of the arch.

"I've lost my job," he announced.

"You haven't! What happened?"

"Let's walk, and I'll tell you."

"Which way?"

"This way." He led her away from Little Sherreen, out into the real ZuLaysa. They paused to buy jukkha of the first vendor they met and, as they walked, they ate the sweet, nut-studded paste, probably dirty as a sewer but nonetheless delicious. In between bites he spoke, presenting a tactfully edited account of his interviews with Shivaux and vo Trouniere.

"And there you have it," he announced in conclusion. "I have no income, no employment, and no prospects here in Aveshq."

"Are you sorry?" she inquired, with careful unconcern.

"What do you think?"

"There is still time to undo what you have done."

"Time, yes. Inclination, no."

"Then it seems that you must leave Aveshq."

"So it seems."

"You are troubled at the thought of going."

"In many ways. There's nothing else in all the world to compare with Aveshq. In leaving this place, I'd leave part of myself. Most troubling thought of all, however, is the thought of asking you to come with me. Could I expect so much? This is your home, these are your people, and you are hereditary sovereign here. If you choose not to go, I'll remain."

"To fill the empty days as best you can?"

"Don't underestimate my resources, Ghochanna. I'll contrive to keep myself occupied."

"I believe that you would. But you will not need to, Renille. I'll come with you, and gladly."

"Your home, your rank, your people—"

"Mine no longer. OodPray is saved, and I rejoice for my mother's sake, and my own. If only I could be certain that these Vonahrish kites will carry on with the renovation, with you no longer present to crack the whip—"

"No fear. I've handed Assistant Secretary Shivaux's letters over to Ziloor, who'll crack the whip as well or better than I."

"Excellent. As for my rank, that is already lost. And my people? They would, if apprised of the facts, regard me as the rightful property of NiraDhar of Dharahule." Correctly interpreting his expression of incomprehension, she explained, "Before I fled OodPray, Mother had written to the Ghochallon NiraDhar, formally relinquishing her parental responsibility in his favor, and thus granting him absolute authority over my person and property. As long as I live within the borders of Aveshq, what is mine belongs to NiraDhar, up to and including the Ivory throne. So you see, you do not deprive me of my home—that was done by another."

"Your poor mother. She must have regretted that."

"Yes," Jathondi agreed quietly. "I believe she did. But let us not speak of an act best forgotten. Let us speak instead of the future. Where shall we go?"

"Anywhere we like. Vonahr?"

"No! Never there!"

"Neraunce, then? Nidroon? Strell? Hurba? Lanthi Ume?"

"Lanthi Ume." Jathondi reflected. "Sunshine, canals, marvelous palaces. Yes. I think I should like that."

"Lanthi Ume it is, then. We'll have to live modestly, but we'll do well enough. I have a little money from my parents—"

"Renille, we'll not lack. See here." She opened the carpetbag, affording a brief glimpse of glittering rainbow contents.

"What is that?" Renille remembered to close his mouth.

"Mother's best jewelry." Jathondi shut the bag. "Paro delivered it to me, at her request. In return, of course, I freed him."

"Paro brought this? Unbelievable that he didn't simply run off with it."

"What a peculiar notion. You really *are* Vonahrish."

"And you've been carrying a king's ransom in gems through the streets of ZuLaysa?"

"Well, I couldn't very well leave them lying around in my lodgings while I was out, could I?"

There was, he had to admit, a certain logic to that. They walked on, into a street lined with dignified stone houses, of the sort owned by wealthy native merchants. Distant thunder boomed softly, the rain resumed, and his wide umbrella sheltered them both. The world was gray, and dim, and drowning around them.

"Not the happiest of conclusions," Renille observed. "The two of us forced out of Kahnderule, and the land left in thrall to a foreign power."

"Today, perhaps," Jathondi admitted. Her eyes traveled to the nearest house, where a workman, indifferent to the rain, was up on a ladder chiseling away at the ushtra carved into the stone above the front door. As she watched, the symbol fell piecemeal, its fragments vanishing instantly into the mud. "But tomorrow?"

Born and raised in Fanwood, New Jersey, Paula Volsky majored in English literature at Vassar, then traveled to England to complete an M.A. in Shakespearean studies at the University of Birmingham. Upon her return to the United States, she sold real estate in New Jersey, then began working for the U.S. Department of Housing and Urban Development in Washington, D.C. During this time she finished her first book, *The Curse of the Witch Queen,* a fairy tale for children that developed into a fairy tale for adults. Shortly thereafter she abandoned HUD in favor of full-time writing. She continues to reside in the Washington, D.C., area, with her collection of Victoriana and her almost equally antique computer.

The Governor stepped forward to read off the names of the prisoners, the long list of their gaudy crimes, the record of conviction and condemnation, and finally, the collective order of that Disinfection designed to rid the world of sorcerous poison. To all of this, the assembled citizens listened devoutly. There was no particle of impatience visible upon any face in the crowd, but only an unobtrusive shifting of weight and shuffling of feet, to mark the eager restlessness of those who had heard such lists and orders, time and time again.

The Governor concluded. The seven prisoners were conveyed up the makeshift stairs to the rough wooden platform overhanging the volcanic cauldron. From that height, in swift succession, they were flung down into the boiling water. Tremendous splash followed splash.

Not everyone in the audience enjoyed an unobstructed view. Those positioned at the very foot of the cauldron sacrificed some spectacle for the sake of exciting immediacy. Others, farther off, often witnessed more, with the best of visual, aural, and olfactory experiences naturally belonging to those exalted personages occupying the bleachers.

But Tradain's view from the tower cell was better yet, surpassing even the Dhreve's. From his vantage point, he could see the entire stage and everything on it; soldiers, Governor, jurists, scaffolding and cauldron, violently boiling water, and violently struggling victims.

They didn't struggle for long, however.

Rav liMarchborg died almost at once. Already much weakened, he succumbed swiftly, losing consciousness within seconds of his immersion. Zendin, hitherto nearly undamaged, fought with a vigor that might actually have won him escape, but for the opposition of the soldiers. Half a dozen thrusts of assorted poles were required to foil Zendin's remarkably persistent efforts to climb out. At last, a well-placed blow thwacked the boy's temple, and thereafter, all resistance ceased. For a while, the five retainers shrieked and thrashed energetically enough to satisfy the most demanding connoisseurs of agony, and then their cries faded, and their bodies went limp. Presently, seven flaccid forms tumbled in silence through the churning water.

Tradain's hands were locked on the iron bars. He couldn't release his grip, which was curious, because there was nothing more to see.

Realms Of Fantasy

The biggest, brightest stars from Bantam Books

Maggie Furey

A fiery-haired Mage with an equally incendiary temper must save her world and her friends from a pernicious evil, with the aid of four forgotten magical Artefacts:

AURIAN ___56525-7 $6.50

HARP OF WINDS ___56526-5 $6.50

SWORD OF FLAME ___56527-3 $6.50

Robin Hobb

One of our newest and most exciting talents presents a tale of honor and subterfuge, loyalty and betrayal:

ASSASSIN'S APPRENTICE: Book One of the Farseer

___57339-X $6.50/$8.99 Canada

ROYAL ASSASSIN: Book Two of the Farseer

___37563-6 $13.95/$19.95 Canada

Katharine Kerr

The mistress of Celtic fantasy presents her ever-popular Deverry series (most recent titles):

DAYS OF BLOOD AND FIRE ___29012-6 $5.99/$7.50

DAYS OF AIR AND DARKNESS ___57262-8 $5.99/$7.99

- -

Ask for these books at your local bookstore or use this page to order.

Please send me the books I have checked above. I am enclosing $____ (add $2.50 to cover postage and handling). Send check or money order, no cash or C.O.D.'s, please.

Name _____

Address _____

City/State/Zip _____

Send order to: Bantam Books, Dept. SF 29, 2451 S. Wolf Rd., Des Plaines, IL 60018.

Allow four to six weeks for delivery.

Prices and availability subject to change without notice.   SF 29 3/97

Realms Of Fantasy

The biggest, brightest stars from Bantam Books

Michael A. Stackpole

An antique warrior, from 500 years in the past, is resurrected to save his kingdom from an evil he unwittingly propagated:

ONCE A HERO ___56112-X $5.99/$7.99

Paula Volsky

Rich tapestries of magic and revolution, romance and forbidden desires:

ILLUSION ___56022-0 $5.99/$6.99
THE WOLF OF WINTER ___56879-5 $5.99/$7.99
THE GATES OF TWILIGHT ___37394-3 $12.95/$17.95

Angus Wells

Epic fantasy in the grandest tradition, of magic, dragons, and heroic quests (most recent titles):

LORDS OF THE SKY ___57266-0 $5.99/$7.99
EXILE'S CHILDREN: Book One of the Exiles Saga
___29903-4 $5.99/$7.99

- -